Collide

Also from Megan Hart
and Spice Books

NAKED
SWITCH
DEEPER
STRANGER
TEMPTED
BROKEN
DIRTY

From MIRA Books

PRECIOUS AND FRAGILE THINGS

MEGAN HART

Collide

Spice

Recycling programs for this product may not exist in your area.

COLLIDE

ISBN-13: 978-0-373-60557-6

For questions and comments about the quality of this book please contact us at Customer_eCare@Harlequin.ca.

www.Spice-Books.com

Printed in U.S.A.

First, to JNB—HAYYY GURLL HAYYYYY!
Thanks for the late-night streamin' marathons
and the mutual appreciation of all the things that
make us a pair of duty hooahs.

To DPF for putting up with me.

And, of course, to Joe. Without you this book wouldn't exist.

Oranges.

The smell of oranges drifted toward me. I put a hand on the back of the chair nearest me and searched the countertop for fruit in a basket. Something, anything, that would explain the smell, which was as out of place in this coffee shop as a Santa suit in the sand. I didn't see anything that would explain the scent, and I drew in a deep breath. I'd learned a long time ago there was no point in trying to hold my nose or my breath. Better to breathe through this. Get it over with.

The smell passed quickly, gone in a few blinks, a couple of heartbeats, replaced by the stronger odor of coffee and pastries. My fingers had tightened on the chair but I didn't even need the support. I oriented myself before letting go of the chair to finish moving toward the counter where I'd been heading to add sugar and cream to my coffee.

It had been almost two years since my last fugue. That one had been equally as mild, but the fact this one had been barely a blip didn't offer much comfort. I'd had periods in my life when the fugues had come hard and fast and often, essentially crippling me. It was too much to hope they would go away, but I didn't want to go back to that.

"Hey, girl, heyyyyyy!" Jen called from the booth she'd snagged just inside the Mocha's door. She waved. "Over here!"

I waved and finished adding the sugar and cream, then wove my way through the jumble of chairs and tables to slide into the booth across from Jen. "Hey."

"Ooh, what did you get?" Jen leaned forward to peer into my coffee mug as though that would give her some idea about what was in there. She sniffed. "German chocolate?"

"Close. Chocolate Delight." I named one of the two featured coffees. "With a shot of vanilla-bean syrup."

Jen smacked her lips. "Mmm. Sounds good. I'm going to choose mine. Hey, what did you get to eat?"

"Blueberry muffin. Should've gone with the chocolate cupcake, but I thought maybe that would be too much." I showed her the plate with the muffin.

"Too much chocolate? As if. Be right back."

I stirred my coffee to distribute the syrup, extra sugar and cream, then sipped, enjoying the extra sweetness most people didn't like. Jen was right. I should've gone for the cupcake.

Jen had picked the wrong time to get in line. The midmorning rush had begun, customers lined up four-deep, all the way to the front door. She threw me an annoyed look and a shrug I could only laugh at in sympathy.

The coffee shop had been pretty empty when I entered, but customers who were put off by the line had started snagging tables while they waited to take their turns. I waved at Carlos over in the corner, but he had his earbuds settled deep and his laptop already open. Carlos was working on a novel. He sat in the Mocha from ten to eleven every morning before he went off to work, and on Saturdays, like today, he sometimes stayed longer.

Lisa, her backpack bulging with textbooks, took a table a few seats away and wiggled her fingers at me without noticing Jen's semifrantic waving for me to ignore her. Lisa sold Spicefully Tasty products to pay her way through law school, and though I'd never found her sales pitches annoying, Jen couldn't stand them. Today, though, Lisa seemed preoccupied, focusing on setting out her books and notepad, already clicking her pen as she shrugged out of her coat.

We were the Mocha regulars, like some sort of club. We met up in the mornings before work, in the evenings on the way home and on the weekends, bleary-eyed from the nights before. The Mocha was one of the best parts of living in this neighborhood, and though I'd only been a part of the club for a few months, I loved it.

By the time Jen got back to our booth with her tall cup of something that smelled both minty and chocolaty and her plate of something oozing and gooey, the crowd had settled. The regulars had found their usual spots and the people who'd just stopped in for takeout had bought and left. The Mocha was full now and buzzing with the hum of conversation and the click-clack of keyboards as people took advantage of the free Wi-Fi. I liked the hum. It made me conscious of being there, present. In the moment. This moment.

"She didn't try to hit you up for some sort of cream-cheese spread today, huh? Maybe she got the hint." Jen offered me a fork, and though I wanted to resist, I couldn't help taking just a taste of her brownie.

"I actually like Spicefully Tasty stuff," I said.

"Pffft." Jen laughed. "Get out of here."

"No, I do," I insisted. "It's expensive but convenient. If I ever really cooked, it would be even better."

"You're telling me. All that money for a bunch of spices I can buy two for a buck at the dollar store and mix together myself. Not that I do," Jen added. "But I could."

"Maybe next month." I sipped more rapidly cooling coffee, savoring the richness of the cream. "Once I get some bills paid off."

"You'll have better things to…oh. Niiiiice. Finally." Jen's voice dropped to a murmur.

I turned to look where she was staring. I caught a glimpse of a long black duster, a red-and-black-striped scarf. The man carried a thick newspaper under one arm, which in these times of smartphones and webnews was a strange enough sight to make me look twice. He spoke to the girl at the register, who seemed to know him, and took his empty mug to the long counter where all the self-serve carafes of coffee were.

In profile, he was gorgeous. Sandy-blond hair tousled just so, a sharp nose that wasn't overpowering. Crinkles at the corners of his eyes, the color of which I couldn't see but suspected were blue. His mouth, lips pursed in concentration as he filled his mug and added sugar and cream, looked just full enough to be tempting without being too lush.

"Who's that?" I asked.

"Girl," she said in a low, breathy voice. "You don't know who that is?"

"If I knew, would I be asking?"

The man in the black coat passed us so close I could smell him.

Oranges.

I closed my eyes against that second wave of scent, the taste of coffee so strong on my tongue it should've blocked out everything else but didn't. I should've smelled coffee and chocolate, but I smelled oranges. Again. I bent my head and pressed my fingertips to the magic spot between my eyes that worked swell for headaches but did nothing for fugues.

But no swirling colors seeped around the edges of my vision as I opened my eyes again, and the scent of oranges faded the farther away he got. I watched the man in the black coat take a seat facing away from us. He shook out the paper, spreading it open across the small table for two, and put his coffee down to take his coat off.

"You okay?" Jen leaned forward into my range of vision. "I know he's fucking hot and all, but damn, Emm, you looked like you were going to pass out."

"PMS," I said. "I get a little woozy this time of month."

Jen frowned, looking skeptical. "That sucks."

"You're telling me." I grinned to show her I was okay, and thank God I was. Not a hint of even a minor onset like the one that had hit me earlier. I'd smelled oranges because that man smelled of them, not because of some misfiring triggers in my brain. "Anyway. Who is he?"

"That's Johnny Dellasandro."

My expression must've been as blank as I felt, because Jen laughed.

"*Garbage? Skin? The Haunted Convent?* C'mon, not even that one?"

I shook my head. "Huh?"

"Ooh, girl, where've you been? Didn't you have cable TV growing up?"

"Sure I did."

"Johnny Dellasandro was in all those movies. They showed them a lot on those late-night cable shows like *Up Past Midnight*. They were slumber party standbys."

My mom had always been too nervous about me spending the night at someone else's house. I'd been allowed to go to the parties so long as she picked me up at bedtime. I'd had slumber parties at my house, though. "Sure, I remember that show. But that was a long time ago."

"Blank Spaces?"

That sounded a little more familiar, but not enough. I shrugged and looked over at him again. "I never heard of that one."

Jen sighed and looked over her shoulder at him, then leaned forward, lowering her voice and prompting me to lean closer to hear her. "Johnny Dellasandro, the artist? He had that series of portraits that became famous back in the early eighties. *Blank Spaces.* Sort of like the *Mona Lisa* of the Andy Warhol era."

I could maybe have picked out a Warhol painting in a museum if it had been lined up alongside a Van Gogh, a Dali, a Matisse. But other than that… "Was that the guy who did the soup cans? Marilyn Monroe?"

"Yeah, that was Warhol. Dellasandro's work wasn't quite as kitschy, but it did go a little more mainstream. *Blank Spaces* was his breakout series."

"You said 'wasn't.' He's not an artist anymore?"

She leaned forward a little more, and I followed. "Well, he has a gallery on Front Street. The Tin Angel? You know it?"

"I've been past it, yeah. Never been inside."

"That's his place. He still does his own work, and he has a lot of local artists there, too." She gestured around the Mocha, hung with samplings of local art, some of her pictures among them. "Better stuff than this. Every once in a while he has some big name in for a show. But he keeps it real low-key, low-profile. At least around here. I guess I can't blame him."

"Huh." I studied him. He was flipping pages of the paper so slowly it looked like he was reading every single word. "I wonder what that's like."

"What?"

"Being famous and then…not."

"He's still famous. Just not in the same way. I can't believe you never heard of him. He lives in that brownstone down the street, by the way."

I tore my gaze from Johnny Dellasandro's back and looked at my friend. "Which one?"

"Which one." Jen rolled her eyes. "The nice one."

"Oh, shit, really? Wow." I looked at him again. I'd bought

one of the brownstones on Second Street. Mine, though it had been partially renovated by a previous owner, still needed a lot of work. The one she was talking about was gorgeous, with completely repointed brickwork, brass on the gutters and a fully landscaped yard surrounded by hedges. "That's his place?"

"You're practically neighbors. I can't believe you didn't know."

"I barely know who he is," I told her, though now that she'd been talking about it, the title *Blank Spaces* sounded more familiar. "I'm not sure the real estate agent mentioned him as a selling point for the neighborhood."

Jen laughed. "Probably not. He's a pretty private guy. Comes in here a lot, though I haven't seen him lately. Doesn't talk a lot to anyone. He keeps to himself."

I drank the last of my coffee and considered getting up to take advantage of the bottomless refills. I'd have to walk right past him, and on the way back I'd get a full-on view of his face. Jen must've read my mind.

"He's worth a peek," she said. "God knows all of us girls in here have made a trip past him a few times. So has Carlos. Actually, I think Carlos is the only one he's ever talked to."

I laughed. "Yeah? Why? Does he like guys?"

"Who, Carlos?"

I was pretty sure Carlos was straight, judging by the way he checked out every woman's ass when he thought they weren't looking. "No. Dellasandro."

"Oooh, girl," Jen said again.

I liked the way she called me that, like we'd been friends for a long time instead of only a couple months. It had been hard moving here to Harrisburg. New job, new place, new life—the past supposedly left behind and yet never quite gone. Jen had been one of the first people I'd met, right here in the Mocha, and we'd fallen into friendship right away.

"Yes?" I studied him again.

Dellasandro licked his forefinger before using it to turn the page of his paper. It shouldn't have been quite as sexy as it was. I was letting Jen's excitement color my impression of him, which had been really too brief for it to be so intense. After all, I'd only had a glimpse of his face and had been staring at his back for less than fifteen minutes.

"You have to come over and watch his movies. You'll see what I mean. Johnny Dellasandro's like…a legend."

"He can't have been that much of a legend, since I've never heard of him."

"Okay," Jen amended. "A legend in a certain crowd. Artsy people."

"I guess I'm not artsy enough." I laughed, not taking offense. I'd been to the Museum of Modern Art a few times in New York City. I definitely wasn't the target audience.

"That is a sad, sad shame. Really. I'm pretty sure watching Johnny Dellasandro movies ruined me for regular boys forever."

"That's not exactly a compliment," I told her. "As if there is such a thing as a regular boy, which frankly I'm beginning to doubt."

She laughed and dug again into her brownie with another glance over her shoulder. She lifted her fork, heavy with chocolaty goodness, in my direction. "Come over tonight. I have the entire DVD box-set collection, plus the earlier ones, and what I don't have we can stream from Interflix."

"Ooh, fancy."

She grinned and bit off the brownie from her fork. "Girl, I will introduce you to some seriously good shit."

"And he lives right here, huh?"

"I know, right?" Jen glanced over her shoulder one more time.

If Dellasandro had any idea we were so scrutinizing him, he didn't show it. He didn't seem to pay any attention to anyone, as a matter of fact. He read his paper and drank his coffee. He turned the pages one at a time, sometimes using a finger to scan down the print.

"I wasn't sure it was him, you know? I came in here to the Mocha one morning and there he was. Johnny fucking Dellasandro." Jen gave a happy, entirely infatuated sigh. "Girl, I seriously almost surfed out of here on a wave of my own come."

I'd been drinking when she said that, and started laughing. A second later, choking when the coffee went into my lungs instead of my stomach. Coughing, gasping, eyes watering, I put my hands over my mouth to try and shield the noise, but it was impossible to be entirely quiet.

Jen laughed, too. "Hands up! Put your hands up! That stops coughing!"

My mom had always said the same thing. I managed to get one hand halfway up and the coughing eased. I'd earned a few curious looks, but none, thank God, from Dellasandro. "Warn me before you say something like that."

She blinked innocently. "Like what? Wave of my own come?"

I laughed again, this time without the choking. "Yeah, that!"

"Trust me," Jen said. "After you see his movies, you'll understand what I mean."

"Okay, fine. You have me convinced. And pathetically, I have no plans for tonight."

"Girl, if not having plans on a Saturday night makes you a loser, I'm one, too. We can be losers together, eating ice cream and squeeing over old soft-core art movies."

"Soft-core?" I looked past her to where Dellasandro had nearly finished his paper.

"You wait and see," Jen said. "Full frontal, baby."

"Oh, wow. No wonder he doesn't want to talk to anyone

here. If I were famous for dangling my dingle I might not want anyone to notice me, either."

It was Jen's turn to burst into laughter. Hers turned more heads than mine had, but still not Dellasandro's. She drew a finger through the chocolate on her plate and licked it off.

"I don't think that's it. I mean, I don't think he likes to brag about it or anything, but he's not ashamed. Well, he shouldn't be. He made art." She was being serious. "I mean, for real. He and his friends were known as the Enclave. They're credited with changing the way art movies were viewed by the general public. They made art movies that actually got shown in mainstream theaters. X-rated theaters, but even so."

"Wow." I didn't know anything about art but that sounded impressive.

And there was something about him. Maybe it was the long black coat and the scarf, since I'm a sucker for men who know how to dress like they don't care what they look like and yet manage to look damned good. Maybe it was the way he'd smelled of oranges as he passed me, not a scent I normally liked—in fact, one I despised because of the way it usually preceded a fugue. Maybe it was the lingering effects of the fugue itself, minor though it had been. Often after experiencing one I found the "real" world went brighter for a little while. Kind of intense. Somehow, even when the fugues were accompanied by hallucinations, coming out of them was even more intense. I hadn't had one like that in a long time, hadn't had even a hint of anything similar in this last one, but the feeling now was much the same.

"Emm?"

Startled, I realized Jen had been talking to me. I didn't have a fugue to blame for my inattention. "Sorry."

"So, tonight? I'll make margaritas. We can get a pizza." She paused, looking distraught. "That is sort of pathetic, huh?"

"You know what's pathetic? Getting all dressed up and going

to a bar hoping to get hit on by some loser in a striped shirt who smells like Polo."

"You're right. Striped shirts are so 2006."

We laughed together. I'd gone out with Jen to the local bars a couple times. Striped shirts were still pretty popular, especially on young frat boys who liked to buy Jell-O shots from scantily clad girls because they hoped those girls would think they were playahs.

Jen glanced at her watch. "Crap. Gotta run. Meeting my brother to take our grandma out grocery shopping. She's eighty-two and can't see well enough to drive. She makes our mom crazy."

I laughed again. "Good luck."

"I love her, but she's a handful. That's why I need my brother to come along. See you tonight, my place. Around seven? We don't want to start too late. Got a lot of movies to watch!"

I couldn't imagine wanting to watch more than one or two of the films, but I nodded, anyway. "Sure. I'll be there. I'll bring dessert and some munchies."

"Great. See you!" Jen stood and leaned in close to say, "Dare you to get a refill now! Quick, before he leaves."

Dellasandro had folded his paper and stood. He was putting on his coat. I still couldn't see his face.

"I dare you to casually wait until he leaves and you go out just after so he has to hold the door for you," I said.

"Good plan," she said. "Too bad I can't just casually wait around for him. I have to dash. You do it."

We both laughed and Jen headed out. I watched her go, then watched Dellasandro return his empty mug to the counter. With his paper tucked under his arm, he headed for the restroom in the back of the Mocha. It was a good time for me to get a refill, since I'd paid for them, but I wasn't really in the mood for more coffee. I had no plans—the day stretched out before me with nothing to tempt me away from the Mocha, and yet I'd forgotten to bring something to read or even my computer to surf the Net. I had no reason to stay and a house full of unpacking and cleaning to finish. I probably had a message from my mom to return, too.

I put my own mug on the counter and let my lustful gaze roam over the pastries. I'd bake some brownies at home instead. They'd be better from scratch, anyway, even if the ones at the Mocha did come with a half-inch-thick layer of fudge frosting I had no idea how to replicate. My stomach rumbled despite the muffin I'd had. Not a good thing.

"Get you something?" This was Joy, one of the tersest people I'd ever met. She certainly didn't live up to her name.

"No, thanks." I hitched my purse higher on my shoulder, thinking I'd better head home and make myself an egg salad sandwich or something before I got hypoglycemic. Going without food not only made me cranky, it could tempt a fugue, and after the one this morning I wasn't about to do anything to bring on another. Caffeine and sugar helped fend them off, but my empty stomach was effectively counterbalancing the oversweetened coffee.

Dellasandro reached the Mocha's front door only seconds after I did. I'd pushed open the glass-fronted door, making the brass bell jingle, and felt someone behind me. I turned, one hand still holding the door so it wouldn't swing shut, and there he was. Black coat, striped scarf, wheaten hair.

His eyes weren't blue.

They were a deep green-brown hazel. And his face was perfect, even with the crinkles of time at the corners of his eyes, the glint of silver I could see now at his temples. I'd thought he was maybe in his late thirties, a few years older than me when I'd first seen him, though obviously his career in the seventies meant he was older than that. I wouldn't have guessed it even now, knowing. His face was beautiful.

Johnny Dellasandro's face was art.

And I let the door slam right in it.

"Jesus Christ," he said as he stepped back.

His voice, pure New Yawk.

The door closed between us. Sun reflected off the glass, shielding him inside. I couldn't see his face anymore, but I was pretty sure I'd just pissed him off.

I pulled on the handle as he pushed it open, the door's sudden give making me stumble back a couple steps. "Oh, wow, I'm sorry!"

He didn't even look at me, just shouldered past with a low, muttered curse I couldn't quite make out. The edge of his paper hit my arm as he passed. Dellasandro didn't pay any attention. The hem of his coat flapped in a sudden upswell of wind and I gasped, breathing in deep, and deeper.

The scent of oranges.

"Mom. Really, I'm fine." I had to tell her this not because it made her worry less, but because if I didn't say it, she'd definitely worry more. "I promise. Everything's fine."

"I wish you hadn't moved so far away." My mom's voice on the other end of the phone sounded fretful. That was normal. When she started sounding anxious, I needed to worry.

"Forty minutes isn't far at all. I'm closer to work now, and I have a great place."

"In the city!"

"Oh, Mom." I had to laugh, even though I knew it wouldn't make her feel any better. "Harrisburg's only technically a city."

"And right downtown. You know I heard on the news there was a shooting just a few streets over from you."

"Yeah? And there was a murder-suicide in Lebanon just last week," I told her. "How far is that from you?"

My mom sighed. "Emm. Be serious."

"I am serious. Mom, I'm thirty-one years old. It was time for me to do this."

She sighed. "I guess you're right. You can't be my baby forever."

"I haven't been your baby for a really long time."

"I'd just feel better if you weren't alone. It was better when you and Tony—"

"Mom," I said tightly. "Tony and I broke up for a long list of very good reasons, okay? Please stop bringing him up. You didn't even like him that much."

"Only because I didn't think he could take good enough care of you."

She'd been right about that, anyway. Not that I'd needed as much taking care of as she thought. But I didn't want to talk about my ex-boyfriend with her. Not now, not ever.

"How's Dad?" I asked instead, so she could talk about the other person in her life she worried about more than she had to.

"Oh, you know your dad. I keep telling him to get himself to the doctor and get checked out, but he just won't do it. He's fifty-nine now, you know."

"You act like that's ancient."

"It's not young," my mom said.

I laughed and cradled the phone to my shoulder as I opened one of the large boxes I'd put in one of the unused bedrooms. I was unpacking books. I wanted to make this room my library and had set up and dusted off all my bookcases. Now I just needed to fill them. It was a task I knew I'd be glad I'd done after I finished but had managed to put off for months.

"What are you doing?" my mom said.

"Unpacking books."

"Oh, be careful, Emm, you know that can kick up dust!"

"I don't have asthma, Mom." I pulled off the layer of newspaper I'd laid on top of the books. I'd packed them not in the order I'd arrange them on the shelves, but just so they'd fit best in the box. This one looked like it was mostly full of coffee table books I'd picked up at thrift stores or received as gifts. Books I always meant to read and yet never did.

"No. But you know you have to be careful."

"Mom, c'mon. Enough." Now I was starting to get irritated.

My mom had always been overprotective. When I was six years old, I fell off a jungle gym at the school playground. Those were the days before schools used recycled tires as mulch, or any kind of soft material. Other kids broke arms or legs. I broke my head.

I was in a coma for almost a week, suffering a brain edema, or swelling, that doctors hadn't been able to relieve by standard methods. My parents had been on the verge of agreeing to an experimental brain surgery when I'd opened my eyes, sat up and asked for ice cream.

The lack of coordination or loss of limb use the doctors had predicted never happened. Nor did memory loss or any discernible brain damage. If anything, I had trouble forgetting, not remembering. I'd suffered no long-term affects—at least, not physical ones. On the other hand, I'd learned to get used to the fugues.

She and my dad had thought they'd almost lost me, and nothing I could ever have told her about that time in the darkness could persuade her I hadn't even come close to leaving. I'd tried once or twice, when I was younger, to reassure her. To get her to let go, even just a little. She refused to listen. I guess I couldn't blame her. I had no idea of how it felt to love a child, much less fear you'd lost one.

"I'm sorry," she said.

The good thing was, my mom knew when she was getting out of control. She'd done her best to make sure I didn't grow up a stilted, fearful child, even if it meant biting her nails to nubs and going gray before she turned forty. She'd allowed me to do what I needed to for my independence, even if she did hate every second of it.

"You could come up once in a while, you know. I'm really not that far. We could have lunch or something. Just you and me, a girls' day."

"Oh, sure. We could do that." She sounded a little brighter from the invitation.

I didn't think she'd actually take me up on it. My mom didn't like to drive long distances by herself. If she did come, she'd bring my dad along. Not that I didn't love my dad, or want to see him. In many ways, he was easier to get along with than my mom, because no matter what anxiety he had, he kept it to himself. But it wouldn't be a girls' day out with him along, and he tended to get cranky about staying too long when he wanted to be home in his recliner watching sports. I didn't even have cable yet.

"I saw him a couple days ago, Emm."

I paused with a large book on cathedrals in one hand. I'd have to adjust the shelves in one of the bookcases if I wanted to stand this book upright. It was meant for a coffee table, for display. I flipped through the pages, considering if I should just sell on Craigslist. "Who?"

"Tony," my mom said impatiently.

"Oh, for God's sake, Mom!"

"He looked good. He asked about you."

"I'm sure he did," I said wryly.

"I got the feeling he was wondering if you'd...met someone."

I paused in unpacking, with another heavy book in my hands, this time one called *Cinema Americana.* Another yard-sale find. I was a sucker for a bargain, books my downfall. Even ones about subjects I had no interest in. I guess I always had the notion I'd tear out the illustrations and put them in frames to hang on the wall. Proof I really did have no appreciation for art.

"Why would he even think that?"

"I don't know, Emm." A pause. "Have you?"

I was about to say no, but a flash of striped scarf and a black coat filled my mind. The floor tilted a little under me. I gripped the phone tighter. The book was suddenly too heavy in my sweating hand; I dropped it.

"Emm?"

"Fine, Mom. Just dropped a book."

No swirling colors, no citrus scent biting at my nostrils. My stomach churned a little, but that could've been the leftover Italian food I'd had earlier. It had been in the fridge a little too long.

"It wouldn't be such a bad thing. For you to meet someone. I mean, I think you should."

"Yeah, I'll make sure every guy I meet knows my mom thinks I shouldn't be single. That's a surefire way to get a date."

"Sarcasm isn't pretty, Emmaline."

I laughed. "Mom, I have to go, okay? I want to finish unpacking these boxes and do some laundry before I go to my friend Jen's house tonight."

"Oh? You have a friend."

I loved my mother. Really, I did. But sometimes I wanted to strangle her.

"Yes, Mother. I have an honest-to-goodness friend."

She laughed that time, sounding better than she had when the conversation started. That was something, anyway. "Good. I'm glad you're spending time with a friend instead of sitting home. I just… I worry about you, honey. That's all."

"I know you do. And I know you always will."

We said our goodbyes, exchanged I-love-yous. I had friends who never told their parents they loved them, who'd never said the words after elementary school. It was something I was glad I'd never grown out of and that my mother insisted upon. Even if I knew it was because she was afraid not saying it would somehow mean she'd have lost her chance to tell me one more time, I liked it.

The book I'd dropped had opened to someplace in the middle, cracking the binding in a way that made me sigh unhappily. I bent to pick it up and stopped. It had opened to chapter called "Seventies Art Films," on a full-page, glossy black-and-white photo of an unbelievably gorgeous face staring directly at the camera.

Johnny Dellasandro.

"Which do you want to watch first? What are you in the mood for?" Jen pulled open the door on what proved to be a cabinet full of DVDs. She ran a fingertip along the plastic cases with a ticka-ticka-tick and stopped at one, looking over her shoulder at me. "Do you want to ease into it or plunge right in?"

I'd brought along the *Cinema Americana* book to show her and it lay open on the coffee table in front me, opened to the page of Johnny's gorgeous face. "What's this picture from?"

Jen looked. *"Train of the Damned."*

I looked at it, too. "That picture is from a horror movie?"

"Yeah. Not my favorite of his. It's not very scary," she added. "But he does get naked in it."

Both my brows raised. "Really?"

"Yeah. Not quite full frontal," she said with a grin as she bent and plucked a movie from the shelf. "But, man, those seventies foreign movies were pretty graphic sometimes. It has a lot of blood and gore in it—will that bother you?"

I'd spent so much time in hospitals and emergency rooms that nothing much bothered me. "Nah."

"*Train of the Damned,* it is." Jen pulled the DVD from its case and slipped it into the player, then tuned the television to the right channel and grabbed the remote before taking a place beside me on the couch. "The quality's not so good, sorry. I found this one in the bargain bin at a dollar store."

"You're a super Dellasandro fan, huh?" I shifted to keep the bowl of popcorn from spilling and leaned to take another look at the picture.

I hadn't told Jen about letting the door slam in Johnny's face, or how I'd already spent an hour staring at this photo, memorizing every line and curve, dip and hollow. His hair in the picture was pulled back into a thick tail at the base of his neck, longer than it was now. He looked younger in the picture, of course, since it had been taken something like thirty years ago. But not much younger.

"He's aged well." Jen peered over my shoulder as the first wobbly sounds of music filtered from the TV's speakers. "He's a little heavier, has a few more lines around his eyes. But mostly, he still looks that good. And you should see him in the summer, when he's not covered up with that long coat."

I sat back against the couch and pulled my feet up beneath me. "Haven't you ever talked to him?"

"Oh, girl, hell, no. I'm too afraid."

I laughed. "Afraid of what?"

Jen used the remote to turn up the sound. So far, the only thing on the TV screen had been a title dripping blood and a shot of a train chugging along a dark track winding through tall and jagged mountains. "I'd word-vomit all over him."

"Word…ew."

She laughed and put down the remote to grab a handful of popcorn. "Seriously. I met Shane Easton once, you know him? Lead singer for the Lipstick Guerrillas?"

"Um, no."

"They were playing at IndiePalooza one year down in Hershey, and my friend had scored backstage passes. Ten or fifteen bands, something like that. Hot as all hell. We'd been drinking beer because cups were a dollar fifty and the water was four bucks a bottle. Let's just say I was a little drunk."

"And? What did you say?"

"I might've told him I wanted to ride him like a roller coaster. Or something like that."

"Oh, wow."

"Yeah, I know, right?" She sighed dramatically and popped the top on a can of diet cola. "Not my most shining moment."

"It could've been worse, I'm sure."

"What would be worse is if instead of never having to see him again I bumped into him all the time at the coffee shop and the grocery store," Jen said. "Which is why I'm keeping my mouth shut around Johnny Dellasandro."

The train—I assumed it was of the damned—let out a shrill whistle and the movie cut to an interior scene of people dressed in the height of late-seventies fashion. A woman in a beige pantsuit and huge hair, gigantic glasses covering half her face, waved a hand heavy with rings at the waiter pouring her a glass of wine. The train shuddered, he spilled it. It was Johnny.

"Watch what you're doing, you damned fool!" The woman spoke in a thick accent. Maybe Italian? I couldn't be sure. "You spilled on my favorite blouse!"

"Sorry, ma'am." His voice was dark and thick and rich…and totally out of place in the movie with that New York accent.

I giggled. Jen shot me a look. "It gets better when he takes her into the sleeping car and bangs her."

We both giggled then, and ate popcorn and drank cola, and made fun of the movie. As far as I could tell, the train became damned when it entered a tunnel that had somehow become connected to a portal to hell. There was no explanation for why this happened, at least none that I could figure out, but since at odd times the movie shifted into Italian with badly translated

English subtitles—with Johnny's voice being oddly dubbed in a much higher, swishier voice—I might easily have missed something important.

It didn't matter, really. It was entertaining, with lots of blood and gore as Jen had promised. Lots of eye candy, too. Johnny ended up stripping out of his waiter's uniform to battle foam-and-latex demons. Shirtless and covered in blood, his hair slicked back from his face, he was still breathtaking.

"I said, 'Get the hell back to hell!'"

It was a classic line, delivered in Johnny's thick accent and accompanied by the blast of his shotgun exploding the demons into tiny, dripping bits. And followed, incongruously, by a long, explicit love scene between him and the woman in the pantsuit, set to bouncy porn music and ending with the woman somehow getting pregnant with a demon baby that tore up her insides and tried to attack its father.

"So...Johnny was...the devil?"

Jen laughed and scraped the bottom of the popcorn bowl. "I think so! Or the son of the devil, something like that."

The credits rolled. I finished my drink. "Wow. That was something."

"Yeah, bad. But the sex scene. Hot, right?"

It had been. Even with the porny music and stupid special effects, even with the discreetly placed cushions that blocked even a glimpse of Johnny's cock but left the woman's hairy bush in full view. He'd kissed her like she was delicious.

"Good acting," I said offhandedly.

Jen snorted and got up to take the DVD out of the player. "I don't think it's acting. I mean, I think he's a much better artist than he ever was an actor. And the way he kisses...he fucks someone in just about every movie he's in. I don't think there's much acting going on. It's all pure Johnny."

"When did he make all these movies, anyway?" I got up to

stretch. The movie had been short, only a little over an hour, but watching it had felt like much longer.

"Dunno." Jen shrugged. "He made a bunch in the seventies, then stopped for a while. Fell off the face of the earth. Then came back with the art and, so far as I know, only acted in one or two things after that. Mostly guest spots on TV shows. He was on an episode of *Family Ties,* if you can believe that."

"Did he fuck someone?"

"He did!" Jen laughed. "But I don't think they showed his cock. For that you have to watch…this."

She pulled out a DVD with a plain red-and-black cover, one word on the front. *Garbage.* She was already putting it in the player as she talked.

"Okay. I'm not going to tell you anything about this movie in advance. I don't want to ruin it."

"That sounds scarier than *Train of the Damned!*"

She shook her head. "No. Just watch. You'll see."

So we watched.

Garbage had even less of a plot than *Train of the Damned.* From what I could tell, it was about a group of misfits living in an apartment complex a lot like the one on the TV show *Melrose Place.* The kind seen in so many movies shot in California—a few buildings painted teal or green surrounding a pool. In this movie, the complex was called the Cove. Run by an office manager who I was pretty sure was a three-hundred-pound man in drag, the Cove's other residents included the slutty heroin addict Sheila, mentally disturbed porcelain figurine collector Henry, unwed mother Becky and a bunch of other random characters who didn't seem to have names but came and went in the background no matter what else was going on.

And, of course, Johnny.

He played…Johnny. Male prostitute. The tattoo on his arm had been crudely drawn, probably inked with a homemade tool: *Johnny.*

"I wonder if his name's Johnny in every movie?" I said, and was promptly shushed.

It wasn't a good movie, if I were going to judge by the acting or writing. In fact, I couldn't be sure there was any writing at all. It seemed mostly ad-libbed, which meant there wasn't much acting, either. It looked more like a group of friends had gotten together one Saturday afternoon with a camera and a bunch of weed and decided to make a movie.

"I think that's basically what happened," Jen said when I told her my theory. "But fuck me, look at that epic ass."

Johnny was naked for most of the movie. Something happened with a trick gone wrong, a drug overdose, a miscarriage. A body in the pool and then put into the garbage. I couldn't have told you what happened if you'd held me down and threatened me with a live tarantula.

All I could see was Johnny Dellasandro. His ass. His abs. His pecs. His delicious nipples. He was built like an Adonis, muscular and lean…and golden. God. He was naked and sunburnished, with just enough hair to make him manly and not so much it looked like you'd have to get a Weedwacker to get at his cock.

And he really did fuck everyone in the movie.

"Look at that," Jen murmured. "I swear he's really fucking her."

I tilted my head to get a better angle. "I think…wow. That's… Is he hard? Omigod. He's got a hard-on! Look at that!"

"I know, right?" Jen squealed, clutching at me.

I hadn't been this excited about an erection since my first boy-girl party in eighth grade, when I got to go in the closet for Seven Minutes in Heaven with Kent Zimmerman. My stomach dropped the way it does just before that first hill on a roller coaster. Heat stole up my chest and throat, into my cheeks.

"Wow," I said. "That is…just whoa."

"Girl. I know. Can you believe it? And just wait…there!

Yesssss," Jen said, falling back onto the cushions. "Full frontal."

Just briefly, but there it was. Johnny's cock in all its glory. He was talking as he walked and I couldn't decide if I wanted to try and listen to what he was saying or just accept my utter, complete perviness and stare at his dick. The penis won out.

"That is some peen," I said, my voice filled with admiration.

"You know it." Jen sighed happily. "That man is fucking beautiful."

I tore my gaze from the TV to look at her. "I can't believe you're so into him and you've never talked to him. Word vomit or not. It has to be worth a try."

Jen shook her head. Johnny wasn't on-screen at the moment, so we weren't missing anything important. She gestured toward it.

"What would I say? 'Hi, Johnny, I'm Jen, and by the way, I love your cock so much I put it on my Christmas list'?"

I laughed. "What, you think he'd mind?"

She gave me a look.

"Is he married?" I asked the more practical question.

"No. I don't think so. Honestly, aside from the movies I don't really know all that much about him, personally." Jen made a frowny face.

I laughed again, harder this time. "Some stalker you are."

"I'm not—" she hit me with a pillow "—a stalker. I just appreciate a nice body, is that so wrong? And I do like his art a lot. I bought one of his pieces," she added, like she was sharing a secret.

"Yeah?"

She nodded. "Yeah. His gallery is really cool. Lots of neat little pieces, nothing too expensive. And in the back room he has different collections. A couple years ago he was showing his stuff. He doesn't always. I mean, he usually has his stuff included among all the other pieces, and he never displays it like it's a big deal, you know?"

I'd never been in an art gallery, so I had no clue, but I nodded, anyway. "Can I see it?"

"Sure. I, um, have it in the bedroom."

I laughed yet again. "Why? Is it dirty?"

I hadn't known Jen all that long, just for the few months since I'd moved to Second Street. I had not, as yet, seen her look embarrassed about anything, or shy. She was pretty up front with everything, which was why I adored her. So when she couldn't meet my eyes and gave that little, shameful giggle, I almost told her I didn't need to see what had made her feel like she couldn't share it with me.

"No, it's not dirty," she said.

"Okay." I got up and followed her down the short hallway to her bedroom.

Jen's apartment had been decorated in IKEA chic. Lots of spare, modern pieces that all matched and maximized the small space. Her bedroom was the same, painted white with matching teal and lime-green accents on the bed and curtains. Her apartment was in an old building, with walls that weren't always quite straight. One, in fact, was curved, with big-paned windows reaching from floor to ceiling and overlooking the street. On one wall she'd hung several of her own paintings. On the opposite wall she'd hung several framed posters of prints even I, the art idiot, recognized—*Starry Night, The Scream.*

In the center of those was a black-and-white photograph, maybe an eight-by-ten, in a thin red frame. The artist had painted over the photo with thick, three-dimensional strokes, highlighting the lines of the building I recognized as the John Harris Mansion from down on Front Street. I'd spent time looking at a lot of what people had determined art and wondered why on earth they thought so, but I didn't have to spend a second pondering it about this picture.

"Wow."

"I know, right?" Jen walked to the wall to stand in front of it. "Pretty cool, huh? I mean, you look at it, and it's not like it's anything special. But there's just something about it…."

"Yeah." There definitely was. "And it's not even dirty."

She laughed. "No. I just like having it in here where I can look at it first thing in the morning. Does that sound lame? Oh, God, that sounds totally lame."

"No, it doesn't. Is this the only piece you have by him?"

"Yeah. Original art's expensive, even though he'd priced this pretty reasonably."

I had no idea how much pretty reasonable was and it seemed a little nosy to ask. "It's nice, Jen. He's really good."

"He is. So you see…that's another reason why I don't talk to him."

I looked at her with a smile. "Why? Because you like his art and not just his ass?"

Jen snickered. "Well, yeah."

"I don't get it. You think he's superhot, you're a big fan… why not just say something?"

"Because I guess I'd rather have him take a look at something I've done and think it's good without me gushing all over him. I'd like him to respect me as an artist, and that's not going to happen."

I walked to the wall featuring her paintings. "Why not? You're good, too."

"And you don't know anything about art, remember?" She said it without malice, following me to look at the pictures. "They'll never hang in a museum. I don't think anyone will ever make a Wikipedia entry about me."

"You never know," I told her. "Do you think Johnny Dellasandro knew when he was making those movies that one day he'd be famous for showing off his ass?"

"It's a pretty epic ass."

"Let's go watch another movie," I said.

By two in the morning we'd only made it through one more because we'd paused and rewound so many scenes so many times.

"Why didn't you start with this one?" I demanded after the third time we'd watched Johnny slide down a naked woman's body with his mouth.

Jen shook the remote at me. "Girl, you have to build up to this shit. You can't just go in full force on this stuff, you might give yourself an aneurysm."

I laughed, though the fact I probably did have an aneurysm that could kill me at any time, no matter what the doctors said, made the joke a little less funny. "Play it again."

She reversed the DVD half a minute and played it again. Johnny called the woman a dirty whore, and in his accent it came out sounding like "duty hooah." It should've made me laugh.

"So fucking wrong," I said, rapt as Johnny-on-the-screen moved his mouth down her naked body again, over her thigh, then moved up to grab a handful of her hair and turn her around. "I should not like that, right?"

"Girl, just give in to it," Jen said dreamily.

In the movie, he called her a hooah again. Told her she was dirty, filthy. That she deserved to be fucked like that, didn't she? That she liked it, being fucked that way, by him.

"God," I muttered, squirming a little. "That's..."

"Hot, right?" Jen sighed. "Even with the funky seventies sideburns."

"Definitely."

We made it through to the end of the movie and I had no idea what the plot had been, just that Johnny had been naked for over half of it and he'd had sex with most of the other characters, men and women. Oh, and that I was in desperate, urgent need of some "alone time."

"Another?" Jen was already getting up, but I stood, too.

"I need to get home. It's really late. And if we sleep in too late tomorrow," I added, "we won't make it to the coffee shop. We might miss him."

"Oh, Emm." Jen blinked, looking solemn. "I've infected you, haven't I?"

"If this is a disease," I told her, "I don't want to find a cure."

Jen lived close enough to me that walking was no problem, at least during the day or in good weather. But in the middle of an oddly frigid Pennsylvania winter and in a neighborhood that was a little dicey, I'd driven the couple blocks. My normal spot was taken when I got home, probably by the girlfriend of the guy who lived across the street. Grumbling, eyes heavy, I drove down to the next block to take someone else's spot and hoped I didn't come out to find a nasty note on my windshield. Since there was very little off-street parking, the jockeying for spots could get brutal.

It was something like serendipity, however, because when I got out of my car I realized I'd parked almost directly in front of Johnny Dellasandro's house. There was a light on upstairs, the third floor. Most of the houses on this street had the same floorplan, so unless he'd done some major reconstruction inside, that light was shining from a bedroom. In my house, someday, I intended it to be the master bedroom with an attached bath. He'd done enough work to his place that I suspected that's what his was.

Johnny Dellasandro in his bedroom. I wondered if he slept naked. I wasn't quite sure I was up to Jen's standard of surfing down the street on a wave of my own come, but it was close there for a second. I definitely had a clit pulse. I fantasized happily all the way down the block and into my own house.

There's never been any rhyme or reason behind why the

fugues come. The things that set off seizures or migraines or bouts of narcolepsy in other people are only haphazard triggers for me. This is good because it means I don't have to avoid intense emotion, or chocolate, or any of a dozen other common triggers. It's bad, of course, because whatever causes the fugues hits me randomly and without warning, and even if I wanted to avoid whatever caused it, I couldn't.

I hadn't had a fugue in nearly two years, and now the scent of oranges told me I was going to have a third in less than twenty-four hours.

In the bathroom. Brushing teeth. Staring at my reflection in the mirror but seeing Johnny's face as he made love to a woman with hair the color of mine. My eyes. My breasts under his hands, my clit beneath his tongue.

Staring at the mirror and then, like Alice…through…

"Watch what you're doing! You spilled my coffee." I say this in a thick accent, not my own voice, but it doesn't feel put on. It feels right on my tongue and teeth and lips. It feels sexy.

"Sorry, ma'am." The waiter dabs at my thighs with a white towel. His fingers brush too close to my belly, linger too long. "Lemme get that cleaned up for you."

"I think you need to compensate me." I say this with a straight face and flip my thick, dark hair over my shoulder.

"Ma'am?" He's not stupid, this young man in the white waiter's coat.

The train rocks beneath us.

"Come to my cabin later tonight and make sure you're prepared to adequately compensate me for the ruin of my slacks."

His only answer is a smile. I finish my meal with my own smile, making it difficult to enjoy the food. I'm not hungry any longer, anyway. Not for dinner.

In my cabin I wait for the knock at the door, and when I

open it, there he is. Not in his waiter's uniform now, but a pair of dark trousers and a yellowed white poet's shirt. Peasant wear, but I don't care. Peasants make great lovers.

"Just look," I say, pointing to the dark stain on my white slacks. I've deliberately done nothing to clean them. "See what you did, you clumsy man?"

"I can pay for them, ma'am…."

"That won't do at all. These pants are pure silk, made by my personal designer. They're irreplaceable."

"Then what?" He's properly challenging.

He has long, thick, dark blond hair clubbed into a tail at the back of his neck. When I loosen it from the tie, it falls over my fingers and hands. It's rougher than silk.

"Clean them."

With a sullen look he pulls a handkerchief from his back pocket and, with a flourish, pushes me a few steps until the backs of my knees hit the edge of the bed, which has been turned down for the night. He swipes at the stain on my pants without looking away from my eyes. I shudder at his touch.

"No," I say, low and throaty. "Use your mouth."

He goes to his knees so slowly it's like watching butter melt. He's smiling, but his eyes are hard. He closes them just before he puts his mouth to the stain.

I can feel the heat of his breath through the thin cloth, and I shudder again. My knees want to buckle, but I put my hand on the wall to keep myself standing. I can feel the train's vibration in my fingers and palm.

His hands move up to grab my ass and hold me still. He looks up at me, his face inches from my crotch. I wonder if he can smell me.

"That good enough?" he says.

"No," I tell him. "Not nearly good enough."

His fingers grip and pull. Silk shreds. I'm suddenly bare from the waist down, my slacks torn and dangling in his fists. I have only a moment to react before his mouth is on me again. My bare flesh this time. My pussy. He sucks at my clit, nuzzling, and I cry out. He slaps my ass lightly, and I don't know if it's to keep me still or make me cry out louder. Then I'm on my back and he's over me, his cock pressing my lips.

"Take it," he says. Brutish and cruel. My cunt throbs and I turn my face. He grabs my hair, holds me still. Then, gently, softly, he rubs his cock over my pressed-closed lips. "Take it."

And I do.

All of it. Thick and hot, hard. Down the back of my throat. I suck him in, greedy for it. I suck and lick and stroke, and he fucks my mouth like it's my cunt, and I swear I get as much pleasure from it.

He's not even touching my clit and I feel the buildup there of pleasure. Like electricity. Like fire. I'm pumping my hips and moaning around his cock. My hair is in my face and he strokes it back, then grips a handful of it to set a slower pace.

I want him to touch me but I don't need him to touch me. I'm going to come in a minute or two. I can feel it. And then he's pulling away, stealing that delicious cock from me, and I do more than moan, I cry out.

"Lookit you," he says in a voice full of triumph and yet tender, too. "Lookit you. Begging for it. Such a whore."

I love the way he says it, like it has two syllables. Suddenly, I don't know why we're on a train, why he's a waiter and I'm some sort of…countess? Or duchess? Some sort of rich bitch with too much money and an itch. Everything that made sense when this started is now a jumble.

All I know for sure is that I don't want this to end. His hand comes down to caress my cheek. His thumb slips between my lips and I suck it gently before biting. He laughs, pulls me up, settles me onto his cock like I weigh nothing. Now there's nothing between us and he's inside me, all the way.

The train rocks us. He rocks us. His hands, strong hands, grip my ass and move me. His mouth takes mine. We kiss for the first time, and I want to drown in the taste of him. His tongue strokes mine. Our teeth bump. He laughs again.

"You like that?"

"I like that," I tell him. I don't have an Italian accent anymore.

When I look in the mirror, I don't see my face. I don't even see our reflection, fucking so prettily on this sleeping-car bed. The mirror is more like a window, only it doesn't look out to the passing scenery. Instead of mountains, I see walls. I see a woman.

The woman is me.

She is there, I am here; we're the same and I look into the eyes of my lover, this waiter whose name is…

"Johnny."

I came out of the fugue with his name on my lips and the smell of oranges so thick and cloying in my nose and mouth I leaned over the sink and gulped water straight from the tap. I stood, heart pounding, eyes wild, face dripping. I looked at the mirror, but all I saw was myself.

Hallucinations weren't new. When I was a little girl, in the first few years after the accident, I'd had a hard time differentiating between the fugue world and the real world. I could tell when I was dreaming, but not when I was having a fugue.

It didn't help that no matter what doctors my parents took me to, none of them could figure it out, either. The brain is still a vastly underexplored landscape. I wasn't having seizures, though in the worst fugues I did sometimes lose motor control along with consciousness. And I didn't have pain, except for the rare few times when I fell during one of the blackouts and hurt myself.

As I got older, I learned to tell when a fugue was coming on. I never learned to notice inside of one if I was hallucinating or not, though I did learn to tell what had been hallucination once I came out of it. And I always came out of it, even if I didn't always hallucinate. Sometimes I just stayed blank, unblinking, unmoving, for a few seconds while the world passed around me and whoever I was talking to thought my mind had wandered.

Actually, that was how I felt about it. That my mind wandered, while my body stayed behind. I'd learned to catch up quickly in conversations with people who didn't know me well enough to realize I'd gone blank for a few minutes. I'd adapted.

Most of the time, the hallucinations were boldly colored, often loud. Often a continuation of what I'd been doing as the fugue hit, just slightly off. I could spend what felt like hours inside the fugue and come out of it within a minute, or spend a much longer time dark and have no more than a few seconds' worth in the dream state.

I'd never, until this early morning, had such a vivid, intense hallucination of such a sexual nature.

I was taking a little time to recover. Wallowing in my bed on a Sunday wasn't out of the ordinary, but the fact I'd grabbed my laptop and brought it under the covers with me was. Normally I kept my bed a sanctuary, a place for sleep, not work, and though I loved my laptop like it was the conjoined twin I carried in a basket after our cruel separation, I preferred using it at my desk or on the couch. Now, though, I used the track pad to scroll through another list of search results.

Johnny Dellasandro, of course. I had the fever. Bad.

He had a current website for his gallery. The only mention of his acting past were the three words, "independent film star" in his bio along with a rather extensive listing of his more recent professional accomplishments. There were store hours, a list of upcoming events. A photo of Johnny, smiling into the camera and looking for all the world like he wanted to fuck whoever was on the other side of the lens...*thud*. Be still my little horny heart.

There were other pictures of him, too, most of the handshake variety. Johnny with the mayor, with a local radio DJ, with a president of some museum. And then, a little more surprisingly, of Johnny with celebrities. Row after row of clickable thumbnails enlarged into shots of him next to some of the biggest movie stars of the sixties and seventies. Rock stars.

Poets, novelists. A bunch of familiar faces next to his. In most of them, they were both looking at the camera, but there were a few more candid shots, and in those, whoever he was with invariably looked at him like they wanted to eat him. Or be fucked by him. I couldn't blame them.

Maybe he wasn't so ashamed of his dingle-dallying past, after all. More searching turned up a half dozen interviews done on blogs that didn't appear to have very many readers. Not that I was surprised. Any monkey with a computer can make a blog, and even though Johnny might've achieved a certain level of notoriety, it was still within a fairly small realm. He didn't sound like he regretted anything he'd ever done, at least not in the interviews he'd done in the past few years, and while those had focused more on his current work, inevitably a few questions would slip in about his early movie-making days.

"I don't regret any of it," Johnny told me from a video clip taken at some awards show I'd never heard of.

The film was shaky, the sound bad, and the people walking past in the background looked a little scary. Whoever was filming also asked the questions, their voice androgynous and too loud in the microphone. Johnny didn't seem terribly interested in being interviewed, though he did answer a few more questions.

I settled back onto my pillows, laptop on my knees. Wikipedia did indeed have an entry on him, complete with links to dozens of articles in magazine and newspaper archives. Reviews of the films and entire websites devoted to discussing them. Links to places his art had hung, or was hanging. There was literally a day's worth of research collected in this one webpage alone. If anyone Googled me—and I did myself a few times a month just to see what was out there—the only thing they'd find would be a list of accomplishments belonging to some other woman with my name. The question was not why there was so much information available about him, but how I'd lived for more than thirty years without being aware he existed.

I shut down the computer and set it aside, then lay back on the pillows to think about this. I was deep in crush, the worst I'd had since sixth grade when I discovered boys for the first time. Worse than the secret love affair I'd had with John Cusack inside my head since the first time I saw *Say Anything*. My feelings for Johnny were a combination of both—he was someone I'd seen in movies, therefore, not "real," yet he lived down the street. He drank coffee and wore striped scarves. He was accessible.

"Snap out of it, Emm," I scolded myself, and thought about getting out of my warm bed and shivering my way to the shower. I couldn't quite make myself.

I didn't want to think about the three fugues I'd had the day before, but thinking of the hallucination I'd had featuring Johnny in all his bare-assed glory, I had to think about the fugues, too. Two minis and one slightly larger. None had lasted long, but it was the frequency that worried me.

I was thirty-one years old and had never lived on my own before these past few months. I'd never worked farther away from a job than I could walk, because I was either not legally allowed, or was too afraid, to drive long distances. I'd spent my life dealing with the repercussions of those few, fleeting moments on the playground, but now I'd finally had a taste of the independence all my friends had been granted.

I was terrified of losing it.

I knew I should call my family doctor, Dr. Gordon, and tell her what had happened. She'd known me since childhood. I'd trusted her with everything—my questions about my first period, my first forays into birth control. But I couldn't trust her with this. She'd be obligated to report the possibility of a seizure, and what then? I'd be back to no-driving status, and I couldn't have that. I just couldn't.

I did, however, call my mom. Even though I'd only spoken to her the day before, and even though I'd been so happy to move out of her house, to stop needing her so much, she was still the first person I turned to. The phone rang and rang at my parents' house, until finally the voice mail kicked in. I didn't leave a message. My mom would panic if I did, and she'd probably just check the caller ID, anyway, note I called and call me back. I wondered where she was, though, before noon on a Sunday. She'd barely ever left the house on Sundays. I liked to sleep in. My mom liked to bake and garden and watch old movies on TV while my dad puttered in the garage.

I'd spent so many hours dreaming of days like this—waking in my own bed, my own house. Nobody around me. Just me, with no place to go and nobody to answer to. Nothing to do but my own laundry, using my own detergent, folding it or leaving it piled in the basket if that's what I wanted to do. I'd dreamed of being an adult, living by myself, and now that I had it, I was suddenly, unbearably lonely.

The Morningstar Mocha would help with that. There I was part of a community. I had friends. I hadn't made specific plans to meet Jen there, but I knew a quick text message would tell me if she were going to show or not. And if she didn't, I could take my laptop and settle in with the bottomless cup of coffee or a pot of tea and a muffin. I could play around on Connex, or instant message friends who were also online.

Oh. And I could sorta-kinda-maybe-just-a-little-bit stalk Johnny Dellasandro.

A quick text to Jen settled the plans. We'd meet in half an hour, just enough time for me to shower and dress and walk to the coffee shop, including the time it was going to take me to shave my legs, pluck my brows and figure out what I was going to wear. Because yes, it was important.

★ ★ ★

"Hey, girl, hey!" Jen's greeting made me laugh as she waved across the crowded Mocha. "I saved you a spot. What took you so long? Couldn't find a place to park?"

"Oh, no, I walked." My teeth were still chattering. January in Harrisburg isn't quite the Arctic Circle, but it was cold enough to freeze a polar bear's balls.

"What? Why? Oh, yeah. Snowplow?"

"I love that I can follow that conversation." As if parking wasn't enough of a hassle on my street, when the snowplow came through and covered the cars and people dug them out, leaving behind their empty spots, it could get ugly when someone took one. That wasn't why I'd walked, though. I shrugged off my coat and hung it on the back of my chair as I tried to casually scan the room for sight of the delicious, delectable Dellasandro. "But no. I just felt like walking."

"I've heard of taking a cold shower, but that's a little overboard."

I blew into my hands to warm them and slipped into my chair. "I need to work off some of this ass if I'm going to keep eating muffins for breakfast."

"Girl." Jen sighed. "I hear you."

We commiserated in silence for a moment about the collective size of our butts, though frankly I thought Jen had a supercute figure and had nothing to worry about, and I knew she thought the same of me.

"Love the top," she said after the moment had passed. Then she laughed and lowered her voice. "I bet he'd like it, too."

"Who?"

"Don't you even pretend you don't know who I mean!"

I looked down at the shirt, a simple sweater of soft knit that buttoned all the way to a pretty scoop neck. "I like the way it makes my collarbones look. And it's not all cleavagy, like I'm trying too hard."

"No, not at all," Jen agreed. "And that color is awesome on you."

I beamed. "I love your earrings."

Jen fluttered her eyelashes at me. "Are we finished being gay for each other? Because if not, I was going to say I think your necklace is pretty."

"This?" I'd forgotten what, exactly, I was wearing on my throat. I wasn't usually the sort to switch out jewelry. My job at the credit union meant I had to dress nicely for work every day, with a strict dress code, and I'd gotten tired of trying to coordinate every day. As I tugged the pendant so I could see it, the chain broke and slithered into my fingers. "Oops!"

"Oh, shit." Jen grabbed at the pendant, catching it before it could fall onto the table. She handed it to me.

"Damn." I studied it. Nothing special, really, just a small, swirled design. I'd picked it up on the bargain table at my favorite thrift store. I cupped it now, the metal curiously warm in my palm. "Ah, well."

"Can you get it fixed?"

"Not worth it. I don't even think it's real gold."

"Too bad," Jen said brightly. "Otherwise, you could take it to one of those places that buys gold for cash! I got invited to some home party thing my mom's neighbor's having. It says they'll take gold fillings…teeth attached!"

"Gross!" I put the necklace into my coat pocket.

Jen laughed and seemed about to say something else, but her chuckle caught and broke. She looked over my shoulder, eyes wide. I knew better than to turn around.

I didn't have to. I knew it was him. I could feel him. I could smell him.

Oranges.

He eased past us. The hem of his long black coat brushed my arm, and I turned into a fifteen-year-old girl. The only reason I didn't giggle out loud was because my throat had gone so dry

I couldn't make a peep. Jen didn't say a word, either, just stared at me with raised brows until Johnny'd passed.

"Are you okay?" she whispered, leaning close. "You look like you're going to pass out. You're all pale!"

I didn't feel like I was going to. I didn't feel pale. I felt red-hot and blushing. I swallowed the cotton on my tongue and shook my head, not daring to look over her shoulder to watch him place his order at the counter. "No. I'm okay."

"You sure?" Jen put her hand over mine to squeeze. "Really, Emm, you look..."

Just then, he turned around and looked at me. I mean, really looked. Not a quick glance, eyes sliding past me like I didn't exist. Not a double take, either, like the sight of me had frightened him. Johnny Dellasandro looked at me, and I was already half out of my chair before I realized I couldn't just get up and go to him.

Jen glanced over her shoulder, but he'd already turned back to the counter to take the plate with the muffin on it from the counter girl. He wasn't looking at me any longer, and I didn't know how to tell her he had been. *If* he had been—it was easy in those few seconds to convince myself I'd imagined it.

"Emm?"

"He is so fucking beautiful." My voice didn't sound like mine. It sounded hoarse and harsh and full of longing.

"Yeah." Jen's brow furrowed and she glanced at him again.

He'd moved to a table toward the back and looked up at the sound of the bell over the door. Jen and I both looked, too. A woman about my age, maybe a year or two older, moved directly toward the back of the room without stopping even at the counter. From my place at the table it was easy to see her slide into the chair across from Johnny and to watch her lean forward so he could kiss her in greeting. My stomach dropped all the way down to the toes of the boots I'd spent twenty minutes agonizing over.

"Well, fuck," I said miserably.

Jen looked back at me. "I don't recognize her."

"No. Me, neither."

"She's not a regular," Jen continued, affronted. "Jesus, at least he could go with a regular!"

I didn't feel like laughing but I couldn't help it—her logic was so very flawed. "Why don't you go over there and challenge her to a dance-off or something."

Jen shook her head and looked at me seriously. "I don't think so."

I opened my mouth to protest that I was kidding, but the way Jen looked again back at Johnny and the woman, then at me, stopped me. She wasn't smiling. I felt studied. A different kind of heat crept up my throat and cheeks, somehow guilty this time.

"No," she added. "I don't think so."

My cell phone vibrated in my pocket and I pulled it out. "It's my mom."

"Go ahead and take it. I'm going to grab some coffee and a piece of cake or something. You want a muffin and a bottomless cup, right?"

"Yeah, thanks." I dug in my purse for a ten-dollar bill she waved away, and I couldn't argue with her because I was already thumbing my phone's screen to take the call. "Mom. Hi."

"What's wrong?"

"Nothing's wrong—why do you always think something's wrong?" I should've felt more annoyed by her question, but the truth was, it was good to hear the concern in my mom's voice. It was good to be so loved.

"You called me before noon on a Sunday morning, that's why I think something's wrong, Emmaline. You can't lie to your mother."

"Oh, Mom." Sometimes she sounded so much older than she was. More like a grandma than a mother, and yet I knew from photos and stories that she'd been a true child of the sixties. More so even than my dad, who wasn't above getting a little tipsy at Christmastime and who'd confessed to me once that he thought pot should be legal.

"So. Tell me?"

"Nothing's wrong," I assured her. My eye caught Johnny again, but he wasn't looking this way. He was in intense conversation with that woman, both of them leaning in toward each other in a way that could only mean intimacy. I tore my gaze from them and focused on my call. "I just thought I'd see what you're up to."

"Oh." My mom sounded nonplussed. "Well, your dad and I went out to breakfast at the Old Country Buffet."

"You…went to breakfast?"

At the counter, Jen was only a few feet away from Johnny, but she didn't even look like she was trying to take a peek, much less not-so-casually overhear their conversation. It was still going full-force, based on his expression and the set of his companion's shoulders. I couldn't see her face, but her body language told me everything I needed to know.

"Sure. Why, aren't we allowed?" My mom sounded a little strange, a little shorter in her response than I was used to.

"Of course you are. Mom, are you feeling okay?"

"I'm supposed to be asking you that," she said.

And there it was, the subject that would never go away. It wasn't fair to call it an elephant in the room. You were supposed to be able to ignore those.

For one long instant I thought about telling her. Not the bits about the sex on the train and being some sort of 1970s Italian movie queen. I was sure my mom didn't want to hear about that. But the small blank moments, the scent of oranges. I didn't, though. Not only because I didn't want to worry her, but because I didn't want to prove her right.

"I'm fine, Mom. Really." My throat closed on the lie, and

my eyes smarted. I was glad we had the distance of satellites between us. I'd never have been able to get away with it face-to-face.

"Where are you? I hear a lot of noise."

"Oh. The coffee shop."

My mom laughed. "Again? You're going to turn into a cup of coffee soon."

"Better that than a pumpkin," I told her as Jen wove her way back to our table balancing two plates and two empty mugs. "People who love coffee say they can't live without it. Pumpkins just get made into pie."

"Oh, you crazy girl," my mom said fondly. "Call me tomorrow?"

"Sure, Mom. Bye." We disconnected just as Jen sat down, pushing my plate and mug toward me.

"Your mom must be pretty cool," she said.

"She can be. Oh, God. Chocolate fudge chip with fudge icing? This isn't a muffin. This is a new pair of jeans in a bigger size."

Jen licked a fingertip. "It's what he likes."

I didn't have to ask her who "he" was. I wondered if I'd ever have to ask again. "Yeah?"

She grinned. "Some stalker you are."

Our conversation turned from the tantalizing topic of Johnny Dellasandro, maybe because he was actually there and could've overheard us, or because he was with a woman, therefore making any fantasies about him sort of lame and pointless. Or maybe because we had other things to talk about, me and Jen, like our favorite television shows and books, about the cute guy who delivered pizzas in our neighborhood. About all the things good friends talk about over sweets and caffeine.

"I should get going," I said with a sigh when I'd polished off that sinful muffin and finished my third mug of coffee. I patted my stomach. "I'm going to burst, plus I have laundry to do and some bills to pay."

"Nice quiet Sunday afternoon." Jen sighed happily. "The best kind. See you in the morning?"

"Oh, probably. I'm sure I'll swing by here for a coffee to go. I know I should make my own at home, but...I can't ever get the brew to taste right. And it seems like a waste to make a whole pot when I can only have one cup."

Jen grinned and winked. "And the eye candy here is so much nicer."

There was that, too.

She ducked out before I did, and not because I was lingering overlong trying to get a look at Johnny. I did take one last glance over my shoulder at him as I pushed the door and made the bell jingle. I was hoping he'd look up, but he was still locked deep in conversation with that woman, whoever she was.

It wasn't until much later that night—bills paid and laundry washed, dried, sorted, folded and put away—that I thought to look for the necklace in my pocket. I searched them all, even the ones of my jeans, though I knew I hadn't put it in there. No necklace. Somewhere, somehow, I'd lost it.

Like I'd said to Jen, it was no big deal. It wasn't a piece I'd had any sentimental ties to, and I was sure it hadn't been expensive. Still, the fact I'd lost it disturbed me. I'd lost things before. Put them down when I was having a fugue and didn't remember it. I'd found things that way, too. Once, I'd walked out of a store clutching a fistful of lip balms I must've grabbed up from a bin. I'd been too embarrassed to tell my mom I stole them. Every once in a while I found one in a pocket of a coat or a purse. They'd lasted me for years.

I hadn't lost the necklace in a fugue, I was almost certain of that. I'd walked home from the Mocha with the wind so cold in my nostrils it had frozen my nose hairs, making it possible but not likely I'd missed any scent of oranges. On the other hand, it was possible I'd had a fugue without that warning sign. Lots of people with seizure disorders never had any warning, or memory, of what had happened.

This thought sobered me faster than a high school kid pulled over by the sheriff on prom night.

Blinking fast to keep the tears suddenly burning my eyes from slipping out, I took a long, slow breath. Then another. By the time I'd focused on the third, in and out, I felt a little calmer. Not much, but enough to slow the frantic pounding of my heart and quell the surging boil in my guts.

I'd discovered alternative medicine a few years ago when traditional techniques could no longer diagnose whatever it was the fall had done to my brain. I was tired of being stuck with needles and taking medicine that often had side effects so much worse than the benefits they provided, it wasn't worth taking them. Acupuncture couldn't diagnose my problem any better than Western medicine could, but I found I'd rather use it than fill my body with potentially toxic chemicals day after day. Guided imagery and meditation didn't get rid of my anxieties altogether, but the practice of them definitely kept me in a better mood. And since I'd discovered through lots of trial and error that I was more likely to experience a bad fugue when I was overtired, overstimulated, overstressed or overanything, I'd incorporated meditation into my daily routine as a preventative measure.

I thought it worked. It seemed to, anyway. I'd been fugue-free for the past two years, anyway, until just lately. And even these three had been so minor, so inconsequential…

"Ah, shit," I said aloud, my voice harsh and strained.

My reflection in my bedroom mirror showed pale cheeks, shadowed eyes, lips gone thin from the effort of holding back a sob. The fugues had never been painful, yet having them hurt more than anything in my life.

I blew out another breath, concentrating while I changed

quickly into a pair of soft pajama bottoms and a worn T-shirt with a picture of Bert and Ernie on it. I'd bought it at Sesame Place when I was in junior high and had only rediscovered it while packing to move here. It fit a little tighter than it had back then, but it was comfortable in more than the size. It was a piece of home.

Changed, I settled onto my bed with my legs crossed. I didn't have a fancy mat or any sort of altar, and I didn't light incense. Meditation wasn't so much spiritual as it was physical for me. I'd studied a lot about biofeedback over the years, and while I doubted I'd ever be able to consciously control my heart rate or brain wave patterns the way some accomplished yogis did, I believed meditation did help. I could feel it.

I rested my hands on my knees, palms up, thumb to fingertips. I closed my eyes. I didn't chant the traditional Om Mani Padme Om or even any of the other traditional phrases. I'd found something that worked better for me.

"Sausage and gravy on a biscuit, yum. Sausage and gravy on a biscuit, yummmmm."

I let the words flow out of me on each exhalation. With each inhalation, I tried to stop myself from testing the air for the scent of oranges. It took me a lot longer than it usually did to put myself into a state of calm. At last my muscles relaxed. My heartbeat slowed to its normal rate.

I let myself fall back onto the pillows. All brand-new. The comforter was, too, as was the mattress and the bed. My new bed, one I'd never shared. I uncrossed my legs, stretching without opening my eyes. Cradled in the softness of the bed, loose and relaxed, it seemed natural for my hands to drift over my belly and thighs. My breasts.

I thought of Johnny. I'd memorized every detail of his face from seeing him at the Mocha, and every detail of the rest of him from the movies Jen and I had watched and the photos online. He had dimples at the base of his back and one dimple on his left cheek, just at the corner of his mouth. I'd like to lick those dimples.

My breath soughed out of me as my fingers slid across the skin of my belly, bare from where my shirt had pulled up. I didn't usually need visual aids to bring myself pleasure. Porn was all right, I had no problem with it, but it all seemed sort of random and senseless to me. Even supposedly woman-oriented porn didn't make much sense to me. I got more turned on reading sensually explicit novels or even listening to music than I ever did watching dirty movies or looking at pictures.

Now, though, I fixed on the image of Johnny's face. His golden brows, arched over those yummy green-brown eyes. That mouth, a little thin but easily quirked into a smile. At least, in his movies, that was. I hadn't yet seen him as much as quirk the corner of his lips in real life.

"Johnny," I whispered, thinking I should be ashamed or embarrassed to be saying his name aloud to myself this way but not feeling anything but warmth.

Even his name was sexy. A boy's name, a nickname, not a name for a grown man who was, I realized, probably my dad's age. I groaned and clapped a hand over my eyes.

It didn't stop me from thinking about him. He might be the same age as my parents, but I had no trouble imagining him as a lover. I'd never had a fetish for older dudes—if anything, I freely admitted to a certain amount of ogling of younger men on a daily basis. My office overlooked the campus of a local college, and my coworkers and I often enjoyed our lunches while watching the boys on their way to class. But Johnny's age didn't matter. Intellectually, I knew he was "too old" for me. My head knew it.

My body was another matter.

My hand stroked down my belly to cup between my legs, the heel of my palm pressing my clit. I sighed. I used a finger to idly stroke myself through the soft material of my pajamas, then slid my hand inside the elastic waistband. This was my pleasure, solo.

It was Johnny I thought of, obviously. Scenes from his movies knitted with still shots and the sound of his voice. I wondered how it would sound if he said my name. Would he groan it the way he did on film, fucking the actress with whom he'd had a child? Would he whisper it against my skin, his tongue working its way down my body to center on my clit the way my fingertip circled just now?

I wanted to undress him. Strip away the long black coat, the scarf. Use it to cover his eyes while he laughed and, patiently, allowed me to unfix the buttons of his shirt from their holes and slide his arms from the sleeves. To unzip and unbutton his pants and slide them down those long, muscled thighs. I wanted to kneel in front of him and nuzzle at the softness of his pubic hair, golden and darker than the hair on his head. I wanted to take that nice, thick cock in my mouth and suck until he got so hard I couldn't fit him all the way in.

My hand was moving faster. My cunt wet. I slipped a finger down to get it slick, then up again, while my other hand cupped a breast and pinched at my nipple. I thought of Johnny while I made love to myself. His eyes, nose, ears, mouth. His delicious nipples. I wanted to lick and bite them. I wanted to hear him say my name, and beg me to fuck him.

"Yes," I murmured.

My back arched, hips pushing upward against the sweet pressure of my hand. I wasn't easing toward climax, more like hurtling toward it. I hadn't done this in a long time. Since before the last time I'd had sex, as a matter of fact, and that had been about three months ago. I didn't want to think about that now. I wanted to think about Johnny.

"Emm," he said in my ear, and I didn't startle. My eyes didn't open. I breathed in the scent of oranges and gave myself over to his touch.

My hands found the spindles of my headboard and I grabbed them. The wood creaked at the strength of my grip. It was slick under my palms, my fingers slid, but I held tight. The bed dipped beneath his weight.

He kissed me.

Openmouthed, slow and sweet and hot, just the way I'd imagined it. Johnny tasted like nothing and everything I'd ever loved or wanted. I breathed him in, sucking gently on his tongue. Our teeth bumped, sending sparks of sensation through me, and a giggle. My eyes fluttered, but he gave a warning noise.

"Don't," Johnny said, and I kept my eyes shut tight.

When wet heat centered over my clit, I let out a noise of my own. Low and urgent. I said his name. He laughed against me, and it was just the way I'd imagined it. His lips pressed me through the thin material of my pajama bottoms. He worked my clit with his lips, and the barrier of cotton only enhanced the pleasure.

I wanted to feel him on me. Skin on skin. I wanted him inside me, balls deep. I wanted him fucking me while I drew gouges in his back with my nails and urged him on.

None of that happened. Johnny used his mouth and fingers to stroke me toward orgasm, and that turned out to be pretty fucking good enough. Pleasure filled me. Overflowing. Electric. I jerked with it and let go of the headboard so my fingers could find that thick, beautiful hair and burrow into it.

I came from Johnny's mouth and hands, and with his voice murmuring encouragement, but when my hand reached down I found nothing but my own body. Orgasm arced through me. My eyes opened. I cried out, wordless and yearning, and my voice slid into a moan.

I swallowed the taste of him.

I was alone.

I looked like shit. Hair lank, shadows under my eyes, skin blotchy. I'd managed to leave the house with mismatched socks, too, a fact I was hoping nobody would notice unless I pulled up the legs of my trousers to show off the mistake. I'd slept terribly, my night filled with dreams that were nothing like fugues.

I sat at my desk, gripping a mug of cooling coffee and staring at my computer screen without doing much. I had an appointment with my acupuncturist after work and didn't see much point in pretending to accomplish anything for the next hour. Fortunately, I had nothing too pressing waiting for me. I'd been expecting a lot more work when I took this job at the credit union, but compared to my days as a teller, then assistant bank manager, my new job was as easy as a two-dollar hooker who takes coupons.

I did rustle up enough energy to check my personal email. Among the forwards of stupid jokes and pictures of strange street signs my mom sent, there was a message from Jen. The subject read simply, "Read This."

So, like Alice being offered a piece of the caterpillar's mushroom, I did.

It was a link to a blog specializing in reviews of obscure

horror movies. It had an entire section devoted to Johnny's films, even the ones that weren't horror. I was surprised to see he'd made only fifteen movies, total, as the wealth of information on the internet had made it seem like way more than that. Reading through the descriptions, I realized it was because so many of them had been recut or released under alternate names, or in foreign versions. There was a clickable list for each one, each link leading to a separate page with still pictures, video clips and information about the movie. Also, Buy links. Some of the movies were readily available, if you knew where to look, and at dollar-bin prices. Others…

"Whoa." I said this with respect and awe.

One hundred and seventy-five dollars for a dubbed DVD of some obscure film I hadn't ever heard of. Plus shipping. I slid my tongue over my teeth as I contemplated this, and then the triple-digit number (not including the decimals) currently in my checking account.

$175 for a J.D. movie. I texted to Jen.

Can u believe it? She answered almost instantly.

I believe it, bb. Which one?

Night of A Hundred Moons.

Holy shit! Grab that shit up, girl. Nobody ever has a Hundred Moons!

Then, a second later:

(I)

It took me a minute to figure out what that was, but when I

did, it made me laugh. It was a moon of the bare butt variety, not the celestial. Nice.

Have u seen it?

I typed.

Never. Not even in bootleg clips.

Do u want to?

R u kidding? YES!!!

One hundred and seventy-five dollars could be a lot or a little bit of money, depending. It wasn't much for a car repair, for example, though it wasn't a little, either. It was just about right for a really tiny television set, a bit too much for a pair of shoes and a ridiculously reasonable amount for a week's vacation at the beach.

It was way too fucking much for a DVD.

I was already clicking on Add to Basket. My heart hung up when the website froze, the small scroll bar at the bottom stuck just an eyelash width from the end. I clicked, clicked again. Nothing happened.

It took me two or three frantic, sweaty moments before I realized I had to click the My Cart link to see that I had, indeed, managed to add the movie. I added the shipping, which was frankly outrageous, as well as some other random handling fee. I couldn't even look at the total as I typed my credit card number into a definitely unsecured website, risking my entire identity just to get my hands on what would assuredly turn out to be a crappy copy of a bad movie.

I printed out the receipt and made sure a copy of the order had also appeared in my email before I dared to navigate away from the site. Then I sat back in my desk chair, heart still pounding, palms still sweating. I felt like I'd run a mile pursued by dogs. Or zombies. Or worse, zombie dogs. I felt wrung out and anxious and something else, too. Unreasonably excited. I texted Jen.

Bought it.

Get the fuck out!

Yes. Girls' night when it comes?

It won't be the only thing coming. Call me when you get it.

I said I would and slipped my phone into my purse so I could head out for my appointment. It took me only ten minutes to get from my office to the alternative medicine center, a trip that had taken me forty-five when I lived with my parents. In another five I was in the quiet room on my back, a soft pillow beneath my head.

I have eclectic musical tastes, but "spa" music usually didn't do it for me. Yet I couldn't deny it was relaxing, the soft chimes and woodwind instruments. That was the point, after all. To relax the patients. And I tried, I really did, but the harder I tried to put everything out of my mind, the more I thought.

I knew the treatment would help even if I couldn't stop the hamster wheel of my brain from spinning. I just didn't want to be there, stiff and aching, anxious. I wanted to melt into the table and let the needles do their work the way they'd done for the past couple of years…and then I was thinking again, worrying again, that this time the treatment would fail. That I'd be back to suffering through the insult of a brain that made me see, hear, smell and touch things that weren't there. Or worse, that gave me blank spots in my memory, moments in which anything could've happened. I wasn't sure which was worse, experiencing things that hadn't happened, or not remembering things that had.

The music changed from the soft tinkle of water and a flute to something low, almost moaning. I'd never noticed vocals in any of the music the office played. Now I couldn't ignore them.

A cello. A woman's breathy voice. The plucking of strings.

And then, though I'd always specifically requested no aromatherapy treatments during my acupuncture…the inevitable scent of oranges.

"No," I muttered, and clung to consciousness with every single brain cell I had.

When the fugues had first started, I hadn't known how to determine one was on the verge. As the years had passed, I could predict the onset with enough time—sometimes only barely, but usually enough—to prepare for it. I had never yet mastered fending one off. In fact, I'd learned it was better not to try, because they seemed to last longer and be more intense, with a longer recovery time, if I fought them. I couldn't help it now, though. It was the worst betrayal to go dark here, with the needles in my shin and collarbone, supposedly aligning my qi and keeping me centered in this world. My muscles strained, defeating the purpose of everything I'd come here to do.

There was nothing I could do. The scent of oranges swirled around me. I closed my eyes, tense, and waited for my world to shift and change or simply go black around me. I gripped the table and felt the needles in my side shift and pinch.

Nothing happened.

I pressed my eyes closed tighter, my senses heightened. I heard the squeak-squeak of wheels, the soft click of the door opening. I opened my eyes, turned my head toward the sound.

It was Dr. Gupta, who greeted me with a smile and a pat to my shoulder.

"I apologize for being a little late to remove the needles, Emm," she said. "We had a little accident out in the hallway. Someone came to clean it up, but there's quite a mess. Be careful when you go out there."

She plucked needles from my skin as she spoke, slipping them into the red sharps container marked with the biohazard symbol. Then she took hold of my arm and helped me sit. She handed me a paper cup of water.

"How do you feel?"

I didn't want to tell her about the fugue I may or may not have fended off. I breathed in. The scent of oranges had faded, though not disappeared. My mouth squirted saliva, lips puckering at the memory of the citrus taste. I hadn't eaten oranges in years, unable to stomach them, but this gustatory illusion was unusual. Mostly I just smelled the oranges, I didn't taste them.

"Tired," I said.

"That's to be expected. Are you dizzy? Drink some water."

I did, not because I was dizzy but to wash away the lingering taste of citrus. She took the cup from me and tossed it in the trash, then gripped my elbow to help me off the table. I waited half a minute, used to the way the floor sometimes tilted at first when I'd just finished a treatment. It didn't today, but I rested a moment longer than normal, anyway.

"Emm. You sure you're all right?" Dr. Gupta is a tiny, dark-haired woman with big dark eyes. She reminds me of that old newspaper cartoon *Dondi*.

"Sure. Fine." I gave her my brightest smile to convince her.

Dr. Gupta didn't look convinced. She drew another cup of water from the cooler and handed it to me. "Drink that. You're a little pale. I think next time we'll concentrate on a super Ming

Men instead of the Shen Men. We'll do some energizing in addition to the tranquilizing."

I'd been having acupuncture treatments for three years now, but that didn't make me anything like an expert. In fact, I was more of the "I don't need to know how it works" school of thought. I'd never studied the mechanics of it, or the philosophy.

"Sure," I told her.

She laughed. "You have no idea what I'm talking about. That's okay, so long as it works, yes?"

"Yes." I drank the water, though by this point my back teeth were swimming.

She patted my shoulder again. "I'll see you in a month, unless you have something you need taken care of before then."

She left me to rearrange my clothes. Standing in the quiet room with the soft music playing, I should've been way more relaxed after a treatment. Instead, I felt electric. Buzzing. Not bad, exactly. And not the way I often felt after having a fugue, sort of fuzzy and disoriented for a few moments.

This feeling was more like an ache in my chest. An anticipation, not quite anxiety. No pain. There was never pain associated with any of this.

When I left the office, the smell of oranges once again assaulted me. I braced myself in the doorway, jaw clenched…until I saw the cleaning cart and the jug of citrus-scented cleaner, cap open, and the floor still gleaming from it. The woman at the cart saw me look and smiled apologetically.

"We spilled almost the whole jug," she explained, holding up a mop. "But it's okay, you can go past now."

She couldn't have had any idea about why I was laughing, but she laughed, too. I wanted to give her a high five as I passed her, but restrained myself. I couldn't keep the grin off my face, though, as I stopped at the front desk to make my co-pay and book my next appointment.

"This is what I love about my job," said Peta, the receptionist.

"Taking my money?"

"No." She shook her head. "Seeing how people come in here full of pain and leave full of peace."

I paused with my checkbook still in my hand. "That's a great way of saying it."

She dimpled. "Maybe I should put that on an inspirational poster, huh?"

"Maybe. But…it's true, isn't it?" I felt more at peace, certainly, once I'd learned the smell hadn't been the harbinger of a fugue, after all.

"It really is. Take care, Emm, see you next month."

I waved at her as I went out, my steps more springy and my heart lighter. Behind the wheel of my car I took a few more deep breaths to center myself out of habit. When you've had your license taken away because the authorities fear you might spaz out and cause an accident while you're driving, you tend to better appreciate your ability to drive yourself when you are allowed. But as I pulled out of the parking lot, I realized the buzzing, churning tumble in my chest hadn't really gone away, just faded.

Bad tacos for last night's dinner, maybe. Too much coffee on an empty stomach. I gripped the wheel and checked my eyes in the rearview mirror. A little wide, but the pupils weren't pinned or anything funky like that. My vision wasn't blurry. I wasn't smelling anything but my own cologne from where it had rubbed into my scarf.

Nevertheless, I drove slowly. Carefully. Taking no chances at yellow lights or intersections. By the time I got to my street, my fingers ached from gripping the wheel and my back hurt, too, from my too-tense posture.

"Motherfucker," I muttered when I saw that someone had once again taken my spot. I really needed to get some lawn chairs and set them up when I left, the way my neighbors did.

I drove farther down the street and found an empty spot. The last time the plow had gone through, a thigh-deep pile of snow had been pushed into someone's shoveled spot. The vehicle that usually parked there, a blue SUV, could no longer fit. I spotted it parked a block farther down and felt no guilt at squeezing my much smaller car into the space. I considered it karma.

The fact I'd once again parked in front of Johnny's house was a nice little bonus, one that had me humming under my breath with glee and buzzing in an entirely different way. I paused after I'd closed my car door to study his house. When had I ever felt this way before?

The answer was, never. I'd had crushes before, plenty of them. In seventh grade I'd thought I would die unless a sophomore named Steve Houseman liked me back. I hadn't died. And even then, when I'd gone to sleep every night wishing on every star I could see that he'd look at me like I was a real girl and not some junior high geek, I hadn't ever felt like this.

The curb was icy, but the sidewalk in front of Johnny's house was bare and well-salted. Unfortunately, his neighbors weren't as conscientious. I was so busy trying to peek through his windows without making it obvious I was a pervert, I didn't pay attention to where I put my feet. I hit a slick patch and slid, arms wheeling. I'd never been a gymnast, but I managed a pretty nice split that had me gasping in gratitude I was wearing a skirt, even though I tore my stockings.

So focused on keeping myself from totally wiping out and doing a face plant into the pile of filthy snow, I didn't pay attention to the man who'd just crossed the street and stepped up onto the curb in front of me. I caught a flash of a black coat, a striped scarf. I had time to think, *Oh, shit, it's him,* before I took another step and slid with that one, too.

We collided hard enough to snap my jaws together. I caught my tongue between my teeth and tasted blood. I looked into Johnny's face, those green-brown eyes so close I could count his lashes. He had a mole at the corner of one eye I'd never noticed before. He grabbed my upper arms.

I smelled oranges.

I was falling.

"Hey, foxy mama."

The man in front of me gripped my upper arms to keep me from falling. I'd tripped on a loose piece of concrete in the sidewalk. I stared at it, thinking there was something wrong.

And then I knew.

Holy shit, it was summer. The man in front of me, Johnny. And he was…young.

"You okay? You having a bad trip or something?" He laughed and shook his hair out of his eyes. "Trip. Sorry."

The moment Dorothy steps out of her black-and-white house into the Technicolor glory of Munchkinland is one of the greatest in movie history. I was Dorothy now, my eyes wide, legs trembling. I looked around at the way my world had changed and ducked instinctively in case a house was getting ready to fall on me. I'd have fallen if Johnny hadn't held me up.

"Chill, little sister," he said in a kind voice, and led me to the porch stoop where he eased me onto the heat-soaked concrete and sat beside me, my hand in his.

The colors were all so bright. I heard music, the steady disco thump of a song my mother had sung to me when I was a kid. A woman in short shorts and a tube top roller-skated past us, jumping effortlessly over the crack that had tripped me up. Her hair flew behind her in a long, gleaming wave.

A garbage truck rumbled past on the narrow street lined with wide cars all in shades of brown and green. It said New York City Municipal Services on the side, and I swallowed a sudden rush of saliva.

Bright sunshine. Heat. And yet I shivered, teeth chattering even as my butt scorched against the steps. The backs of my calves were worse, having no protection but my ripped panty hose. I hissed and shifted.

"Chill," Johnny said again, soothingly.

I didn't smell oranges. I smelled car exhaust and the faint whiff of sewage, probably from the alley next to this house or the garbage cans lined up along the curb. I smelled sun-baked concrete. I smelled him, too.

I leaned closer without thinking to take a long, deep breath of his neck. His hair tickled my cheek. He smelled like a man should—not like cologne but clean skin, a little bit of summer sweat, fresh air. He smelled better than I'd ever imagined he would, and I'd imagined he'd smell pretty fucking fine.

"Hey," Johnny said softly.

Blinking, I pulled back, the heat in my cheeks and throat having nothing to do with the summer sun beating down all around us. I'd just sniffed him like a dog testing out a fireplug. During my fugues lots of things happened that didn't in real life; I behaved in ways I'd never have done while conscious and never felt embarrassed about it the way I did now.

"Sorry," I managed to say, and tried to pull away, but his hand holding mine kept me anchored onto the step.

"No sweat. What's your name?"

He was even more beautiful than he'd looked in pictures. It wasn't fair to compare this young Johnny to his older version, but I couldn't help it. This Johnny smiled at me, while the older one never had. He ducked his head a little now, peering at me from the silky fringe of long bangs.

"You have a name, right?"

"Emm," I said. "My name's Emm."

"Johnny." He lifted our hands and shook them before letting them drop, this time to his thigh.

I felt his skin beneath the back of my hand. I shivered again. I blinked and breathed. This was a fugue. I was imagining all of this. Somewhere else I'd gone dark.

"Oh." The word eased out on a moan and I closed my eyes. "Johnny."

I meant the one in winter, in the black coat. The one I'd run into and was now likely making a fool of myself in front of.

"Yeah. That's me." He shifted, our thighs touching. "I don't know you, but you seem to know me. How's that?"

This was a fugue, I reminded myself. It wasn't real. But no matter how hard I tried, I could sense nothing but this now. This place. This man in front of me. No glimmers of anything else, even though I knew it had to be there, in front of me, if only my brain would let go of me long enough to get back to it.

I didn't want to get back to it, I realized, looking at Johnny's smile. It was for me, that grin. So was the appreciative gaze he swept over me, his eyes lingering on my breasts a second too long before he focused briefly on my mouth and licked his lips. When his gaze swept up to meet mine again, I got lost in those eyes.

"You don't talk much, huh?"

"I just… This is a little…" I couldn't explain.

He laughed and stroked the back of my hand with his thumb. "You must be on some pretty good shit. But you should be more careful. This neighborhood, it ain't so great. I mean, I live here and all. But you don't. I'd have seen you around here before. Are you new, or just visiting?"

"I was just walking past." It wasn't a lie.

"You want to come inside? Gotta bunch of friends over, just hanging out. Having a little party. C'mon," Johnny said, as though I needed any persuasion. "You'll have a good time, I promise."

He stood, tugging me onto my feet. The earth didn't rock. I didn't spin. With Johnny holding my hand, I wasn't going anywhere but wherever he took me.

His house here in 1970s New York was a tall brownstone a lot like the one in present-day Harrisburg. It had to be newer, but it wasn't as nice on the outside. Inside, it was so similar to my own I let out a low murmur of surprise as we entered the foyer. Stairs in front of us led up, a long and narrow hall pointed toward the kitchen and an arched doorway to our right led into a formal living room. A beaded curtain hung in the archway.

I heard music, louder in here, from upstairs. I heard voices, too. I smelled pot.

"C'mon in." Johnny linked his fingers through mine and tugged me down the hall toward the kitchen, where a group of men and women sat around a wooden table or leaned against the counters to watch another man cooking something on the stove. "Hungry? Candy's cooking."

At the sound of his name, the man at the stove turned and flashed a grin of straight white teeth. He bent his head, Afro waving, as regally as any king welcoming a subject, his stirring spoon a scepter. "Welcome, welcome, sister. We got enough to feed you, if you're hungry."

I was hungry, intensely so. My stomach rumbled. I'd never been hungry in a fugue before. Oh, I'd eaten and drank, but never from need. I put my free hand, the one not still clutching Johnny's, over my belly.

My clothes hadn't changed. I looked down at the familiar friction of material under my fingertips. I was even wearing my winter coat, though it had come unbuttoned. No wonder

I'd been so hot outside. No wonder everyone was looking at me so strangely.

"You can take that off," Johnny offered.

I nodded and let him help me out of it. Women's lib might be going strong, but Johnny was still a gentleman. He hung my coat on a hook behind the door and put his hand on the small of my back as I stood under the scrutiny of everyone in the kitchen.

"This is Emm," Johnny said, like he brought strangers home all the time. He probably did. "That's Wanda, Paul, Ed, Bellina and Candy's at the stove. Say hi, everyone."

They did, in a chorus, while I stared and tried to keep my mouth closed. I didn't recognize Wanda or her name, but Bellina Cassidy was a playwright, her shows performed on Broadway by casts of the biggest names in theater. Edgar D'Onofrio had been a celebrated poet who'd killed himself sometime in the late seventies. Paul was probably Paul Smiths, the photographer and moviemaker who'd directed a handful of Johnny's early movies. And Candy…

"Candy Applegate?"

Candy looked at her with a grin. "That's me."

"You have a restaurant," I said. "And that cooking show on TV."

The room bubbled with laughter. I was looking at the Enclave. I licked my mouth and tasted sweat.

"Naw, girl, that ain't me." Candy shook his head and dipped the spoon back into whatever was simmering so deliciously on the stove. "Must be some other Candy."

"No, it's you," I said, but shut my mouth up tight before I could say the rest.

Fugues were never like dreams, which I could sometimes control. I'd never been able to fix the course of what happened when I was dark. Sometimes that meant they were scarier than nightmares. Other times, like now, I just had to remember this wasn't real and I could do nothing about it. I could tell them I knew the future, but I'd only look crazier than I probably already did.

Johnny, in fact, was studying me. "Feed her, Candyman."

"I'll feed her," Candy said.

And they did. A great, steaming bowl of some spicy, meatless stew. We all ate it over fragrant, sticky rice and sopped up the gravy with thick slices of homemade bread. I had to stop to taste everything twice, not because I was greedy or hungry, but because it tasted so, so good.

We all ate a lot. Laughing and joking. Talking about politics and art and music I knew only from history lessons or the classic rock station. They dropped names casually—Jagger, Bowie, Lennon. They dipped bare fingers into the communal pot and ate with their hands. They passed a pipe without telling me what was in it, and I smoked some of it because, after all, none of this was real.

Through it all, Johnny watched me from across the table. I watched him, too. I hadn't asked what year this was and knew even if I did it wouldn't matter. By the length of his hair, I guessed Johnny was about twenty-four. This made me older than him by about seven years. He didn't seem to care.

I definitely didn't.

We ate and talked and laughed. Someone brought out a guitar and started to play a song I was surprised I knew the words to. Something about flowers and soldiers, and where had they gone. And then they sang "Puff the Magic Dragon." I'd never known it was about marijuana.

Sometime during all of this, our places around the table changed. I ended up next to Johnny instead of across from him. Our thighs pressed together. Our shoulders brushed when he leaned forward to grab up a slice of Candy's bread, or to refill my glass with the kind of rich, red wine I avoided in real life.

Johnny turned his face toward me and smiled. And I kissed

him. Just a brush of lip on lip, his breath warm and soft against me. He smiled into the kiss and his hand came up to cup the back of my neck beneath my hair.

Nobody noticed, or nobody cared. By that point I think most of them were drunk and high. Ed had passed out, his head on the table, snoring softly. Johnny squeezed my thigh beneath the table.

"Take me someplace," I whispered into his ear.

He looked into my eyes for a moment, curiously. Then he nodded. He took me by the hand and led me from the table. We didn't say goodbye, and I didn't look back. We went up the long, narrow stairs, our hands linked loosely. My hand trailed the banister. I looked over the side, to the floor below, then up to the floor above. Stuck between, Johnny leading me, woozy from the food and whatever was in the pipe…I followed.

But at the top of the stairs, I led. I kissed him. I pushed him back against the wall, my leg cocked between his thighs, against his crotch. His belt buckle, something huge and metal, pressed my belly through my skirt. I slid my hands up his front, over the slick-smooth fabric of his ugly-patterned shirt. And I kissed him, long and smooth and hard and slow and deep.

He looked at me curiously again when I pulled back. "Who are you?"

"Emm." I wasn't slurring, but my voice was definitely hoarser than usual. I tasted him when I swiped my tongue across my lips.

"Emm," Johnny said, as though considering something important. "That's your name, all right. But who are you?"

"Nobody," I assured him.

Our bodies pressed together. His hands fit on my hips. Downstairs, I heard the burble of laughter and music. Smelled the tang of weed. Here, up here, it was quiet.

I'd been away too long. Any minute I would start to fade from this place and wake, maybe blinking away only a few seconds of time. Maybe on my knees, or worse, my face, on the ground. Maybe I wouldn't wake at all.

The first door in the hallway, just to Johnny's left, was cracked open enough to show me a bedroom. I took his hand and pulled him toward it. Through the door, to the bed, which was neatly made up with a blanket of orange, ribbed fabric. My grandmother had used bedspreads just like that one. I sat on the bed and spread my legs. My skirt, too long for this era, dipped between my thighs, and I pulled it up inch by inch, watching him watch me.

I pulled the fabric up over the torn remnants of my panty hose and crooked my finger at him. "Come here."

Johnny, grinning, was already unbuttoning his shirt. He tossed it to the floor and then crawled up over me. Our mouths locked. His tongue stroked mine. I cradled him against my cunt, my legs open wide to accommodate him. My fingers drew circles on the bare flesh of his back.

I rolled him onto his back and straddled him. I hooked fingers into my nylons and tore them to keep any barrier from between us, but his jeans were still there.

"Cock blocked," I murmured, and tugged at his zipper.

"What?" Johnny laughed and put his hand on mine to help me pull down the zipper.

"Your jeans. They're cock-blocking me. Take them off."

He laughed again. I wanted to eat it up, that laughter. His mouth. All of him. I bent to kiss him with my hair hanging down all around us, and when he was naked underneath me, myself still clothed, I covered his body with my kisses.

He didn't protest when I nipped and sucked, or when I licked. He didn't protest when I lifted my skirt and pulled my panties aside to slide down on his cock. And Johnny didn't protest when I fucked him, sweating, both of us concentrating hard, not speaking, not even kissing, as the pleasure built higher and higher and crashed over us both.

He only protested when I got up to leave, but by then it was too late. The edges of this place were fading. Shaking in the aftermath of my orgasm, I kissed him. My skirt fell down around my knees. Johnny held my hand and made a wordless noise of complaint, but I tugged my fingers gently from his and stepped backward out the door, closing it behind me.

And then I woke up.

Chapter 06

My knees hurt. Throbbed and stung. Blood oozed from several scrapes. My panty hose had indeed been shredded, but on this sidewalk now, not from me tearing them away in order to get at naked Johnny.

He had one hand on my elbow, the other at my hip, holding me in place. "You all right?"

I blinked rapidly, putting myself in place. I knew where I was. I knew who I was. Most importantly, I knew *when* I was.

"Fine. I slipped on the ice. I'm sorry, did I hit you?"

My breezy explanation wasn't cutting it with him, I could tell. How long had I been dark? I hadn't conveniently glanced at my watch before the fugue.

"You should be more careful," Johnny warned, sounding stern.

I could still taste him. I swallowed against the flavor of his mouth and skin. We were standing too close for strangers, which is what we really were. He let go of my hip but kept hold of my elbow, and I was grateful because my legs had suddenly gone trembling and weak.

"You look like shit. You better come in here."

Yew bettuh come in heah.

From anyone else I'd have laughed a little at that accent, but on Johnny it was utterly drool-worthy. I couldn't say anything, could only let him pull me along and up the brick stairs, through his front door. And then I stood inside Johnny's house.

It was beautiful, of course. I hadn't expected anything less. I stood on his parquet wood floors, my panty hose shredded and the hem of my coat dripping. I hadn't noticed that before, that I'd gotten wet. I looked at my feet and the growing puddle of dirty water, then at him.

"Oh, God. Sorry."

Johnny had been hanging up his long black coat and that scarf on a brass hook on the wall just inside the door, and he turned to give me an up-and-down look that left me feeling totally lacking. "You should come into the kitchen. Get a drink. You look like you're going to pass out."

I felt white-faced and shivering, certain I looked like shit just as he'd said. "Thanks."

"C'mon." Johnny made a shooing gesture down the hall toward the kitchen, then followed me. "I'll make you a cuppa tea. Unless you want something stronger?"

"Tea's fine. Good. Thank you." I sat in the chair he pointed to, at a table that couldn't be the same one my brain had created, no matter how much it looked like the one in my fugue.

Sometimes, not every time, I did come out of a fugue this way, disoriented and a little sick. Most of the time it passed quickly. Today, I had to take slow, shallow breaths and sip at the air to keep my stomach from revolting up my throat.

Johnny moved around his kitchen in silence. He filled the kettle and settled it on the gas range. The burner hissed and sparked without lighting until he fiddled with something, and then the blue flame whooshed up, high.

"Damn thing," Johnny said, but not to me.

Word vomit. That's what Jen had called it. I'd laughed at her then, but understood it now. I had to clench my jaw tight to keep myself from blurting out the most random, insane thoughts crossing my mind and, even then, didn't quite manage.

"You have a beautiful house."

Johnny grunted as he pulled a couple of oversize mugs from a cupboard and set them on the counter. He opened a tin canister marked Tea and filled a small mesh ball with leaves. Another cupboard produced a ceramic teapot.

"You've done a lot to it," I continued.

My dad was fond of saying that only a fool speaks just to fill silence. I wasn't making my dad very proud now. Nor did I seem to be impressing Johnny.

"How long have you lived here?"

"Fifteen years," Johnny said finally, after he'd poured boiling water into the teapot and brought it to the table. He covered it with a knitted cozy and put the mugs beside it. He took a trip to the fridge and brought out half-and-half.

Johnny was making tea for me. This was more surreal and harder to believe than finding myself in the late 1970s had been. I sat with hands linked in my lap, watching as he sat across from me and poured the tea. He added three spoonfuls of sugar and a generous dollop of half-and-half to one mug, then pushed it toward me. I wrapped my hands around it but didn't dare drink for fear I'd spill it all down my front and embarrass myself even more.

"It's nice," I said. "The house, I mean."

He looked at me. "Drink your tea."

I blew on it, then sipped. It was perfect, exactly the way I'd have made it myself. My stomach settled. Then it grumbled.

Johnny hadn't drunk a sip. He got up, went to the counter, pulled out a package of cookies from a bread box and set them on the table, too. "You need more sugar."

"I'm okay, really."

He took a cookie from the package and set it on the table in front of me. "Eat that."

If he'd said it with a smile, cajoling, I'd have eaten it. It was my favorite kind, and I was hungry, craving sugar. But something in his tone and look made me ornery.

"No, thanks."

Johnny shrugged and snagged a cookie from the package. He held it between his thumb and forefinger, turning it like a magician getting ready to do a coin trick. He studied it, then looked at me. It crumbled when he bit it, and when he licked the crumbs off his lips, I had to concentrate on the mug of tea in my hands. The surface of the liquid shook the way the glass of water trembled in *Jurassic Park,* announcing the presence of the T. rex. I was pretty sure there weren't any dinosaurs here.

"Suit yourself," he said.

It was stupid not to eat it, so I did after another half minute. Sweetness exploded on my tongue, and though it might've been the placebo effect, my stomach instantly settled and my head stopped swimming. I licked melted chocolate from my fingertips and took a long, slow swallow of tea.

The fugue was fading, the memory of Johnny's taste replaced by tea and chocolate. I didn't want to let the sensations go, but they'd become slippery as a fistful of spaghetti and no more easily gripped. I sighed and took another cookie when he pushed the package toward me.

"They're not very good." Johnny didn't say it like an apology, just a fact. "Homemade's better."

"Homemade is always better," I agreed. "But I guess you have to take what you can get, huh?"

"Yeah." He didn't crack a smile. He sat back in his seat, gaze shuttered, mouth thin and straight without even the hint of curve. "You got some color back in your cheeks."

"I'm feeling a lot better, thanks. This was just what I needed." I lifted my mug and pointed it toward the cookies, praying I didn't have chocolate smeared on my mouth or teeth.

"Yeah. I know. You okay now?"

I nodded. "Yeah. Thanks. Thank you."

Johnny gave an unsubtle look at the clock on the wall. "You live here, in the neighborhood?"

"Yes. I just moved in a few months ago. Down the street," I added. "Number forty-three."

Word vomit. I was about to fall prey to its insidiousness. Fortunately, Johnny cut me off before I could spew out anything really embarrassing, like an offer to take him home and fuck him until we both saw stars. Unfortunately, he also stood in a way that made it obvious I was supposed to leave.

I paused on the front porch. "Thanks, Mr. Dellasandro."

He'd kiss me now, I knew it. Or I'd kiss him. He'd push me up against the wall and put his hand under my skirt. We'd fuck right there on the stairs....

"Be more careful out there," Johnny said, and closed the door in my face.

He hadn't even asked my name.

"You didn't." Jen sounded horrified and fascinated at the same time. "He took you into his house? And gave you a cookie? Damn, girl...did he ask you to sit on his lap, too?"

"No, God, no. Too bad."

"Really." She shook her head and held up a skirt she'd pulled off the rack. "What do you think of this?"

"Hideously ugly." I fingered the fabric, a polyester blend in shades of orange and green. "And yet appealing."

"I know, right? How about this?" She held up a dress, which had been made to look like a shirt and skirt but was really one piece. "It has a matching belt."

"And it's half off," I said with a glance at the tag. Wednesdays were price-reduction days at the Salvation Army. Jen and I had made it a weekly date. "Where are you going to wear it?"

"Oh. To work, I guess. With a pair of supercute boots. Maybe hem the skirt a little. I love the sleeves."

The sleeves were pretty awesome, cuffed tight at the wrists with the rest blousy. It wasn't a look I thought I could pull off, but it would suit her. "It's artistic."

"You think so?" She held up the dress again. "Yeah. I guess it is."

She put it in the cart and we inched down the aisle. The store was always crammed with shoppers on Wednesdays, making it nearly impossible to navigate with a wonky-wheeled cart unless we both maneuvered it. I pulled out a sleek black dress with a scoop neck and an A-line hem. It also had a glittery broach. Bonus! I stuck it in the cart, even though I had no place to wear a dress like that. At five bucks, half off, I couldn't resist.

"Cute," Jen commented. "But listen, tell me more about Johnny. What's his house like? Did he come on to you?"

"Gorgeous. And no way. If anything, he couldn't wait to get me out of there."

"Bummer." Jen pulled a blue sleeveless tank dress from the rack. "This is a great color."

"Yeah. I guess I couldn't be surprised. I mean, I did nearly knock him over on the street like a huge, giant doofus."

Jen laughed. "But you managed not to ask him if you could bite his epic ass, right?"

"At least there's that. Hey, I'm heading over to the shirts." I couldn't look at any more dresses. I'd end up spending twenty bucks on vintage finery I'd never wear.

I have a theory about thrift-store shopping. I've spent hours going from store to store in search of something specific, but I've never gone away from a thrift store empty-handed. For whatever reason, whenever I shop at a thrift store, no matter what I want, I find it. When I wanted an emerald-green cardigan sweater, an item that was both out of season and not in a trendy color, I found the perfect one at the Salvation Army. When I needed a jean jacket to replace the one I'd left behind in a hotel, I had my choice of ten or so from the local church bargain basement store. I think there's some higher consciousness involved, or maybe it's a matter of perception that allows your eyes to be opened at just the right time. To see things you wouldn't have noticed before.

Like the T-shirt in my hand. White cotton, faded from hundreds of washes. I'd plucked it from the rack because of the fabric's softness, though I wasn't looking for a T-shirt. I'd grabbed it because of the material, but what made me hold on to it was the design on the front.

It was the poster for one of Johnny's movies. *Dance with the Devil* was the English name, but this had been filmed in Italy. I recognized the artwork from my internet research. Johnny on a motorcycle, in a black leather jacket, hair blowing back from his forehead, cigarette in his mouth. Very James Dean. Very sexy. Also, very rare.

The tag on it was for one dollar, which put the reduced price at fifty cents. That made up for the hefty price I'd paid for the out-of-print DVD, and yet I hesitated, hovering between shoving the shirt back on the rack and walking away and gripping it tight with two fists and knocking down everyone in my way to get to the cash register.

Perception or higher consciousness? What had placed my hand on this shirt just now? If I'd come across it a few weeks ago, would I have pushed it aside in favor of the peasant blouse with the tags still on just beyond it? The shirt crumpled in my fingers as I clutched it.

The world tipped, just a little.

"Hey, what did you find?" Jen looked over my shoulder.

The world steadied. No orange smell, no wavy lines around my vision. No fugue. I let out the breath I'd been holding and held up the shirt.

Her eyes widened. "Get the fuck out of here. Is that *Dance with the Devil?* On a fucking T-shirt?"

I looked at it. "Yes!"

"Girl." Jen got solemn. "I don't know where you're getting your Johnny mojo, but damn. That shirt looks real. I mean, not like someone did it themselves with a homemade iron-on. I've never even seen them advertised anyplace. Let me see the tag."

I showed her. She puffed air between her lips and handed it back to me respectfully. "Tag looks old, too. I think this is an original promo piece or something."

"Could be." I held the shirt close to my chest with two hands. "I'm buying it."

"Of course you are. You'd better. That shit is probably worth something." Jen nodded. "Not that you'll sell it, I guess. You're going to wear that to bed, huh?"

I laughed. "Probably. Definitely, yeah."

"Johnny on your boobs," she said a little dreamily. "Can't blame you there."

After that find, there wasn't anything else that could top it. We paid for our stuff and parted ways in the parking lot. Night had fallen. The air smelled like snow. Jen was talking about something, going out, meeting up on the weekend for something or other, but I couldn't concentrate very hard on what she was saying. The T-shirt felt too heavy in the plastic grocery bag dangling from my wrist, and it had nothing to do with its weight.

She waved and got in her car. I got in mine. I drew in breath after breath of frigid air, making sure there was no scent of oranges, nothing but the odor of old fries from the grease-spotted bag in my backseat. Nothing wavy in my vision except from the moisture now dotting my windshield.

By the time I got home, my fingers ached from clutching the wheel. My head hurt, too, from concentrating so hard on the road. For a change, the spot in front of my house was empty, and I took it even though I'd grown to like parking in front of Johnny's house.

Inside, I threw everything I'd bought that could be washed into the washer and set aside the items that would require dry cleaning. The T-shirt I held in my two hands for much longer than necessary. The shirt had been washed before, I could tell, and the print on the front barely faded. It was probably safe to machine wash, but I took out a bucket from beneath the sink instead, and swished it around in Woolite, rinsing in cool water and hand-wringing it gently before hanging it on a drying rack.

Too much effort and care for a T-shirt, I thought. It wasn't yet time to switch the laundry from washer to dryer, so I went to the kitchen to eat. I could see the drying rack every time I walked past the kitchen doorway, and I looked at it each time.

I dreamed of him that night, but they were normal dreams. Disjointed, confusing, full of leaps and jumps that didn't happen in the fugues. I didn't know I was dreaming in them, either, even when he kissed me. Even when he told me to get lost. Then Johnny faded in and out of now-Johnny's clothes in the dream and was replaced at one point by an actor whose name I didn't know but who'd been on the last commercial I saw just before bed.

Restless and wakeful, I got up in the darkness and made my way to the laundry room, where I found the T-shirt, dry and a little stiff, smelling clean. I took it back to bed with me and held it as close as I used to hold my blanky. If I dreamed again, I didn't remember it.

I didn't meet up with Jen at the Mocha the next morning, though it was crowded enough without her there. I didn't have more than a few minutes to pick out a muffin and grab a coffee before work, and I almost reconsidered the stop when I saw the long line. Still, by the time I'd figured out I ran the risk of being late, I was almost at the head of the line. I crossed my fingers and prayed to miss the morning traffic.

I was thinking of him, of course. Johnny had fully infiltrated my brain. So when I turned, coffee in hand and muffin in the other, my car keys jangling, I had to blink a couple times before I could make myself believe he was really there. He'd paused by the newspaper rack to check out a copy of the *New York Times* and was just tucking it under his arm when I stepped in front of him.

"Hi," I said.

I wasn't sure what I expected, but it was something entirely different than a blank stare and a blatant brush-off. Johnny didn't even acknowledge me with a nod. He pushed past me without a word and stepped up to the counter to pay for the newspaper, leaving me behind with my face virtually slapped. I must've worn my distress as obviously as a neon sign, because

Carlos gave me a sympathetic glance from behind his open laptop. He was there early today.

"Hey, don't worry about it," he said quietly as Johnny wove back through the crowd and out the front door, black coat flapping around his ankles. "He's like that to mostly everyone. I mean, he doesn't like being fawned over."

"I wasn't fawning over him. Jesus." I frowned, watching Johnny through the glass. "I was being friendly."

Carlos shrugged. "I'm just saying. He does get some pretty loony fans once in a while. I guess he's being cautious."

"I am not," I said tightly, "a loony fan."

Carlos's brows raised, and he grinned. "No? You and Jen look at him like you want the Mocha to put him on the menu."

Heat spread across my cheeks. "Oh, God. That obvious?"

"Nah. I don't think he notices, if that's what you're worried about. He's just leery. I mean, I've seen some chicks who practically rip off their shirts and try to mount him right here!" Carlos shook his head as though he couldn't decide if the thought disturbed or excited him. "Old chicks, Emm. Like in their fifties, old. You, in comparison, are a very hot young chick."

"Gee, thanks." I could no longer see even a hint of Johnny's black coat. I took a drink from my coffee and eyed Carlos. "Jen says he was nice to you."

"Maybe because he knows I don't want to fuck him. Or even if I did, it's not the same as being in love with him because of some stuff from a long time ago."

"Why not?" I knew Johnny'd had some sexual fluidity in his past, but had never claimed to be gay or even bisexual. He'd called himself "straight but openminded" in more than one interview.

"Who knows, maybe he doesn't find dudes as threatening, in general. Maybe we're easier to put off. Or maybe he was just in a good mood that day. I don't know."

Carlos's assessment, as close as it was to truth, stung. "I never said I was in love with him. Besides, last week I bumped into him outside his house and he invited me in for tea."

"Tea? Get out of here." Carlos flapped a hand, scoffing.

"I'm serious." I hadn't slipped a paper liner on my cup, and my hand was starting to burn. I switched, almost crushing my muffin in the process. "I sat in his kitchen and drank his tea, and today he can't even say hello? That's just...well, that's douchy, that's all."

Carlos shrugged, looking back toward his laptop. "Man's got issues, what can I say? If it makes you feel any better, it's not just you."

That made me feel worse. I didn't want to be treated the same way Johnny treated everyone else. I wanted to be...special.

"Later," Carlos called after me, though I'd moved away without saying goodbye. "Don't let it get to you, Emm!"

But I was. My coffee tasted bitter without the extra sugar and cream I normally added but had forgotten. My muffin, when I looked into the brown paper bag, had crumbled into bits. And I was late for work.

"All I said was hi," I grumbled under my breath.

I thought about it all day long as I sat at my computer, entering data into spreadsheets, answering calls and emails. Putting out fires. Probably starting a few, too; I was too distracted to notice.

I'd ended up in banking by accident. I'd gone to Lebanon Valley College in my hometown so I could live at home and walk to school if I had to. Annville's a tiny town bordered to the north and south with farms but blending east and west into the towns next to it. I was limited in my job choices within walking distance of my parents' house. Pizza shop, gas station, movie theater...bank. The bank had the best hours, pay and benefits, and I didn't have to rely on my parents to give me a ride. I'd worked there all throughout college and then after when my inability to drive limited me even more severely.

After a few years I'd advanced to bank manager. I liked my work. I liked numbers. I liked my new job, working for the Pennsylvania State Employee's Credit Union, even better.

But not today.

Today I counted the minutes until I could go home and check the mail to see if my DVD of *Night of a Hundred Moons* had arrived. Unfortunately, the mailbox was empty yet again. My stomach sank like the *Lusitania*. I actually checked twice, as though a package could possibly be hiding in the shallow box somewhere out of sight. Then, disappointed, I let myself into my dark and chilly house.

I didn't even have any calls on my answering machine, not that I ever had many. Most people who wanted to get in touch with me rang my cell if they tried at home and didn't reach me. Apparently, today I wasn't even popular enough for that.

I took a long, hot shower, head bent to let the steaming water pound down on my shoulders and back. Tension had twisted my muscles. I needed strong hands to unkink the knots. Sadly, unless I wanted to pay for it, I was out of luck. My skinned knees stung as I ran a razor over them.

So of course I was thinking about Johnny again.

What the hell was his problem? Okay, so I understood that it might be annoying to have random strangers compliment him on his cock. Even if he wasn't ashamed of his art movie past, it *had* ended more than thirty years ago. I could respect him not wanting to live on the bragging rights of work he'd done so long ago, or off a body that had now aged. I could respect him not wanting to be worshipped for his looks. What I couldn't get behind was him blowing me off like he'd never made me tea just the way I like it and offered me cookies. That was douchebaggery of the highest degree, and I didn't want to believe he was a big bag of dicks. I was too much in crush for that.

Johnny could have no idea of the late-night movie marathon

Jen and I'd had. He couldn't know of the fugues and the dreams. And no matter how anyone else had ever behaved to him, I hadn't. No matter what I'd thought or what had gone on in my subconscious, I hadn't acted on it. I hated that he'd lumped me in with loony fans who stalked him in the Mocha. Hey, I hadn't moved into my house to get closer to him, for fuck's sake. We were neighbors.

My stomach rumbled at the memory of the cookies. What had he said? Homemade's better? And wouldn't it be neighborly of me to offer him some?

In a few minutes I had an array of baking materials spread on my kitchen island. I'd bought this house in part because of the kitchen, which the former owners had refurbished and updated—not in colors I liked or top-of-the-line appliances, but they'd added this island that doubled as workspace and eating area. I didn't have a kitchen table.

I had all the ingredients. I even had mixing bowls and measuring cups. What I didn't have was a recipe. Not a good one. Not the best one. I had pieces of it stored away in my Swiss-cheese brain, but I'd never actually baked my grandma's chocolate chip cookies on my own.

My phone was already to my ear, my mom on autodial, when I realized I hadn't spoken to her in about three days. Three. I couldn't remember ever not speaking to my mom for more than two days or so in a row. If I didn't call her, she called and left me messages until I called back.

She'd answered before I could contemplate this too much. "Hello?"

"Mom, it's me. Emm," I felt suddenly compelled to say, as though she had more than one daughter.

"Emmaline. Hi. What's going on?"

She hadn't asked me what was wrong. That was both a relief and a concern. "I need grandma's chocolate chip cookie recipe."

"You're baking?"

"Well...yeah." I laughed. "Why else would I need it?"

"I haven't made cookies in forever," my mom said.

I paused in shaking the bag of flour into the tin I hadn't been using before. "Really? How come?"

"Well...your dad and I have been trying to cut back on sweets. Get ourselves in shape."

"Oh." I didn't think anything of that. My mom put my dad on a diet a couple times a year and often vowed to do the same for herself, but both of them liked to eat and not exercise, a family trait I'd unfortunately inherited. "How's that going?"

"Oh, you know your dad. He says he's sticking with it, but I know he's sneaking burgers and fries."

"Maybe if you made him cookies once in a while he wouldn't," I offered, and we both giggled, knowing there was no way my dad would replace burgers and fries with cookies, no matter how good they were.

"I found it." My mom sounded triumphant. "I stuck the paper in the back of that cookbook Aunt Min got for me a few Christmases ago."

"Which one, the low-fat baking one?"

"Yes."

"Mom, why would you put a chocolate chip cookie recipe in that cookbook?"

"Because," my mom said as though I were a fool for even asking, "I knew I wouldn't look for it there."

We both laughed again. Nostalgia swept me. I'd spent so many evenings baking cookies with my mom, or rolling out crust for fruit pies and potpies. My mom was an excellent cook and had taught me well, but I hardly ever cooked for myself. I missed that. I missed her.

"Emm? You're not getting a cold, are you? Or, God forbid, the flu? You should take that...what's that stuff called, your cousin told me about it. Oscillating something. Like a fan."

She meant oscillium. "I'm okay. What's first?"

She didn't follow up with that, and I paused again. My mom *never* just let something go. If she even had a hint that there might be something wrong with me, she shook it to death like a puppy with a stray sock.

"You have all the ingredients?"

"Yep."

"Shortening?" My mom sounded suspicious. "Eggs?"

"Yes, Mother."

"Because, Emmaline, you know you can't make cookies without eggs."

As once I'd tried. "You'll never let me forget that, will you?"

"Never," my mom said. I heard the smile in her voice. I heard the love.

I sniffled but put my hand over the mouthpiece of the phone so she wouldn't hear. I didn't want my mom to worry about me. Then again, I didn't want her to not worry about me, either.

She walked me through the measuring and mixing as she kept me up-to-date with family gossip and stories about our neighbors. Her neighbors now, no longer mine. She told me about running into old school friends I hadn't even spoken to in years aside from the casual Connex wall post.

"You spend more time with my old friends than I do," I told her as I finished scooping the last blob of dough onto a baking stone and slid it into my embarrassingly clean oven. I licked the spoon.

"You'll get salmonella," my mother warned.

"How did you know?"

"I know you, Emmaline. I'm your mother. Oh, I have to go! My show's about to come on. Bye, Emm. Love you."

She hung up before I could even ask her what show she meant. The fact I had no idea proved all the more how much had changed since I'd left home. And that was a good thing,

I reminded myself as I disconnected the call and set the timer on the oven. The last few months between my decision to take the job in Harrisburg and move out on my own and the day I'd moved had been horrible.

Most mothers and daughters I knew had weathered their share of arguments. Daughters had to grow away from their moms. To go to school. Move out. Become women. I'd become a woman under my mom's watchful, too-protective eye, and had chafed at it even as I knew I had no choice. When my doctor had declared me seizure-free for more than a year and thus able to drive, instead of getting better, my mom's concerns had grown worse. I didn't blame her for them. I understood why she was so nervous. I'd been effectively disabled by the injury to my brain, and there was no cure. Only treatment. Only fingers crossed and prayers said. Only hope.

Even so, it had been unbearable living at home for those few months after I accepted the new job and before I was able to settle on and move into my house. She'd hovered, scolded and worried me nearly to madness. We'd fought harder and longer than we ever had during my adolescence. There'd been more than one night when I went to bed fuming and woke still angry, and I'm sure she felt the same way. She was afraid to let me go, and I was afraid of never being able to stand on my own. Now, here in the house I could only afford because of all the years I'd lived rent-free when my friends had been paying out to landlords, I wanted to call my mom back and tell her how sorry I was for being so snotty every time she'd worried about me.

Instead, I licked cookie dough straight off the spoon and dared salmonella to find me. It tasted extra good for being licked in defiance of everything my mom had ever told me, and because I knew I really shouldn't eat cookie dough when my pants were already a little too snug. I was a rebel with a spoon.

By the time the cookies finished baking my kitchen smelled gorgeous and my stomach felt a little queasy. I sipped at some ginger ale and laid the cookies out on a pretty plate I'd picked up at the Salvation Army for a dime. It had roses on it and gold around the rim, and I could've sold it on eBay for a hundred times what I'd bought it for. It was another example of my thrift-store theory. I'd gone in looking specifically for housewares to stock my new house and found an entire box of mismatched but complementary plates for ten cents apiece.

I had plenty of plates. I could give this one up. On the other hand, it was pretty enough that anyone who got a plateful of cookies on it might feel compelled to make sure he returned it to me.

I could be so sneaky sometimes.

"Hi—" The rest of my sentence cut off as Johnny's door opened and didn't reveal Johnny.

The older woman stared at me for a long moment, a sour look on her face. When at last she spoke, it was with a shake of her head. "You here for him, I guess."

"Um, Johnny Dellasandro?"

"That's who lives here, ain't?" Her thick Pennsylvania Dutch accent sounded out of place here in the "big city," though I'd heard it plenty back home. "You'd better come in."

I stepped over the threshold and wiped my boots carefully on the mat, not wanting to drip dirty snow water on his beautiful floors again. I held my chin and the plate of cookies high. I'd covered them with some festive red plastic wrap I'd bought reduced after Christmas.

The woman looked at them, then at me. "You made these for him?"

"I did. Is he here?"

"He likes chocolate chip cookies." She smiled then, and it transformed her from grumpy gnome into beaming fairy godmother. "Come on back the hall, *wunst*. He's upstairs doing something arty. I'll get him for you."

"Thanks." My stomach in knots, I followed her to the kitchen.

She opened what in my house was a closet, but here turned out to be a set of back stairs, and hollered up them. "Johnny!"

Her voice echoed, but nobody answered. She looked at me, still standing in my buttoned-up coat, plate of cookies in my hands. She shrugged.

"Johnny Dellasandro!"

No answer. She sighed and heaved herself onto the bottom stair, which jutted out at a forty-five-degree angle from the staircase. She put her hand on the door frame and leaned out of sight, then screamed his name so loudly I took a step back.

"That'll get him," she said with a nod and a grin, and dusted her hands as though she'd just finished a particularly difficult task. "When he's working it's like his ears get filled with cotton."

"I don't want to disturb him." He'd already made a practice of giving me the stink eye. If I took him away from his art, I could only imagine the reaction I'd get.

She flapped her hands. "Pshaw. He's been working all day long. He needs a break. And some cookies from a pretty girl."

I smiled. "I don't want to interrupt, that's all."

We both turned at the thud of footsteps on the stairs. I saw his feet first, bare toes. My own toes curled. Then the hem of a pair of faded jeans, hem ragged. Then Johnny stepped onto the last step and paused in the doorway. He looked perplexed.

"Whatchoo shoutin' fooah?"

Fuck me, I loved that accent.

"You have comp'ny. For mercy's sake, Johnny, put a shirt on!" The woman sighed and put her hands on her hips, shaking her head.

Not on my account, I thought, trying hard not to stare and not sure exactly where to look if it wasn't at those delicious nipples.

Fuck, his abs were hard, too. He might not be young, but he was still superfit and in better shape than some of the younger dudes I'd been with.

"Hi," I said, relieved my voice didn't shake or catch. I couldn't do anything about the blush, but hoped my cheeks simply looked rosy from the cold and not from embarrassment.

Johnny stared at me. The woman looked from him to me, then back, and sighed. She took the plate of cookies from my hands and held it up to him.

"She brought you cookies, *dummkopf.* You," she said to me, "take off your coat and sit yourself."

Her tone showed she was used to being obeyed, but I waited until he stepped off the stairs and all the way into the kitchen before I sat. I didn't take off my coat, though. Johnny, casting a glance over his shoulder at me, crossed to another door that did prove to be a closet, where he hooked a hooded sweatshirt off the back and put it on. I mourned a little but was relieved at the same time. I was less distracted that way.

"Now, I'm off, finally. Your dinner's still in the oven and your groceries are all put away. I left your bills on the desk and your other mail in the basket," the woman said.

"Thank you, Mrs. Espenshade."

She flapped her hands again. "It's what you pay me for, ain't? Now I'm leaving and I'll be back on Friday to take care of the cleaning. Don't forget now."

"I'll be here," Johnny said, looking at me.

"I don't care if you're here or not. Maybe you should be away, then I could get more done." She chortled at that and shook her head again. She patted my shoulder as she passed me. "Don't let him eat them all by himself."

"Good night, Mrs. Espenshade," Johnny called after her, but her only reply was the slamming of the front door.

"Hi," I said again into the painful silence that followed. "I brought cookies. Chocolate chip. They're homemade."

"Why?"

"Because they're better." I smiled.

He didn't. He didn't open them, either. Nor did he sit. Johnny stood against the counter, arms crossed over his chest.

I was too warm in the kitchen with my coat on, my scarf tucked tight around my throat. I didn't dare unwind it, though. Mrs. Espenshade might've welcomed me in, but Johnny definitely wasn't.

"I mean, why'd you bring me cookies?"

"To say thank you for helping me out the other day. For the tea. Because you had crappy prepackaged cookies and I knew I could give you better." My voice rose a little with each sentence, and I had to bite off my words to keep from sounding too strident.

Something flickered in his gaze, some indiscernible emotion passed over his mostly impassive face. "Okay. I'll eat them later."

He was dismissing me yet again. This time felt even worse, because I'd come bearing gifts. Because I'd thought, somehow, it would make a difference. I got up from the table.

"I live right down the street," I said, too loud. Too bold.

Again, Johnny's gaze flickered. "Yeah? It's a nice street. Lots of people live on it."

My mouth thinned. "I guess they do."

Silence stretched between us, but it wasn't quiet. It was full of the beat of my heart, the hitch and shift of my breath. It was strung tight with tension, thrumming like a plucked guitar string. I moved out from behind the table.

"*My* kitchen has an island," I said with a lift of my chin that meant nothing to him and everything to me. "I'll show myself out."

"I'll walk you."

"You really don't have to. I can find my way." I spun on my heel and stalked down the hall toward the front door.

Johnny padded after me on bare feet and got there just about the same time I did. It could've been because his legs were longer, but I think it was because, despite my insult, I was hanging back in hopes he'd show me some tiny measure of interest. Even a scrap. And realizing this made me so angry I grabbed at the doorknob and yanked, not knowing it was locked. Foiled in my grand exit, I let out a low, angry noise. I turned on him.

"I said I could find my way out."

Johnny, looking into my eyes, reached around me to unlock the door. My eyes fluttered at his closeness. The brush of his breath on my hair, the heat of his body. I wasn't too angry to get a little thrill, even though I hated myself for it. I hated more that he could see it on my face, that lust. It didn't matter if he was used to it. I wasn't used to it.

"Here," he said. The lock clicked. He didn't move away for one interminable second. Then he stepped back, freeing me to move.

"They're good cookies," I said flatly. "For whatever that's worth, which apparently is nothing."

My voice was hard, and he blinked. "I'm sure they're great."

"You're welcome." I opened the door.

Cold air rushed in, frigid enough to force the breath from my lungs in a small gasp and bring tears to my eyes. Or maybe it wasn't the cold air. I drew myself up and forced myself to walk, head high, down his front steps and onto the sidewalk that he'd made sure was heavily salted and ice-free.

When the door didn't shut behind me, I turned to look back. Johnny stood silhouetted in the doorway, golden in the light spilling out around him. He'd put one hand up high on the door frame, the other on his cocked hip. He had to be cold, what with his feet bare and nothing on beneath his sweatshirt, still mostly unzipped. But he didn't go inside.

"You know, I thought maybe you didn't talk to anyone

because you were a little shy. Or maybe because you were cautious."

His head cocked to match his hip. "Oh, yeah?"

I put my hands on my hips. "Yeah. I mean, I know it must be a pain in the ass to have people bugging you when you're just trying to have a cup of coffee and a muffin."

"Yeah. That can be a real pain in the ass," Johnny said slowly.

I narrowed my eyes, wishing I could read his expression. "But you know what?"

"What," Johnny said, and damned if he didn't sound amused.

"I don't think it's because you're shy or because too many people bug you, because let's face it, most people don't even know who you are anymore. Or they don't give a damn."

His shoulders lifted and fell at that—a laugh or a shrug, with his face in shadow I couldn't tell. "What about you?"

"I know who you are," I told him.

"Yeah," Johnny said. "But do you give a damn?"

I turned at that, my fists clenched. Then I turned back and forced myself to say, "Yes. I do."

"Why?"

I didn't know why. It was more than the ass, the face, the long-past fame. It wasn't his art. It wasn't his house, his money. It wasn't even his coat or that long scarf I loved.

It was the heat of summer, and it was the taste of him I knew I couldn't know. It was the feel of his hair in my fingers and his cock up deep inside me, and it was the sound of his voice saying my name when he came.

It was the smell of oranges.

I made it home before it took me. To my front porch, anyway, my fingers fumbling with the key in the lock. I wasn't much for praying, but I did mutter under my breath to whatever entity would listen to at least let me get inside before I went dark.

I opened the door.

I went anything but dark.

Brilliant sunlight blinded me. I threw a hand up over my eyes and stumbled on a floor slick with wax, not ice. I breathed in heat, and a cacophony of sounds and smells assaulted me.

The tang of pot and sting of cigarette smoke pushed aside the smell of oranges. I heard laughter and music and the cry of a child. I blinked, rubbing at my eyes.

I'd gone through the looking glass again, this time right into Johnny's house. The door hung open behind me. Had I even knocked? Nobody had answered. Nobody seemed to even notice I was there.

I closed my eyes to orient myself, but only for a second. Then I shrugged out of my coat as fast as I could, hung it on a coatrack along with my scarf. I fluffed my hair. I checked my clothes—a pair of boot-cut jeans and a button-up blouse.

It wouldn't pass for seventies summer fashion. I had a cami on underneath, though. The voices in the kitchen rose and fell as I stripped out of it quickly, then with a second thought took off my bra and tucked them both into the sleeve of my coat.

It felt strange, going without a bra. My nipples poked at the soft fabric of my camisole. I felt free but self-conscious.

A baby wearing only a saggy diaper and a white onesie came crawling down the hall as fast as he…or she—I couldn't tell the gender—could and was followed by a laughing woman with long, dark hair that fell to her waist. She wore a one-piece shorts jumper made of terry cloth in bright yellow. My eyes hurt just looking at it. She scooped up the baby and flubbered its belly until the baby screamed with laughter, while I stood, awkward and caught.

"Oh, hey," she said languidly when she caught sight of me. "Who're you?"

"Emm."

"Sandy." She hitched the baby onto her hip and held out a limp hand for me to shake. "Groovy."

I wasn't sure if this was a greeting or a statement on my clothes, or maybe just a philosophical observation. "Um, I'm looking for Johnny."

"Oh, yeah, that's cool. He's in there, back in the kitchen, you know. Unless he owes you money or something." She had a strange, nasally voice, an accent like his. On her it wasn't quite as charming.

"Thanks." I didn't want to push past her, especially since she was now studying me up and down.

"Whadja say your name was?"

"Emm."

"Emm." Sandy looked a little blank for a second. "We never met before, did we?"

"No. I don't think so."

She shrugged and hitched the squirming baby higher. The

scent of dirty diaper wafted toward me and I took an unconscious step back. Sandy wrinkled her nose.

"Gee, all this kid does is eat, sleep and shit. I guess I'd better give her a bath." Sandy moved past me and up the stairs, babbling baby talk.

I went to the kitchen with my heart pounding and palms moist. I was already smiling in anticipation when I saw him. He was sitting in the windowsill, tipping beer in a brown bottle to his lips, a cigarette in one hand. He'd held his hair off his face today with a red bandanna folded into a thick band.

He was so beautiful it hurt to look at him.

He stopped in midlaugh and jumped off the windowsill when I came into the room. He put his beer down and stuck the cigarette in the throat of the bottle. The room fell silent as everyone turned to look at me. Candy was there, not at the stove this time. And Bellina, along with a bunch of people I didn't know. Ed fixed me with an intense look, cutting off his own words before turning to face the woman he was talking to. Weird, but I wasn't paying that much attention to him.

"Johnny," I said, breathless.

"Emm." He moved toward me like nobody else was even there.

His hand fit perfectly around the back of my neck. He tasted of beer and smoke when he kissed me, and somehow it wasn't disgusting but just right. His tongue stroked in and out of me; my knees went weak. I didn't care that we weren't alone. I didn't care that his hand was on my ass, kneading, or that he'd pulled me up close to him.

"Hey," he said, sounding a little breathless himself when he broke the kiss.

Our faces were very close together. I fell into the depths of his eyes and swam there for a bit as everything stopped and started around us. He smiled. I smiled, too.

"You came back," he said. "Thought I'd never see you again."

I had no good answer for that, so I kissed him again. "So, you're glad to see me?"

"Hell, yes. You ran outta here so fast last time I never got your number."

"Oh..." I hesitated. Everyone had gone back to their own discussions, not paying attention to us in the doorway. "I don't really have a number."

Johnny shrugged. "Oh, yeah, that's cool. Ours got turned off a while back, too. Paul says he'll get it turned on next time he gets paid for a gig."

"If you don't have a phone," I whispered into his ear, giddy from this, "how were you going to call me?"

Johnny nuzzled into me. "Phone booth down the street."

"Ah." Of course. Phone booths. A little dizzy all at once, I clutched him to keep from swaying. I was reminded of the TV show *Life on Mars,* about the cop who gets shot and wakes up in the 1970s while his body's in a coma in present-tense time.

I wasn't in a coma...not quite. But I wasn't sure how much time I had. I looked over his shoulder, but nobody was paying attention to us. They all had their own thing going on, which made sense, didn't it? I didn't need them. I just needed him.

"Take me upstairs," I said into his ear, and tugged his lobe between my teeth.

"You want to split? I can dig that."

I snickered. I couldn't help it. "Dig it" was so quaint, so seventies sitcom. So...sort of sexy, really, when he said it, not like he was trying to toss around slang for effect but like that's just how it came out. Natural. Everything about him was natural.

"You're so different," I told him in the hallway as he linked his fingers with mine.

Johnny gave me a glance. "Than what?"

"Never mind." I couldn't explain that I meant he was different than himself. "I like it."

His grin lit up his face. He put his hand on the newel post and swung around a little, one foot on the stairs. "Where've you been, anyway? I looked all over for you. You don't live around here, huh? You just visiting again?"

"Just visiting," I agreed.

We stopped to kiss at the top of the stairs. My fingers tangled in the silk of his hair. I tugged the bandanna free so his hair fell over his eyes, and when I kissed him the fringes tickled my face.

"You are something, all right," Johnny said in a low, mystified voice.

I remembered where his bedroom was, but stopped at the doorway as Sandy came out toting the baby on her hip. She paused and looked at both of us blankly. Then she shrugged and held out the baby for Johnny to look at.

"I gave her a bath and everything. Now I'm gonna feed her a bottle."

His arm slid around my waist and held me tight against him, hip to hip. "Yeah, sure, that's great."

Sandy pursed her lips and shook her head a little. "Well, see ya."

Inside the bedroom, the door closed, we made our way to the bed where I pushed him back and he fell down onto it, bouncing a little before pushing himself up on his elbows to look at me. I pulled my camisole off over my head and stood bare-breasted in front of him. I tugged open the zipper of my jeans, toed off my shoes, pushed down the denim along with my plain cotton panties and stood before him naked.

I'd never felt so beautiful as I did at that moment, with Johnny's gaze upon me. Never before, but always, always after. When he looked at me, it didn't matter if I felt rounder in places than I wanted to be, or if my breasts weren't of porn-star proportions. It was the time, I thought, cupping them and flicking my thumbs over my nipples to get them hard. Back then women could be normal-size.

There was something else different about the women he was used to. Johnny's gaze focused on my pussy, which I'd shaved just a few nights before. Not bare—I hated feeling as if I looked like a schoolgirl. I'm a woman, and women have hair. But I had trimmed my bikini area and left a landing strip, mostly for convenience rather than fashion, since I was due to get my period in a few days.

Johnny dragged his hand across his mouth, pulling at his lips and leaving them sheened with saliva. Sitting on the edge of the bed, he was at the perfect height when I moved to stand between his legs. His hands found my ass as he looked up at me, eyes a little glazed.

Drunk, I thought. But not from the beer he'd been drinking when I found him in the kitchen. Drunk on me.

I ran my hand over his head and tugged off the bandanna. I tossed it onto the bed. His hair fell over the back of my hand when I wove my fingers in it. My fingers tightened in it, and I pulled to tip his head back.

"Johnny." I said it just to say it. Just because I could.

"Yeah, baby." His voice was low and throaty. Full of sex.

"Johnny, Johnny, Johnny..." Laughing, I tipped his head back farther.

He laughed, too. His hands moved, stroking my ass, the dimples at the small of my back, my upper thighs. "Yeah, Emm. I'm right here."

"So am I."

"I see that." When I released him from my grip, he nuzzled against my breasts and found my nipples with his mouth. He sucked gently, one and the other, and looked up with a grin when I gasped. "You like that, huh?"

"Yes." A sudden, vivid memory of him saying those exact

words in one of his films came back to me. My cunt pulsed. "Does that make me a whore?"

I said it in my Central Pennsylvania accent, hard on the *r* at the end. Nothing like the way he said it. Johnny paused in exploring my breasts to look up at me again, brow furrowed.

"A what?"

"A...whore," I said, my voice gone breathy with painfully urgent excitement.

"A...whore?"

Fuck. The way he said it made the Fourth of July explode in my pussy. I bit my lower lip and still couldn't quite keep in the gasp. "God."

His chuckle sounded perplexed. His hands stopped roaming for a moment on my rear. "Do *you* think you're a whore?"

A hooah. "Christ, that shouldn't be so fucking sexy," I said.

Johnny blinked, ducking his head for a moment as his shoulders shook with laughter. "That turns you on, huh?"

"Yes. Say it again."

He stopped laughing when he looked up at me. Something dark skittered in those green-brown eyes. He licked his mouth, wiped the back of it with his hand again. His voice got lower. "You wanna be a whore for me?"

I didn't want to be a whore for anyone. I just wanted to hear him say it. I wanted to see him look at me that way. My fist tightened in his hair again. This time, he winced.

His hands gripped my hips, hard. "That it? That what you like?"

"You make me like it."

He was stronger than I'd expected. I was on my back on the bed in half a second, my hands pinned above my head while Johnny looked down into my face. His denim-clad thigh rocked slowly on my bare cunt. The rough fabric sent shivers of pleasure throughout me—or maybe it was just his eyes, his mouth. His voice.

"You like that? Huh?"

"I like it."

He nudged his thigh a little higher. "Does that get you wet for me?"

"Yes," I breathed.

I never spoke out like that, but this, I reminded myself, wasn't real. It was all fantasy. All made up. All of this was nothing more than some misfiring neurons in my mangled brain.

With the hand not holding my wrists, Johnny yanked open his belt. He shifted. I arched my back, tipping my hips, waiting for him to enter me—but he surprised me instead. Johnny moved his mouth down my body, over the slopes of my breasts and belly. He slid his hands beneath my ass and lifted me to his mouth, his tongue stroking over my clit before he fasted his lips there and sucked gently.

I shuddered and said his name. Johnny said nothing, just got to the business of eating my pussy.

I'd never seen this in any of the movies.

Oh, they'd hinted at his oral prowess. Soft-focus shots of women writhing as he lapped at their skin. Off-centered shots of his head at waist-level, then cuts of the women's faces contorted in ecstasy, all of them crying out his name. But none of the movies had actually shown him licking and sucking between their legs. I had no images to call on.

This was all me.

He did it with his eyes closed. He made small groaning noises. The sound a man makes when he feasts on something delicious, a meal that completely sates his hunger. He sampled my clit for a while before sliding a finger inside. Then two. I cried out.

"So fucking wet," Johnny muttered against me.

Pleasure coiled spring-tight in my belly. Heat rose, flushing up my chest and throat to my cheeks. His mouth burned on me. Electric. I shifted my hips under him, unable to stay still.

I didn't notice how he'd pushed his jeans down, only that he had. I tasted myself on his mouth when he kissed me. My mouth was already open when I gasped as he entered me, and I drew in his breath and made it my own.

Johnny buried his face against the side of my neck and slid slowly deeper into me. He settled there without moving for a second or two, then pushed up on his hands to look into my face. He looked bemused. I smiled and pulled him down to me for another kiss.

"You are something," he said.

Then he began to move. This was different than the first time had been, with me on top, both of us moving so frantically. This time was slower. This time took forever.

I'd never been able to come in the missionary position, not without sliding a hand down to give myself some help. Then again, I'd never been with a man who moved the way Johnny did. In, out, each thrust added to a subtle twist of his hips that hit me just right. And he kissed me, oh, God, how he kissed me. Sweet and soft, then harder, his tongue stroking, lips nibbling. I was caught up on a wave of sensual onslaught, and I gave myself up to it without holding anything back.

I came once in slow, rippling waves. I came a second time after he'd rolled us so that I lay on my back, him on his side, fucking into me at an angle. And finally, when he shifted us again so that I was on his lap, his back pressed against the headboard, my thighs pressed to his hips, I came again. I bit into his shoulder when I did, my body jerking. Sweat glued us and the scent of our fucking wiped out everything else.

He came inside me with a grunt. He stroked hands down my sweat-slick back, and pushed the tangled strands of my hair, sticking to my cheeks, off my face. He breathed out and held me close.

"Johnny, I—oops!"

"Jesus, Sandy," Johnny snapped, not bothering to grab up a

sheet or make any attempt to cover us even as I cringed against him. "I told you to fucking knock before you come in here."

"Sorry! I just needed to get my bag! Jesus, Johnny, you could've locked the door you know. Gawd." Sandy huffed and went to the dresser to grab up a huge straw bag with bamboo handles. The contents clinked and shifted inside as she stuck her hand on her hip, the bag hung from her wrist. "I'm going."

"Who's got the kid?" Johnny looked over my shoulder, his hands keeping me still.

"I called my mother to come get her." Sandy gave me a look. "What was your name again?"

"Get the fuck out of here, Sandy. Jesus Christ." Johnny shifted as though he meant to push me from his lap and get up, and Sandy jumped back, hands up.

"Okay, okay! Jesus! Chill out, man. It's all cool. I ain't trying to mess with your scene or anything."

"Get out," Johnny said.

Sandy left, closing the bedroom door behind her. I didn't move. I wasn't sure I could move. Johnny looked up at me.

"Sorry," he said. "She's a moron."

I got off him then, feeling sticky and slick. We hadn't used a condom, and I marveled more at the details my mind was providing more than the fact I'd fucked him bareback. I settled onto the mattress next to him. I hadn't paid much attention to Sandy before, not with Johnny in front of me, touching me. The look she'd given me, though, told me a lot.

"So. Sandy?"

"Yeah?" Johnny stretched to snatch a pack of cigarettes from the nightstand, offering me the pack and shrugging when I shook my head. He lit a cigarette and drew in the smoke, exhaling on his next sentence. "What about her?"

"Do you have something going on with her?"

"She's my old lady." Johnny shrugged and moved in to kiss me again. "But she's cool, don't worry."

"Wait a minute." I frowned, a hand on his chest holding him back. "Your old… You mean your wife?"

"Well, yeah. Nah. We split up a while ago, just haven't signed the papers yet. Now she just comes around once in a while to bring the kid."

"Wait a minute," I said again. This hurt my brain. I took the cigarette he offered this time and took a drag. I'd only smoked a couple times before, but I managed not to kill myself with coughing. "She's your wife. That was your kid?"

"Yeah, that's Kimmy, my daughter."

"You couldn't have split up too long ago," I pointed out. "She's only what, ten months old?"

"Something like that. Yeah." He took the cigarette back and eyed me through a veil of smoke. "You got a problem with that? I mean, it ain't like we're still together. Like I said, she's cool with what I do. She does her own thing."

I wasn't sure I was cool with it, but what could I say? I came in off the street and fucked him in a house full of strangers, in a time before I'd even come into this world. I shuddered, thinking of it. Somewhere out there my parents hadn't even met yet. I didn't exist in this world, and Johnny'd already been married and had a kid. His daughter was older than me.

"Hey. You okay?" Johnny pushed the heavy weight of my hair off my shoulder and down my back, now not so sticky that the sweat was drying.

"Yeah, sure. I'm great. It's all cool." I couldn't even be jealous, just annoyed with my mind for tossing up crap like an ex-wife who didn't know boundaries.

"Cool." This seemed enough for him. Naked, Johnny smoked and sighed, leaning back against the headboard. He shot me a glance. "You're not running away this time."

I looked around the room and drew in a long breath, but all I smelled was our fucking and his cigarette. "No. Should I go?"

He smiled and leaned to kiss me, lingering. "Hell, no. You stay here. We'll get Candy to cook us up something good. Paul's coming over later to do some work on a project. You should stay."

I bunched up a couple of flat pillows—no memory foam here—and stretched out beside him. "What kind of project?"

"An art project. You like art, Emm?"

"I... Sure." It wasn't really a lie. I was convinced I'd like art if I could ever appreciate it.

Johnny laughed and stubbed out his cigarette in an ashtray on the nightstand. He stretched out an arm behind me, pulling me closer to rest my head on his chest. It was a better pillow than the others had been. "What kind of art do you like?"

"Oh, umm, Van Gogh, I guess. Dali."

He snorted. "Those guys."

I looked up at him. "What kind of art do you like?"

He shrugged. "I know it when I see it. Anyway, Paul, he's not doing something like that. Not painting and shit. He's got a movie camera. He's going to make another one of his movies or something. I dunno. I told him I'd help him out again."

Johnny and Paul had made three or four of these homegrown art films, all even more plotless than the foreign horror films had been. I'd only caught bits and pieces of them on the internet, since Jen didn't own them and I hadn't yet managed to get through the entire queue on Interflix. Some of them weren't even available on DVD.

"I've seen them."

He cocked his head to look at me, curious. "You been in one of his movies? Is that your bag?"

"Oh, no. I meant... Never mind what I mean."

"You are something," Johnny said again. "I just can't figure out your scene, you know?"

"I don't have a scene." He kissed me, then looked into my

eyes like he was trying to seek out all my secrets. I pulled away. "What's the movie about, Johnny?"

He shrugged again and yawned. "Hell if I know. I just said I'd help him out, you know? Help him do his thing. He's got the camera and the money. He's got some rich-ass bastard behind it, too, says he'll get it in all the cinemas."

At least this gave me a better idea of what year we were in. The first of Paul's movies had been made in 1976. All of them, from what I could recall, were made over a year-and-a-half time span.

Johnny ran a hand over my hair. "Paul's an artist."

"So are you."

"Me? Hell, no." He laughed at that. Hard. "I can't draw worth shit. Can't sing. I'm not even a very good actor. The only thing I guess I'm good at is posing for pictures."

Pitchahs. I laughed softly. "You *are* pretty."

Johnny snorted. "Yeah, well, pretty is as pretty does, huh? It pays the bills, I guess. And it beats stealing cars."

"You won't be doing it forever," I told him.

The clock on the dresser ticked very loudly as silence fell between us. As he stared at me. Johnny's gaze took in everything about me. He slid a hand beneath my hair, cupping my neck, but didn't pull me closer.

"No," he said. "I know that. You can't think to do something like that forever, you'll end up on the street."

"You won't end up on the street," I said.

"What are you, a fortune-teller?"

"Something like that. Sure." I took his palm and held it up to trace the lines there. I had no idea about palmistry, or cards, or any of that. But I did know his future. "I see fame and fortune in your future."

"Good, good. That's good." Johnny leaned forward to stare down into the mysteries of his palm as though he could see what I wasn't really seeing.

"And…love." The word slipped out of me on a breath.

He looked at me. "Yeah? You see love?"

"I see love for you, yes." My voice had gone dreamy and thick. I traced another line on his palm, making it all up and yet convinced, somehow, I was telling the absolute truth. I looked deep into Johnny's eyes, captured by his gaze, held tight to this place and time, at least for that moment, which was maybe all I could really expect.

He pulled me closer and kissed me, long, lingering, slow and sweet. "I like the sound of that."

We kissed for a while without urgency. Lying with him in that big bed, the pillows and sheets tangled all around us, all of this had taken on a magical soft focus, sort of like in his movies. His cock rose up hard between our bodies but he seemed in no hurry to fuck again—and that was okay. Different, unexpected, but okay. It was enough to be there with him, making out like we had no place to be and all the time in the world.

Which of course, I did not. My bladder twinged, first of all, an event that had never happened in my fugues. Laughing, I twisted from Johnny's insistent grip and left the bed to pad on naked feet to the bathroom. I turned from the doorway to look at him. I blew him a kiss. And when I turned back and stepped through the doorway, I stumbled and fell and ended up on my hands and knees in my front hallway.

I was still naked.

Chapter 10

My phone was ringing, harsh, discordant and insistent. Shaking so hard my teeth chattered, gooseflesh like braille on my skin, I stood. Immediately, the floor shifted beneath me. My stomach lurched, too.

I made it down the hall to the kitchen where I plucked the phone from its base and held it with a shaking hand to my ear. "Hello?"

"Hi, honey, it's Mom. Listen, I was wondering if you had that black dress we got for you to wear to that Christmas party a few years ago, because I'd like to borrow it."

I swallowed against a surge of bile. Sometimes I came out of a fugue with an upset stomach or a sharp headache, but this didn't feel like that. This felt like terror.

"Mom?"

"I checked your closet for it, but I couldn't see it, so I thought maybe you took it with you."

I slid down the wall and ended up on my cold kitchen floor, my bare ass freezing. I drew my knees up to my chest and wrapped my arms around them and put my face down. The phone pressed into my ear. I swallowed again and again before I could answer.

"Yeah, I think I have it. It might be in a couple of things I haven't unpacked yet."

"Do you think you could look for it?"

"Right now?"

"Well, whenever you get the chance," she said.

"Sure." My voice sounded rough and raspy. I cleared my throat. "I can do that."

"Good. So, what else is exciting up there in the big city?"

My stomach was settling, my headache fading. I was still freezing but not quite ready to move off the floor in case I set myself off again. "Nothing. The usual. Nothing, really."

"Well, maybe you can come down next week," my mom said. "You can bring the dress and we'll get some dinner. Maybe see that new Ewan McGregor movie. I hear he shows his butt."

My laugh came out a little strangled but genuine. "He shows his butt in every movie."

"Gotta go. Dad's waiting. Bye, honey, love you."

And like that, just like that, she hung up on me. My mom never hung up on me without asking me if something was wrong. Without worrying just a little.

I got up off the floor. I put the phone back in the base. I went upstairs and ran the shower as hot as I could stand it. It stung when I got in, but I was still so cold I needed the heat. I rubbed my hands together under the spray, then hunkered down in the center of my shower and let the water pound over my back until I stopped shaking. I stayed in there until the water turned lukewarm.

By the time I got out, I felt better enough to wrap myself in a thick robe and go down to my kitchen for something to eat. Toast, jam and tea. An invalid's dinner. I didn't feel sick. I was no longer in pain. Hell, I could barely remember how it had felt when I went to my hands and knees in my entryway, naked.

Belly full, I searched my entryway. No clothes. Hesitantly,

I opened the front door and looked there, but if I'd somehow gone outside starkers and run around the neighborhood, I hadn't left the clothes conveniently on the front porch. I'd left Johnny's house just after 8:00 p.m. The phone showed my mom had called at 8:17. Considering the walk should've taken less than five minutes, I'd been dark for fewer than another ten. Not long enough to get into much trouble or get very far, and yet though I checked behind the bushes on either side of my front porch, all I turned up was some rotting leaves that hadn't been covered by snow.

I'd stepped through my front door and, the next thing I knew, was naked just a few feet inside it. I stood in front of the door, my robe dragging on the ground, and looked around. My unused formal living room to the right, stairs immediately in front of me, the hall to the kitchen and dining room straight back. How long would it take me to strip, make a trip to some other place in my house, and make it back to the front door? And why would I have done something like that?

In college, I'd had a friend who liked to drink too much. He didn't just pass out, he blacked out. He could be up and talking to you, holding a perfectly rational conversation, and not remember a word of it. He could go from alert to unconscious in seconds. Sort of like me and my fugues, except while I often had vivid, rich fantasies during them and knew I could react to my environment even while dark, that was only for a few seconds and only if I wasn't down too deep.

I'd never, not so far as I could remember, been dark for longer than a minute or two while also maintaining the appearance of consciousness. And while I might've been able to answer simple questions, enough to keep the person I was with unaware I was having a fugue, anything more complicated than "yes," "no" or "uh-huh" quickly revealed the truth. I'd certainly never gone and done anything while I was dark for longer than a few minutes, and even then, it was never anything more than sitting down or taking a few steps.

I counted the steps and the minutes from my door to my living room. To the kitchen. To my bedroom and back again. No clothes. No signs I'd been staggering around, making mischief.

I went back out onto the front porch and looked at the sidewalk, unsure if I hoped to catch a glimpse of a pile of clothes under the streetlamp or not. All I saw was Joe, the guy who lived with his wife one street over and who liked to walk his dog around the block. Plastic Baggie in his hand, he waved.

I pulled my robe closer around my throat and waved back. The frigid air was sucking all the heat out my front door. My feet were bare, so I couldn't go to him. I had to holler.

"Hi!"

"Hi, Emm. How's it going?" Joe looked cold.

The dog, Chuckles, stopped to sniff my lawn and lift his leg against one of the raggedy bushes I'd eventually have to remove. I didn't really mind. Even if his dog pooped on my grass, Joe always picked it up.

"Good. Fine. Um, have you been out at all tonight? Before now?"

Joe looked down at the dog, then back at me. "You mean with Chuckles?"

"Yes. Around the block?"

"Yeah, I'm just heading home now. Why?"

"Did you…see me?"

Joe said nothing for a few seconds as my face heated, feeling extrawarm against the chilly wind. "Should I have?"

I forced a laugh. "Oh, no. I was just wondering if maybe you saw me someplace else other than my house tonight."

Joe hesitated again. "Are you okay?"

"Oh, sure, sure." I flapped a hand as though greeting a semi-stranger in my bathrobe and bare feet on a glacial winter's night from my front doorstep was entirely normal. "I was out for a walk earlier, that's all. I thought I saw you guys but I waved and...it wasn't you."

"Oh." Joe tugged the dog's leash to keep him from going into the neighbor's yard, because she did mind even the tiniest sprinkling of pee. "Nope. Not me. It's too cold to be out here for long."

"Right. Well. I guess it was someone else, then. Sorry!"

"No problem. Good night." Joe waved again and set off down the sidewalk.

"Night," I called after him faintly, and shut my door.

The credit union had a generous sick day/vacation time policy, and though I hated using up time I could've spent at the beach lying in my bed instead, I called work the next day, claiming I had the flu. I did feel feverish and achy, but not really sick. I couldn't stop thinking about the night before.

Even when they'd been at their worst, I'd always counted myself fortunate that my fugues weren't harmful. They could've been dangerous if I went dark while I was driving or operating machinery or something like that, which was why I hadn't had a driver's license for much of my adult life. But no matter how frequently I went dark, no tests had ever shown any evidence of further brain damage. I remained a medical mystery, files thick with test results and reports, but no real conclusions. My brain had intermittent, irregular and unpredictable erratic activity that seemed controllable with medication and alternative medicine, but nobody had ever found evidence it was getting worse.

So. What had changed? Had the stress of moving out on my own tipped me somehow into another level? Had something burst, a clot or aneurysm? In my bed, covers clutched to my chin, I shuddered. Would I know if something like that happened? Would I have pain?

Maybe I'd just go dark and never come out of it.

Maybe I was overreacting, taking a page from my mother's book. I forced myself out of bed and into the shower where I ran out the hot water again. Then I made myself eat some soup and toast, more sick food, though I wasn't really sick. After that I made myself a plate of my mom's homemade macaroni and cheese from the store of containers in my freezer she'd sent along with me. And after that, tummy full of carbs and fat, I felt a little better.

I knew I should call Dr. Gordon and get in for some tests, just as I knew that no matter what they showed, she'd feel obligated to make a report to the state. There went my license for another year. And yes, I knew it was irresponsible of me not to tell her, but I could take public transportation to work and most other places I needed to go, thank Saint Vitus, the patron saint of epileptics. Except I didn't have epilepsy. I didn't know what I had.

I was hardly ever home on weekdays, so the rattle-thump as I passed my front door scared me until I realized it was the mailbox outside. I opened the door, catching the mail carrier halfway down the sidewalk. I grabbed the yellow package slip from the box and waved it, catching her attention.

"Hi!"

She smiled. "Oh, you're home. Lucky you. I have a package for you that won't fit in the box. I was going to take it back for pickup later."

"Lucky me." I handed her the form. She gave me the package, a flat-rate envelope with an unfamiliar return address. "Thanks."

Inside, I ripped open the envelope. A DVD fell out into my palm. *Night of a Hundred Moons.* My stomach dropped a little, just like it did on the crest of a roller coaster's first hill. I studied the front of the case. It looked photocopied, and poorly not professionally produced. I flipped it over. Same on the back, the art and text a little faded and askew. Inside, the disk was plain silver with a printed label affixed.

Huh.

I hadn't looked too carefully before buying it, but Jen had said it was a really rare and hard-to-find movie. I didn't like the idea that I'd somehow purchased a pirated copy, but it was too late now. I could only hope it would play in my DVD player.

I should've called her. I'd promised to. But Jen would be at work now, and I was home alone. Sick days were meant for watching movies all day long in bed, and with this burning in my hand, there was no way I could even wait until tonight to watch it with her. I was sure I'd want to see it again, anyway. She didn't have to know it would be my second viewing. Or hell, I was sure she'd understand. She'd watched all of Johnny's movies long before she got me hooked on them.

Upstairs in my bedroom, I finally set up the DVD player my parents had bought me this Christmas just past, a present meant to celebrate the fact I was moving out and would need my own appliances. I'd ended up taking along their old one, too, since I'd bought them a Blu-ray player. Since moving into my house, I'd only ever watched movies in the living room, determined to live like an adult and not some lame-ass still living in her parents' basement.

I didn't feel lame now. I felt decadent, actually. Owner of two DVD players, two televisions, home on a workday and ready to lounge around in bed watching art films. It was so far from last year at this time when I'd still been sneaking in after midnight as though I had a curfew and refusing to let my boyfriend sleep over. Well, now I had my own place and no boyfriend, but I thought it was a good trade-off.

I got myself some ice cream—double chocolate fudge—and tucked myself under the thick comforter with the remote in hand. I settled back onto my pillows.

I pressed Play.

I knew that house. I knew that kitchen. I knew those people. Candy, Bellina, Ed, even Paul. And Johnny, oh, Johnny, wearing a tank top and jeans that should've looked outdated and ridiculous but fit his ass so right I had to appreciate them.

They sat around his kitchen table, smoking and talking, while the camera cut from one face to another. The sound was awful, the music tinny and out of sync. The continuity was bad, too, like they'd simply shot the scene once but from all different angles, and bits of conversation had been dropped while the camera shifted. There was a plot, at least, or some semblance of one, even though they all spoke in stilted sentences that sounded nothing like their actual conversation.

I stopped, ice cream melting on my tongue. I put the bowl on the nightstand and turned up the volume. I recognized these people from seeing them on the internet, didn't I? In still shots from this very movie. And my mind had filled in the rest. So I couldn't know how they actually sounded, none of them but Johnny, and he was a better actor than any of them and the only one who could really pull this off.

With the movie on pause I could study the scene more carefully. I didn't know that clock on the wall, or the number of cabinets, but I hadn't counted them, had I? Hadn't paid much attention to anything but Johnny during the fugue, because he was who my brain wanted to create. The rest of this was all…

"Shit," I muttered aloud. "Shit, shit, shit. Where did I see this? How did I see it?"

I took the movie off pause and hopped out of bed to get my laptop. I searched the film and found the site I'd ordered it from, along with a few other obscure sites I hadn't read as thoroughly before. With one eye on the TV screen, I scrolled through pages of horrible light on dark text and blinking .gifs I had to make sure not to stare at too long. They'd have given someone without brain injury a seizure.

According to one site, *Night of a Hundred Moons* had been a staple of late-night cable during the eighties, particularly popular with shows like *Up Past Midnight,* which I could vividly remember watching at every sleepover I'd ever had even if I didn't actively recall any of Johnny's films. I paused the movie again, comparing it with one of the still shots on the site. I knew that table, that kitchen, those people, but of course I did. I'd seen them before, some time I didn't remember.

I let out a chocolate-scented breath I hadn't realized I was holding. My brain took bits and pieces of whatever I'd experienced and wove them together into fiction. It was what happened. This was no different than any of the others, just more vivid and realistic because of my crush on Johnny. I wanted it more, that was all.

It still didn't explain how I'd ended up naked on my floor, but I didn't want to think about that now. I put the laptop aside and concentrated again on the movie. In it, Johnny had left the kitchen for what must've been the back garden and a swimming pool I hadn't known was there. He stripped down, naked, tipping his face to sunlight that turned him golden.

The camera fucking loved him. Loved fucking him, too. Whoever had filmed this looked at Johnny with the eyes of a lover, traveling over the length of his body and lingering on all the places I wanted to kiss and bite and suck and lick—for real, not in fantasy. He swam the length of the pool, body not obscured by crystal-clear water, legs scissoring and muscles flexing.

This part of the film seemed to be better edited, shots not just cutting at random but flowing. He came out of the water in slow motion and flipped his hair back, off his face.

I came a little bit, with a groan that would've been embarrassing if I hadn't been alone.

I frowned in the next minute. Sandy, wearing only a skimpy T-shirt and a pair of panties, was waiting for him when he came out of the water. She'd pulled the hem of her shirt up and through the neckline to bare a belly I was catty enough to notice wasn't flat and firm. I'd done the same with my shirt when I was a kid running around in the summer, but never as a woman. I reminded myself this movie was easily thirty years old and being a bitch about a woman whose tits were surely now someplace around her belly button would only come back to haunt me later.

"Hey, Johnny," Sandy said in that same irritating nasal voice she'd had in my fugue.

Fuck, it was annoying. Of all the things my brain had had to retain, why that? On the other hand, I thought, watching as Johnny hoisted himself out of the pool, I guessed I had to take the good with the bad.

"Hey," Johnny said.

"Come outta there, I wanna talk to you."

Johnny didn't move, just looked her over with one eye squinted shut against the sun. "What do you want?"

"C'mere." She reached to toy with his hair, and though I knew it was a movie, I was glad to see him pull away.

"Leave me alone," Johnny said. He jerked away when she reached for him again, but when she slid down behind him and wrapped her arms and legs around him, her fingers tweaking at his nipples, he didn't try too hard to escape. "I said leave me."

"No."

They tussled a little, but she didn't let go and he didn't get up. Her hand drifted lower but he stopped it by slapping it flat against his belly and holding it there. Smiling, she nibbled at his neck. He didn't smile. Johnny looked stone-faced, water dripping down his temples and cheeks to hang off his chin in shimmering drops.

"Being around you makes me feel so sexy, Johnny. I feel so sexy now."

"Good for you." He wasn't budging.

Not when she licked him, not when she tweaked his nipples, not even when she slid a hand below camera level into his lap.

"I said no." Johnny's face twisted in an echo of my current expression. He shoved her off, finally, and got up to stalk naked to a chair and grab up a towel.

I was hard-pressed to find a reason for this scene. Knowing Sandy was his wife, or ex-wife, whatever, only made it worse. I was jealous. I laughed out loud at that, though it sounded shaky and nothing like my regular laugh. I was jealous of something that had happened in a movie filmed before I was born.

"Lame," I told myself.

It didn't feel lame. Watching them together, it felt the way I had in eighth grade when the boy I had a crush on asked someone else to dance. I wanted to fast-forward through the movie, or at least through this scene. Even Johnny's naked ass wasn't enough to get me past the sick, twisty feeling in my gut.

My ice cream had melted and the heat had kicked on, making the comforter too heavy. I kicked it off and lifted the remote to scan ahead, when it happened again.

I went dark.

Chapter 11

"Hey." Johnny's voice turned me from the hedgerow I found myself in front of. "Where'd you run off to this time?"

If I opened my mouth, I'd babble, so I pressed my lips closed on a smile I hoped looked real. Johnny's hair, slicked back and wet, looked familiar, as did the jeans and tank top. He came toward me with a slight grin.

"You missed Paul," he said. "He just left. He'll be back tomorrow sometime, says he has more to shoot."

I couldn't speak. I let him pull me closer and kiss me. I let him twirl a strand of my hair around his finger and tug. But I couldn't speak.

"What? You mad about something? You ain't mad about that stuff by the pool, are you? That wasn't anything. That was just for the movie."

The movie. The pool. I'd just watched Sandy put her hands all over him.

I found my voice. "With Sandy?"

"Yeah. But it was just…look, she's still got a thing going on for me, but it doesn't matter. It's just at thing, you know?"

"I know." I did know. I had a thing for Johnny myself.

"Anyway, it was just something they wanted us to do for the

movie, that's all. She wanted to make it more, make it real, but I told her and I told Paul, I'm not into that scene, you know? Not with her, anyway. But you weren't around. Too bad, huh?" He grinned. "I coulda helped make you famous."

"How...how long was I gone?"

Johnny shrugged. "Coupla hours? I gotta tell you, Emm, I figured you'd disappeared again, just run off. But you left your stuff behind. How'd you do that?"

He looked me over, a frown tipping his mouth for the first time since he'd seen me. "What are you wearing?"

I had on a pair of fuzzy sleep pants with Batman on them and a baby-doll T-shirt. Sick-day clothes. I'd showered but done nothing with my hair, and it hung in still-damp sheaves, heavy down my back.

"Kiss me," I said instead of answering him. "Just kiss me."

And he did. Long, and soft and slow and sweet, just the way I wanted it and the way I needed it. The way I knew he would kiss me in my real life, if only I could ever convince him to try. I pulled away, knowing I must look tousled and glazed. Love drunk.

Johnny cocked his head, eyes narrowed. "Emm?"

The world was shifting under my feet again. Slip-sliding away, as Paul Simon said, but I doubted he'd ever had something like this happen to him. Fuck. Had that song even been written yet? I didn't know.

"Kiss me, Johnny," I said.

He did again, over and over, while the world spun so fast I was sure I'd fly right off. His hands caressed me, slid up under my T-shirt to cup my bare breasts and tweak my nipples. We kissed in that garden, in the bushes, like a pair of lovers trying hard not to get caught.

I could smell the chlorine on his skin and something tropical, maybe tanning oil. I smelled the broken branches and leaves from where we'd crushed against the bush. I smelled all of this and, under it, the sick-making scent of oranges. It made bitter saliva squirt into my mouth.

"I have to go," I told him when I could no longer fight it off.

"But you'll come back, right? Promise me you'll come back." Johnny took a fistful of my hair and held me tight, leashed. "I'm not letting you go unless you promise."

"I promise!" The words spun out of me on a gasp. "I do. I'll be back."

"Good," Johnny said, and kissed me again. "So, I'll see you?"

"Yes," I told him. "Yes, yes, yes, Johnny."

I let him go, even though he was all that kept me standing. I smiled and waved. I turned and walked through the garden and out to the sidewalk in front of his house.

I blinked.

My bed. TV still on, movie still playing, still showing the same scene. My nipples were still tight, my clit throbbing. My breath caught in my throat as I fell back on the pillows.

I cupped my breasts, but there was no warmth there from any touch but mine. I'd imagined him kissing me, touching me. My body had reacted and still was.

I slid my hand under my waistband and found my cunt, aching and empty and slick. My clit pulsed as I circled it with my fingertip. My hips shifted, pushing upward as I stroked myself. I stopped, staring up at the ceiling that should've been blocked by Johnny's face but wasn't. And wouldn't ever be.

"Dammit, brain. Not fair."

I slid my tongue across my lips and imagined the taste of him. I looked at the screen, where Johnny was now lying on his stomach, naked, on a bed with his eyes closed. Sleeping. Dreaming, it looked like, by the way his lids twitched, and he let out a moan.

Fuck. It went right through me. It was full of sex and longing, that moan, much like the one slipping from between my lips. On the TV, Johnny was dreaming, but I was awake. Not dark. This, my hand on my clit, was real. The orgasm building inside me, my belly muscles getting tight, that was real. The bed beneath me, my own slick heat coating my fingers as I fucked myself, all of that was real. And my orgasm, finally, that was real, too.

I ventured out just after five o'clock, when it no longer felt so scandalous to be up and about when I was supposed to be home in bed. The walk to the Morningstar Mocha was just long enough in the cold air to get my blood pumping, and the exercise had me feeling better after my comfort-food overload. I was going to destroy all that good effort with a piece of cake and a sugary latte, but I didn't care. I needed the sugar and the caffeine.

"Hey." I tossed a glance at Carlos. "Are you always here?"

"Free internet," Carlos said with a shrug. "Saves me close to fifty bucks a month. That's more than enough to cover the cost of my coffee and doughnuts."

"You obviously don't drink enough coffee and eat enough doughnuts."

He shrugged again and pointed at the laptop. "When I sell my novel, I'll treat you all to lattes."

"It's a deal." I peeled off my gloves and shoved them into the pocket of my jacket, which was not the right weight for this weather but…well, I'd lost my coat along with my favorite pair of jeans. I looked around the almost-empty coffee shop. "Who's been in today?"

"Not your boyfriend, if that's what you're hoping." Carlos gave me a smug grin.

I ignored it. "How about Jen?"

"Haven't seen her. You're her bestie, not me."

I pulled out my phone with a flourish and tapped out a text

asking her if she planned on stopping by. "Do you *have* any friends?"

"Good one." Carlos's grin was nicer this time.

I gave him a smug grin of my own and went to the counter for a double white-chocolate peppermint-stick latte with full-fat milk and a slice of coffee cake. I could practically hear the buttons on my fat pants screaming in protest, but I didn't care. Sugar and caffeine had helped in the past with the fugues. Indulging was worth a few extra hours on the treadmill.

I took my coffee and cake to a table toward the back just as my phone buzzed from my pocket. I sent up a prayer to thank whoever was the patron saint of phones that my precious iPhone hadn't been in my pocket when I lost my clothes, and thumbed the screen to read the message from Jen. She was on her way. I wasn't sure what I planned to tell her about *Night of a Hundred Moons*. I wasn't sure I could watch it again. Maybe I could just lend it to her.

I sipped the hot, sweet coffee and picked a lump of cinnamon sugar from the top of my coffee cake. I people-watched. The Mocha was a good place to do it, since it was on a street set in the heart of a residential district. The crowd was varied, too, young and old, trendy hipsters in line behind classy old broads with red lipstick and leopard coats. I spotted familiar faces from my few nights downtown. Harrisburg's a city, but a small one, no matter what my mom thought.

By the time Jen arrived, pink-cheeked with sparkling eyes and a grin I had to return, I'd finished my cake and drank half my coffee. I was buzzing from both, but there was no hint of oranges. Not topsy-turvy world. Nothing shifted or slipped away from me. And, of course, there was no Johnny.

And I wanted there to be. Even if it meant going dark. The thought startled me, yet I wasn't quite surprised.

"What's up?" Jen said as I stood to greet her with a hug only really good friends merited. "You look confuzzled."

"I… No, I'm fine. Just a little tired. I stayed home from work today."

She withdrew, making a face. "Ew! Not the flu, is it?"

"No."

She leaned closer. "Trouble in lady-parts land?"

I laughed. "No. Just tired. Bad headache. I think it was more a mental health day than anything."

"Girl, I need one of those so bad. I've had it with preschool kids and their runny, snotty noses and poopy pants."

"Wow, and here I thought the youth of the world was in good hands."

She shook her head. "The fuck was I thinking, getting a job in a day-care center? I thought the hours would be good. And I like kids. Hell, I love my nieces and nephews, and since my womb will probably dry up and fall out before I ever meet someone to have some of my own with—"

"Oh, shut up. God. You're what, twenty-five? Twenty-six?"

"It's all downhill after twenty-five, Emm," Jen said so seriously I thought she meant it until she cracked up.

"Gee, thanks, so what does that make me?"

She waved a hand. "Ah, you're fine."

"Fine as in old?"

"How old are you?" She shrugged out of her coat and hung it on the back of her chair, but didn't sit.

"I'll be thirty-two."

"Huh." She thought on that for a minute. "Well, I guess you could always adopt."

"Bitch," I called after her as she headed for the counter to place her order.

Back again in a few minutes with her drink, Jen looked me over. "You know I was kidding."

"I know. I don't think I'll ever have kids, either. It's okay."

"No? Really?" She blew on her coffee to cool it before sipping and winced, anyway, as she burned her tongue.

"No." I hadn't told her about the brain stuff. I wasn't sure this was the right place or time to reveal it now. "Not that I have to worry about it."

"You never know. You could meet Prince Charming tomorrow," Jen said.

"Well. The same goes for you. You never know what might happen."

She looked around the Mocha and frowned. "Yeah, well, I doubt it's going to happen here."

We both laughed at that and looked up as the bell jingled. I froze. Jen's laughter eased into a happy little sigh. We both looked at each other and then away, fast, to keep ourselves from laughing.

Johnny's coat brushed our table as he passed, and I let my fingers creep over the spot to caress it. I caught Jen looking at me. I shrugged.

"You," she said, "have it worse than I ever did."

"I got the movie today." I pitched my voice low, too aware of him only a few feet away. After he'd so rudely dispatched me from his house after the cookie incident, I didn't want him to overhear me talking about him like the sort of goggle-eyed fan he thought I was.

"*Hundred Moons?* Wheeee!" Jen hushed herself, though Johnny didn't seem to have heard. "Kick. Ass. When can I come over and watch it? Oh, wait. You did already, didn't you?"

"I'm sorry," I admitted. "I had to."

"Oh, girl, it ain't no thing." Jen lifted her cup in my direction. "I'd have been all over that bitch the second I got it out of the envelope. So. How was it? It's superhard to find, but it's supposed to be amazing."

"It was..." The truth was, I could barely remember the actual movie. "I guess if you're an art movie critic you could probably find a lot of good things to say about it. The cinematography and stuff, or maybe the existential meaning of the plight of youth in modern society."

"Shit like that," Jen said solemnly, "is why we are friends."

"No, seriously," I told her. "It was pretty much like the others but with more random moments."

Jen lowered her voice and flicked her gaze toward Johnny, who'd taken his coffee to a table directly opposite us on the other side of the room. "At least tell me he's naked in it."

"Completely."

"Then it's worth it," she said. "Because damn, naked Johnny Dellasandro cannot fucking be bad."

"His wife's in it. His ex-wife."

"Which one?"

"He has more than one?"

"I think he's had three or four," she said with another surreptitious look.

He had to know we were talking about him, or looking at him. How could he have missed it? We were worse than a pair of giggly girls in the back of the room passing notes about the hot substitute teacher.

"How did I miss that?"

"Maybe you only Googled pictures of his cock."

I tossed a napkin at her. "Shhhh!"

Jen laughed into her hands. "Sorry!"

"He's not married now, is he?"

"I don't think so."

"Dating anyone?" I asked.

Jen's brows raised. "My stalking does have its limits. I mean, I don't think so. If he is, he doesn't bring her around here. Though he was with that chick last week, and I have seen him out and about a few times with her."

"Shit." I sounded miserable and didn't try to hide it.

"Oh, girl," Jen said, sympathetic. "Look at you."

I frowned and licked my finger to pick up the last bits of sugar from my plate. "I know. Pathetic, right?"

"You should talk to him. Just say hello or something."

I sighed and risked a glance, but Johnny was deep inside his book, the title of which I couldn't see. "I sorta kinda did that."

"And?"

I looked at her, coming clean. "I took him some cookies as a thank-you for that day I slipped on the ice."

"You *fucked* him!" Heads turned. Not his, thank God. Jen lowered her voice to a hiss. "You fucked Johnny Dellasandro?"

"No! No, no," I amended as my cheeks turned to infernos. "He didn't want to have anything to do with me, actually. In fact, when I went to give him the cookies, he wouldn't even eat one. He was a douche bag, actually."

"No." She sat back in her chair, slumping, defeated. "I mean, he's always sort of standoffish, but to be a douche bag? That's so disappointing. Did you tell him you wanted to ride his face or something embarrassing like that? Because that's probably what I'd do."

"No. I just made him some cookies because he'd mentioned he liked homemade cookies."

She scoffed. "Who doesn't?"

"Apparently, Johnny Dellasandro doesn't. Or at least not mine. And if he won't even eat my cookies, I sincerely doubt he'd be interested in eating my pussy."

Jen burst into laughter, and I followed, even though I wasn't really trying to be funny. We both guffawed until even Johnny turned to watch us. Our eyes met, his somber and mine I could only imagine as full of glee. I could've sobered at the look he gave me, but I didn't. Screw him, I thought. I'm not going to pretend I'm intimidated.

"Ah, well, I have to run. Taking Grandma to the hairdresser."

Jen sighed with the last remnants of her laughter and got up. "When can I come over to watch the movie?"

"Thursday?"

"That's good with me. You want to watch it again?"

I hadn't been sure, but I nodded, anyway. "Duh!"

"Cool. See you Thursday." She laughed, shaking her head, and muttered, "Cookies," as she left.

I sat there a minute or two longer, braving the energy to face the cold outside, now dark. I stalled by making a trip to the restroom. When I came out, Johnny was gone. He hadn't gone far, though, just outside the Mocha's front door. He was lighting up a cigarette.

I stopped when I saw him. I almost said hello, then thought better of it. Then thought again. I'd say hi to a stranger I passed on the street; I shouldn't make Johnny be anything less. Or anything more.

"Hey," I said, casual.

He nodded and blew smoke out into a thin stream that was whisked immediately away in the wind. The smell bit at the inside of my nose, but at least it wasn't oranges. I gave him another look, willing myself not to leap into his arms and make a bigger fool of myself, though once my teeth started chattering it was hard to look like anything else.

We had to walk in the same direction, and without words we fell into step next to each other. It was the longest three blocks I'd ever walked, and possibly the coldest.

I never wanted it to end.

By the time we got to my house, though, I was shuddering with cold. My jaw gritted to keep my teeth from clattering. My nose raw. I couldn't feel my fingers. I turned in at my front walk, and I thought Johnny would keep going without a word the way we'd walked the whole way home.

"You should have a better coat," he said.

I turned to look at him. "What?"

He was almost finished with the cigarette and pointed at me with the butt. "Your coat's not warm enough. You should have a better one."

"I, um, misplaced my other coat," I told him.

He studied me for what felt like a very long time. "Yeah?"

"Yeah."

"Well," Johnny said as he backed up a couple steps on the sidewalk, "you should get yourself another one."

And that was all. I watched him walk down the sidewalk to his own house. He didn't look back. Not once.

Chapter 12

So it wasn't a marriage proposal. I still went to bed with my head and heart buzzing. I slept hard, no dreams, and woke refreshed. No strange smells, nothing shifting around. I felt better than I had in weeks, the difference subtle and unnoticeable if I hadn't been so focused on every small twinge of my body.

After work I found the dress my mom wanted and decided on a whim to drive it down to her. Harrisburg was only a forty-minute drive to Annville and it wasn't like I had anything better to do. Or worse. And...I wanted to see my mom. With everything that had been happening, I needed to sit at the old kitchen table, drink some chocolate milk. Be babied, just a little.

But when I got there, the house was dark and quiet. No car in the drive. I let myself in the front door, feeling like a guest even though I used my own key. "Hello?"

No answer. I checked my watch. It was just after 7:00 p.m, by no means late at night, but for my parents it was the equivalent of one in the morning. I put my keys in my bag and set it on the chair just inside the front door out of habit, though my mom had always yelled at me to put my stuff away. I had no place to put it now.

I didn't live there anymore.

"Mom? Dad?" I hung the black dress, still covered in plastic from the last time I'd had it dry-cleaned, on the coatrack. "Hello?"

The crunch of car tires alerted me to someone pulling into the drive, and the next minute the electric garage door opener rattled the decorative plates hung on the dining room wall. I stepped through into the kitchen just as my mom came through the door from the garage.

She screamed. Loud. I screamed, too.

"Emmaline!"

"Mom!" I started laughing. "Didn't you see my car out front?"

"I wasn't expecting you," my mom said, a hand over her heart. She was puffing. "You scared the breath out of me!"

"Sorry." Chagrined, I moved forward to hug her as my dad came through the door. "Hi, Dad."

My dad greeted me with an absentminded kiss and a hug. He pushed past us and down the hallway toward their bedroom as though my visit were nothing special. God, I love my dad.

My mom held me at arm's length and looked me up and down. "You look thinner."

"I wish. But you definitely do." I'd seen her only a month or so ago, but she'd lost weight. She wore a tracksuit and had dropped a gym bag at her feet when she screamed. "Were you at the gym?"

My mom looked at the bag, then her clothes, then at me. "Yes. Your dad and I figured we'd better get in shape."

My mom had never been fat. Just pleasantly rounded, thick in the thighs and full in the chest. It was strange to see her cheeks more hollowed. I'd brought the dress thinking there was little chance she'd fit in it, but now it looked as though it might actually be too big.

"Wow," I said. "I should take a page from your book."

It was her pet phrase, and I sounded just like her. My mom laughed and hugged me tight. I closed my eyes and hugged her back just as hard.

"Oh, my baby girl. I've missed you."

"Mom," I said out of habit, not because I really minded.

"What are you doing here?" she said when we pulled apart.

"I brought the dress."

"Oh, right. Good!" My mom beamed. "Let me just take a quick shower and I'll try it on. Have you eaten yet? I'm going to throw together a salad for Dad and me, but there's some leftovers in the fridge."

"No, I'm fine."

I did pull open the fridge to get some milk, but when I opened the cupboard to look for the chocolate milk mix, it wasn't there. And the table itself, I realized when I looked it over, was new. The same shape and size as the other one, but definitely different. I put the milk back and sat down heavily in a chair that was different, too.

"So, what do you think?" My mom came into the kitchen almost shyly, wearing the dress. It fit her perfectly, only a little baggy in the chest. She twirled slowly.

"It looks great."

"You think so?" She tugged at the neckline, which was way lower than anything she usually wore. "It's not too revealing?"

"No. Not at all. With your hair up and a pretty necklace, it will be great. You'll need different shoes." I pointed to her thick ankle socks, and we both smiled.

"Good. Well, that's taken care of, then." She smoothed the dress over her belly and turned from side to side to catch her reflection in the mirror hung on the back of the basement door. "Saves me having to buy one."

"What are you wearing it for?" I thought she'd say a wedding or something.

"Oh…" My mom chewed her lower lip for a second before looking at me with shining eyes. "Your dad's taking me on a cruise for our anniversary."

"What?" My jaw dropped.

"Yep. And there's a formal dinner night. This will be perfect."

Could. Not. Process. "A cruise. You and Dad?"

"Yes," she said. "An Alaskan cruise!"

Not even to the Caribbean, which was at least closer. "Wow. That's great, Mom."

"We haven't taken a trip together, just the two of us…well… probably not since our honeymoon."

Because of me. She'd never say it, and I knew lots of parents who'd never taken a vacation without their kids when the children were small, but my parents had stuck close to home for long years after their friends had all started hopping off on weekend getaways. And cruises.

Suddenly I was choked up, on the verge of tears I didn't want my mom to see. "Sounds like fun. When do you leave?"

"Oh, not until March. That's why we joined the gym. Marianne Jarvis, you remember her, right? Well, she said that cruises stuff you so full you come back ten pounds heavier. I thought we should get rid of at least ten before going." My mom smoothed the front of the dress again.

"I'm sure you'll have a great time. And you look great, too."

She studied me then. "Emm? Are you okay?"

No chocolate milk. A new table. My mother in a black cocktail dress, looking younger and prettier than I could ever remember. These were the changes that had happened since I'd moved out, and I didn't want to ruin her excitement with my own fears.

"You always ask me that. And what do I always say?"

"You always say you're fine," my mom answered.

"So, I'm fine."

"Okay, let me go get changed out of this. Are you staying for long? I can heat up something for you."

"I have some things to get out of the basement, if that's okay."

She gave me a funny look. "Of course it's okay, honey, this is still your house. It will always be your house."

I made it to the basement before bursting into tears I stifled with my fist. The battered love seat I'd left behind was still there and I sank onto it with both hands clapped over my mouth to keep even the tiniest sound from escaping. I rocked, weeping for reasons I couldn't really understand. I'd wanted to be independent. So why did I feel abandoned instead?

I forced myself to stop before I disintegrated entirely. The breakdown was mawkish and self-serving, not to mention selfish. And stupid. It was also dishonest, because I knew very well if I'd told Mom flat out that I'd been having fugues again she'd have hog-tied me to a kitchen chair and refused to let me leave until I made a doctor's appointment, and maybe not even then.

I wanted to tell her so she could pet and pamper me. I didn't want to tell her because I knew she would. I couldn't really have it both ways; that was my burden to deal with, not hers. I was almost thirty-two years old, and it was time to stand up on my own.

I hadn't left a whole lot behind, but there were a few plastic bins full of miscellaneous crap in the crawl space. Old yearbooks and photo albums, some treasured dolls, that sort of thing. Stuff I hadn't thought I'd want to look at again and yet found myself thinking of as I unpacked the boxes in my new place. Okay, so it was silly to want to see my old My Friend Mandy doll sitting on the bookshelf the way she had for all the years I'd lived at home. I'd left those things behind precisely because I wanted to have a grown-up house, but it felt too bare without those pieces of my childhood.

I pulled the bins out of the crawl space and opened each to make sure they were the right ones. I didn't want to drag my mom's Christmas decorations by mistake. Everything was there, just as I'd left it when I packed it all up months ago. And on the top of the third and final bin...

"Hey, Mom?" I asked on the way up the stairs. She appeared at the top in her regular outfit of jeans and a sweatshirt, an oven mitt on her hand. "Did you put this in my bin?"

"Georgette? Yes. I found her behind the love seat when I was doing some cleaning down there. I figured you'd want her."

I held up the stuffed koala bear that fit just right in the palm of my hand. Her fur had worn off in places, and one eye had been carefully glued back on after being lost for an entire day. My grandpa had bought her for me while I was in the hospital after falling off the jungle gym. I could still remember waking up to find her tucked against my side, a new and unfamiliar toy I'd quickly grown to love more than anything else.

"I can't believe I forgot her." I pressed her to my heart.

"Now you can take her along," Mom said.

"Yes," I said. "I'm going to."

I took her home sitting on the seat beside me. When I got out of the car, I put her in the pocket of my coat, an old one I'd picked up from my parents' house since I still hadn't found my other one. Then I took one bin from my trunk and heaved it up the sidewalk to my front door.

Someone had left me a package. Well, a brown paper grocery bag. I set down the bin and fumbled for my keys while I nudged the bag with my toe. I'd forgotten to replace the bulb in the light fixture over my door, so the bag's contents were shadowy and mysterious. I shoved open my door, set the bin inside on the rug so it wouldn't get snow on my clean(ish) floor. Then I brought in the grocery bag.

It was my coat.

More than that, it was my clothing, folded neatly. Bra, panties, socks, T-shirt. My favorite jeans. Only my boots were missing. I searched the bag for a note and found nothing.

"Shit," I breathed. "Shit, shit, shit."

Someone had taken pity on me, but who? Where had I gone wandering, naked and dark, and what had I done? I found myself feeling my body all over, as though I'd be able to tell what misadventures I'd gotten up to now. I had a friend in college who would always put a tampon in before she went out, even if she didn't have her period. She said that way, if it went missing, she'd know she'd been up to something even if she couldn't remember. I'd never tried that trick, but my womb twinged, anyway, as I remembered what my mind had told me I was doing during that time.

The clothes smelled of cedar as I shook them out. A small piece of paper fell from inside the folds of my shirt. It fluttered to the floor, sawing and drifting on the current of air coming in through my still-open front door, which I closed before bending to pick up the paper. It was a receipt for dry cleaning, pretty tattered and yellowed, looking old.

There was a name on the receipt.

"Shit, shit, shit." This I said aloud and closed my eyes tight, hoping to open them and discover I was imagining this. I opened them. "Shit!"

The name on the receipt was, fuck my life, Johnny's. I groaned and crumpled it, then thought better of it and smoothed it into my palm. I put it in my pocket.

My cell phone rang. Jen. "Hey, girl."

"Hey," she said. "Listen, would you mind if I bagged on our date night? I feel like a major douche about it, but, well…I have a real date. Not that a date night with you isn't real," she added hastily.

I laughed. "Of course I don't mind. Who's the date with?"

"His name's Jared," she said. "Get this, he's a funeral director."

"Whoa. Well, at least he has a job, which is more than I can say for my last lame-ass boyfriend."

She giggled. "Yeah. Anyway, we were supposed to go out on Friday night, but he's on call at weird times and asked if I minded going out on Thursday instead."

"How'd you meet this guy?" I shoved my clothes back in the grocery bag, glad to have them back but not ready to face what they meant. "I never heard you talk about him before."

"I'm almost embarrassed to say it."

"Girl, when are you almost embarrassed to say anything?" I laughed.

"I met him at a funeral. My grandma's sister Hettie died a couple months ago. Jared took care of her."

"He asked you out at your great-aunt's funeral? Whoa." I couldn't carry the bin and talk on the phone at the same time, so I went to the kitchen to put the kettle on, Georgette in my other hand. I set her on the table.

"No. Not then. I made a connection with him on Connex. The funeral home has a fan page."

"What?" This stopped me dead, no pun intended. "You're kidding me."

"Girl, I am not even. It's actually not as bad as you'd think. It's more like an information page, though it is sort of weird to become a fan of a funeral home. But we started talking that way, and then he asked me out."

"Maybe I need to hang out more often on Connex." I didn't mean it. Connex was such a time suck, even for someone with my currently slow social calendar.

"He's so cute, Emm. And really funny, too."

"Good for you! Have fun on Thursday, and don't worry. Really. I told you, the movie's not that good."

"Awww, any movie with Johnny in it's got to be good," she said, but without the conviction she used to have.

Jared must be really, really cute, I thought, but didn't begrudge her.

"You sure you don't mind? Sistahs before mistahs and all that?"

"Hell, no," I told her. "At least one of us should be getting some action."

"It's just a date," Jen said, but I heard excitement in her voice.

"Have fun," I told her again. "I'll expect a full report on Friday."

"You got it."

We hung up just as my kettle started whistling. I poured the hot water over some loose tea in a tea ball, then went out to bring in the rest of my bins while it steeped. On the street, a car passed me and pulled up in front of Johnny's house. I busied myself with rearranging my trunk while I peeked to see who got out.

Johnny did, of course. So did the woman I'd seen him with at the coffee shop. He waited to help her over the ice, a solicitous hand on her elbow. Jealousy, irrational and useless, reared up inside me, and I slammed the trunk lid so hard the sound of metal-on-metal rang out clearly all the way down the street. They both turned. I pretended to be busy with my bin.

I didn't own him. My pieced-together fantasies didn't give me a single right to any feelings whatsoever about what Johnny did with his life or his time. We weren't really lovers. Hell, we weren't even friends.

Even so, I muttered a string of curses as I unpacked the stuff I'd brought from home and spread it around my house. A few Little Golden Books on a bookshelf and a framed drawing I'd done as a kid on the wall in the living room. I paused to look at it. It wasn't half-bad, which was probably why my mom had framed it. I was more artistic than I thought.

I'd signed my initials in the lower right corner—E.M.M. for Emmaline Marie Moser—and I smiled the way I always did when I saw my name that way. I had clever parents.

I'd drawn a house, along with a man and a woman in front. The woman was a princess or a bride, or maybe both. It was hard to tell by the fluffy pink dress and veil, and the flowers in her hand might've suited either. She and the man next to her were holding hands, their smiles single-line curves stretching from ear to ear. He looked more like a prince than a bridegroom, since he wasn't wearing a tux but a long black coat with a long, striped scarf.

I looked again, closer. Long black coat. Long striped scarf. My stomach flip-flopped. I reached for the picture, the glass dusty and spotted, the wooden frame loose at the corners.

That was my house. This one. Tall and narrow, three windows on one side of the front door, one on the other. Okay, so it could've been any house, but it looked like mine.

And then, I saw the TARDIS. I'd missed it the first time, the blue shape partially obscured by the out-of-perspective trees. Oh.

"Hello, Doctor." I touched the figure again. Mystery revealed. I'd been a huge Doctor Who freak as a kid. No disrespect to any who came after him, but Tom Baker would always be my doctor.

The Doctor, not Johnny.

"Freak," I said fondly to my eight-year-old self, and hung the picture up again.

There was still the matter of my clothes to figure out, and it ate away at me all day at work until I could do nothing but conjure up all the worse scenarios. At least whatever I'd done hadn't been illegal. Or I hadn't been caught. I hadn't ended up on the evening news or, so far as I could tell, YouTube. Or YouPorn, thank God.

Though if any of that had happened, at least I'd *know* what I'd done.

There was no way around it. I had to talk to Johnny about it. He'd returned the clothes; it wasn't like he was pretending it hadn't happened. Whatever it was.

Fuck my life.

I didn't go to his house with a plate of cookies this time. I had no idea if a peace offering would be appropriate, and I didn't want to intrude any more than I'd apparently already done. I went to his gallery instead.

The Tin Angel on Front Street took up most of one of the grand old mansions that had been split up into offices. It wasn't empty when I went in, which was something of a surprise for a Thursday night. I shouldn't have assumed that just because I had no appreciation of art that nobody else would, either. Couples carrying glasses of wine and plates of cheese and grapes wandered the rooms and murmured over the prints hung on the walls and sculptures displayed on pedestals. Soft music played.

Great. I was crashing his party. What I at first thought was some sort of special reception turned out to be a regular Thursday night event, though, as I overheard one couple talking about how they'd been there the week before to pick up a housewarming gift for friends. This week, apparently, they were looking for a birthday present.

I took my time, wandering the unevenly sized rooms. The floors of stripped and stained wood gleamed, and even though none of the walls seemed quite plumb, the soft off-white paint and windows hung with gauzy netting made up for it. Fairy lights hung on potted trees and crisscrossed the rooms with higher ceilings.

"This place is gorgeous," I mentioned to an older couple who looked like they'd stepped out of the pages of a fashion magazine. I was glad I'd come straight from work. At least I was wearing a skirt and heels instead of jeans and boots.

"Oh, it's amazing what Johnny's done with this place, isn't it?" the woman said. "Just look at some of these pieces. Hard to believe you could find anything like this in Harrisburg, of all places. Who knew there was so much local talent?"

"Is that what he focuses on mostly?" I thought Jen had said something like that.

"Yes. And his own work, obviously. You're familiar with Johnny's work, of course." The man with her had wandered off, maybe to refill his cheese plate. The woman waved her glass of wine in my direction.

"Of course."

Truthfully, of all my internet stalking, the one part of Johnny's life I'd paid little attention to had been his artwork. I knew a little of his history, but not much else.

"We're so fortunate to have an artist of his caliber, and his support of the local arts community has been so amazing." She was a little drunk. She leaned in to me. "And what a looker, huh?"

I drew back in distaste. "Yeah. Is he here, do you know?"

"Johnny's always here on Thursdays. This is *his* place," she said, like I was a fucking moron.

A foron I might very well be, but I wasn't going to be a coward, too. I thanked her and kept moving, room by room, until I saw him. He was standing in the very back of the very last room, talking to a group of people I assumed were artists, based on their eclectic appearances.

He was smiling, even laughing, and, oh, how beautiful he was. The wanting was a burning in my gut, sudden and fierce, but I welcomed the pain of it as what I deserved. I hung back in the doorway for a moment, watching him interact with the group surrounding him, and more jealousy speared me. Not sexual, this time. If Johnny was flirting it was subtle enough to keep me from seeing it. But he looked as if he genuinely liked the people he was with, and I wanted to be one of them.

He looked up. Saw me. His smile didn't fade, his laughter didn't break. He didn't wave me in, but he didn't look as though he wanted me to leave, either. If anything, he looked like he'd been expecting me all along.

I passed the time looking over the art in this room while his admirers all paid their respects and left one by one, until eventually we were the only two in the room. I felt him behind me before I turned, and I stayed staring at the piece in front of me for some long, silent moments while I tried to get up the courage to speak.

Johnny didn't wait. "You like that one?"

I glanced from the corner of my eye but didn't have the guts to face him. "It's nice."

"Nice? To hell with nice. Art isn't nice. Art's supposed to move you."

I looked at him. "I'm sorry, I don't know a lot about art."

Johnny laughed, not unkindly. "What's to know? You think you need a fancy degree or, what, a beret, to get art? Nah, you don't need any of that. You just have to feel it."

"Well," I said after a moment, "I guess I'm not feeling much of anything about it."

"Me, neither," Johnny said. "I just hung that there because that kid needs some cash to pay for school, and some people like that kind of thing."

I laughed and turned to face him. "Really?"

"Really."

We both studied it for a moment longer.

"I wanted to thank you for the clothes," I finally said.

Johnny said nothing. The music was fainter in this room than it had been in the others. I could still hear the buzz of conversation in the other rooms, the clatter of heels on the wooden floors. But in here, we were still alone.

"I told you. It's cold out there. You need a good coat."

"Johnny—"

His eyes flashed, but I wasn't going to call him Mr. Dellasandro. "It was nothing. Don't worry about it."

"Where did you get them?" I moved two steps closer, noticing that he took only one back. I didn't want anyone to hear this. I wanted to be closer to him.

"You left them at my house," Johnny said.

My gut twisted hard, and I swallowed a tinge of bitter bile. "Oh. Shit. What happened? What did I do? I mean…oh, God, this is so embarrassing. This is so—"

Before I knew it, he had me by the elbow and had walked me through a small door into a tiny office, where he sat me on a hard-backed chair, pushed my head into my lap and drew me a paper cup of water from the cooler.

"Breathe," Johnny said. "And, Jesus, if you have to puke, do it in the can."

I didn't have to puke, but the world had spun in an alarming way. Not like I was going to go dark, that was always more of a slip-sliding sideways thing. This was most definitely like I'd spent too much time on the merry-go-round. I sipped the water and drew in a breath.

"You're as white as paper. Drink more of that water."

I did. "I'm sorry. But I have to know."

"You don't remember?" His accent deepened when he was concerned, I noticed. He lost the *r* at the end of his words.

I shook my head. "No."

He rubbed at his face, then pinched the bridge of his nose. He sat on the edge of the small desk. I was close enough to touch his knee, but I didn't.

"Was it…bad?" I'd spent so much time lately on the verge of raw emotion, I didn't realize I was going to cry until the tears had already started. "Pleasc, Johnny. Please tell me it wasn't bad."

"Hey, hey," he said. "Don't cry."

His embrace was warm and as familiar as his every gesture, though I knew it was my mind just filling in the blanks. I didn't care. Shamelessly, I took advantage of his pity and pressed up against him, my cheek to the front of his shirt. I could hear his heartbeat, and it steadied me.

Johnny's hand stroked down my back and through my hair. "Shh. It wasn't anything bad."

I shuddered against him with relief. I closed my eyes. "I'm so, so sorry for whatever it was."

Johnny didn't say anything, just held me. His heartbeat sped up. His fingertips circled on my back, and my heartbeat bumped faster, too.

I took a deep breath. My story wasn't secret, it simply wasn't something I told most people right off the bat. I hadn't even told Jen yet, and she'd become the best friend I had. But I had to tell him, to explain, even though I knew it would make him look at me with pity I wouldn't be able to stand.

"When I was six, I fell on the playground and hit my head hard enough to knock me out. I was in a coma for a week."

His hand stopped moving. He didn't move away, but I felt every muscle in his body go stiff. His heartbeat got faster, but he didn't say anything.

"I suffered undetermined brain damage that fortunately didn't result in the loss of any of my motor skills or anything. But it did leave me with the tendency to…blank out. Sort of like seizures. They usually last only a few seconds but can last for a few minutes, too."

"Fugues," Johnny said.

Startled, I pulled away to look at him. "What?"

"They're called fugues," he said.

"Yeah. How did you know that?"

"I know lots of things," Johnny said.

I'd moved away a little bit, but he was still holding me, and there was no way I was giving that up. My belly pressed his belt buckle in a way that made my knees weak. "I call them fugues, yes, though medically they've been diagnosed as everything from petit mal to grand mal seizures. I'd stopped having them, until a few weeks ago. They came back. That night at your house."

"You went blank," Johnny said. "Your face went blank."

"Oh, God," I said miserably. "How mortifying. And what else did I do? How did I end up—"

"Don't worry about it," Johnny interrupted with a flash of his green-brown eyes. "I told you, it wasn't bad. You couldn't help it, right?"

The last thing I wanted was for him to look at me like some sort of medical freak. Abnormal. Disabled. "No, but—"

"Then don't worry about it. It's forgotten."

He hadn't let me go. His gaze burned into mine. I'd thought I knew that intense stare, but seeing it on-screen was incomparable to being subject to it in real life. Both of us, I realized, were breathing faster. Belly to belly, his arms around me, all it took was for me to tip onto my toes so my mouth could reach his.

I kissed him.

Just a brush, I wasn't bold enough to try for more than that, so when his mouth opened under mine and he pulled me harder against him, I gasped into his mouth. Our tongues met, slip-sliding and sideways, and the earth tilted, but I clung to him and kept myself from falling.

At least, that's what I thought. In the next second I was a few feet away from him, my mouth still wet from his and my heart beating so fast it made thunder in my ears. There wasn't much room for him to retreat, but he'd backed up against the desk and held me at arm's length.

I whimpered when he let me go.

It was a stupid, raw and thoroughly embarrassing noise, but what was one more humiliation on top of all the others? I clapped a hand over my mouth, anyway. My eyes felt wide enough to see the whole damned world.

Johnny shuddered and turned half-away from me. “Go on. Get outta here.”

“But—”

“Emm,” Johnny said, startling me to silence. “I said get out. Please.”

And I did, taking two stumbling steps back to cross the threshold, standing in mute compliance when he shut the door in my face. Shaking on weak knees, the taste of him still on my tongue, my heart still beating so fast I thought I might really pass out, I turned on my heel and smiled.

He knew my name.

Chapter 13

The euphoria lasted about thirty-seven seconds, just long enough for me to remember that I'd kissed him, and he'd pushed me away. Fortunately, nobody'd seen me come out of his office, so I didn't have to face anyone with *rejection* stamped all over me. I left the Tin Angel without even looking at any of the rest of the art.

Johnny didn't come to the Mocha on Monday.

Or Tuesday.

Or Wednesday.

By Thursday, I'd convinced myself I'd scared him away for good, though I didn't dare tell Jen. I hadn't told her about the kiss, and I wasn't sure if it was because I was worried she'd feel like I was trying to steal something she could really claim first, or if I just didn't want to admit he'd pushed me away. She knew something was wrong, though. Good friends can do that.

"So," she said over sandwiches that weren't as good as the Mocha's morning selection of baked goods. "Spill it. What's up?"

"Why should anything be…up?" I lifted the slightly soggy croissant and took off the iceberg lettuce. "Look at that, what a shame. This sandwich calls for nothing less than baby radicchio."

"Uh-huh." Jen had already taken the crusts off what the Mocha had called "PB & J for Grown-ups." We hadn't figured out what that meant.

I sighed. "I have something to tell you, and I don't want it to get between us, that's all."

"Girrrrl," Jen said on a sigh. "What on earth?"

"Well..."

She waited. I tried, I really did, but it was too hard to confess it. Some things are too hard to tell even a best friend.

Suddenly, her hand covered mine. "Is it something really that bad? You can tell me, Emm. Honestly. Are you sick or something?"

I turned my palm upward to squeeze hers. I wanted to tell her the truth about everything—my fucked-up brain, the fugues, ending up naked in my living room. I just couldn't. I knew she'd understand, at least about the fugues, but I didn't want her to have to. "No. That's not it."

"Then what?"

"I sort of did something and I'm not sure how you'll take it."

"Did you put up some naked picture of me on Connex or something?"

I laughed. "No. God, no."

"Then I'm pretty sure I'll be okay with it, whatever it is." Jen let go of my hand to take a bite of her sandwich. "Huh. Crunchy peanut butter and exotic jelly and costs as much as about fifty regular pb and j's. Is that what makes it for grown-ups? I should've had the turkey."

"I kissed him," I said.

She swallowed, throat working, then rinsed her mouth with a swig of milk before finally managing to answer. "Who?"

I guess my face gave her answer enough, because her eyes went wide.

"Yeah," I said before she could say anything else. "I was so stupid."

"How? Where? What happened? Oh, my God, what was it like?" Her squeals turned heads.

I gestured at her to shush, and told her in a lowered voice the whole story, leaving out the bits about the hallucinations I'd had while dark. She listened without interrupting, only occasionally shaking her head. When I'd finished, I bit into my sandwich so I could keep myself from saying more.

"Oh, girl," Jen said finally. "That is some messed-up shit right there."

"I know," I said miserably. "And this sandwich sucks."

She laughed. "Yeah, you know there are a dozen other places we could meet for dinner."

"Yeah…I guess I wanted to come here because… Well, you know."

"I know." She licked a smear of jelly from her thumb. "I can't blame you. I mean, I knew you had it bad, but I didn't know you had it for realsies."

"It's not for realsies," I pointed out.

"Are you sure?"

"He pushed me away. Dudes don't push away women they're kissing if they're into them."

"Sometimes they do," Jen said. "He might've had a reason you don't know about. Maybe he's got a girlfriend."

I snorted. "That would actually be a worse reason than if he's just not into me."

"You think so?" Jen didn't look convinced.

"Yeah. If he's not into me, which I'm sure he's not, I can just move on. But if he's super into me but can't be with me because he's with someone else…"

"I see your point," she said. "That would suck."

I laughed, feeling a little better at having confessed. "And also totally unlikely. He pushed me away from him like my mouth was poison. Shit, that's embarrassing."

"That really is," Jen said.

We looked at each other for half a minute before busting into cackles of entirely inappropriate laughter. It was good, though. Made me feel better than any sympathetic words or assurances could have.

"You're not pissed off?" I asked.

"Hell, no, why would I be?" Jen looked genuinely confused.

"Well…because…it's Johnny."

She snorted laughter again. "It's not like we were together and he dumped me for you, or anything. I wouldn't want to have to hire ninjas to cut holes in your favorite jeans."

"But you liked him first."

"What, are we in sixth grade? Girl," Jen told me seriously, "you are going to kick me so hard for saying this, because I know you won't believe me, but I think he does like you."

"No way."

She nodded. "Yeah. I think so. I was in here one day last week when you weren't, and he came in. He looked around. He looked at me, girl, straight on, but it was the empty seat across from me he was seeing, if you know what I mean."

"Get out of here! Why didn't you tell me?" I felt instantly guilty for sounding accusatory when I'd just gotten finished feeling guilty about trying to nab her crush.

"I didn't think anything of it until you told me this, but it makes sense now."

"I told you he pushed me away when I kissed him, and you think you remember him looking for me here?" I shook my head with a sigh. "Sorry, that's really reaching."

"Hey. What happened before the kiss?"

I thought about how he'd held me against him and stroked my hair. "He was just being nice."

"You think dudes are just randomly nice like that?"

"Some are! Oh. God." My stomach dropped out. I put my face in my hands.

"Shew, girl, it ain't no thing!" She poked me until I looked up.

I couldn't tell her that I had, in fact, fucked Johnny seven ways to Sunday. In my head. That it had been sweet and dirty and gorgeous, and that I'd already worried that somehow my fantasies had been spurred by something my unconscious body was doing.

The jingle of the Mocha's doorbell made Jen look over my shoulder. I didn't have to turn to see who it was. I could tell by the way her eyes widened and the look she gave me, her mouth clamped tight on a smile. I stiffened, closing my eyes briefly. I heard the shuffle of shoes on the floor. I waited for the brush of his coat as he passed me. I opened my eyes.

Johnny stood at our table, looking down at both of us.

Jen, to give her credit, looked barely surprised. I made sure to keep my mouth shut instead of allowing myself to gape like an idiot. We stared up at him. He stared down at us.

"Girls," Johnny said with a nod, and moved on toward the counter.

That's when I discovered that being acknowledged was actually hideously worse than being ignored.

"Wow," Jen said quietly. "He hardly ever says hello to anyone."

"'Girls'?" I whispered, watching him, though he hadn't done so much as glance back while he waited for his order. "'Girls'? Like we're twelve?"

She laughed gently. "We *are* a lot younger than him."

I put my face in my hands and groaned under my breath. "Girls. Like we should be wearing knee socks and penny loafers with our hair in pigtails."

"Maybe he's got a schoolgirl fetish thing," she teased.

"Gross." I peeked at her through my fingers and watched as Johnny took his coffee to one of the back booths and settled into it, facing away from us. At least there was that. I didn't have to make sure our eyes didn't meet.

"He never said hi to me before, that's all I'm saying." Jen gave me a lifted brow. "And he said 'girls,' plural, but he was only looking at you."

I didn't let hope get a foothold. "Dude, I went all dead zone on him in his house, then I went to his gallery and tried to make out with him. He probably figures he'd better throw me a bone so I don't, like, boil his bunny or something."

Jen laughed, loud and long. "That's a good one."

"I mean it!"

The doorbell jangled, and a few moments later, Johnny was no longer alone in his booth at the back. The woman who joined him was the same who'd been there before. Glossy, glamorous…and looking annoyed. She didn't order anything at the counter, just sat across from him and started peeling off her leather gloves as she stared at him with a sour look on her admittedly pretty face.

Jen had glanced up as she passed, now looked over her shoulder to see where she'd gone, and looked back at me. "He does seem to have a thing for younger women. But no wonder we're girls, compared to her."

"She's not that much older."

"At least seven or eight years, ten if she's had work done, and, girl, those clothes say she has."

I didn't really feel better by picking apart the woman who might or might not've been dating the man I was so crazy for I was actually going…crazy. "Whatever. If they're together, they're together. It doesn't make anything that happened or didn't happen with us any better."

"Does it make it worse?" she asked pointedly. "You said it would. If he were with someone."

"Only if he really wanted to be with me instead, and wasn't because of some other woman."

"You know what?" Jen said with a sigh as she pushed her plate away. "I think you overthink it. Why not just get a bottle of wine, something sugary and chocolaty and take it over to his place. Wear something nice but not too nice, you know. Apologize to him for what happened, or what didn't happen, and see where it goes from there."

I snorted under my breath. "Yeah. How about not."

"Why not?"

"I already tried to make a peace offering. See how well that went."

"You're so pessimistic!"

It was my turn to give her a look. Jen shrugged and gave another glance over her shoulder before leaning forward to whisper, "I'm just saying."

"I feel like enough of an idiot as it is, Jen. No. I'm just going to avoid him. Totally avoid him."

"Good luck with that," Jen said as she looked over her shoulder again before giving me another wide-eyed, brows-raised glance.

Johnny had gotten up, his companion with him. He waited like a gentleman for her to sweep past us. She didn't bother to even spare us a second's attention, but he hesitated at the table. He didn't say anything this time. Just met my eyes for the length of time it took for universes to be born from the dust of an imploding sun. In other words, half a second. Then he was gone, following her out the door and leaving me behind, breathless and sick-stomached and full of yearning.

"Oh, girl," Jen said sympathetically. "You are in so much trouble."

I didn't get more than a few steps inside my front door when it hit me like a citrus tsunami. My eyes watered from the stench of oranges going soft and moldy. Always before, the smell had been fainter than this. Softer. Not a bad smell, for all it portended. But this was an assault on my nostrils, and I reeled from it.

I put my hand out, blindly reaching for the newel post, but my fingers slipped past the carved wood. I stumbled forward a couple steps and clapped a hand over my mouth and nose, trying hard to keep the stench from permeating me any further. The smell was on my skin.

Disgusted, I tore my hand from my face and rubbed it frantically on my clothes, but it only got worse. It rose all around me, a miasma. I couldn't get free of it, because it wasn't just around me. It was in me. It was on me.

It *was* me.

The world tipped and I went with it, onto my hands and knees, just like I'd been thrown off a merry-go-round, or jumped from a swing and landed wrong. Just like…just like…

Just like I'd fallen.

"Hey."

The soft, low voice shook me into opening my eyes. I knew that voice. I knew the touch of that hand on my arm, even though I couldn't see him. I knew it was Johnny before I even opened my eyes.

"Hey," I said, blinking in the bright summer sunshine.

Heat assaulted me, and a thousand different smells, none of them oranges. I gulped in deep breaths while struggling not to show how shaken I was, even as I wondered if it mattered. What would Johnny do, here, if I went to the ground shaking and twitching, if I babbled in a strange tongue. If I acted crazy?

He was carrying a paper sack of groceries in one arm, and he shielded his gaze from the sun with his free hand. "You're just in time for the party."

He sounded a little distant. Wary. The look he was giving me wasn't much warmer.

"Great!" I, on the other hand, sounded too brightly warm, too falsely cheerful.

"You coming in?" He settled the bag on his hip, still shielding his eyes. He looked me up and down. "Get out of that coat, maybe?"

No wonder I was sweating. I still wore my winter coat, though not the one Johnny'd returned to me. Though it was my favorite and most flattering coat, I hadn't been able to bring myself to wear it instead of this one. Residual and misplaced mortification. I wore a scarf, too. And gloves.

"Right." My laugh was brittle. "I bet you're wondering why I'm wearing this."

"Not really, no."

We stood there in silence while I sweated. Johnny took his hand away from his face. The sun beat down on both of us, but it lit him up like a diamond. Like the sun. Too bright and beautiful to look at head-on.

"Come inside. Get a drink before you pass out from the heat. Jesus," Johnny said after another half minute. "C'mon, Emm."

I followed him into the house and down the hall and into the kitchen, which for once was quiet and empty. It was cooler, too, though the breeze came in from the open windows, not from any artificial air-conditioning. I had to remember it was the seventies, probably during the energy crisis, when central air was a luxury even people who could afford it didn't always use. I marveled again at the details my mind provided.

Johnny put away the contents of his bag while I took off my heavy clothes and sighed in relief. My shirt, a thin plaid with faux mother-of-pearl buttons, was fine once I undid a couple of the snaps and rolled the sleeves up to my elbows. I fanned my face and lifted my sweat-heavy hair from my neck, wishing for a clip or a hair tie.

"Here." Johnny tossed me a thick piece of leather with a wooden dowel piercing it.

I looked up at him, not sure what to say. "What's this?"

"It's yours," he said. "For your hair."

I'd never seen it before. I turned it over and over in my fingers, feeling the smooth leather. It had a design embossed on it, some sort of flower with a vine. I looked up at him again. "It's mine?"

"Yeah." Johnny shrugged. "You left it here the last time."

"Are you sure? Because..." I didn't want to put anything like this in my hair, not if it belonged to someone else. And yet I did want to put my hair up, get it off my neck.

"I'm sure," Johnny said with another shrug. "But you don't want it, don't use it."

I remembered I had an elastic band in my pocket, and I pulled that out instead. "It's okay, I have this."

He shook his head a little, at last smiling. "Whatever you want."

He leaned against the counter, watching as I twisted my hair on top of my head. He wore a bandanna again today, probably for the same reason I was tying mine up. I liked the way his hair fell into his eyes, but he probably didn't.

"So," I said after another long minute in which we stared at each other without speaking. "When's the party?"

"When isn't the party?" Johnny said with a laugh.

He still hadn't gotten me that drink yet, and I needed it. I swallowed over sandpaper and winced. The sweat on my skin was drying. My heartbeat, which had been steadily thud-thumping since I opened my eyes, now bumped up a little bit when I looked into his eyes.

"C'mere," Johnny said.

I stood, slow motion, and moved through the syrup of the air toward him. I drank his kiss as though it were water, though it did nothing to cool me. His hands stroked up my bare forearms to clasp me just above the elbows, and even that small touch forced shivers all through me. My nipples went instantly, almost painfully hard. A pulse of desire throbbed between my legs, insistent.

Johnny broke the kiss but didn't pull away. "How come whenever you leave, I'm never sure you'll be back again?"

I had an idea of why that might be, but I shook my head. "I don't know."

He licked his mouth, his eyes on my lips, then dipped in to kiss me again. Softer, this time tongue probing gently as one hand went to the nape of my neck. We fit together, his ins matching my outs. I slipped a hand inside his shirt, my palm flat on his gorgeous belly. The muscles leaped under my touch, and Johnny laughed under his breath.

"It makes me crazy," he said.

I stopped kissing him. I cupped his face in my hands and looked into his eyes, searching for something. I didn't know what. "It does?"

"Hell, yes. Every time you disappear, I think it will be the last time I ever see you. And I don't want to never see you again, Emm. I don't care if..."

"If what?" I asked when he didn't go on. "What, Johnny? What is it?"

"I don't care if this can't last. I just want as much as I can while I have it."

I blinked rapidly, my eyelids fluttering. I kissed him, then looked into his eyes once more. "I don't understand...what makes you think...?"

"You told me," Johnny said. "You don't remember, I guess, the way you don't remember you left the hair clip. But you did."

I took a step back, but his hand snared my wrist as the other went to my hip, and I was grateful for the support. I might've fallen, otherwise. I might've gone sprawling on his none-too-clean kitchen floor. Instead, Johnny drew me close against his chest, his chin against the top of my head. He wrapped his arms around me, tight, as though he didn't intend to let me go.

It was the way he'd held me in his office, the embrace the

same, but without the shame. I knew this time if I tipped my face to his, he'd kiss me long and hard and slow and deep, and he wouldn't push me away after. I shuddered again.

None of this was real. I would always go away. This could not last.

It absolutely sounded like the truth, though I couldn't imagine myself telling him any of it. What purpose would it serve to tell a dream he wasn't real? I knew this was only some strange mix-up in my brain, some impulse traveling from one nerve to another and getting diverted like a train off the rails. I knew none of this was really happening, that I was probably still on my hands and knees on the floor of my front hall, and if I were lucky I'd come back to myself there and not naked in a stranger's house.

And then I knew something else. I didn't want to lose this. I didn't want the reality in which Johnny pushed me away or, worse, looked through me. I wanted this time, this place.

When he loved me.

"I'm not going anywhere," I told him, and offered my mouth again.

He kissed me, murmuring, "Yes, you will. You always do."

"Then let's enjoy the time while we have it," I whispered into his mouth.

"Yeah," Johnny said. "Time."

It wouldn't have surprised me if he'd laid me on the kitchen table and fucked me right there, but before either of us could even move that way, the back door swung open and Candy, carrying two bags of groceries, barged in followed by Bellina and Ed, also carrying food and bottles of wine.

"Looky-look," said Bellina, her voice husky from too many cigarettes. She raked me up and down. "Didn't mean to interrupt."

She hadn't said it with malice, and I only smiled into Johnny's kiss before I reluctantly pulled away. "Hey, Bellina."

"Give us a hand here. Candy's got a lot of food. We're having ourselves a real party," said Ed. He looked stoned already.

"Yeah, a party in my house." Johnny didn't sound put out. "Nice of you guys to come over."

They all laughed. Even I got the joke. This was Johnny's house, but they might as well all live there. Like a commune. Or a hive.

We worked together putting away the food, every package a new surprise to me. Cans that didn't have pop-tabs, brands I didn't recognize. Everyone laughed and joked around me, and at first I joined in, but with every new item we pulled from the bags, or I spotted in the cabinet or fridge, I got quieter.

Normally, I'd never have made myself so at home in someone else's house, but here there seemed very little regard for personal space or possessions. I went from cupboard to cupboard, looking at the boxes, bags and cans. I opened the drawers to peek at silverware. I studied the Tupperware containers stacked haphazardly on shelves. And then, as they all watched me and pretended they didn't, I turned slowly in the middle of the kitchen and looked at all of them.

I checked the calendar on the wall.

"There's so much," I said aloud, not caring what they thought.

Because what could they think? Nothing but what thoughts I gave them. They could do nothing but what actions I provided. All of these people were puppets, this place the stage I'd built. And yet I stood and stared, sweat sliding down the line of my spine, and I shivered.

Johnny linked his fingers in mine. Held me tight. He kept me from shaking when I looked at him, his smile making everything else go away.

"Let's go upstairs," Johnny said. "C'mon, gorgeous."

"Ooh, Emm, watch out. He's going to ask if you want to see his etchings." Ed snickered as he lit a hand-rolled cigarette with a familiar tangy smell.

"How about it, Emm?" Johnny tugged my hand, never looking away from my eyes. "You wanna go upstairs with me now?"

"Yes." One small word, forced from a dry throat.

I didn't care if they were all staring, or what they might think. I wanted to go upstairs with Johnny, of course. I wanted to strip him naked and kiss my way up from his ankles to his chest, and every sweet inch in between. I wanted to slide him deep inside me and ride him until we both came and collapsed, exhausted and sweaty.

When I lived with my parents I'd been responsible for very little. My mother, despite my protests, had insisted on doing my laundry. I gave them money toward the bills but didn't have to spend the time paying them. I didn't even cook for myself most of the time, and any grocery shopping I did was often done with my mom and thus only half the effort. When I lived at home, I'd had a lot more free time that moving into my own place had eaten up with mundane tasks like changing the toilet paper and cleaning up after myself. I wouldn't have traded it for anything, but it had meant I'd forgone some of the time-wasting habits I'd had when I lived at home.

Playing the Sims was one of them. I'd spent hours at the computer lost in that virtual world—building houses, creating families, watching them live, work, sleep, eat, fall in love, marry, have children…even die. I'd been the God of that universe, sometimes but not always benevolent. The maximum number of Sims that could be played on any one lot was eight, but I consistently failed at keeping more than three of them happy, with all their needs met, and along a positive life path. I wasn't a very good God.

I wanted to go upstairs with Johnny because suddenly being

in that kitchen was making my brain hurt. All those pieces. All those details. All those people. I wasn't a very good juggler, either. All the balls were in the air, and I stood there with my hands out, ready but not expecting to catch them all.

"C'mon," Johnny said again. His eyes flashed. He backed up, grinning but ignoring the catcalls and lewd comments from his friends. "I want to show you my etchings."

He wasn't lying. In his bedroom he pulled a leather-bound sketchbook from a drawer and flipped it open to show me a pencil drawing, a series of lines and shading. I studied it. I wasn't familiar enough with his work to know if this was something I should recognize.

"You're good," I said sincerely. Even I knew enough to see that.

"Nah. I'm just a scribbler."

Johnny stretched out on the bed beside me as I sat cross-legged, flipping pages. He had photographs slipped into some of the pages, mostly small but a few eight-by-tens. I pulled one out and studied it with more familiarity than I'd been able to give his art.

"Nice ass," I teased, waving the picture at him.

Johnny laughed and lay back with his hands behind his head. "That ass paid for a coupla month's mortgage on this house."

The photo, black and white, was of Johnny, nude, posed like a classic Roman statue. Minus any fig leaf. His face in profile was serious, his body tight and toned, his ass mouthwatering. I found another from the same series, this one a little creased and bent. Also full frontal.

"You should be more careful with these." I spied a signature in the corner of the print. "Wow. Are these signed?"

"Yeah. Paul took those."

I knew that, of course, though the name hadn't risen immediately to my mind. I'd seen the first one online, the second one in cropped and grainy versions that did nothing to show off the real beauty in the picture. And the others, the sheaf of a dozen other shots, all glossy and signed, I'd never seen at all.

I looked at each one carefully, seeing more than just his body. It was luscious, yes, but there was more to it than that. The shots weren't cheesecake, or even gay porn, though that's where I'd seen them before, on sites dedicated to such things. I put them carefully in order. These pictures told a story, one to the next.

"You should take good care of these," I said when I saw a shot I'd once seen in an online auction, going for close to four thousand dollars. "Signed like this and stuff."

Johnny pushed up on an elbow. "What for? They ain't worth nothing. I did them as a favor to Paul. He paid me a couple hundred bucks, that's all. He hasn't even used them for anything."

I flipped it over and saw a poem scribbled on the back. I remembered, then, why the picture in my hand had been selling for so much money, and it wasn't the custom-made frame and matting. "Ed wrote this?"

"Yeah, he's always writing shit down on stuff."

Everything's worth more after the artist dies. Ed D'Onofrio had killed himself. He'd slit his wrists and drowned in a swimming pool. I hadn't paid much attention to his death, just that it had spurred the breakup of the Enclave, leading its members to all pursue their own projects and achieve success or failure.

My throat dried and I looked at him. There was another bit of information I'd gleaned from my online stalking. After Ed died and the Enclave broke up, Johnny'd broken, too.

Some accounts said he'd simply holed up out of grief. Others claimed it had gone further than that. That he'd actually gotten hooked on heroin, gone to rehab, been committed to a mental facility. That he'd come out of it clean and dry and, arguably, not crazy, and that sometime after that he'd started creating art, real art, the kind critics wet their panties for. I'd never found confirmation of the rehab or institution part, though it was proven fact he'd become a respected artist in that time frame.

Johnny sat up to take the picture from me, then the book. He put them both aside and pulled me into his arms. "Don't worry about that stuff now."

In my real world, flirting was something I'd never really gotten the hang of. I had no trouble talking to men. My problem was more that I was too straightforward, too practical, too honest. The subtle dance of back-and-forth my friends did with potential lovers had always escaped me. I wasn't sure it had ever stopped me from getting dates, but it had gotten me into trouble more than once when something less than bluntness might've served me better than being forthright. Honesty in dating wasn't always the best policy.

Here, with this Johnny, the one with longer hair and a younger face, I discovered my ability to flirt. To vamp. I felt my mouth curve up in a saucy, sexy smile, felt the lift of my brow, the parting of my lips. Come-hither eyes.

"What should I pay attention to, then?" Even my voice shifted and went sultry.

"Me."

"Oh, really? You?"

He was already taking my hand and putting it on his crotch, where he moved it in slow circles on his hardening cock. "Yeah. Me. Right here."

I laughed and shifted closer to push him back on the bed and straddle him. I pinned his wrists, one next to each ear. I leaned in to kiss him but pulled away just as he leaned to kiss me back. He snapped his teeth at me, growling.

"No," I said. "Not so fast."

Johnny lay back, eyes flashing, but he didn't try to get away the way I knew he could with a simple push. "What are you going to do to me?"

"What do you want me to do to you?"

"Anything you want," Johnny said with a sly grin. "Everything you want."

I tilted my head, looking him over, then glanced over my shoulder at the book he'd tossed aside. I let go of his wrists and sat up. "I want you to pose for me."

He blinked, smile fading into confusion. "Huh?"

"Like in those pictures, Johnny. I want you to pose for me."

"Are you going to take my picture?" He sounded teasing and amused.

"No. I don't have a camera."

"Draw me?"

I laughed hard at that. "Oh. No way."

"So…you're just gonna look at me?"

"Oh, yes," I told him as my heart started up its thumping in anticipation. "And maybe some other things. But yes. Looking, to start."

I slid off him. Johnny, still grinning, got up and stood at the side of the bed. First came his shirt, off over his head and tossed to the floor without a second glance. He was good at this. I rolled onto my belly and put my hands in my chin to watch him.

"Keep going," I said.

Johnny ran his hands over his chest and belly. "You sure?"

"Yes," I began, but the word turned to a shivering mess of stuttering syllables when he rubbed his thumbs over his nipples.

"You like that?"

I nodded. "Love it."

He licked a fingertip and circled his nipple, then drew it down his belly. "That?"

"Yes," I whispered.

His grin got broader even as his gaze heated. His fingers went to his belt buckle, and he teased it open. He slid the belt from the loops—thwap, thwap, thwap. He held it in his two hands, snapping it taut. "You like that, huh?"

"I love it."

"You like leather?"

Leathah. I nodded. "Oh, yes, Johnny. A lot."

He tilted his head to look at me, then tossed the belt aside to unbutton his pants. His zipper. He eased his jeans down over his naked hips and thighs. No underwear. His cock, thick and half-hard, shifted between his thighs as he pushed the denim over one foot, then the other. He stood there, naked and beautiful, and I yearned for him so fiercely my body actually ached from the wanting.

"Pose." It was a demand that sounded like a plea.

He did. Twisted his hips, turned his face, curled his arms. Muscles worked and shifted under his sun-burnished skin. His lines became curves; curves turned to planes. He turned in place, showing me that epic ass and the dimples just above it.

I pushed myself up on my hands. "Turn around. Slowly."

I got off the bed as he obeyed. Fully clothed, I stood in front of him. We stared into each other's eyes. We weren't smiling. This had become business of the most serious sort. This had become something more than play. This had become everything.

I put my hands so lightly on his hips he shouldn't have been able to feel me, nor I him. The fine hairs on his skin stood on end, and the heat of him touched me. I drew my palms up his sides, then around and over his chest and belly, all with that microscopic distance between his skin and mine.

Johnny shivered. "Emm."

"Shh."

I drew my phantom touch over each of his thighs. Moving around him, his back, his shoulders, his ass. Down over the sweetness of the skin behind his knees. His calves. To his front again I moved, and cupped the air around his shins before getting to my knees in front of him.

I touched him then for real. My hands cupped his ankles. Johnny groaned. I slid my hands up his legs, shins, knees, calves, thighs. I let them rest on the backs of his thighs, just below the curve of his buttocks.

His cock was hard now. In front of my face. I wanted to taste him. Still holding him, though he'd made no attempts at moving, I leaned in to nuzzle against his thigh. I let my tongue flicker along his balls, then the base of his shaft. He twitched, and his hand came down to tangle in my hair, but other than that, he stayed still.

I took him into my mouth slowly, savoring each inch. I sucked gently and used my hands to move him in and out of my open, willing mouth at my own pace. His fingers tightened in my hair, and he groaned.

I paused to look up at him. "You like that, huh?"

He smiled at my echo of his question. The tight hold on my hair softened and he smoothed a hand over my head, then my cheek. "Yeah. I like it."

"Good." I bent back to the pleasure of letting him fuck my mouth.

And it was sweet, that pleasure. It wasn't the act, but Johnny who made it so. The way he sounded and moved, the way he said my name as though I were the most precious gift he'd ever been given.

I knew he'd had blow jobs before, maybe even some more skilled, maybe even some more enthusiastic. Yet when I looked up at him, his face twisted with his desire, I didn't see a man who was used to this, or who was taking it for granted. Johnny looked down at me with marvel in his eyes, as though all of this were a dream. A fantasy.

Not real.

He came into my mouth, and I swallowed the hot, slick taste

of him without even a wince of protest. Funny how it worked that way here. With him.

His eyelids fluttered. He murmured my name. His hips pushed forward, his cock throbbed. And wonder of wonders, I came, too, in a slow, rolling rush of sensation unlike any orgasm I'd had.

I started laughing.

There on my knees, which were beginning to hurt, and with the taste of him still on my tongue, I laughed. I nuzzled forward again, against his softening cock, and kissed him there. Then I let him help me to my feet, and I kissed him.

"Emm, Emm, Emm," Johnny said.

"Mmm," I whispered into his mouth. "I like it when you say my name."

"Emm," he said again.

He pushed me back toward the bed, but before he could lay me down and do whatever delicious, wicked things he'd planned, the door flew open. Sandy came in, already babbling. She didn't even stop when she saw the pair of us.

"Johnny, listen, I gotta talk to you," she finished up, putting her hand on her hip.

"Sandy," Johnny said in the voice of a man who's gone beyond all patience. "Get the fuck outta here. Jesus."

"Not until you give me some money."

"What? I got to pay more money for you? What happened to the two hundred dollars I gave you last month?"

"I'll…just wait outside," I told him, moving away, though he'd tried to snag my wrist.

"You, stay," Johnny told me. To Sandy, he said, "You, go."

She crossed her arms over her chest and stuck out her lower lip, the perfect picture of a sullen pout. "No."

"Jesus, Sandy. You're really gonna get it, you know it?"

"You see that?" she said to me. "That's too much. He's threatening me. What kinda guy is that, threatening the mother of his kid? It's bullshit, I say. C'mon, Johnny. Just give me some money and I'll go."

"What do you need money for, anyway? I thought you were living with your mother? And I give you money for Kimmy, don't tell me you spent all of it already. What does that kid need, gold-plated diapers?"

"I need it," Sandy insisted. Her gaze slid over me, calculating. "I need it for something."

"For what?"

"For…an abortion," she told him with her chin lifted, mouth thin but quirked on the ends like she didn't mean to smile but couldn't help herself.

It seemed like my cue to leave. Not from jealousy—how could I be jealous of something that was created from my own imagination? But because whatever was happening between them didn't need to involve me, because I didn't want to be a part of it, I moved toward the door. I couldn't actively control what happened in here, not like taking a handful of threads and weaving them together or pulling them apart the way I might in a real dream. But if I didn't see it, it didn't happen, or so I thought.

Johnny tugged my arm but let go as I kept walking. "Emm. Don't go."

I looked over my shoulder at him. "No, baby, you need to deal with this."

It seemed like the right thing to say. His eyes lit. He grinned. He let me go. I walked past Sandy without giving her the benefit of a glance. Women know how to cut each other that way, and though I wasn't jealous, I was definitely not interested in giving her any attention.

I walked out the door.

I ended up in my living room.

Chapter 15

At least this time I wasn't naked.

I was, though, breathing hard. My stomach twisted. My head hurt so bad I cried out, low, and stumbled to the couch where I lay down and clutched a pillow. The world didn't spin, thankfully, but it took a long few minutes before it settled.

I sat up slowly. "What the fuck."

I sounded miserable. I felt it, too. Not so much physically, not after a few minutes, anyway. The damage in my brain had never made me feel bad physically, other than lately. It wasn't my gut or head that made me feel this way, though. It was knowing that, even though the fugues were getting worse, possibly something had broken free inside my brain, that I might at this moment be bleeding out into oblivion....

I didn't want the fugues to stop.

I liked being in a place where someone like Johnny Dellasandro was into me, where I didn't worry about stuff like condoms and pregnancy, or hell...shaving my legs, for that matter. Or paying bills or exercising. But most of all, where Johnny put his hands and mouth all over, where he put his delicious cock up inside me, where I could touch him and kiss him and know he wanted it just as much from me as I wanted from him.

What I wanted right now, though, more than anything, was another hot shower. I stayed in there a really long time and felt only a little better when I got out. I combed my hair, slathered my face with cream. Pulled on a faded T-shirt that hit me midthigh and was thin enough to cling to every ample curve the mirror insisted on showing off. I studied my reflection, side to side, smoothing my hands over my breasts and belly and hips. I never wanted to hate my body the way so many of my friends seemed to, the way movies and television urged us normal-size gals to do.

"Work out harder," I advised myself, sucking in my belly and cheeks to give an illusion of shadows. But I knew I wouldn't. I knew that even if I did, there'd be one too many muffins in the Mocha, too many scoops of sugar in my coffee, because sugar and caffeine had always done what pills had only sort of stopped.

My wet hair had dripped all down my back, giving me a chill. I threw on a Lebanon Valley College sweatshirt and a pair of thick, rainbow-knit knee socks and went downstairs to make myself a cup or three of hot chocolate. I had a book and a bed in my future, if not a movie playing on my laptop at the same time. A quiet evening in.

Then the doorbell rang. I didn't believe my ears at first, convincing myself it had been the neighbors' bell even though I'd never mistaken theirs for mine before. When it rang again, followed moments later by a knock, I took my cell phone from where I'd left it charging on the counter and gripped it tight in my palm, ready to thumb in a swift 9-1-1.

I'd clearly been watching too many horror movies.

I didn't have a peephole or whatever they called those fancy windows to the side of my door, though it did have an annoying and useless transom window above it. I vowed to remedy all that as soon as I could, not that it did me any good now, standing in my foyer with wet hair and no panties on, with the night sky pressing in on the transom and a stranger knocking so persistently.

The knock came again. Phone in hand, I slid back the chain lock and then the dead bolt. I cracked open the door. And then I swung it wide.

"Hi," Johnny said, looking supremely uncomfortable and totally handsome in his long black coat with the scarf that made me want to wrap myself in it.

I found my voice faster than I thought I would. "Hi."

We stared at each other, neither of us moving.

"Can I come in? It's freezing out here."

"I… Yeah, yes. Of course! Sure!" I stepped aside to let him in, along with a swirl of air the temperature of snowflakes, and closed the door behind him.

He turned to look at me. "I know it's late."

"It's not that late. It just gets dark so early now. It's not too late. Really." I forced myself to shut up.

Why couldn't I be with real, present-time Johnny the way I was with his imaginary-past counterpart? What had happened to the vixen, the vamp who knew how to flirt and how to take control of the situation? Instead, I stood and stared and practically scuffed the tile with my rainbow-clad toes and muttered, "Aw, shucks."

"You mind if I take off my coat?"

"Of course not. I'll hang it up for you." I took it from him, then had no place to put it. We stared at it in my hands, silence awkward and brittle between us. Finally, I hung it carefully over the stair railing where the newel post would keep it from falling off.

"Do you want to come in? I was making—" the kettle whistled "—hot chocolate."

It was what a girl would drink, I thought, trying to see what

Johnny thought and finding nothing on his face but the beauty time hadn't faded. I thought about offering him something more sophisticated. Like a liqueur, or something fancy I whipped up all casual like, with special tools and ingredients I just happened to have on hand.

"Sure. That'd be great, thanks."

He didn't move, waiting for me to lead. So I did, wondering too late if my shirt was too short, if my ass cheeks were hanging out. If he was looking at them if they were.

"Make yourself at home." I gestured at the bar stool set up along the raised island I loved so much. "Do you want hot chocolate? Or something else? I could get you, um, juice or…a beer?"

"Nah. Hot chocolate sounds great. Good for a night like this."

"Yeah, the temps have really dropped, huh?" I took powdered milk and cocoa from my cupboard. Sugar. Vanilla. Marshmallows. Chocolate chips.

Johnny watched as I assembled the ingredients along the counter. "That's some setup."

It was easy to smile at him, and somehow smiling took some of the edge off. "I call it lazy man's gourmet cocoa. Except, well, I'm not a man. And it's not really gourmet…"

Word vomit again. I swallowed my explanation. Tried again.

"It's faster than boiling milk," I said. "And I hate the way skim milk gets when you boil it. And when it's scalded, gross. This way, using the powdered milk, the cocoa is as creamy as using milk, but without the gross parts."

"And the rest?"

"That," I said with a grin, "is all just bonus."

Johnny smiled, too, though slowly, as though he'd almost forgotten how. "Sounds good."

I handed him an oversize mug emblazoned with a skull and

crossbones, and took down my favorite mug for myself. It was also oversize, with a picture of the TARDIS on it. I mixed the cocoa in a glass mixing bowl, the kind with a handle and a spout and a nifty plastic lid. I even used a fancy whisk.

Johnny watched, saying nothing. I pretended I didn't notice. I also pretended I wasn't as clumsy as I was when I knew he was watching me.

I poured the steaming cocoa into the mugs and pushed the marshmallows and chocolate chips toward him. "Here. You can add your own bonus."

"I think this is good like this."

"Really?" I plopped three marshmallows into my mug, where they rapidly melted and spread sugary white goodness all over the cocoa. I added a handful of chocolate chips. "It's reallllly good."

Johnny took a marshmallow and put it in the cocoa, then a few chocolate chips. "Shit."

"No, no, much better than that." I sipped and watched him through the steam. "You'll like it, I promise you."

He lifted his mug and tasted, then nodded. "Yeah, it's good."

I was grateful for the island between us. I leaned a hip against it, sipping slowly so we could both act like the hot liquid took up so much attention it was impossible to talk. I even took my time blowing on it so I didn't burn my tongue. Usually I was so impatient I scalded myself.

"So," Johnny said after a few more minutes filled with awkward silence broken only by the sound of us both blowing on our cocoa and slurping.

I waited. He didn't go on. He put his mug down, though, and then his hands on the counter. He looked at me, but not the way he did in my imagination. In the fugues, Johnny looked at me like I was something special he couldn't quite figure out how he'd been lucky enough to get. Now he looked at me as if he simply couldn't figure me out.

"Yes?" I played at being calm and composed, but inside my guts were doing jumping jacks.

"I've been wanting to talk to you."

I couldn't help it. I started laughing. Softly at first, just a giggle, then another and more until I had to cover my mouth to hold back a full-on guffaw. I managed to squeak out a "Really?"

I'd seen his smile so many times in photos, in movies and in those magic times when I was dark. It looked the same now, but different, too. He was holding back a little.

"Yeah. Really."

My laughter eased, my belly muscles hurting a little but in a good way. I wiped at the corners of my eyes. "So talk."

"I just thought we should discuss what happened at the studio."

This sobered me, though not totally. "Uh-huh."

"And that you should know why…it won't work."

It wasn't something I'd never heard before, or never said, but it wasn't at all what I thought he'd say. I put my mug on the counter and licked my mouth, not wanting to face him with chocolate smeared on my lips. "What won't work, exactly?"

He still had both his hands on the countertop, and now his fingers twitched. "Us."

"Ah." I wasn't much good at flirting, but I wasn't any better at faking a lack of interest. "Why not?"

Johnny blinked, his smile growing infinitesimally wider. "Emm."

My breath hitched when he said my name. I wanted to close my eyes and drift on that sound, that single syllable. I didn't, though. I kept my gaze on his, not looking away because he wasn't, either.

"Johnny." I couldn't disguise the longing in my voice, and wouldn't have wanted to even if it had been possible.

He groaned, under his breath but still audible.

The sound shot pleasure all through me, tingly and unexpected. I felt my eyes go wide. My nipples hardened a moment later. My clit pulsed. I was glad I'd put down my mug, because I'd have dropped it, otherwise. As it was, I had to put both my hands on the island top to keep my knees from buckling. It was that intense, the sensation. That powerful.

"I should go," Johnny said a half moment later, before I'd had time to fully process the noise he'd made.

He was half out of his seat when I moved around the island to stand in front of him. "Wait."

He sat back in his seat like I'd pushed him, though I wasn't even close enough to touch him. Not yet. "Emm…"

"Oh, fuck me, I love the way my name sounds coming out of your mouth," I said without thinking.

He groaned again. His throat worked as he swallowed. He looked a little wild-eyed. I could see his pulse throbbing at the base of his throat, just once, twice, quickly.

Four or five steps separated us, at most. I took three of them, my feet sliding on waxed wooden floors, the hem of my T-shirt riding up too high for modesty. I wanted to smell him. I didn't think about how it looked, my sudden approach. I didn't care.

"Emm," he said again, and this time it didn't sound like a warning or a protest.

It sounded like an invitation.

I moved. He shifted. His chair was high enough that when I slid between his parted knees, they pressed my hips. I leaned close, eyes half-closed, and breathed deeply. Johnny didn't move away, didn't move closer, just stayed as stiff and rigid as stone.

I opened my eyes. I was so close to him I could see the

speckles in his eyes. I could count his eyelashes. I could see the tiny speck of marshmallow at the corner of his mouth.

But I didn't kiss him.

He kissed me.

Eager, open mouths, tongues sliding, teeth clashing. It was perfect. His hand came up to cup the back of my neck, his fingers tangling in my hair, and I gasped into his mouth at how much I wanted him. He tasted so fucking good, I wanted to eat him.

The chair rocked alarmingly when I straddled him, but his arm went around me, his hand grabbing my ass as his feet hit the floor and kept us from tipping. My shirt rode up. His belt buckle was cold against me, the denim of his jeans deliciously rough. When his hand met my bare flesh, Johnny groaned again, louder, and broke the kiss just long enough to mutter my name again.

I cupped his face in my hands and broke the kiss to look into his eyes. Our mouths were still so close that when I spoke, my lips brushed his with every word. "What about this isn't working?"

His other hand moved down to my ass, and both squeezed gently. The chair rocked again, but I didn't worry it would tip over. I squeezed my thighs against his hips and drew my thumb over his lower lip.

He drew it into his mouth and sucked gently before biting it lightly. "None of it. All of it. Whatever. I can't think straight with you on my lap like this."

"I could be on your face instead," I said.

Johnny muttered an expletive so garbled I couldn't be sure if he were cursing or praying. He kissed me again. His mouth punished mine, and I took it gladly. I was slipping a little, shifting on his lap as he moved to keep the chair from tipping, me from falling. It was messy and it was lovely, but I had to get off him or else find myself on the floor with him on top of me, and not in the way I wanted.

With my feet braced on the floor, our mouths still fused, I could reach between us to press my palm against the bulge in his jeans. I'd never been so bold as this, never, except with him. There…and here.

He put his hand over mine and broke the kiss. "Jesus."

I took the time to catch my breath. I didn't take my hand away. I looked into his eyes, his pupils gone wide with desire. There was no faking that. I licked the taste of him from my lips and remembered the flavor of him coming down the back of my throat. I shivered and the world tilted, not as though I were going dark. Just faint.

"I want you so much." My voice broke on the edges of my honesty, and as with everything else that had happened, I didn't care. Not about propriety, or dignity, or pride.

I turned the hand on his crotch upward, capturing the one he'd put over it. I moved it between my legs, against my hot, slick flesh. I rubbed his fingers over my clit, already hard, and down farther, sliding. I pushed his fingers inside me and shuddered, never looking away from his eyes.

"See?" I said.

Johnny moved his hand, fingers stretching me oh-so-fucking-good. Deep inside, he curled them a little, hitting some hidden spot I'd read about but never bothered with. Every nerve in my body zapped. My other hand found his shoulder, my fingers digging into him as I kept myself from falling. His thumb pressed my clit just right, just perfectly, just the way I knew he'd do it. The way he'd done it in my head.

He moved his ass to the edge of the chair so his feet more firmly met the floor. He kissed me again, fucking me with his hand as his other gripped me tight at my hip to keep me upright. I leaned against his thigh, not caring about how awkwardly I had to tilt my head to keep both his mouth and his hand working on me. I lost my focus on his dick, helpless to do anything but ride the wave of desire already getting ready to crash.

I was so wet his fingers had no trouble sliding in and out, and he moved them slowly, pushing inside, curling and withdrawing, while his thumb gave delicious counterpressure. I rocked against his touch. I sucked his tongue and took his breath when he moaned. I couldn't keep my eyes open now; pleasure had made them too heavy. I couldn't speak, either. I could only give myself up to this.

And he gave me all of it. His mouth, his fingers. His voice, muttering my name into my ear when he left my lips to slide his mouth along my jaw and put the flesh of my throat between his teeth.

My orgasm hit me like a freight train, hard and fast and without mercy. I buckled with the force of it, but Johnny kept me upright. I opened my eyes as it started, and my gaze found his face. He wasn't smiling. His gaze had gone dark and heated, his cheeks flushed, lips parted and wet from mine.

As the pleasure faded, I realized my fingers had cramped on his shoulder. I let go. Aftershocks rippled through me as he withdrew his fingers and I belatedly noticed I'd been on my tiptoes. I let myself rest flat-footed, knees still weak.

"Wow," I managed to say.

When I angled my face to kiss him again, though, he turned just enough that my lips would've hit his cheek if I'd been persistent enough to keep going. I wasn't. After all that, I was smart enough to stop myself.

"I'm sorry," Johnny said, and pushed me gently away. "I can't."

He stood. I moved. He left.

Chapter 16

"…and I think I might need a new suitcase," my mom said, continuing a conversation I hadn't been able to focus on for the past twenty minutes.

It hadn't mattered. She'd been content to chatter on about the upcoming cruise while we wandered the mall, and I'd been content to mutter an occasional "uh-huh" when she paused to pretend she was asking my opinion. I should've known better than to believe I was fooling her, though. She was just waiting for the right moment to confront me, and it turned out to be over frozen yogurt in the food court.

"So," she said, digging her spoon into a mess of vanilla and berries. "What's going on?"

I had a dish of chocolate and fudge in front of me but so far had only painted my spoon with it instead of the inside of my stomach. "Hmm?"

"Emmaline," my mother said warningly. "I know something's up. Talk to me."

I opened my mouth to spill it all. The fugues. The situation, in a much-censored version, with Johnny. Everything I'd have told her before I'd moved away hovered right there on the tip of my tongue, but my eye caught the pile of bags at her feet and I swallowed every single word.

My mom was going on a cruise with my dad. A vacation, without me. The first they'd ever had in all their years of marriage. I knew my mom well enough to suspect, if not know a hundred percent, that all it would take would be one simple sentence and she'd cancel her trip. I didn't say it.

I said instead, "Oh, it's boy troubles, Mom."

She brightened. "Really?"

I had to laugh, though each chuckle hurt my heart. "Don't sound so excited, sheesh."

"Boy trouble means there's a boy," Mom said with a lick of her spoon.

"You act like I never had a boyfriend before."

"You haven't talked about anyone since you moved," she told me.

I swirled my spoon around and around, making a soup of my frozen yogurt. I had no appetite for it but ate a bite, anyway, knowing that not eating it would alarm her more than anything else. I shrugged.

"So. Tell me."

"Well, he's not a boy, for one thing."

My mom was silent for a minute, and when she spoke it was with forced casualness. "Is he…a girl?"

I laughed wholeheartedly at that. "Um, no."

"Oh. Okay. Because you remember Gina Wentzel, don't you? I think she was a year or two ahead of you in school. Her mother works at Weis Markets."

I knew if I waited just long enough, this story would have a point. "Yeah, I knew her. She was a cheerleader."

"*And* a lesbian!"

I laughed again. "Oh, Mom."

"It's true. Her mom told me herself. Said she was with some woman she met while she was working in Arkansas."

"Because Arkansas is filled with lesbians?" I asked after a pause, trying to connect the pieces and failing.

"I have no idea," my mother said. "I'm just telling you what her mother told me. They're thinking of adopting a baby together."

"Um, good for them?" I remembered Gina as a slightly slutty blonde who'd once made a rude comment about my clothes but who'd otherwise never really crossed my path.

"Oh, it's fine for them," my mom said with a nod and another lick of her yogurt. "It would be fine for you, too."

"If I were a lesbian?"

My mom pointed at me with her spoon. "I'm just saying, your dad and I would love you just the same, even if you were a lesbian. I mean, imagine how that girl on the radio's parents must feel."

The fact I could no longer so easily follow my mom's non sequiturs saddened me. "What girl on the radio?"

"That 'I Kissed a Girl' girl. Imagine what her parents must've thought about that."

"I'm sure they're proud of her, too, Mom."

"Well, your dad and I are proud of you, Emmaline. No matter if you're a lesbian or not." My mom's eyes glistened with tears, though she was smiling. "You've grown up so beautifully. I mean, I always hoped, but never thought… I mean, we weren't sure…"

"I'm not a lesbian," I said to fend off any emotional breakdowns. I was already close to an emo outburst of angsty sobbing brought on by PMS. I didn't want to break down here in the food court or encourage my mom to do the same.

"So, boy trouble? But not with a boy. A man, then," my mom said with a shrug as though I were merely splitting hairs.

"Well, yeah. He's a man. He's not a boy. At all." I frowned, thinking of how Johnny had called me a girl.

"I guess that's fine. You're in your thirties now. Time to date men, I guess." Mom smiled. "So, what's he like?"

"We're not dating. I mean, I like him a lot..." I sighed, clearing my throat to keep the emotion shoved way down deep. "He doesn't like me."

"Then he's a jerk."

"Gee, Mom, thanks, but I think you're a little biased."

She smiled again and scraped the last of her yogurt from her cup. "Doesn't matter. I'm your mother. If I say some boy—sorry, some man—is a jerk for not liking you, I'm allowed. What's his name?"

"Johnny."

She scoffed. "That's not a man's name."

"It's sort of... I guess he got stuck with it early on and now everyone knows him by that. That's all. I don't think he'd be a John. He's just...Johnny. It fits him, actually."

"Are you sure he doesn't like you?"

I thought of how he'd pushed past me, leaving me alone with my T-shirt up around my hips and my kitchen smelling of sex. "Yes. I'm sure."

"He's a jerk. Forget about him."

"I'm not sure I can, Mom. He's pretty unforgettable."

"Any man," my mom said with a glower, "is forgettable."

I sighed. "Not this one."

"Oh, Emm. Honey. I hate seeing you like this. Why do you always let yourself get so worked up?"

I laughed even though it hurt my throat. "Geez, Mom, where's the support?"

"I said he was a jerk, didn't I?"

I laughed again. "He *is* a jerk."

"But you like him," my mom said sympathetically. "I can tell."

"He's just...special," I told her with another sigh. I swirled my yogurt again but couldn't manage to eat it, even to save her from worry. "He's different. He's so talented. So talented, so well-traveled. He's lived so much, Mom, he makes me feel like some backwoods bumpkin. Like…well, like a girl."

"You *are* a girl," she pointed out.

"I'm a woman," I said.

She looked at me, eyes soft. "I know you are, honey. And there's no boy…or man, for that matter, so special that you should ever feel like that."

I really love my mom.

"I know. I can't help it. He's just so… Gah!" I stabbed my now unfrozen yogurt. "Stupid! He's stupid! Stupid Johnny Dellasandro."

My mom chuckled, then paused. "Why does that name sound familiar?"

"He's an artist," I offered, knowing that would be an unlikely connection for her to make. "He has a gallery in Harrisburg called the Tin Angel."

"No, that's not it." She pulled a package of wipes from her bag and busily cleaned each finger.

"He was…an actor," I added hesitantly.

Her brows raised. "A famous actor? Like…Tom Cruise?"

"Not quite like that. But pretty famous, yeah," I said, thinking of the articles, the websites, the fan pages. "A long time ago, though."

"How long ago?" She sounded suspicious. She looked suspicious, too.

"Um…" I hedged. "In the seventies."

My mom sat back in her chair, arms crossed. "I assume he wasn't a child actor?"

"No."

"Oh, Emmaline!" She stopped, brow furrowed. "Not the guy who's in all those late-night cable movies? The ones where he shows his…you-know-whats?"

"Um…"

"Emmaline Marie Moser," my mother said, aghast.

No matter how old you are, the use of your three names will always be shaming.

"I can't believe you." She hitched forward in her chair, voice lowered like we were talking about something filthy. "He's got to be as old as your dad, at least!"

"He's not," I insisted. "Dad's fifty-nine. Johnny's only fifty-seven."

"Oh, God. Oh, my God." She put a hand over her heart, then shook herself. "Thank God he doesn't like you. He *shouldn't* like you! If he did he'd be more than a jerk, he'd be a…pedophile!"

"Mom!"

"He's too old for you, Emmaline!"

"Mom," I said, quieter. "I'm almost thirty-two years old. It would hardly make him a pedophile."

"Still too old for you," she said stubbornly.

I frowned. "You'd be okay with me dating a girl, but not an older guy?"

This stumped her. She glowered further. At least she was scolding me, not fussing over me.

"He doesn't like me," I repeated.

"Then he's a jerk!"

"Oh, Mom." I laughed, shaking my head. "Yeah. He's a jerk. And it's good he doesn't like me."

I thought of how much he hadn't liked me when his fingers were deep up inside me, making me come, and had to study my melted yogurt very carefully. There are some things you just never want to share with your mom, no matter how much you love and get along with her, or no matter what else you could share. I forced myself to eat a bite of creamy, chocolate fudgy goodness, but didn't enjoy it.

"You really like him, huh?" She knew me too well. It was annoying.

"Well...yeah. I told you..."

"He's special. I know. But aren't they all, at first?"

I looked up at her. "They don't stay special?"

She smiled, her gaze going a little dreamy. "Some do. I mean, I still think your dad's pretty sexy."

I wrinkled my nose. "Um, hello, not your bestie here. That's my dad."

She laughed. "You asked."

I was glad their marriage was good. I was a lucky daughter to have parents who loved each other. And it wasn't wrong to want that, I knew it.

"C'mon. If chocolate doesn't make you feel better, maybe some retail therapy will." My mom got up to toss her trash, and I followed.

"Yeah, too bad I'm broke."

"Emm, if that's a blatant way of getting me to buy you a pair of shoes, that stopped working in eighth grade."

I smiled and gave her puppy eyes as we gathered her packages and left the food court behind. "No, it didn't."

"Just don't tell your dad. He's already having a freak-out about this trip," my mom counseled me.

I didn't really want or need her to buy me anything, but it was nice to know she might be persuaded to. "What's he freaking out about?"

She started telling me, but a kiosk just past the food court stole my attention from her. I'd passed it dozens of times without a second look, never having a need for a hand-tooled leather belt or bracelet, but today...today, as so much seemed to be lately, was different.

"Wait a minute," I murmured even as my mom, still chatting, kept walking toward the bookstore. "Mom, hold on."

"Hey," said the boy working at the kiosk. He was supercute, with emo bangs over one eye and a hint of guyliner that would've set my heart aflutter not too long ago.

Now he just looked too young.

"Hey," I said. "Can I see one of those?"

I pointed at the hair clips. Made of molded leather in a half circle and punctured through two drilled holes by a small, spiked dowel, they were nothing like I'd ever bought or would ever have worn. At least, not here, in this now. But apparently my mind thought they'd suit me, because it had manufactured one for me in one of the fugues.

"Sure." He hooked one off the rack with a finger and held it out. "They can be personalized, too."

I glanced up at him as I took the clip. I paused. He was totally giving me the once-over, and it felt good. Really good. I hadn't been looked at like that since…well, since the last time I went dark. I frowned.

"I don't need it personalized." I slid the wooden dowel in and out of the holes, trying to remember if this was like the one in my fugue. I hadn't paid much attention to it and couldn't recall if it had any designs on it.

"It would look great on you." He sounded sincere. "You have really thick hair."

"Thanks," I said after a second. I touched the ponytail hanging over my shoulder. I did have thick hair, sometimes too thick for a regular elastic band. They were always breaking at random moments. "I'll take it."

I paid him less than ten bucks for it, which wasn't quite pocket change for a hair clip but was less than what I'd seen some go for. I tugged the elastic from my hair and it fell around my face and shoulders in a familiar weight before I gathered it in my fingers and twisted it on the back of my head and clipped it in place. I turned my head from side to side, testing to see if it would slip out, but it seemed to be holding firmly.

"Looks great," he said. "Sure you don't want it personalized? You could get a picture, or your initials. Something like that."

"What are you buying?" my mom, back from her trip to the bookstore, said. "Oh, my God, Emm. What is that thing?"

"It's a hair clip."

She laughed. "I wore one just like it when I was dating your dad. Good Lord."

I smiled. "Did you have yours personalized with your name?"

She laughed again. "I don't think so. I think it had a flower on it. I think they all had flowers on them. Or maybe they were marijuana plants, I don't remember."

The kiosk guy choked laughter behind his hand. I knew I shouldn't have been so shocked, but I was, anyway. "Mom!"

"What?" she said, all innocent. "I'm not saying I smoked it. I'm just saying there were a lot of things with that picture on them. That's all. Emm, c'mon, it was the seventies."

"I definitely don't want a picture of weed on my hair clip." I looked at him. "How much to personalize it?"

"Free," he said. "Which is why, you know, you should do it. Because it's included."

"How about my initials, then," I told him. "E.M.M."

It took only a few minutes, but when he handed it back to me he looked apologetic. "Something got screwed up with the machine. I put in your initials but I must've hit the wrong code, because it came up with this."

Flowers and vines. It was still pretty. It was familiar, and I swallowed a bitter taste. "Actually, this is fine."

"You sure? I can make another one…."

"No." I shook my head. "This is fine."

He gave me the clip along with something else. His phone number. I waited until we'd passed out of sight before I tossed it in the trash.

"Why'd you do that?" my mom asked. "He was such a cute boy."

"He was a cute boy," I said.

But I didn't want a boy. I wanted a man. I wanted Johnny.

"You sure you want to go in there?" Jen asked. "You know there's a shitton of other places we could go, Emm. The Mocha's coffee isn't *that* good."

I set my jaw and hunched my shoulders deeper into my coat, turning my collar up against the wind. I studied the Mocha from our place across the street. I'd been standing there for ten minutes, waiting for her. I hadn't seen Johnny go in. Hadn't seen him come out, either.

"No. I'm not going to let that son of a bitch ruin the Mocha for me. Fuck that noise. Fuck Johnny Dellasandro, too, whoever the fuck he thinks he is," I said grimly. The sour taste of each word clung to my tongue like the flavor of milk gone bad. Nasty.

"Sure, I get it." Jen shivered, staring across the street.

The temperatures had dropped over the past few days, promising even more snow. The clouds couldn't have more perfectly mirrored my mood. Since Johnny'd left me standing in my kitchen a couple days before, I'd been alternating between mortified despair and slowly simmering, self-righteous fury.

"It's just..." She trailed off.

I looked at her. I couldn't feel my nose. Or my toes. Or the back of my neck, since I'd pulled my hair up in my new hair clip, stupidly exposing my flesh above the security of my scarf. I didn't want to stand on the street corner like some two-dollar whore, which is exactly how he'd made me feel. "You don't want to go in?"

"I don't want you to go in," my friend said, "if it means you're going to get upset."

I had to answer slowly to keep my teeth from chattering. "Do you think I'll cause a scene? Because I won't, Jen. I'm not a scene kind of girl. But I'll be fucked with a barbed-wire dildo before I'll let him keep me out of our place. That's *our* place, and it was before I ever knew he existed."

"Ouch." She winced and laughed.

"Up the ass without lube," I added, not feeling much like laughing but letting a small giggle escape, anyway. "C'mon, it's freezing out here. I don't care if he's in there, I just want something fattening."

"Right on," Jen said. "If you're sure. I mean, a barbed-wire dildo up your ass seems pretty sure to me, but I want to be sure you're sure."

"I'm sure." I couldn't hold back the chattering now, and the words bit out of me between the clatter. "Really. I don't know what his problem is, but he can suck it."

"Ooookay." She howled with laughter and clapped her hands together. "Let's go."

He wasn't inside, which made the whole conversation pretty anticlimactic. We placed our orders and took them to a table, where we peeled ourselves out of our layers and wrapped our hands around steaming mugs to warm them. I still didn't feel much like laughing, but with Jen across from me, it was fairly impossible not to give in to the giggles.

"So, how's it going with the funeral director guy?" I asked her as I licked melted marshmallow topping from the mint-chocolate latte I was trying. It had a peppermint stick in it, and even a couple months after Christmas, who can resist that?

"Ohhh, girl," Jen said. "I like him."

"Wow. That's good, right?"

She twirled her spoon in her latte and shrugged. "I guess so."

"Why just you guess so?"

She sighed. "Well, you know how it is. You like a guy. A lot. He likes you. It's going great. I'm just waiting for it to all turn to crap."

"Awww, why would it?" I asked.

She shrugged again. "Because that's what happens."

"Not always," I said, then added, "or so I hear."

"Yeah, I know, right? Love is sorta like Sasquatch. Or alien abduction. You hear a lot about it happening to other people, but there's no real evidence of it. Girl, that shit's scary." Jen made a face.

I sighed, my smile fading along with my good humor. "So's love."

"Oh, Emm. I'm sorry. It sucks that he's being such a dick." My friend squeezed my hand. "Cute blouse, by the way."

"Nice subject change." I looked down at the shirt I'd picked up at the Salvation Army. It had poofy sleeves banded tight at the wrist and a matching bow at the throat. "It was fifty percent off because it's so ugly."

"It's like a shirt and a vest combined. Verrrry retro."

I laughed. "The pockets aren't real, either."

Jen looked over my shoulder and sighed. "So much for the subject change."

My muscles went tight, my back straight. "It's him, huh?"

The bell jangled. I imagined rather than felt the whisper of cold air along the back of my neck. I turned to look at him, expecting him to ignore me as usual and not going to let him get away with it without at least a little bit of guilt.

Johnny stopped at the table. He nodded at Jen but looked at me. "Emm. Hi. Can I talk to you?"

I ignored Jen's breathless squeak and the kick she gave me under the table. I folded my hands over my mug and looked up at him without the slightest hint of a smile. "You're talking to me, aren't you?"

He didn't look taken aback, or abashed, both reactions I'd have quite thoroughly enjoyed. Johnny tilted his head just a bit. "Privately."

"I'm with my friend right now."

"Actually," Jen said apologetically, though I didn't believe for one second she was sorry, "I have to get going. I promised Jared I'd call him."

I narrowed my eyes at her but couldn't force her to stay with me when she was already getting up and putting on her coat. "Betrayer," I muttered.

"Nice seeing you," Jen said to Johnny.

He smiled at her. "You haven't been into the gallery in a while."

She stopped, looking stunned. "I, um..."

"I'm having a new-artists show in a month or two. You should bring me something to look at for it."

Both of us let out surprised squeaks that time. Johnny didn't look surprised. Patiently, he waited for an answer.

"Sure, okay," Jen said hesitantly. Her smile got wider. "Yeah, sure. I could do that!"

"Bring it by sometime in the evening this week. I'll be there until seven."

"Great. Okay." She nodded and gave me a look full of wonder and excitement I wasn't about to sully with my own pissed-offedness. "See you, Emm."

"Later." I waited until she'd gone and he'd slid into her seat before I glared at him. "What was that all about?"

"What?" Johnny pushed Jen's mug out of the way and

steepled his fingers together on the table in front of him. He hadn't bothered to take off his coat, maybe not planning to stay long.

"How do you even know she's an artist, anyway?" I didn't want my drink anymore and spun the half-melted peppermint stick around and around.

Johnny's brows lifted. So did one corner of his mouth. I hated that smile. It tempted me into returning it, and I didn't want to. Silently, he pointed along the Mocha's back wall, hung with the photos and art for sale, some of them Jen's.

"I didn't think you'd have noticed," I said coolly. "Not to mention paid any attention to who she was."

"You think I don't know who's in here and who's not?" Johnny's smile hadn't reached full power yet, but I could tell it was on its way. "You think I just come in here and drink my coffee without noticing everything?"

"Yes. I do." The peppermint stick snapped in my fingers and I let both pieces slide into the chocolaty coffee.

"Well," Johnny said in a low voice, "I don't."

His gaze was unflinching. His smile crept up another fraction. I bit the inside of my cheek, hard, to keep myself from giving in to his attempt at charm.

I smelled oranges.

Against my will, my eyelids fluttered. I drew in a swift breath, not on purpose but from unconscious reaction. The smell got stronger. I stood, pushing my chair back with a loud scrape.

"I have to go."

"Emm," Johnny said, standing, too. "Wait."

I didn't wait. I went dark. I fell into it headlong and came up gasping, like I was kicking up from miles below the surface of a still, silent lake.

I wasn't cold. I was hot. I was in a bathroom, porcelain

sink cool under my palms, gripping it. Water running. I was sweating, salty drops of it on my upper lip when I licked it.

I cupped some water and drew it to my mouth, drinking. Gulping. I splashed my face, not caring I also wet my blouse and even got the front of my high-waisted jeans wet. I looked at my reflection. Wild eyes, dripping face.

I turned slowly, looking around. There was nothing so convenient as a calendar to show me the date but the shower curtain of red, orange and lime-green geometric patterns clued me in. Well, that and the fact that only a minute ago I'd been in the Mocha, getting ready to storm out, thinking, *Fuck Johnny Dellasandro, the arrogant prick.*

Now, here, I was also thinking about fucking Johnny, just not in the same way. I dried my hands on a towel that wasn't quite clean. I pushed open the bedroom door. Johnny, naked, lounged on the bed in a tangle of sheets.

"Hey, babe," he said, then stopped, frowning. "Why'd you get dressed?"

I looked down at my clothes. "I—"

"Shit." He laughed. "Sandy'll be pissed you're wearing her clothes. But, ah, who cares? That shirt looks better on you. She doesn't have the tits for it."

I was still angry; this didn't make it better. I put a hand on my hip, not caring this was a fugue and I was essentially arguing with myself. "And why are Sandy's clothes in your bathroom, huh? Why the fuck does that bitch waltz in and out of here like she owns the place? Like she owns you? And yet you can't give me the time of day?"

Johnny sat up, not bothering to cover himself. "What the hell are you talking about?"

I breathed hard and deep, disoriented enough to grip the doorway tight. "Her. Sandy. Your wife, remember her?"

"I told you, we split up." Johnny got out of bed and padded toward me on bare feet.

His body was gorgeous. His hair like silk as he pushed it off his face and drew me close. He kissed me.

"Don't be mad, baby," Johnny murmured against my mouth. "C'mon. Get undressed. Come back to bed."

I pushed his chest until he stepped away from me. "No."

His expression clouded. "Jesus, you chicks. The fuck's a guy gotta do for you? You go into the bathroom all fucking smiles, you come out looking like you want to kill me."

"How long ago?" I demanded.

"How long ago what? We split up, like, a year ago."

"No. How long ago did I go into the bathroom?" I forced the words out across a dry tongue and numb lips.

"I don't know. Five, ten minutes ago?"

"Oh, God." I wasn't just *back* in the world I'd constructed out of wish fulfillment and an overdose of internet stalking. I was back and forth inside it.

I stumbled into the bathroom where I bent over the sink and swallowed convulsively, sure I was about to heave up every bit of my peppermint latte. With my eyes closed I couldn't see him, but I heard the shush-shush of Johnny's feet on the tile and felt his hand on my shoulder. Without opening my eyes, I fumbled open the faucet and ran my fingers through cool water to press them against my forehead and cheeks.

"You okay?" His fingers made soothing circles on my back. "What's wrong?"

"Heat. It's the heat." The words slipped out of me, and I wondered why I lied.

"Take a drink." His hands kept smoothing over my back.

I did feel better with his touch, but my fingers gripped the sink and I didn't move until I could be sure I wasn't going to puke. Then I splashed my face again and, dripping, turned to him. "What is this, Johnny?"

"What's what?" He took a towel from a drawer and gently wiped my face. He cupped my chin in his palm and looked into my eyes before kissing my forehead. He pulled me against his chest, his arms around me.

I didn't care if it was too hot to snuggle, or that his bare chest beneath my cheek was sticky with sweat. I pressed my lips to the skin there. I tasted salt and sex.

"This. Us."

He laughed. "I don't know. What do you want it to be?"

"I want it to be everything, Johnny." My voice broke.

"Hey," he said softly. "Hey, shhh."

I didn't quite cry, but my body shook with tension and he must've thought I was weeping. It was nice, him holding me this way. A nice echo of what had happened the day in his office, except that here I knew if I kissed him, Johnny would kiss me back.

"So why can't it be?" he said after a minute.

The air in the bathroom was heavy with heat and moisture. Breathing it took effort. Speaking took effort, too.

"Because none of this is real."

"Hey." He pushed me gently away without letting go of my upper arms. Holding me steady. "Don't say that. It's real. I'm right here, you're right there—"

"No." I shook my head. I ran my hands over his chest and belly. "You're not. I'm not. This isn't real at all."

"Then what is it?" He tilted his head and gave me a faint smile. "It feels real to me."

He slid his hand up to cup my breast through my blouse. "This feels real."

He took my hand and pushed it down to hold his half-hard cock. "This feels real, too."

I pushed away from him, half turning. With the sink at my back I had no place to go. "It would feel real to you. You're always real to yourself. The problem, Johnny, is all of this is inside my head. I'm making it up. None of it's real. It's all just something that's going on in my brain."

He didn't laugh. He didn't try to pull me closer, but he didn't move so I could get away. "Emm. Look at me."

I did. He was so beautiful, so young. Smooth face, unlined. Was it wrong to see such beauty in his youth, especially when I had the memory of his real face to overlay the one in front of me? The lines at the corners of his eyes, the silver at his temples, those were things about the real Johnny I found utterly delicious, but there was no denying that the man in front of me was in his yumfuckable peak.

"What's not real about this? I know we haven't known each other very long, but…"

"It's not that." I shook my head. My hair had started to slip from the clip binding it in a coil to the back of my head.

I reached up and pulled it out, then held the curved leather on my palm to show him. "This is real. I bought it because of something you said to me here. That I left it here, that is was mine."

He looked confused. "You did? When?"

"You told me," I said, "in the kitchen. That this was mine, though I'd never seen it. That I'd left it here. Then I saw it in the mall and I bought one like it, because it reminded me of you. That's crazy, Johnny. Maybe I'm crazy."

"We're all a little crazy. It's okay." He smiled.

I didn't. I threw the leather clip into the sink, where the leather turned dark with wet. I looked at him again.

"None of this is real, and it can't last."

"Shit." He frowned. "Some things last. Don't make this over before it's even started."

"But it is over!" I shouted.

He backed up a few steps, eyes narrowing, fists clenching just a little, like he thought I might hit him. He had been married to Sandy, a woman I could totally see punching a dude in the nuts when he was naked. I, however, wasn't that sort of woman.

"It's over," I whispered. "Because it never started. Don't you get it?"

"No. I don't get it."

"This isn't real." I threw out a hand to gesture at the bathroom. "We aren't. Somewhere, you're shaking…shaking…"

I was shaking, but not from nerves or a seizure, but as though a phantom hand were pushing me back and forth.

"Emm?" Johnny sounded alarmed.

"Shaking me," I whispered hoarsely, then louder, "shaking me out of it."

"Out of what?" Johnny cried, reaching for me. "Jesus, Emm, you're scaring the shit out of me."

"Shaking me out of the dark. Bringing me back." I pushed past him. "I'm going."

"Where are you going?" he called from the doorway as I pushed myself to walk at a steady pace through the bedroom, not knowing where I was going.

Knowing it didn't matter.

"Are you coming back?" he cried. "Emm! Tell me you're coming back!"

"I don't know," I said over my shoulder as I opened the bedroom door. "I never know."

And then I was blinking, my vision momentarily blurred, and Johnny's hand was on my shoulder.

"Emm," he was saying quietly. "You have to believe me when I say I'm sorry."

"For what?" I asked stupidly. I'd missed something important. I gave a pointed look at his hand, and he took it away.

Johnny paused before answering. "You were…gone…again, huh?"

My chin went up a little. "It was nothing."

"Sure, it's something," he said, but before he could say more his phone rang from his coat pocket.

He reached for it, and I took the chance to get up while he was answering. He gestured at me to wait, but I didn't. I grabbed up my coat and bag and pushed away from the table without even tossing my trash. Let him toss it. I had to get out of there.

I took the long way home. The cold felt good on my hot face, even though by the time I got back to my house I couldn't feel my nose. Or my toes. The sky had gotten even darker, thick with clouds. The air tingled with the promise of snow.

My phone rang as soon as I got through the front door. I had caller ID. "What do you want?"

"Is that how you always answer the phone?"

"Only when it's you," I told Johnny.

He laughed, and I hated that he could find humor in my anger. "I've never called you before."

"Maybe you shouldn't have called me this time, either."

"Emm. I'm sorry. I had to talk to you."

I clenched my fists, one at a time, switching the phone from hand to hand to get some feeling back into them. "Why?"

"You know why."

"Actually, I don't." I put the kettle on, thinking to make some hot tea and decided to make cocoa instead. Then, thinking of the last time I'd made hot cocoa, I decided again on tea.

"What happened the other night…I was wrong."

"Damn right you were wrong." I twisted the burner on and, finally warm enough, unbuttoned my coat.

"I'm sorry," Johnny said. "I shouldn't have let things get that far."

"No, what you should be sorry about is walking out afterward like I was some bargain basement *hooah.*" I paused, realizing I'd unconsciously imitated him.

Johnny was silent for a long few seconds. "I didn't mean to make you feel like that, Emmaline."

It was the first time he'd ever used my full name, though it wasn't the first time I'd ever heard him say it. The sound of it was too strong a reminder of the havoc my brain was wreaking. I turned off the burner and poured myself a mug of peppermint tea before the water in the kettle had even boiled.

"Well. You did," I said.

The sound of his sigh tickled my eardrums through the phone. "I'm sorry."

"Make it up to me," I said.

Sometimes in silence you can hear an expression, but I couldn't this time. Was he smiling again, crinkling his eyes at the corners? Frowning, so that his brow furrowed between his eyes with that little divot I wanted to smooth away with my thumb? Or was he giving the phone that frankly assessing look he'd given me a few times?

"How?"

"You could take me to dinner, for a start," I told him, giddy with my own boldness and yet suddenly, completely certain this was how it had been meant to go all along. "I like Italian food."

"Dinner, for a start. And then what?"

"Let's start with dinner. I'll see if I'm sufficiently mollified," I told him.

This time, I heard his smile as clearly as if I'd been able to see it. "What time should I pick you up?"

"Seven-thirty tomorrow."

"Be ready," Johnny said.

"You're the one who needs to be ready," I told him. "Ready to convince me you're not an asshole."

I heard the soft chuff of a laugh. "I'll do what I can."

"See you tomorrow, Johnny," I told him, and hung up before he could reply.

He showed up at my door with flowers. This was one of the differences between being taken out by a man and not a boy. This was the promise of a real date, not just a hookup. Not beer and wings at a bar with some sport playing on the big screen and buddies dropping by the table every few minutes to slap my date's hand and check me out not so surreptitiously. This was something special.

"You look nice." Johnny handed me the bouquet of lilies and daisies, two flowers I'd never have put together in one bunch.

I lifted them to my nose. "Thanks. These are pretty. Let me put them in some water and I'll be ready to go."

He stepped inside my foyer. I gestured at him to come with me to the kitchen, where he hesitated in the doorway and I bit back a smile as I filled a glass vase with water and snipped the ends of the flowers before putting them in the vase. When I turned, drying my hands on a paper towel, he was looking at the chair he'd been sitting on the last time.

"Ready?" I asked.

Everything turned inside out when he looked at me.

"I don't think so," he said. "But I guess I'll take you, anyway."

And he did, twenty minutes away to a delightful restaurant I'd heard about but never been to. He opened the car door for me, and the door of the restaurant, and he pulled out my chair at the table. It was first-class treatment all the way, and I ate it up like it was the main course and not the delicious lasagna recommended by the waiter.

I didn't think the conversation would flow. Johnny hadn't exactly proven himself to be a talker—at least, not in the present, real-time. Sitting across the table from me, though, he turned out to have a lot to say on a lot of topics, and I let myself be buoyed by the rise and fall of that delicious voice.

"You're not saying much," he said with a pause to drink some of the excellent red wine he'd convinced me to try.

"Just listening." I sipped wine, too, letting it roll around on my tongue before swallowing.

"How's the wine?"

"Great. I don't usually like red wine, but this is really good." I took another sip, then tore a piece of thick Italian bread into pieces to dip in the flavored olive oil. "Keep talking."

He didn't right away. He studied me across the table. We even had a candle for ambience. The golden glow made highlights in his hair and reflected in his eyes. It reminded me of the first fugue I'd had, seeing him in sunshine.

"What?" Johnny asked.

"You," I said. "You're so..."

"Old?"

"Hush. You're not old. I was going to say handsome."

Johnny sat back in his chair, head tilted, mouth quirked. I knew that look. I'd seen it on his face in his films and in photos. I'd seen it on him in my head.

"I'm old," he said. His phone rang from the pocket of his coat. "Sorry."

I busied myself with dunking my bread in olive oil and my leftover red sauce from the lasagna, and with chewing and swallowing. I savored the flavor of the oil and garlic, thinking how I should've brought some mints or gum. I didn't want to overhear his conversation, but did, anyway.

"Honey, listen… No. Yes, of course I'll be there. I wouldn't miss it." Johnny frowned. "I told you the last time I couldn't make it because… I know he does. Listen, has the kid complained? Because I talked to him just a coupla nights ago, and I asked him if he was okay with me taking him another night. He said yes…. Well, yeah, I know he might feel like he has to, but not because of anything I ever told him…. Honey…I know…. Yes. I will be there. I promise. Have I broken a promise to you?"

A pause. More frowning. I sipped wine to wash down the garlic while Johnny rubbed the edge of his thumb between his eyes.

"Within the past two years?" Pause. "Yeah, I thought so…. Well, don't you push me, either, that's all…. Yeah. I'm sorry, too…. I know. I'll talk to you later."

He clicked off the phone and put it back into his coat pocket, then looked at me with a sigh. "Sorry."

I wiped my mouth with a napkin. "Uh-huh."

Johnny laughed; I loved the sound of it. "You're looking at me funny."

"Don't you know it's rude to take a phone call from another woman when you're on a date with someone?" I didn't know where the sassiness came from, just that I opened my mouth and it came out.

"Another… Oh. Ah." Johnny nodded, still smiling. "Well, you've seen me with her in the Mocha."

I licked my lips and tasted garlic and oil. Johnny's eyes gleamed in the candlelight. He watched my mouth.

"Oh?" I said. "Does that make it any less rude?"

"You like to give me a hard time, don't you?"

I smiled and said nothing.

"She's my daughter," Johnny told me. "Kim."

I had a flashback of a diaper-clad baby smelling of poo and spit-up. "But she's—"

Of course she was no baby any longer. I'd read somewhere about his wife, his child. That was the explanation for why they'd shown up in my fugues. I'd never connected the blurred image of an infant in pictures with the woman who'd met with him in the coffee shop.

"I know," Johnny said, though he couldn't possibly have known what I meant. "Maybe you understand now why I was… Well, why I was a rude asshole."

I didn't, and my face must've shown it.

"It's the age difference," he said quietly, leaning forward.

"That again?" I flashed on what my mom had said, too, and frowned. "Lots of men date younger women."

"Younger than my kid." Johnny shook his head, looking rueful. "Kimmy's at least a coupla years older than you are. And I'll tell you something, Emm, I've only just been a part of her life again for the past coupla years. I know she'll freak out if I bring home a girlfriend who could be her younger sister."

This made so much sense—for someone else. Not for us, and I couldn't even be sure why. "Let me ask you something. Is she married?"

"Yeah. Has a kid and everything. I'm a grandpa." Johnny

grinned at that, and I watched his face light up. "Great kid, too. He's six now."

"Did you tell her who to marry? Or comment on her husband's age?"

Johnny looked at me straight on. "I'm not gonna lie to you. You think I'm an asshole? Well, my daughter thinks so, too. You both have reason to think so."

I regretted making him feel bad even though I still thought it was some kind of fuckery for him to walk out of my kitchen the way he had. I didn't comment, though. I just let him talk.

"Her mom and I split up before she was born. We were both young, figured getting hitched would be fun. When Sandy turned up pregnant, I was all for making a family, but…" He shrugged. "She's kind of impossible to deal with. And I was working with all these people, all these women…"

"You don't need to spell it out for me," I said. "I've seen the movies."

He didn't look ashamed, just tilted his head to study me again. "Yeah. You know."

"That was a long time ago," I said. "Do you think that would matter to me now?"

"The women? No. But the fact I didn't make sure I was a part of my kid's life the way she deserved me to be? The fact I let her mother take her off and expose her to all sorts of shit, even when I knew she was being dragged all over the place?" Johnny shook his head again. "No, Emm, that's something that doesn't get better just because it was a long time ago, or because I was young and stupid. I owed that kid something, and now I'm doing my best to pay her back."

"That is exactly what makes you not an asshole," I said.

He smiled and shrugged. "It's not an excuse. But it's why I did what I did with you that day. It's why I've been trying to avoid you."

I reached for his hand across the table, and he didn't pull it away. I held it out to look at the palm and traced the lines of it with my fingertip like I was telling his fortune, though I could only go back and not forward. "So then how come you're here with me now?"

Johnny closed his fingers over mine, holding my hand tight. "Because no matter where I went, you were there."

"You make it sound like I was stalking you." My words came out in a whisper, throaty and hoarse.

His eyes gleamed again. His thumb rubbed over the back of my hand and I felt that touch all the way through me. "Not stalking me. Just impossible to get away from."

"And you wanted to get away from me?" This stung less than it should've, the words counterbalanced by the heat in his gaze.

"Yeah."

"Why, Johnny? Why would you want to get away from me?"

"Because you scared me."

I squeezed his hand. "I'm not scary. Really, I promise. Bossy, maybe…"

"Bossy, definitely." He squeezed back.

"I just… I can't explain to you why," I told him in a low voice.

All around us, the clatter of forks on plates and low murmur of conversation reminded me we weren't alone, and yet nothing else was in front of me but Johnny's face. We held hands like lovers, though that wasn't quite what we were. Then again, it wasn't what we weren't.

"There's something about you, that's all. I know you've probably had a lot of women tell you that—"

"Hundreds, easy."

I squeezed his hand hard. "Hey!"

He laughed and my grip softened. Our fingers linked. It was a little awkward, stretching across the table this way, but

I didn't want to let go of him. Not now that I'd grabbed him. Held him tight.

"None like you, Emm," Johnny said. "None like you."

I chose to take that as a compliment, even though I wasn't entirely sure he meant it as one. I made it through dinner without embarrassing myself, although every time he wiped his mouth I wanted my cunt to be the napkin. I thought he had to know this about me, but if he did, he made no sign of it. He just talked.

And then…he took me home.

I hesitated on the doorstep, hoping he would kiss me. And he did. On the cheek, soft and sweet, at the corner of my mouth. I tasted garlic and olive oil, but though I opened my mouth, it was too late. He'd already pulled back.

Scent of citrus, carried on the cold night air.

I took one step back.

"Johnny," I said, but it wasn't now-Johnny who answered.

"This good, babe?" he said from behind me in that butter-slick voice, thick and sweet and low, and I turned to face my foyer and wound up rolling over in Johnny's bed.

"Johnny?"

Naked beside him, my body slick with sweat, his hand between my thighs. His fingers moving. And just like that, I was shivering and shuddering, consumed with pleasure.

And just like that, blinking, I pushed myself up from the cushions of my couch. A damp cloth fell from my forehead. Water had run down my cheeks and wet the front of my shirt. My hair was wet.

"What the hell?"

Johnny had been pacing, biting his thumb, and now whirled to sink beside me. "Jesus Christ, Emm!"

He went to his knees in front of me and gathered my hands in his. He rubbed them together. I sat up, but he pushed me to stay still.

"What happened?" My stomach, sick and churning, twisted into knots. I was sure I already knew.

"You went dark."

My mouth opened when he described it the way I always had. "What? How…how long?"

"Fifteen minutes. Shit." Johnny got up to pace again, running a hand over his hair, which then flopped into his eyes. "I was going to call the ambulance in another five minutes."

"Oh, God." I sat up all the way and swung my legs over the edge of the couch. I put my face in my hands, bending forward to combat the faint feeling rushing over me.

I felt his weight beside me. His arm around me. "You fucking had me so worried, Emm. Jesus."

He got up after half a minute and paced again. "I'm calling the doctor."

"No!" I looked up. Johnny stopped. "No. Please don't."

Tenderly, he sat next to me again and took my hands in his. "Emm…I have to. You were out like a light. I shook you, nothing. Said your name. Nothing. Fifteen fucking minutes, Emm. I was so worried."

Alarmed, I heard his voice break and I looked into his eyes. "I'm sorry. But please, Johnny. Don't call the doctor."

"But if there's something…"

I shook my head. "I told you before. This has happened for

years. There's no treatment. And if you make me go to the hospital, they'll do all sorts of tests. I'll lose my license again. Without my license, I can't work. And if I can't work, I can't afford this house. I won't be able to live here anymore. I'll have to move back home with my parents...."

"Shh," he said. "No, you won't."

I shook my head again, fighting tears. "Yes. I will."

"I'll drive you to work."

I swallowed hard. "You're not even... Why would you do that?"

"So you're safe," he said. "So other people on the road are safe."

"No. I mean, why would you make that commitment? Why would you help me like that? We've had one date," I said. "What happened in the kitchen aside, one date. And before that, you barely spoke to me. I mean, I think we've sort of cleared up why, but that doesn't change the fact that you have no reason to get involved with me like this. To make promises."

"To help you?" he asked, and brushed my bangs out of my eyes. "Why wouldn't I help you, Emm?"

"Driving me to work?" I gave a short, harsh laugh and got to my feet. "That's not helping me. That's taking care of me."

"What's wrong with that?"

I turned to face him. "You barely know me."

His mouth opened, but no words came out. He closed it again a moment later. He looked pained. "If you don't let me drive you, I'm going to call 9-1-1 and tell them I found you unconscious. They'll send someone, and you can try to lie about it, but with your medical history, don't you think they'll figure it out?"

"You wouldn't." Tears sparked in my eyes and my throat got tight.

Johnny looked at me seriously. "I would."

"What a shitty thing to do!" I cried, though I knew he was

right. This had gone too far; I'd be wrong to endanger myself and, worse, others.

"I know," he said, and reached out a hand to grab my wrist and pull me a few steps closer to him. "I know. I'm sorry. But I have to."

I let him pull me up against him, and though I tried not to cry, I did. His hands smoothed my hair, over and over, and his breath whispered over the top of my head. I closed my eyes and held on to him, tight.

"But you don't even..." I let the protest trail away. I'd wanted this. Why was I fighting it so hard?

"I want to."

That wasn't what I'd been about to say, but I nodded. My cheek rubbed the front of his shirt. The buttons scratched. I pulled away and tipped my face to look up at him.

"Johnny?"

"Yeah, babe?"

I blinked at the endearment, which sounded so familiar. "Thanks."

He smiled and traced my eyebrows with his fingertip. He took my face in his hands and kissed my forehead. "You're welcome. Hell, I'm home all day, what the hell do I have to do but play chauffeur, anyway, for a pretty girl?"

He'd called me "girl" again, and the "pretty" didn't help. I looked up at him again. "That's really what you think about me, huh?"

He smoothed my hair again. "Isn't it what you are?"

"I'm a woman."

He laughed softly. "What's the difference?"

I licked my mouth and tasted tears. "Come upstairs and let me show you."

Something flickered in his gaze, swift and hot, and faded to be replaced by a strained smile. He didn't say no, though. I took his hand and put it on my hip. Rubbed it up and down my thigh. Before I could slide it between my legs, Johnny took his hand away.

"Emm. Don't."

I frowned. "Why not? You didn't seem to mind the other night in my kitchen."

"That was…different."

"How?" I challenged. "You came over to my house, you walked into my kitchen, and you got me off with your hand. The only thing that's different between then and now is that now we've had a date."

"Are you the sort of girl—sorry, woman—who fucks on the first date?" His accent got thicker when he was agitated.

It was too fucking sexy to be borne. "Only with you."

His eyes flashed again. His tongue crept out, the tiniest hint of pink, to tease his lower lip. He was seriously eye-fucking me; heat had risen between us, and I swore I could feel his cock getting thicker against my thigh. But he shook his head.

"Maybe I'm old-fashioned," Johnny said.

"Bullshit," I breathed, never looking away from his gaze. "You've fucked women whose names you didn't even know."

"That was a long time ago. Things were different then. Doesn't make it right, anyway."

"Are you going to make me beg?" I asked him.

"Jesus, Emm. No."

Everything about him had made me crazy. Unstrung. Undone. I'd never begged a man for anything, never wanted to. Never needed to.

I got on my knees, my cheek pressed to the inside of his knee. His hand came down to touch my hair. I nuzzled against him, the fabric of his trousers a little rough.

"I will," I said in a low voice. "I'll beg you to let me take that beautiful cock down the back of my throat."

Johnny made a noise. A low, groaning fucknoise.

"I'll beg you to fuck me, if that's what it takes." I whispered but had no doubts he heard me. I had my eyes closed, couldn't see him. Didn't have to. His fingers tightened in my hair, not yet pulling. "Please, Johnny. Fuck me."

He pulled me to my feet, one hand still tangled in my hair, the other gripping my upper arm hard enough to bruise. I've never been into pain, but I relished how hard he held me. I wanted him to mark me. I wanted to have proof of this, later.

His eyes were a little wild, his mouth wet when he spoke. "Is that really what you want?"

"Yes!" I leaned toward him, but he held me at arm's length. "It's what I want. I wanted it from the first time I ever saw you."

He groaned again. I knew that sound. His eyes never strayed from mine. He didn't smile. He pulled me closer. Slid a hand between my legs, the heel of his palm pressing my cunt.

It was my turn to moan.

Johnny pulled his hand away, though he stayed close. "You should go to bed."

"I'm trying to get you there."

He shook his head a little. "No, I mean…really to bed. To sleep. You were just… You just had a…"

I knew what he meant, but didn't move. "Sex has never triggered a fugue. If anything, the physical release helps keep them away."

"You," Johnny said, "are fucking with me."

"I'd like to be."

He looked at me with something like wonder, then looked stern. "I'm not doing anything until you've had a good night's sleep and gone to the doctor."

I blinked. "You're holding your cock hostage until I go to the doctor?"

He laughed, low and surprised. "You have a fucking mouth, you know that?"

I smiled. "Only for you."

He tilted his head a little in that familiar way, checking me out as though I'd reminded him of something. "Yeah."

"Take me to bed," I whispered, suddenly tired, my head aching, though no scent of oranges threatened me and I didn't feel faint. Just tired the way I always was at past eleven o'clock at night. "Come with me. Just…be with me, okay?"

He looked past me toward the hall. "I should go."

"What if I need you in the night?" I asked.

He looked back at me. "You think you might?"

I nodded. Johnny sighed, looking toward the hall again, then down to my face. He took it in both his hands, holding me still. His gaze burned into mine, and I tensed, waiting for him to kiss me.

"You want to stay," I whispered. "Just as much as I want you to. No matter what else you think about this, you do. Don't you?"

Johnny sighed. "Just to make sure you're okay. That's it."

I put my hands over his and shifted them so I could kiss his palms before linking our fingers together and holding his hands in front of me as I backed up a step. I led him up the stairs and down the hallway to my bedroom, which wasn't as clean as it should've been, but I hadn't been expecting a guest. I let go of his hands and he stopped just inside the door.

"I'm going to use the bathroom," I said. "Make yourself at home."

In the bathroom I was relieved to see that I didn't look too bad. My hair was messy and my eyes slightly red-rimmed, but that was from the tears, not from going dark. I turned my face from side to side, trying to see myself as he must, but I could only see myself as me.

I washed quickly and tossed my clothes into the hamper, then pulled on my oversize T-shirt. The floor was cold beneath my bare feet and I skipped along the hall until I got to my bedroom. I paused just inside the door. Johnny turned, the copy of *Cinema Americana* open on my desk, one hand holding open the pages. Beside it, I remembered, was a thick folder of glossy shots I'd printed off the internet. Shots of him from his movies, modeling days. Some pictures of his art. The DVD of *Night of a Hundred Moons* was there, too.

"Um," I said. "I'm really not a creepy stalker. I promise."

He flipped the book closed. "You know all that was a long, long time ago."

"I know." I went to the bed and pulled back the covers, then slipped into the sheets with a grimace at the chill. They'd warm up soon, but for the moment I felt a little shivery. I thought of something. "I don't have anything for you to wear. Sorry."

His fingers were already on the buttons at his throat, and he paused. "I can sleep in my shorts. It's okay."

Watching him undress was surreal—like watching a movie and yet totally different. I'd seen him make these very moves in films and grainy clips on the internet. And inside my head when I was dark. Now I knew just how he'd twist his wrist to loosen the buttons before he did it.

Johnny took off his shirt and looked around before hanging it carefully on the back of my desk chair. His chest was still sleek and bare, no hair on it. Still toned—admittedly not quite as muscular as it had been when he was in his twenties, but hell, I was nearly drooling, anyway. Then he undid his belt. His button. His zipper. I realized I was leaning forward, staring, mouth open with anticipation, only when he stopped with his hands hooked into his waistband and didn't push down his black dress trousers.

I closed my mouth. Sat back against the headboard. Surreptitiously, I wiped what I was sure would be drool from the corners of my mouth.

Johnny didn't move. "How about you turn out the lights?"

"What?" I looked at the lamp on my nightstand, but didn't touch it. "Why?"

"Why you need all this light in here?"

There was only the one small circle of light from the lamp, since he'd turned off the overhead light when I was in the bathroom. I studied him. "You know, for a guy who spent most of his career naked, you're charmingly modest."

"Yeah, naked," Johnny said. "I was a lot of fucking years younger back then. It was different."

I was used to being the one who was shy about my body, worried about a little extra baggage here and there. Cellulite. The men I'd gone to bed with had never seemed to care about their back zits, hairy asses, love handles. Johnny's hesitation charmed me, if it were possible to be further charmed.

"It's cold." I patted the covers. "Come to bed."

With a frown, he shoved his pants down, stepped out of them and took off his socks. He might've been worried about time, but he made even that awkward dance graceful. In his dark boxer briefs, he didn't have the body of a twenty-year-old. Nor a thirty-year-old. It didn't matter, he was still Johnny. Gorgeous and luscious.

I held out my hand. "Come to bed."

He did, sliding beneath the blankets and sitting against the headboard. He didn't look at me. I looked at him, though. His chest rose and fell too fast. A muscle ticked in his cheek.

"Johnny, seriously…"

"It's those fucking pictures," he said.

Pitchahs. God, I loved the way he talked. "What about them?"

He looked at me. The dimmish light hid the crow's-feet, the silver in his hair. He looked different, yes. Older, yes. But in a lot of ways it could've been Johnny-then in front of me. My heart skipped as another wave of surreality washed over me.

"I was so fucking young," he said in a low voice.

I put my hand on his shoulder and ran my fingertips down his arm to take his hand. "You're beautiful. You're one of the most beautiful men on the planet."

His mouth quirked a little at that. "Yeah, according to the art mags back in 1978."

"According to a lot of people, even now." I thought of all the fan sites.

"I don't care about what they think."

I circled my fingertip over his wrist and felt the pulse beat there. "According to me."

We stared at each other in silence for a few moments before I twisted in the sheets to turn out the light. Darkness covered us, and I blinked against it. Slowly, silver moonlight filled the spaces, making shadows. Johnny inched down in the bed and pulled me close to him, on my side. He spooned me, and though it wasn't at all the way I wanted to end up in bed with him, I wriggled as close as I could and fell asleep.

Or not asleep.

Chapter 20

I turned in a bed, tangled in sheets that weren't mine. I heard the sound of a toilet flush, the pad of bare feet, and in moments Johnny slid into bed beside me. Naked. I was naked, too.

"You awake?" Johnny ran a hand down my body.

I rolled toward him. "Yes."

"You thinking again?"

"Again?" I laughed softly, snuggling in closer. "Always."

"Whatcha thinking about?"

"You," I said. "This. Us. Everything."

His hand rested flat on my belly. "What about us? This and everything?

"Just that…" I sighed and rolled to face him. I slid my thigh between his to press us as close together as possible. "I don't know how long it will last. That's all."

"You can never be sure anything will last."

"That's the sort of thing you find easy to say in the dark," I told him.

Johnny laughed. "It is dark. And it's true. What, do you want it to end? This, us, everything?"

"I don't want it to. But it does. It will."

"Then we'll just have to make the most of it, won't we?"

As his cock nudged between us, my laugh turned to a sigh. "Yeah. I guess we will."

He kissed me, and I blinked. I ran my hands over his body, over broad shoulders, down a smooth chest. Over his ass, which was no longer naked but covered in soft cotton.

"Johnny?"

"Yeah, babe." It was Johnny-now talking to me. I could tell by the rougher timbre of his voice.

"I thought you said..." I didn't want to cry—I wasn't sad, but my breath hitched in my chest. "I thought you said you didn't want to..."

"Oh, Emm." His hands slid over my body, beneath the hem of my T-shirt, over my bare flesh. "How could you ever think I don't want this?"

He moved over me, pressing me into the mattress. He took my hands, moved them over my head, our fingers linked, to hold me still. I wasn't trying to move, but I liked when he did that, anyway.

We kissed for a long time. Soft and slow. The kisses got deeper and more desperate, but never sloppy. Johnny wasn't a sloppy kisser. He moved his mouth over my face, my throat. He let go of my hands to push up my shirt over my head. He kissed my breasts, sucking gently at my nipples until I couldn't breathe. Then down over my belly, the rough hint of his stubble scratching at my thighs.

When he kissed between my legs, I gasped and put my hand on top of his head. He paused. The bed shifted.

"This is how you like it," Johnny murmured against my skin.

He was right.

He made love to me with his mouth, tongue and lips moving over all the secret parts of me. His fingers slipped inside, stroking. I tilted my hips, giving him access.

My first orgasm rolled over me in slow, shuddering waves. When he kissed me, I tasted myself on him. I pulled him down close, feeling his cock thick and hard through his briefs. My mind mushy with passion, I whispered in his ear, "Condoms in the drawer."

He paused and pushed himself up on his hands to look down into my face. I had a sudden worry he'd protest the use of a rubber—and how disappointed I'd be if we couldn't make love because he refused. But Johnny only shook his head a little and reached into the nightstand for the box of condoms I couldn't even be sure hadn't expired.

We wriggled together, moving, taking off his briefs. Putting on the condom. He got on his knees, getting ready to push inside me, but I put a hand on his chest.

"Are you sure?" I asked.

Johnny kissed me. "I'm sure."

Then he slid inside me, all the way, and we moved together until I came again, this time with a gasp and a cry. He followed me, saying my name over and over again.

This time, when I closed my eyes, I didn't open them until morning.

"Morning," Johnny said from my doorway. He was already showered and dressed. His hair looked good slicked back from his face. He hadn't shaved, but he still looked good. He wore different clothes. "What time do you have to leave for work?"

I scrubbed at my face, sitting. "I have to be there by nine. Leave by eight-thirty. What'd you do, go home and come back?"

"Time for breakfast, then."

I looked at him and laughed. "You did the walk of shame."

"How else was I supposed to get something else to wear?"

"You woke up early, though. Got up in the dark?" I laughed

again and got out of bed. He didn't pull away when I stood on my toes to kiss him. "You were embarrassed."

"I always get up that early."

"You didn't used to," I said, not sure where that came from.

"I used to go to bed a lot later." His hands settled on my hips. "Don't you think you should get dressed?"

"Are you going to make me breakfast?"

"Do you want me to?" He laughed. "No. I'm a fucking bad cook."

"Then you'd better take me to the Mocha," I said.

It was a test. I half thought he'd fail it. But Johnny only nodded and looked me up and down.

"You'd better hurry it up, then. So you're not late for work."

I showered and dressed and put on my makeup, but when I thought to twist up my hair and secure it with the leather clip I'd bought, I couldn't find it, though I searched through my jumbled drawer of hair ties and bobby pins.

"Emm! C'mon!"

"Coming!" I left it, putting my hair in a braid instead and skipping out to follow him.

When we walked into the Mocha together, it was a little like being the prom king and queen entering the gym. Everyone looked. Everyone stared. And Johnny took my hand, our fingers shielded by gloves but still linking tight.

"Hey," he said to Carlos, who hadn't yet set up his laptop. "How's it going?"

"Morning, Carlos." I beamed. It sort of felt triumphant, maybe a little catty, but I didn't care.

Carlos nodded at both of us. "They got pumpkin spice lattes on the board today. They're good."

"I know what I'm getting," I said.

Johnny squeezed me next to him. "Yeah. Me, too."

He drove me to work and it felt a little strange, but not too much. He kissed me in the parking lot and told me to call him half an hour before I needed to leave work.

And that was how it started.

That. Us. Everything.

And it was good. Really good. Johnny was a man, not a boy, just like I'd told my mother.

He did what he said he was going to do. If Johnny told me he'd be there to pick me up from work, he wasn't late. If he promised to pick up something for dinner, he did that, too. Because he worked his own hours, he had more flexibility than I did, which worked out well in my favor, since he insisted I either go to the doctor or voluntarily give up my driving privileges. I accepted his offer to be my chauffeur.

We didn't talk about the fugues, and I was glad for that. If sometimes I caught him looking at me with a curious expression, I ignored it. What we had was good, and real, and it worked.

Johnny's daughter, Kimmy, was a different story. As he'd warned me, she wasn't exactly welcoming. She was, I thought, her mother's daughter, even if I only had my imagination to tell me what her mother was like.

It was Johnny's day to take his grandson, Charlie, who ran through the front door and into Johnny's arms in a whirlwind of small boy, then ran off again just as fast into the TV room to play with the Wii on the big screen. Kimmy stayed in the doorway like she needed to be invited in, something I knew wasn't true.

"Emm, I want you to meet my daughter, Kimmy. Kimmy, this is Emm. I told you about her."

Kimmy looked me up and down with a sniff, then said to her father, right in front of me, "They keep getting younger, Dad."

"Maybe you're just getting older." It probably wasn't the

best response I could've made, but instead of hauling off and punching me in the teeth, Kimmy actually smiled.

"She speaks. Imagine that."

"Kimmy," Johnny said with a sigh, but made no apologies for her. "Christ, lay off, will ya?"

I liked that he wasn't trying to make us into best friends. Not that I'd have minded being friendly with Johnny's daughter, who my mind insisted on remembering clad in a dirty onesie and stinking diaper. Just that I didn't need to kiss her ass to feel important.

"My father," Kimmy said, "has a history of dating dumb blondes. I mean really dumb. Like dirt-dumb."

"I'm not blonde," I said, not pointing out that she, in fact, was.

"Not dumb, either," Kimmy said grudgingly with another sweep of her gaze up and down over me. "Any kids?"

"Kimmy, Jesus," Johnny said.

"Not yet," I told her. "You worried about losing your place in Daddy's affections?"

"No." She smiled grudgingly. "I guess he didn't tell you he's been fixed."

Johnny slapped a hand over his eyes with a groan. "For fuck's sake."

We hadn't ever discussed anything remotely like marriage or children, but that didn't mean I hadn't thought about it. "I didn't know he was broken."

Kimmy laughed. "Dad, God, you should've warned her you've had all the kids you need. Right? Isn't that what you said? You do know he has other kids, right? There's me, I'm the oldest. Then there's Mitchell and what's the other one's name?"

"Logan," Johnny said.

"At least that one's younger than you are," Kimmy offered, like that was a prize.

"I know about Johnny's kids." The internet, of course.

He looked at me, faintly surprised but only for a second. "Give it a rest, Kimmy. Seriously."

"Grampa!" Charlie appeared in the hall, waving a Wii remote. "This one doesn't work. It needs new batteries."

Johnny looked back and forth between us and put up his hands. "I gotta take care of the kid. Emm, toss her out on her ass if she gets mouthy."

My brows rose as he went after Charlie and they both disappeared into the living room. I faced Kimmy. "You know, he's not a bone we have to fight over. I'm not interested in getting in between you or anything. And I have my own daddy, so really, this isn't about that. You should chill out and back off."

To my surprise, she backed down. She actually laughed. "I'm just warning you what you're getting into. You're young, Emm. He's old, that's all."

"I guess that's my business. Are you as kind to warn off all his other girlfriends?"

Kimmy shook her head. "Seeing as how none of them ever lasted more than a couple of months, I didn't have to."

"Huh." I studied her. "We've only been seeing each other for a couple of weeks. Yet I get the special treatment."

She looked at me, hard. "You're the first girlfriend he's ever had around Charlie. I told him a long time ago that he wasn't allowed to trot his part-time fucks through my kid's life. And he never has."

I chewed the inside of my cheek for a second, finding compassion for her. True, I didn't really know her mother but I had read about her on some of those fan sites, and Johnny had alluded to the way Kimmy had been raised. "I have no intention of getting between Johnny and Charlie, either."

"No. My dad's been an asshole in the past, but I trust him with my kid. If you're important enough to him to share Charlie with you, that means something." She looked me up and down again. "You're really not his usual type at all."

I laughed. "I'll take that as a compliment."

Kimmy gave me a grudging grin. "It should be."

"I'm not going to try to be your stepmother."

She rolled her eyes. "As if you could. And please, for the love of God, call me Kim."

We both laughed at that, and from the living room came the sounds of cheering. She looked that way, then back at me. "He's good with Charlie. Really good. Sometimes I'm jealous that my son gets to experience my dad in a way I never did."

"I can understand that."

She shrugged. "Yeah, well, I'm also a grown woman who needs to get over it. And besides, when Charlie's with my dad, that gives me some peace and quiet."

"I can understand that, too."

She nodded slowly. "So long as you know what you're getting into. That's all."

"Thanks for the warning," I said, rolling my eyes in imitation of her. "But I'm also a grown woman. I'm okay."

"Yeah," she said. "You are."

With Kimmy out of the way—sort of—the next hurdle to cross was my parents. Of course I had to tell my mom that we'd started seeing each other. Even though she wasn't calling me every day the way she used to, there was no way for me to hide my new relationship from her. And no reason. I knew she wasn't thrilled about the age difference, but I suspected my dad would be the one less likely to accept Johnny as his daughter's boyfriend. After all, they were close enough in age to be brothers.

A dinner party seemed like a great idea. I could show off my new place to my parents, impress them with my independence and introduce them to my new boyfriend, his daughter and her son all at the same time. I also invited Jen and her new boyfriend, Jared—it was official now!

"Why did I offer to do this?" I groaned, up to my elbows in lasagna that didn't want to congeal and a chocolate cake that had fallen in the center. "This is madness!"

"At least it ain't Sparta," Johnny said from his seat at the island, where he was scooping homemade guacamole onto tortilla chips and downing them like they were going out of style.

"Very funny. You don't think your precious Kimmy isn't going to be noting what a crappy cook I am?"

Johnny laughed. "Do you care what Kimmy thinks of your cooking? She's coming, isn't she? If she really didn't like you, she'd have said, 'Fuck you,' to the invitation. That's more Kimmy's style."

"Yeah, she is more an in-your-face kinda gal, isn't she?" I put the liquidy lasagna back in the oven and washed my hands.

Johnny came up behind me to put his arms around me, fingers linked over my belly. "What, you think I'm not nervous about meeting your folks?"

I leaned against him. "You think my dad's going to try and kick your ass?"

"I guess I have to let him if he does, huh?" Johnny nuzzled against my ear, sending shivers all through me. "Just to keep the peace."

I turned in his arms and linked my hands behind his neck. "My dad isn't going to be thrilled, but my parents will both like you."

"You sure about that?"

I stood on my toes to kiss him thoroughly. "Sure. They're good parents. They want me to be happy. That's what's important to them."

Johnny looked down into my eyes. "Are you?"

"Happy?" I asked, wondering how he could possibly think anything else. "Deliriously."

He might've kissed me then if the doorbell hadn't rung. We pulled apart with a laugh, and Johnny swatted my ass as I headed for the front door. I looked over my shoulder at him, standing there so naturally in my kitchen, and took an extra couple of seconds just to admire him and marvel at how lucky I was before the bell rang again.

Jen and Jared arrived first, bearing a loaf of crusty Italian bread and a bottle of wine. Kimmy and Charlie came a few minutes later, bringing some dessert and a hand-drawn picture Charlie had made specifically for my fridge. I put it in a place of honor with magnets advertising a local pizza shop and caught Kimmy's approving glance as Charlie took his grandpa's hand and started chattering a mile a minute. My parents came last, laden with shopping bags and full of hugs and kisses. I held my breath as Johnny let go of Charlie's small hand to shake my father's.

"Nice to meetcha," Johnny said without a trace of the nervousness he'd earlier claimed.

"You, too," my dad said, then, "How about those Eagles?"

"Robbed," Johnny said, like he knew what he was talking about, and I was glad he did, because I had no clue. "Absolutely robbed."

And that was that.

Charlie charmed my mother, while Kimmy warmed to Jen and Jared for reasons I couldn't discern. She warmed to me, too, after a glass of wine. My dad and Johnny talked sports and politics, two subjects that could easily have led to an argument, but they both seemed to agree on everything.

The lasagna didn't look pretty, but it tasted fantastic, and sitting around my dining room table with all the people in my life who were important, I was glad I'd decided on the dinner party, after all. Every now and then, Johnny would slide a casual arm behind me, give me a squeeze, hold my hand for half a minute. Small, casual touches that made it clear we were a couple. And nobody seemed to mind at all.

"He's nice," my mother said in the kitchen as I dished leftover lasagna into plastic containers and set the pan to soak. "Very nice."

"I know, Mom. Johnny's...great." I turned to look at the sound of her chuckle. "What?"

"I've never seen you like that about a man before, that's all."

I shrugged. "He's different."

"I can see that. Oh, listen here. I brought you some things. Where did Daddy put the bags? Oh, here they are." My mom answered her own question. "Laundry detergent, some cleaning spray..."

"Mom, I do go to the store myself."

"I know, I know, but your dad likes to shop at Costco, and it's too much for us now that you're not home. I just brought you some extra. Look at these cleaning wipes." She held them up. "Antibacterial!"

My hands covered in suds, I turned with a laugh to shake my head at her gift. "Great. Thanks."

Citrus-scented, antibacterial cleaning wipes, just what I needed.

Citrus.

Oranges.

Dark.

Chapter 21

"No. No, no, no, no!" I stumbled forward two steps, my hands still covered in suds from the sink I'd left behind. "Oh, damn it, no."

Darkness. I blinked rapidly, my eyes adjusting. The smell of oranges had faded, replaced by the faint hint of heat and chlorine and motor exhaust—familiar scents. I was back in the world my mind had created for me so I could be close to Johnny.

But I didn't need this now. I had him for real. In my real life. Clenching my fists, I gritted my teeth and concentrated on going back.

Nothing.

I was standing in the side yard of Johnny's town house. From the splashing and laughter I could hear from around the corner, there was a poolside party going on. Maybe they were filming another movie. I didn't much care. I wanted out of here, back to consciousness. Back to my own time.

I let myself into the kitchen, expecting to find Johnny and coming across Ed instead. He was slumped at the kitchen table, a cigarette in one hand and an ashtray full of butts in front of him. Also, a bottle of vodka, almost empty. And next to that, a rolled cloth pouch with a syringe on it.

"Emm. Emma. Emmaline. Emm," he said, not slurring, though his eyes looked red and bloodshot.

He stank, even from across the room. I winced. "Ed. Where is everyone?"

"Swimming. Skinny-dipping. Fucking." His laugh chilled me. "Getting high. Where are they always? What are they always doing? You looking for Johnny, right? He's waiting for you."

"What do you mean, waiting for me?"

"Johnny says you're coming." Ed waved his cigarette and smoke wafted toward me. "Johnny says he's waiting for you. You'll show up. You always do. He's a little drunk, a little high, but he's not fucking. Why isn't he fucking, Emm? Because he's waiting for you."

I frowned and hugged myself, though the kitchen was as sticky-hot as it had always been every other time my mind had brought me here. "Thanks for letting me know. Where is he? Upstairs?"

"He's out by the pool. Paul is taking pictures of him. Naked," Ed added with another chilling laugh that rose the hairs on the back of my neck. "Showing off his ass again. I told you, they're drunk and high."

"And not fucking. I get it." I ran some cold water in the sink and scooped a handful, then splashed my face.

It looked like I was going to have to ride this out, that was all. I almost didn't want to find Johnny here. Somewhere, my mother was talking to me about cleaning wipes. I couldn't do what I'd always done in this place, not knowing she was waiting for me to answer her. Maybe even getting concerned, saying my name, shaking my shoulder. I couldn't fuck Johnny in front of my mother, even if she wasn't really there and I wasn't really here.

"You wanna know what Johnny says about you, Emmaline?"

I looked at Ed. Now I noticed he had a pen and a leather-bound notebook in front of him. It hadn't been there before. All these details, tiny details, making my brain fuzzy.

"What does he say?"

"He says you ain't real. That you're not a real girl, you're made up. Maybe we're all imagining you, I said, but he said not that. Just that you come from someplace else. Is that right, Emmaline? You come from some other place?"

"Yeah, Ed. I do," I answered, tired. "And I'd like to go back to it."

His laugh guttered into a wheeze, and he drew in another breath of smoke. "Good luck with that. Don't we all want to go on to another place?"

The counter dug into my back as I leaned against it. From outside came the sound of more laughter. Quite the party going on. It sounded like fun. More fun than this bizarre and tilted conversation with a man who'd slit his wrists and eventually drown himself in that very pool.

"He says you're from the future."

"What?" This startled me into standing upright. "Johnny says that?"

"He says you told him."

I blinked, then paced the linoleum floor. "That's just crazy."

"Yeah. That's what Johnny says. Says he must be fucking crazy. That we all are. We should all end up in the fucking nuthouse, right? All of us. Johnny says you told him you made us all up. So lemme ask you something, Emmaline. If you made me up, why'd you make me such a fucking mess?"

"I don't know. I don't know what to say to that." Was it a lie to say he was right? What happened when your hallucinations learned that's what they were?

"Just tell me if it's true, that's all." Ed took a long drink from the bottle and toyed for a moment with the syringe, but didn't, thank God, use it. "I just want to know if I'm real. Or not real."

"You are…real," I said, hesitating. "I mean, you're a real person, Ed. But this isn't real. This is just in my head. This conversation isn't real."

"Tonight's the night," Ed said suddenly with a jerk of his chin toward the calendar.

"For what?"

"Making me real, I guess." He nodded as though this made sense, which was more than it did for me. He drank again, finishing the final swallows while the bottle gurgled. "So, who do I blame for all this shit?"

"I don't know. Me?" I spread my fingers. "You could blame me."

He looked up at me with bleary eyes and a crooked smile. "I could, I guess. But I don't think I will. You know I wrote a poem about you?"

I shuddered. "No. I didn't know."

"I did." He pulled his notebook toward him, cleared his throat and read aloud.

She walks in night,
A beauty.
Single, tiny steps on bare toes, shoes left behind.
Puppet-master, girl-made-woman, she comes and goes.
She makes us, and she breaks us, too. Spinning her dreams,
She is what she becomes. She can be anything she wants to be.
Emmaline.

I was no more able to appreciate poetry than I could art, but that didn't sound very good. It sounded sort of pretentious and self-important, the sort of poem Goth kids would read aloud to one another while they refreshed their eyeliner and discussed the layers of meaning. People would make blog posts about it, quoting, without knowing what it really meant.

"It doesn't mean anything," I said sourly.

"No?" Ed sounded surprised and looked it over, running his finger over the words. "You're right. Doesn't mean a fucking thing."

Because he didn't write it. My fugue brain did. And because I wasn't a poet, the poem sucked. That was the truth of all of this. I was the puppet-master, pulling the strings. Making and breaking everything here. And I wanted to be done with making.

I wanted to break all of it.

So, I did.

Bright light. The sound of murmuring voices. I blinked, wincing, something soft beneath my head and something sharp stinging the back of my hand. A weight on the other, fingers held tight.

"Hey," Johnny said softly from beside the bed. "You're awake."

"What?" I struggled to get up, the smell of hospital rushing in all around me. Choking.

The sting on my hand was an IV, and Johnny shushed me. I quieted at once, sinking back onto the pillows. I was still wearing what I'd had on at the dinner party, so at least I hadn't been here long enough for them to strip me down and put a hospital gown on me. My throat was dry, and before I could ask, Johnny had a plastic cup of water for me, with a straw.

I sipped. "What happened? Where are my parents and everyone else?"

"Your mom and dad are probably in the waiting room. The

others went home. Jen wanted to stay, but I convinced her boyfriend to take her home. I'll call her, tell her you're okay."

"Shit," I muttered. "Am I? I went dark, didn't I?"

"Yeah, babe, you did."

"How long this time?"

"It's been about three hours. Your mom didn't wait as long as I did the last time." Johnny laughed, shaking his head. "You were only out for ten minutes before she had the ambulance on its way."

"Oh, God." I groaned and covered my eyes with the hand attached to the IV, which was a mistake because it pulled hard on the port and hurt. "Shit."

"You just went blank," Johnny said.

I looked at him through my fingers. "Just? That's not comforting. Unless you mean it's better than falling down, frothing at the mouth and pissing myself. Then, yeah, I guess it's better."

Tears clogged my voice, and Johnny stood to kiss me softly, even though I tried to turn my face. He kissed me, anyway, and smoothed my hair from my forehead. He kissed my mouth, then my cheek, and squeezed my hand.

"They're going to run some tests on you. And you probably have to stay overnight."

"No," I said. "Absolutely not."

"Emm," he said warningly.

"I'm not staying. You know there's nothing they can do, Johnny. You know it." There was no reason he should, really, since we'd barely ever discussed my problem in detail, but he nodded reluctantly. "But there goes my license. There goes… shit, everything!"

"Not everything," Johnny said quietly. "Not me."

I cried then. He sat and held my hand and handed me tissues. It didn't last long—I didn't have many tears left for situations like this. When it had passed, he kissed me again. I realized something.

"They let you in here with me? Not my mom or dad?"

"She said, your mom said, I should sit with you."

I blinked tear-swollen eyes. "Get out of here. Are you kidding me?"

"Nope." Johnny grinned.

"She must really like you," I whispered, and wept again.

It went on a little longer this time, and again he handed me tissues when the ones I was using grew sodden and fell apart. He gave me water, too, holding the cup for me, though I was anything but an invalid. And then he went to the bathroom and got me a damp cloth to wash my face.

They did, indeed, do tests that went on pretty late into the night. Drew lots of blood. Ordered a CAT scan, which couldn't be done until the tech came in and which I refused, though the attending physician did his best to bully me into it. I had a lot of years of practice dealing with doctors and hospitals, and I wasn't being a pain for the sake of being a jerk. I knew the tests would show nothing. They'd prescribe me some meds, maybe. Keep me longer. Bill my insurance for thousands of dollars, much of which I'd have to pay back since I'd been fortunate enough not to have yet met my deductible.

"I want to go home," I told the doctor firmly. "Look at my records. This has happened before. It'll probably happen again."

I hated admitting that.

"And I have someone who can stay with me," I added, indicating Johnny, who nodded. "I'm not driving. I'll sign myself out against medical advice, if that's what you want."

The doctor, who looked tired and possibly not much older than me, rubbed at his eyes and the scruff of his beard. He sighed heavily. "Fine. Fine. I'll get the discharge order ready."

He pointed a finger at me. "But if you die, I'm going to kill you."

I didn't think I'd be able to laugh, but I did. "Fair enough."

My parents met us in the lobby, my dad looking tired and my mom white-faced. I braced myself for the rush of scolding, her insistence she come home with me, or worse, go home with them. Instead, my mom only hugged me close. She let me go, and looked at Johnny.

"You take care of her," my mother said.

"Yes, ma'am. I will." Johnny put his arm around my shoulders.

But this wasn't enough for me. I couldn't, in fact, believe it. I followed my mom to their car, which was parked next to Johnny's. My dad was already in the driver's seat, and Johnny got into his car to warm it up, leaving us alone.

"Mom," I said.

"Emmaline," my mother said. "That man... Your Johnny..."

"I can't believe you're letting me go home with him," I told her.

She hugged me hard. Tight. I hugged her, too.

"I have to," she said into my ear, then took my face into her hands and held it still so she could search my gaze with her own.

"What?"

She shook her head and looked over her shoulder at Johnny in his car. She shook her head again, brow furrowed, then looked at me. She choked off a sob, shaking her head, trying to get control. Watching her force away the tears made it hard for me to resist my own, but I managed. My mom squeezed my face, then let me go.

"He's a good man. And even though I'm worried sick about you, I'm sure you'd rather have him there than me. So...I'm letting him take you. But you call me tomorrow, first thing!" She shook her finger, then clung to me in another hug. "Oh, my precious girl, it is killing me, but…"

"Thanks, Mom," I said quietly into her ear as we squeezed each other. "Thank you."

"You call me," she said, letting me go. "Tomorrow!"

"I will."

She nodded and hugged me again, but didn't linger. She got into the car next to my dad and shut the door. I could see them both talking, but not hear what they said. Johnny opened his car door, got out, walked around to the passenger side to open it for me.

"So chivalrous," I said when he'd settled back in the driver's seat.

He looked at me. "You sure you don't want to stay?"

I shook my head. "They're not going to do anything, and I feel fine. I just want to go home to my own bed. Get at least a couple hours of sleep. Tomorrow's Saturday. We can sleep in."

Johnny leaned across the seat to kiss me. He stroked my hair. Then, in silence, we drove home. I looked out the window at icy streets, snowbanks. My breath fogged the glass. I fisted my hands in my lap, thinking of the fugue, of Johnny-then and Johnny-now. Wondering how all of this was going to work out. Hating the fact I had to depend on him, and hoping it wasn't going to ruin everything that had just begun.

Chapter 22

At home, Johnny stayed with me while I showered. He didn't say it was because he was worried I'd go dark in the shower and drown or something, but I knew that was why, and though we shared the water and the sponge, I didn't even try to turn this into something erotic. When we dried off and I put on an entirely unsexy flannel nightgown, he tucked me into bed and got in beside me.

I turned on my side, away from him, staring into the darkness without being tired. Johnny's breathing deepened. I felt the weight of him shift as he went boneless into sleep. And I blinked and blinked, the pattern of light coming through the window shifting. The temperature, too. The sheets underneath me.

When he rolled against my back, his hand going flat to my belly, I wanted to turn and face him. I wanted to know if this was Johnny-now or Johnny-then. If I was dreaming, or had gone dark, or if I was just so tired the bed had felt like it was shifting underneath me. But I didn't turn to see him. I didn't speak. And Johnny, whichever one he was, pressed up real against me. Whether it was the truth or a lie concocted by my brain, he was real.

* * *

I went back to work on Monday. Johnny dropped me off and tilted his face for a kiss in the parking lot. I gave it to him, but didn't linger the way I had just a week before. I didn't mean to be grouchy, I didn't want to resist him, but depending on him this way was already wearing me thin in places that hadn't been very thick to begin with.

I did my job with expertise and not enthusiasm. When he picked me up at the end of the day, I got in the car hoping no coworkers would see me. Of course I'd had to report what happened to Human Resources, not because I wanted anyone to know, but because if something happened on the job I had to let someone know what to do. I put on my seat belt without looking at him, and I stared out the window all the way home.

He took me to my house and came in with me, though when I hung up my coat he didn't take off his. "Emm."

I looked at him. "Yeah?"

"Do you want me to go? I can go home."

"No. You can stay."

Johnny gave me a look. "I thought maybe we'd have dinner out tonight. You want to go out to eat? I'll take you anywhere you want."

Normally, I'd have leaped at the offer, but I just shook my head. "I feel like staying in. Vegging out. Get caught up on TV or something."

Johnny put his hands in his pockets. "You want me to go, you should just say so."

"You can stay," I repeated.

"Do you *want* me to stay?" he asked, and I wanted to laugh at everyone who'd ever written or said that Johnny Dellasandro was a dim bulb. Just then he was very bright, so bright I couldn't look at him.

"You can if you want to," I told him, unable to make myself

say more than that because I didn't want to be a liar, and I didn't want to hurt his feelings, either.

"Nah. I'll go home. Get caught up on my own stuff," Johnny said.

He kissed me before he left. At least there was that. He held me close and hugged me until I hugged him back, though it took me a few seconds to bend. He kissed my temple and squeezed me. Then he left.

I watched him go.

I wasn't angry at Johnny, and just then I was pretty furious with myself. I had what I wanted, finally, and I was pushing it away. But I couldn't help it. Johnny wasn't everything I wanted. I wanted a brain that worked, damn it. One that didn't flip-flop me all around and make me no better than a child.

I did, indeed, veg and watch TV. Well, I flipped through the channels, unable to find any one program that could keep my attention. I texted Jen, who replied that she was hanging with Jared, and did I want to come over and hang with them?

I did not.

I went to bed alone and angry, nobody to blame but myself.

Johnny didn't flee screaming from my bitchery, which is what I'd have done in his place. He was infinitely patient with me. Driving me to work, picking me up, sitting beside me silent on the couch while we watched stupid movies or sleeping next to me without seeming to mind that I turned to face away from him every night with barely a kiss.

I didn't want to become this sexless, irritable bag of woe. I hated it, in fact, yet I couldn't seem to break myself out of it. Hanging with Jen didn't help. She was thoroughly head over heels for Jared, who seemed equally as enamored, and of course I was happy for her, but it made it impossible to talk about what was going on with me when our duo had become a quartet Saturday mornings at the Mocha.

Carlos had a clue. He cornered me one morning as I ducked in, leaving Johnny waiting for me in the car, to grab us both a couple of coffees. “Trouble in paradise, huh?”

“What are you talking about?”

“Your face is sour. What, you got him, now you don’t want him?”

I stopped, clutching two paper cups that were so hot they were going to burn me through my gloves. “I don’t know what you’re talking about.”

Carlos snorted. “You don’t look happy, that’s all.”

“It has nothing to do with Johnny,” I told him.

“Yeah? Well, if I were you, I’d make sure he knew it.” Carlos cast a significant glance toward the car idling at the curb. “I mean, a dude like that, he doesn’t really need to put up with any shit, you know?”

I knew it. And as I slid into the car and handed Johnny his cup, I also leaned across to kiss him. He looked at me, surprised.

“What’s that for?”

“I’m sorry,” I said. “I’ve been a bitch.”

He laughed and kissed me. “Yeah. So? I figure you’re a little entitled. Besides, I knew it wouldn’t last.”

Being forgiven, especially for something you know is your fault, is an easy spirit-lifter. “Oh, really? You know that?”

“I knew it,” he said, and pulled into traffic.

“How? What if I’d turned out to be a supermegatwat forever?”

He shook his head, smiling as he cast me a quick glance before putting his eyes back on the road. “Nah. I told you. I knew it would get better.”

I turned in my seat to face him, the seat belt digging into me a little. “How?”

He sighed. "Because you told me, Emmaline."

"I did?" I frowned. "When?"

Johnny hesitated and reached for my hand. He squeezed it. "One time when..."

"I talked when I was dark?" I knew sometimes I did.

"Yeah." He hesitated again, but nodded.

"What else did I say?"

"Nothing. But it's okay, honey, I'm just glad you're feeling better. That's all."

I didn't deserve it to be this easy and told him so. "It's not a good excuse, Johnny."

He was pulling into the parking lot of the credit union by this time, and he put the car into Park before turning to me. "No, it's not. But it's okay. Believe me, I've had my share of asshole moments. I can give someone the benefit of the doubt."

"I love you," I said, and kissed him before the words I'd let slip out could embarrass me. "I mean..."

"I love you, too, Emm," Johnny said.

The kiss was longer and more thorough this time. Tongue. Hands got a little frisky. We were steaming up the windows.

I let my forehead rest against his shoulder for a second. I never wanted to be that girl, the one who said, "Do you? Do you really love me? Do you?" And the funny thing was, with Johnny, I didn't feel like that. If anything, our mutual announcement had felt pretty anticlimactic.

"Do you really?" I asked, anyway.

He kissed my forehead. "Hell, yeah."

I laughed and kissed his mouth. "I love you. Love, love, love!"

"Get outta here," Johnny said. "Before you're late for work, Jesus."

"Ah, there's the grouchy pants I first met," I teased. "That's more like it."

"You like it when I'm grouchy."

"I do. Sort of like Mr. Darcy. All brooding and stuff." I tickled him, and Johnny laughed, pulling away. I caught the end of his scarf and held him still for another kiss. "Say it again."

"I love you," Johnny said.

"Love you, too," I told him, and got out of the car.

That night, in my bed, I didn't turn away from him. "Do you mind sleeping over here so often?"

Johnny, who'd been reading, took off the glasses he didn't like and I privately had been fetishizing. "No. Do you want to stay at my house instead?"

"It's not that." I ran a hand over his hair, ruffling it, thinking of how it felt in my fugues. Rough silk. It felt the same in real life, too. "I just want to make sure you're okay with it."

"Well..." He folded his glasses, then put the book on the nightstand to roll to face me. "I like your place. And I spend all day in mine when you're at work, if I'm not at the gallery. So it's okay."

I traced his lips with a fingertip, not pulling away when he bit it lightly. "I just want things to be fair, that's all."

"Emm," Johnny said, and kissed my palm. "I don't care. So long as I'm in a bed with you in it, I don't really fucking care which one it is."

"You," I murmured, "have a fucking mouth."

He laughed. We kissed. The kiss became a cuddle, then something more. I couldn't believe I'd been passing this up night after night. Okay, so maybe only a week or so of nights. Still, too many. When faced with the delectableness of Johnny's cock rising between us, I found it hard to believe I could ever pass it up again.

"Nice," he said when I stroked him. "Keep doing that."

"This?" I arched a brow and continued the rhythm until his eyes grew heavy-lidded. "You like that?"

"Fucking love it," Johnny said.

"I know something else you'll love." Grinning, I slid down under the blankets, into the dark, and found his cock with my mouth. His groan was muffled but entirely satisfactory when I took him in as deep as I could.

The air was close beneath here, but I didn't care. His scent covered me. Sexy as hell. His erection, thick in my mouth, tasted sexy, too. I lost myself in sucking, licking, even gently nibbling with my lips covering my teeth to keep from biting too hard.

He thrust a little, not too much. Not choking me. I stroked his balls with my hand, then followed the path of my palm and licked him there, too. I grinned against his flesh as I heard another muffled curse. His hand came down to wind in my hair, tugging and pushing gently, setting the pace. I let him. I liked knowing he was feeling good. It made me feel good, too.

I was feeling even better when I used my free hand to slide between my legs and stroke myself. My scent joined his, there in the cave I'd made of bedsheets and blankets. I circled my clit with my fingers, slowly, easing into the sensation.

The air got hotter as I did, too. I moved my mouth along his cock, sucking a little harder at the top when he pushed into my mouth. I used a hand, too, stroking along with every slide of my mouth and lips on his flesh. He'd set the pace, but I teased him every so often by slowing down, swirling my tongue, twisting my grip on his shaft. I was aiming to make this a truly stellar blow job. I couldn't stand the heat, though, and paused to throw off the covers.

Cool air, not cold, flooded over me. I nuzzled at Johnny's cock, feeling him tug my hair a little harder to get me to look up. I did, smiling.

Johnny-then pulled me up to his mouth, his hands roaming. Cupping a breast, tweaking a nipple, replacing his fingers with his mouth while his hand slid down to move between my legs.

I was too stunned to move. I'd had no warning, nothing. And my body wasn't protesting this, not at all.

"Johnny—"

"Shh," he said against my breast, fingers making magic on my clit. He drew me to his mouth again, and I gasped into it.

I didn't want to protest this, but I thought I should. Still, as he urged me to straddle him with his hands on my hips, I did. When he took his cock in his hand and guided it inside me, I let him. When he kissed me, I kissed him back.

Johnny-then.

Johnny-now.

Was there a difference? Just then, swept up in our lovemaking, no. He tasted and felt and smelled and sounded the same.

He thrust up inside me slowly, one hand positioned to rub my clitoris with each movement. Orgasm swelled inside me, made me stupid with desire. Made me not care about anything but what was going on.

Then.

Now.

I let my head fall back, my hair tumbling over my shoulders, tickling. I rode him. We rocked. He made a fucknoise that sent pleasure spiraling through me, and I came with a stutter, a flutter, a shudder.

I sank onto him, my face buried against his neck. Smelling. Feeling. Tasting. With my eyes closed, I didn't know if I was locked in my imagination or back in the real world. His hand stroked over my hair, and he flipped a sheet over us. I kept my eyes closed, my face pressed to his skin.

"That was fucking fantastic," Johnny said.

"It always is."

He laughed. "Yeah. It always is."

"Listen, Johnny..." I licked at the salt of his skin and he shifted at the touch of my tongue. "Thank you."

"For what?"

"For loving me, even when I'm a bitch."

He was silent. Our breathing synced, rising and falling at the same time. His fingers tangled in my hair at the base of my skull. "You're not a bitch, Emm."

"I was angry…not at you. Just at everything. And I might be that way again, Johnny. Because it's hard, knowing that my head could send me spinning at any time."

He was quiet for another second, before he said, "Everyone has bad days."

I laughed a little hoarsely. "Does that make it okay to be a jerk to you?"

He kissed the top of my head. "What do you want me to say?"

"I guess…I just want you to say that you'll forgive me when I'm being a douchenozzle to you."

His entire body twitched and jerked with laughter. "What the fuck is a…. Fuck, Emm. Sure. Okay. I'll forgive you."

He kissed the top of my head again, holding me close. I still had my eyes closed. I was drifting a little, sleepy. Could I sleep inside a fugue? Dream inside a dream?

"I'll forgive you," Johnny said.

Chapter 23

Whoever I'd fucked the night before, I woke up with Johnny-now. We made love again before I forced myself into the shower and then to breakfast. No Mocha for us that morning, just bagels and coffee at my kitchen island. Very domestic. Very sweet. Very normal.

Because it was his night to be working late at the gallery, I asked Jen to hang out with me after work. We hadn't had a girls' night in a long time. First we swung by Arooga's Sports Bar and picked up some crazy amount of hot wings in all different flavors, along with a couple of six-packs of beer. At my house we kicked off our shoes and changed into lounging pants.

"This is another reason we're friends." I pointed at her duck-patterned pj bottoms. "You always come prepared."

Jen laughed. "Girl, do you know how long it's been since I just lounged around in elastic-waist pants getting my feed on? Too long, that's how long."

"What, you and Jared don't hang out in matching pajama pants?"

"Not yet. Do you and Johnny even wear pants?"

I laughed and opened the container and set it out on the

coffee table. "Sure we do. When we're not too busy being naked."

"Yeah, yeah." Jen grinned. "So, spill it. I know it's kinda creepy, but I want to know all the details. All of them!"

"Only if you share yours." I popped the cap on a bottle of Guinness and admired the steam wisping from the top. "Just to be fair and all."

"Girl, I'm pretty sure my details aren't as exciting."

I picked out a wasabi wing and licked my fingers of extra sauce as I gave her a look. "Get out of here. Jared's verrrry cute."

"Oh, he is. But you know, he's no Johnny fucking Dellasandro, that's all." Jen chose an Old Bay seasoned wing and nibbled it.

I paused and put the wing on my plate. "Really, you're not pissed off? I know you said you weren't. But…really, Jen?"

She looked surprised. "Hell, no! I mean, it's not like I ever had a shot with him and besides, honestly, Emm…he was always a fantasy. Not real. I'm happy he's real for you."

I thought of the fugues. "He's a fantasy for me, too."

"Well…yeah." Jen sounded confused, and no wonder. "I'm sure that's part of it."

I wanted to tell her. I wanted to tell someone, and I didn't want to tell Johnny that I'd fallen so hard for his young self before even saying a word to the man he was now. I didn't want him to think it was only the movies and the "pitchahs." I wanted him to know it was him, no matter how it happened, even if…even if I wasn't so certain myself.

"What's up?" Jen licked spices from her fingertips. "Is it… not as good? I mean…is the reality not so good? You can tell me. It'll break my heart, but you can tell me."

"No. Nothing like that. If anything, it's better than I could ever have thought." I drank some beer.

Jen laughed. "Hey, that's better than the alternative, right? I mean, there are times with Jared I'm not sure it's going to work out at all, you know?"

"Really? Why not? Well, I guess I know why not, because of course you can never be sure in the beginning…but why aren't you sure?"

"Okay, babblemonster," Jen said. "What's going on? Really, now?"

"I have to talk to you about what happened at the dinner party," I told her.

She didn't say anything for a few seconds, just drank some beer and licked her fingers clean before picking up another wing. "Your mom told me about the accident. About your seizures."

"Yeah, they're not really seizures. They're blackouts. Fugues. I go dark, that's what it feels like. They usually last just a few seconds. Maybe a minute. I haven't had one that lasted that long in forever."

She nodded as she picked the meat off the bone and ate it. "Your mom said you'd been good for a couple of years, that it was a real surprise. I'm sorry, Emm, that sucks."

"Yeah. It does. I can't drive until I've been seizure-free for a year. Johnny's been getting me back and forth to work." I grimaced. "I hate it, actually. I thought I could finally move away from home, get a better job… It does suck, Jen. It sucks hard and mightily."

She frowned. "So, what now? How've you been feeling?"

"Fine." It wasn't a lie. The fugue I'd slipped into the other night while giving Johnny a blow job hadn't left me with any residual negative effects. "I've stepped up my appointments with my acupuncturist to once a week, and I've made an effort to make sure I get back into my meditation. That helps. Um, sugar and caffeine help, too, so I've been eating a lot of brownies and coffee."

"Lucky you." She grinned.

"I have prescriptions for meds, but I hate taking them because they make me feel fuzzy all the time. And don't really work, anyway."

"I don't blame you. Still—" she finished off another wing, then used a wipe to clean her fingers "—I'm sorry you have to go through this. If I can help, let me know. I can probably pick you up from work a couple nights a week, stuff like that."

I didn't want to cry, but her offer wrinkled my face and stung my eyes. "Thanks. Believe me, I fucking hate having to ask."

"Girl, it ain't no thing," she said with a little rotation of her head on her neck and an accompanying hand gesture. "Fuhrealsies."

I managed a laugh. "It's just…it's about Johnny."

"It bothers him?" She gave me a sympathetic look. "He's not being a dick to you about it, is he?"

"No. The opposite. He's been fan-fucking-tastic about it, totally. Too good, in fact. If you think I hate having to ask you to give me a ride, think how I hate having to count on him to drive me around, even though he offered. Before the dinner party, I mean. He…insisted, actually." I drank more beer. "He knew about the fugues."

I'd told her the story about the cookies, but not the part about ending up naked in my hallway, or of Johnny returning my clothes. I told her now, quickly filling in the missing pieces, adding the part about how I'd gone to the gallery and kissed him, how he'd assured me nothing bad had happened.

"Wow," she said in the silence after I stopped talking. "How come you didn't tell me any of this before?"

"It's embarrassing," I said flatly. "Some stuff is just too much to share. I'm sorry."

She waved a hand. "Ain't no thing, girl, how many times do I have to tell you that? I mean, it would've made the stories a fuckton more interesting if you'd told me everything earlier, but I get why you didn't. So, he's known pretty much all along and he's still with you."

"Yeah." I took a deep breath. "But there's more. Something he doesn't know."

Both her brows raised. She leaned forward. "Oh, yeah?"

I nodded. "When I go dark, I sometimes have hallucinations. Very vivid. Very real."

"Ooh, girl." Jen grabbed up another wing and looked rapt. "Tell more."

"Just after the accident, while I was in the coma, I had really intense dreams about a lot of things. Most I can still remember, though they were jumbled up. Bits and pieces. Random. I dreamed a lot about the Doctor…"

"That makes sense, you were in the hospital."

I laughed. "No, not the doctors in the hospital. The Doctor."

"Doctor who?"

"Yeah, exactly."

She frowned. "Huh?"

I laughed again. "Doctor Who? Science fiction TV show, he had a long striped scarf? There's a new version out now. Daleks? The *TARDIS?*"

"Oh, right, right. I haven't seen it. So, you dreamed about Doctor Who."

"And his long, striped scarf," I said, remembering. "He wore a long dark coat and a long, striped scarf."

"Hey, Johnny wears a long black coat and a striped scarf," Jen said.

I looked at her. "Yeah. I know."

"You think, what, your kiddie dreams made you fall in love with him because of that?"

"No." I shook my head. "It's just coincidence. That's what I remember from the time in the hospital. When I got out, I'd go dark pretty often, sometimes a couple times in a day, usually once a week, then once a month, for the first year or so after. I missed a lot of school but got caught up over the summer because my mom was determined I wasn't going to be held back. And by that time, I'd had a hundred tests that showed nothing, not even brain damage, and they'd started me on meds that kept the fugues from happening. At least, the ones anyone could tell. I got really used to pretending I knew exactly what was going on in a conversation even if I'd missed a couple minutes of it."

She made another face. "God, that sucks."

"Yeah, well. It could've been worse. I could've had permanent brain damage that left me disabled. More disabled," I said, allowing bitterness to edge my words. "Because, yeah, it's pretty much fucked up my life."

She reached for my hand and squeezed it.

"Thanks. Anyway, I'm getting to my point, and that is that as I got older, the dark times often also led to hallucinations. Not really dreams, because they were almost always cohesive, and I almost always knew I wasn't really doing whatever it was my brain told me I was doing. It was really helpful in a way, because if suddenly in the middle of class I found myself in a field of flowers, chasing a butterfly, I knew I was dark and I could try to get myself back right away."

"Can you do that? Make yourself come out of it?"

"Sometimes. Sort of. Other times..." I shrugged, thinking of waking up in the hospital with Johnny holding my hand. "Not."

"Phew." Jen sighed and looked sympathetic, but not pitying.

"Before I moved up here I hadn't had any fugues in over a year, and not any major ones in a couple years. I hadn't had any hallucinations in a much longer time. Maybe three or four years."

"And now?"

"I've been hallucinating about Johnny."

Her brows went up again. "Yeah? Like what?"

"The first one was really just a mess. I was on that train from *Train of the Damned,* and I was the countess or whatever she was. And we were…you know."

"Ooh, girl, you were banging him on the train? That's the kind of dream I wouldn't mind having."

"Yeah." I smiled. "It was good. Except for the part where it meant I was having a fugue, it was really good. But that one was normal. Since then, I've had more. They're not like the others I've ever had. But they're all the same. I'm always at Johnny's house, back in the seventies. Usually there's a party going on. I think sometimes it's the same party, I'm just popping in and out of it at different times. At least, it's always within a few days or hours of the same timeline. And there are other people there. Paul Smiths, Candy Applegate."

"Shit, you mean like from the Enclave? All those people?"

"Yes. Ed D'Onofrio, too."

"The writer? The one who died?"

"Yes. Him." I thought of the last time I'd gone dark, of standing in Johnny-then's kitchen with Ed, watching him self-destruct. "And Sandy."

"His first wife?"

I made a face like I'd tasted something bad. "Yeah. Her."

"She was in *Night of a Hundred Moons* with him, right? Her? Kimmy's mother."

"Yeah. And the thing is, Jen, the really weird thing is, I was having these hallucinations about that movie, people in it and stuff, before I even saw it for myself. I guess I pieced it together from the internet stuff."

"You could've seen it on TV, late-night. Like *Train of the Damned,* maybe you'd seen it a long time ago and hadn't remembered until we watched it."

"I guess so," I said, though that explanation didn't feel quite right. "It's more like I've put together this world, though. Johnny's world, back then. The man he was with the movies and the modeling. The super-sexed-up version of him. And in these hallucinations, I go back to that time and just…fuck him silly."

She laughed. "And this is bad? I mean, yeah, aside from the fact you're having the fugues."

"In my head, we have this great, sexy thing going on. It's all really free. Sex, drugs. Rock and roll. It's this whole other world. But it's not real," I told her. "And it was great at first—if I have to be a brain-damaged freak and suffer blackouts, it's pretty sweet to also get to hang out with Johnny fucking Dellasandro."

"I hear that," she said, again sympathetically and not with pity. "So, what's the issue with it? I know you'd rather not have them at all."

I laughed harshly. "Sort of. It's easier in those dreams. I don't have to worry about anything, and I still get Johnny."

"You have him in real life, too," she pointed out.

"I haven't told him about the hallucinations. I don't want him to think that it's just all about the movies, or the modeling, or about all that stuff he's kind of put behind him, you know? I love Johnny-now," I said. "At least, I think I do."

"Is it so wrong to be into him because of who he was, too?" Jen asked. "Admiring his accomplishments isn't a bad thing. Johnny's not ashamed of what he did, he's just moved on, right?"

"I guess so." I couldn't describe why all of this felt so tangled up and twisted. "I should just tell him that when I go dark, I end up fucking him with his seventies sideburns and long hair. And that it's totally hot, by the way. So fucking hot."

She giggled. "So long as it's not hotter than it is in real life, right?"

"Definitely. And it's not. It's just different. Also, not real," I said drily. "So, you don't think I should tell him?"

"I don't know if you should keep it a secret, but then again, I'm not sure you have to tell him. Would you tell him if the fantasies were about something else?"

"Maybe. Maybe not, if they were as nasty dirty sexy as the ones I have about him."

"You think he might, what, get jealous of…himself?"

I giggled, too. "Maybe. Or just get a weird feeling. And it's not always sex. The last time I went dark I had this whole involved thing with Ed D'Onofrio, and let me tell you, that was just fucking creepy, not sexy at all. I know he's supposed to be a genius of his time and whatever, but his poems freak me out. And get this, I imagined he was writing a poem about me."

"Gross!"

"Yeah. See, I don't want to tell Johnny stuff like that. It's embarrassing and just gross, and it's bad enough he's putting up with me blanking out on him and having to drive me all over and stuff. I don't want to tell him that my brain makes up shit about him and his old friends, you know? It feels creepy to me. It is creepy," I said sort of miserably. "Totally feels like a stalker."

"Which you weren't. At all." Jen rolled her eyes.

"That was different," I told her. "And I blame you."

She laughed and tipped the last of her beer down her throat before setting the bottle down. "Yeah, yeah, I infected you with Johnny-itis. You want a cure, bitch? I didn't think so."

We laughed together. Telling her, at least, had lifted some of the weight from my mind. "You don't think it's totally sick? What I imagine when I go dark? It doesn't mean I'm not happy with what I have now, with him. The real him. Because that's better than anything I even imagined, ever."

"If you were trying to make yourself spend so much time

in this fantasy world, I'd be worried, but you're not. You don't try to make the fugues happen, they just do, right?"

"Yeah. I'd stop them if I could, even if it meant losing the hot seventies smut."

"Well, you said you could always tell if you were in a fugue and not just asleep, right?"

I licked sauce from a wing and swallowed. "Yeah."

"Well, have you ever tried guiding the hallucinations? Like a dream, you know. Some people can make stuff happen."

I thought about it. "No. I usually understand I've gone dark, but I don't try to make anything happen. What good would it do?"

Jen leaned forward, looking serious. "If you could control what happened, maybe you could control when you wake up. On purpose, I mean. If you could get hold of what's going on, change it up, maybe you could end it when you wanted to, instead of just waiting for it to stop."

"You think so?" I leaned forward, too. "Where'd you come up with that? I've been having these things almost my whole life, and never thought about it that way."

Jen waggled her fingers and made a woo-woo noise. "I'm just spooooooky like that."

I hit her with a pillow. "It might work. Do you think it might work?"

"There's only one way to find out," she said. "Try it."

Chapter 24

"This feels stupid." I was on my bed, comfortable with pillows and a knitted afghan thrown over me.

We'd lit candles and had soft music playing. It felt like a seduction, and it was, in a way. Not of my body. Of my brain.

"Shhh! How will you know if you don't ever try?"

"I've never tried to bring on a fugue before. I'm always trying to fight them off, not make one happen."

Jen, in her chair by my bed, shook her head. "Maybe it's like hypnosis. Power of suggestion, that sort of thing. You said you've used guided imagery and meditation. Just do that now. Only if you slip into a hallucination, try to figure out how to change it, so the next time you do go dark, you can figure out how to wake up. Oh, fuck, what do I know?"

We laughed. I yawned. "This is crazy."

"Well, get your crazy ass moving, then," Jen said. "I could be doing some really hot sexting with my boyfriend right now, but no. I'm sitting here trying to get you into your masturbatory nirvana."

"All right, all right!"

Minutes passed. I thought I might drift into sleep, but though I yawned a few more times, I didn't quite doze. My bed was soft and comforting. My pillow cradled me. I walked myself through my meditation patterns in silence.

And then, I sat up.

Johnny's bed. The one back then. Tangled sheets. The smell of sex. The sound of water running from the bathroom.

I got out of bed and whispered, loudly, "Jen!"

No answer. I looked around, thinking maybe my brain had placed her in the room with me, but she wasn't there. I tried again and got only silence in reply.

Johnny padded out of the bathroom wearing only a towel, his bare skin still glistening and his thick golden hair slicked back from his face and hanging wet down his back. "Emm? You say something?"

"No. Just…how long was I sleeping?"

"Couple hours, maybe?" He grinned. "I thought you might miss the party."

"How could I miss the party, it's always going on."

Johnny went to the window and tugged aside the sheer curtain to look down into the backyard. "Not one like this. Lots of people here tonight. Big deal. Celebrities, even."

"Should I care about that?"

He gave me a strange look and tugged off the towel to scrub at his hair. As always, I couldn't look away from his body. He was so beautiful. The only sort of art I could really appreciate.

"I don't know." He shrugged. "I guess not. I don't, really. They come to drink my booze, eat my food, smoke my dope. Fuck in my pool."

"So why do you have these parties, if you don't really like these people?"

Johnny dropped the towel and crossed to me, pulling me to my feet. He looked down at my clothes, the *Dance with the Devil* promo T-shirt, my soft pajama bottoms. He rubbed a thumb over my nipple, caressing his own face. He pulled me a little closer.

"Who says I don't like 'em?"

When he kissed me, I opened for his mouth. Tongue on tongue. But aware that Jen was watching me, I put a finger over his lips and stopped him before we could get any hotter.

"Johnny."

"Yeah, babe?"

"You know there's more to you than just those movies and those photo shoots, don't you?"

He gave me another strange look. "Are you gonna tell me I should be an artist again?"

"Not that you should be. That you are." I looked at the file of his drawings I could see on the dresser. "You're really, really good."

He shrugged. His hands cupped my ass. His cock pressed against me, not quite hard but definitely considering it. "Thanks."

"I mean it."

He put his forehead on mine, looking into my eyes. "Emm, Emm, Emmaline."

I smiled. I was supposed to be guiding this somehow, and not doing a very good job of it. I put my arms around his neck. "Yes, yes, yes."

His gaze searched mine seriously. "When you say that, I almost believe you."

"It's true. You're very talented."

His eyes narrowed the tiniest bit. "Art ain't as easy as acting. Or posing."

"Isn't that what will make it all the more worthwhile?"

He laughed a little. We were moving, not quite dancing. Swaying to the music that had begun drifting up to us from the yard outside. I could hear laughter and splashing. A party was, indeed, starting up.

"I don't know," Johnny said. "Lots of things I think are worthwhile."

"Yeah? Like what?"

"You," he said.

I cupped his face in my hands. "Johnny. You know…this isn't real. You know that, right? Us, now?"

He shook his head slightly. "You're wrong. It's all real. You and me, Emm. This is real."

I sighed. "No, it's not. It can't last. I can't keep doing this."

"Why not?"

It was a simple question, but I couldn't form my mouth on the answers. I tried, I really did, but Johnny stopped my efforts with a kiss that got deeper, harder, longer. I knew I should end it, that I was supposed to somehow be guiding this and making it my bitch instead of the other way around. I was too distracted.

And what could it hurt? This kissing? This fondling? It was good. It felt good. It wasn't hurting us. It wasn't real. I could wake up anytime I wanted. Right?

"Come down to the party," Johnny murmured into my mouth as his hands rubbed my ass. "It'll be fun. Sandy's not coming."

"You bet she's not," I said. If there was one thing I could control about this, it would be that.

He laughed. "Don't let her bother you. She don't mean anything to me. You know that."

"Yeah, aside from the fact she's your ex-wife and mother of your child." I made a face at him.

"Everyone makes mistakes."

"Yeah, well, you should learn from your mistakes, too." I poked him in the chest, then pressed my hand flat over his heart.

I felt it thumping. I felt his warmth, heard his breathing. I could smell him. I let my eyes flutter closed. All of this, so real.

All of it fake.

"I have to go," I told him, because leaving without an explanation, even in a hallucination, felt rude.

"Don't go."

I laughed, not trying too hard to pull away. "I have to!"

"You don't have to. You can stay here with me forever."

His grip tightened on my ass, holding me in place. Unease slipped through me. His gaze was hard, his mouth thin. Not smiling or joking.

"Johnny, don't. I mean it. I do have to go."

He shook his head again. "Why? Why do you always have to go?"

He kissed me, hard. There wasn't anything soft or sensual about it. It was angry, and I pulled away.

"Stop it." I pushed away from him.

This time, he let me go. He swiped the back of his hand across his mouth, then crossed to the chair and grabbed up a pair of jeans he pulled on over his bare ass. He tugged a white tank top over his head, too, and ran his fingers through his hair before tying it into a ponytail.

I watched him with my arms crossed. Angry and feeling stupid, because I'd put myself in this place on purpose, and I couldn't seem to change anything. Well, if I couldn't make him do what I wanted, I could at least wake up.

Except, I couldn't.

I closed my eyes. I opened them. He was still there. I tried again. Nothing.

"Shit," I said miserably.

"Yeah, it's shit," Johnny said.

"No. Not… This isn't…" I shook my head. Even if this wasn't real, I couldn't have him thinking I thought anything that had happened was shit.

Stupid.

Johnny looked out the window again. "Is it because of all that shit out there?"

He'd spoken in such a low voice, I almost didn't hear him at first. I took a few steps closer. I felt the wooden floor beneath my bare toes. I heard more laughter, splashing, music.

Johnny looked at me. "Is it because I'm nothing special?"

"No! How could you even think… How could I?" Because if he was saying it, it meant I was the one thinking it. This was all me, everything here. I shook my head.

"Because I'm afraid, then?"

"I don't know what to say." My mouth moved, words came out, but I wasn't sure where they came from. I blinked again and again, but nothing changed. My heart sped up. Triple thump. I was sweating.

"I mean because I'm afraid of trying to be something more than the guy in those movies. The one everyone wants to fuck but nobody loves. The pretty face with nothing going on behind it. Is that why this isn't real for you?"

"That's not what I mean at all. I don't think that. I know better. I know you, Johnny. I know what you become. Who you are. What you can be. That's all." I swallowed, my throat thick with emotions I couldn't decipher.

I needed to sit but satisfied myself with putting a hand on the back of the chair instead. I touched him, half expecting my hand to go right through him like smoke. Like a ghost. Like the fantasy I knew he really was.

He turned to me. "Then don't go. Stay here with me, okay? Come to the party. Spend the night. Wake up with me in the morning."

"I don't belong here, Johnny," I breathed. "I'm sorry. I just don't."

"But something's keeping you here," he pointed out. "Something's bringing you back."

"Just smoke. Just dreams. This isn't real."

"It's real to me," Johnny shouted so fiercely I took a step back. "It's fucking real to me, Emm, okay? It's been real since the first fucking time you showed up on my doorstep, and every fucking time since! I don't care if you're crazy or whatever the hell's going on, I don't care. Just…stay. Please."

He reached for me, and I let him hold my hands. I let him pull me closer. I let him kiss me, soft and deep. And I felt myself drifting. Giving in. Instead of waking up, I felt myself falling deeper into this dream.

"I'll do whatever you want. Stop making the movies. Hell, I'll stop the parties. I'll get a real job, if you want that. I'll wear a fucking suit and tie, buy a car, pay my bills on time. I'll be whatever you want me to be, Emm. Just don't keep walking in and out of my life, making me crazy."

"I want you to be an artist," I told him. "I want you to be everything you can be, that's all I want. And I want to be with you, Johnny. I just can't do it here."

"Why?" he asked, face pleading.

"Because I don't belong here. I don't belong in this place."

He cupped my breast, thumb passing over my nipple. "You feel real to me here. You feel like you belong."

I put my hand over his. "But…I don't. And whatever this is, it's wrong of me to keep doing it."

"Whatever this is," Johnny said with a humorless laugh. "What is it for you?"

"I don't know."

"Well, I do," he said. "I love you, Emm. And I want to be with you."

"You are with me." Tears slipped over my cheeks. I tasted salt. "We're together. Just not here. Not now."

"Then when?"

"In the future." It sounded crazy, but he didn't pull away. "I'm from the future. I'm crazy. I make all of this up in my head.

It's not real, you're not. This isn't. All of you are something I just made up."

"Stay, anyway," Johnny said.

I tried again to wake. Nothing. I tried to make something else happen. Change the room. Change his frown to a smile. There was only one way to do that.

"Just a little longer," I said. "I'll come down to the party for just a little while."

Had I ever made anyone so happy before? Johnny hugged me. He kissed me. He smiled, which I loved, and he took my hand as we went down the stairs and out the back door. He held my hand as he introduced me to people whose names were familiar even if their faces weren't. He kissed me in front of them. He brought me drinks, which I drank and got tipsy from.

Time passed. The night went on. The party got more raucous. I saw a couple fucking in his pool, just as he'd said. I saw people smoking dope. I saw some shooting up, though I turned away at that, the sight of them injecting their veins disgusting and scary. I saw a lot of things at that party, but everywhere I went, I also saw Johnny.

Had I ever spent so long here before? Maybe something had broken, and if it had, I'd been the one to break it. I'd forced this on myself, trying to figure out a way to stop it, and now I was becoming truly afraid I wouldn't ever get out of it.

People talked to me, and I answered. If they thought I was drunk it was because I slurred my words a little. Weaved a little in my walk. I saw Johnny from across the pool. He was looking at me, expression concerned, while a young woman in a terry-cloth halter top, her breasts like watermelons, tried without success to grab his attention.

Everything was hazy, like it wanted to spin but wasn't. And I couldn't wake up. I took another drink, tossed back a shot in a way I'd never done in real life. Fire burned my gut.

I stumbled into the kitchen through the back door. Ed was there. He looked up, eyes wide, mouth open.

"Holy fucking shit. Where the fuck did you come from?"

"Outside." I looked at the bottle in front of him. The cigarette. The drugs. The notebook.

This was the same as the last time, except the bottle was already empty, the ashtray overflowing, the drugs gone with only the needle left behind. I blinked and went to the sink to splash cold water on my face. Also like the last time.

"Holy fucking shit," Ed said. "You were there. Then you weren't. What the fuck? What the fuck?"

"Maybe you're high," I said cruelly, my voice thick like syrup. "Maybe you're crazy."

"I am crazy," Ed said.

We stared at each other across the kitchen. Heat shimmered between us. That's what I thought. But it wasn't heat, it was something else. Something invisible pulled me, tugging at my belly like a string attached to my guts. I twitched.

"Fucking crazy," Ed said. "You were there, and then you weren't. Did you know I wrote a poem about you, Emmaline?"

"Yeah, you told me."

"You don't like it. You're not impressed."

Something tugged me harder. I went to my knees right there on the kitchen floor. They smacked the linoleum, hard and painfully. I put both hands flat on the linoleum, wondering if I were going to fall. Puke. Pass out? How could I pass out when I was already unconscious?

"Oh, shit," Ed said.

I closed my eyes.

The world shook.

Then the world wasn't shaking, just my bed. Just me. I opened my eyes, blinking, and Johnny's face swam into view. He had my shoulders and was shaking me.

"Emm!" he cried when I focused on him. "The fuck are you doing?"

"She was just trying—" Jen began, rubbing at her eyes.

Johnny glared at her and gathered me close. "Fucking bright idea!"

Jen looked scared. "Is she okay?"

"I'm fine. Johnny! I'm fine!" I pushed him away a little bit so I could catch my breath. "Seriously, lay off."

He cupped my face and looked into my eyes. To Jen, he said, not meanly but not in a voice filled with sunshine and light, "I think you'd better go."

She did, squeezing my shoulder before she left. "I'll call you."

"Yeah," I said, too tired to get up and fight him to go after her, wanting really to just curl up next to him and knowing my friend would understand.

When she'd gone, Johnny kissed me, my face still in his hands. Then he looked into my eyes again. "What the hell were you doing?"

"I was trying to figure out if I could control the fugues," I whispered, hating that I felt ashamed.

He drew in a slow, shuddering breath. Emotions flowed over his face, too many for me to discern. "And can you?"

"Apparently not," I said sourly.

Johnny shook his head. "Don't do it again."

Annoyed, I turned my face from his. "Is that what you want? Me to just do whatever you say?"

"No, Emm." Johnny turned my face gently to face his again. "I just don't want to lose you all over again."

Chapter 25

It felt like something had broken inside me, but it wasn't necessarily a bad thing. Whatever had made my brain skip and jump back and forth from dreams to consciousness seemed to be…not repaired. I wasn't stupid enough to think that. Not fixed. Broken worse, and yet better.

I didn't go dark again for a week in which Johnny hovered over me so mercilessly I thought I might kill him. Then another week passed with me clearheaded. One more. At the end of the month, spring was inching into the air and I hadn't even dreamed of Johnny-then in regular sleep.

I did make an appointment with Dr. Gordon, ostensibly for my yearly woman care, but I had her check out everything else, too, including a new CAT scan. I didn't protest when she suggested it. We talked a little about my night in the hospital and my treatment options, and though I know she wanted to put me back on higher doses of antiseizure meds, I resisted.

"I already have trouble remembering to take my birth control pills every day. Adding in another dose of something else would be a pain in the butt," I said.

Dr. Gordon shook her head. "Are you sure you don't want

to switch over to something a little less difficult for you to maintain, Emm?"

I laughed, which always feels awkward while sitting on a paper-covered table in a flimsy gown. "Nah. I'm okay. I'm in a stable relationship right now, not having multiple partners—blah, blah, blah—and we use condoms, although I think we'll have the talk about STDs pretty soon and get rid of those. Besides, he's had a vasectomy."

She chuckled. "Sounds like you have all the bases covered."

I shrugged. "I don't want to go back on drugs if I don't have to. That's all."

She put her hand on my shoulder. "I know you don't. I know. But as your doctor, I have to at least offer the treatment I feel is best, even if you don't want to follow my advice."

I nodded. Dr. Gordon had known me a long time. "Right. But I think we both know it's not really going to make a difference in the fugues or even in my management of them. They come. They go."

"They come, they go," she said. "I wish we could figure out some better answer than that for you."

Of course she did. So did I. So did my parents, friends. So did Johnny. But none of us were going to find something better, so I had to accept what I had.

My mom had driven me to my appointment, not because Johnny couldn't but because we'd decided to have a mother-daughter bonding day. After my appointment we went to lunch, saw a movie, then came back to my house where my mom was going to sort through my closet and see if any of the stuff that didn't fit me would work for her.

Talk about depressing, giving your mother hand-me-downs because she's losing weight and you're…not.

I was happy for her, though, as I watched her spin around in a long peasant skirt I'd bought on sale and had never worn.

Frankly, never would, and not because it wasn't the right size. It had been an impulse purchase, the color wrong for me, the material not my style. But it looked great on her, and I told her so.

"Oh, you think so?" She smoothed the skirt and spun in front of the mirror again. "I love this. I'd never have picked it up for myself."

"I know. Maybe it was fate I saw it that day at Marshalls."

She checked the tag, as I knew she would. "I'll give you the money for it."

"No, you won't." I shook my head and my finger at her. "No way."

She sighed. "Emmaline."

"Mom, no." I found a blouse in my closet, too, and handed it to her. "Try it with this."

She held it up, then glanced over her shoulder at me. "Oh, before I forget, I have a couple of boxes for you in my trunk. Your dad found them in the crawl space when I was cleaning out some stuff for the church bazaar yard sale. There's a bunch of your things in there."

"I'll go get it." I tossed the rest of the clothes I was sorting onto the bed and grabbed her keys.

The boxes she'd brought were the kind with lids and handles, easily lifted, though whatever was inside made them heavy. I took them all into my living room and left my front door open so the fresh evening air could blow through the screen door. By that time my mom had changed into her own clothes and come downstairs.

"What is all this stuff?" I took the lid off one box and found a pile of papers, books, small toys.

"Oh, things you left behind."

I looked at her. "Did you think maybe I left it behind because I didn't want it?"

She gave me a "Mom" face. "So throw it away. I don't need your junk any more than you do."

I knew she didn't mean it like that, but the words stung and I felt my face twist. My mom saw it, too, because she sat down beside me right away. She took the lid from my hands.

"Emm, I didn't mean it like that."

"It's okay," I said.

"No. Look at me."

I didn't want to; I knew I'd start to cry the second I did. There's something only mothers and daughters can trigger in each other, that bursting-into-tears reaction to emotion. Hallmark card commercials ain't got nothing on moms and daughters.

"Oh, honey." My mom hugged me, stroking my hair. "What's wrong? Have you been feeling sick again? Is it something with that man?"

Funny how she'd been calling him Johnny all these weeks but at the first hint he might be making me cry she called him *that man*. "It's not him. He's great. I mean, I know you and dad aren't sure about Johnny, but it isn't that."

"It's not that I'm unsure about him," my mom said. "I'm just wondering about having a son-in-law who's old enough to be my husband."

I laughed through my tears. "We're not really talking about getting married, Mom. Don't worry."

She gave me a familiar snort that told me she knew better. "We'll see."

"It's not him. And I haven't had any problems lately. The opposite, in fact. Nothing for a month. Dr. Gordon took another CAT scan, but even that was just for the records. She doesn't expect to see anything new."

"Then what, honey? Your junk?"

"I just..." I sighed, plucking at the faded knees of my jeans. "I don't want to move back home ever again, but I don't really like knowing you're glad I'm gone, you know? I mean, don't get me wrong, I totally understand why—"

"Emm!" My mom cried, shocked. "How could you think something like that? Glad you're gone? I should smack you for that."

I flinched exaggeratedly, though I knew she wasn't going to hit me. "C'mon, Mom. You know it's true."

She put her hands on my shoulders and looked into my eyes. "Emmaline, I am happy you've been able to move out on your own, have the life you deserve. I'm happy you've grown into a lovely, independent young woman who is capable of living her own life. But I could never be happy you're gone. And if you ever had to move back home, you'd hate it way more than I ever could."

We both cried a little then, until our tears turned to soggy laughter.

"If you don't want the stuff in the boxes, throw it in the garbage," she told me again. "Most of it's from so long ago you might not even remember it, but I didn't want to just toss it without letting you see it. That's all."

I nodded and sifted through the papers. Old report cards, construction-paper valentines, that sort of thing. A lot of fast-food toys I couldn't believe she'd kept. And then, at the bottom of the first box, a book.

"Oh, my goodness," my mom said when I pulled it out. "I haven't seen that in years."

I hefted the thick paperback, pages yellowed but not falling out of the binding. I flipped through it, noting the dog-eared corners where someone had marked favorite pages. My fingers felt gritty from touching it, and I tasted grit, too.

"This was...mine?"

"Well, it was mine. Everyone had a copy of that book, it seemed. I read it a lot when I was pregnant with you," my mom said fondly, and lifted it from my hands. "Ed D'Onofrio's poetry was really popular for a while, though I really only liked a few of his poems. Well, just the one, of course."

I looked at her. "Of course? Which one?"

My mom smiled. "'In Night She Walks,' silly. You've read it, haven't you? You must've, Emm."

I shook my head. "I don't think it was ever assigned in school or anything like that."

She laughed and flipped to one of the most worn sections of the book. "No, honey. See? 'In Night She Walks.' It's where I first heard your name. It's why I named you that."

My stomach twisted, then lurched, my lunch burning in my throat. I stood so fast the book fell, and I didn't pick it up. My mom looked immediately concerned and stood.

"Emm, what's wrong?"

"Nothing." I forced myself to sit and pick up the book, to scan the page. The poem on the page was different than the one Ed had spoken during my fugue, but it was close enough that there could be no mistaking the similarities. "I just didn't know. I mean, I was surprised."

"I thought you knew," she said. "I was sure I'd told you. But it must've been so long ago, maybe you don't remember. I read that book aloud over and over again when I was pregnant with you, sitting in that old rocker Gran gave me. And I read it to you when you were in the hospital. I guess...well, now that I think about it, after that I didn't read it aloud to you anymore. Maybe we never talked about it."

"It's kind of a strange poem to read your kid, isn't it?" I ran a finger down the lines, then looked at her. "Not like 'Humpty Dumpty.'"

My mom tilted her head. "Honey, are you okay?"

"Yeah, I'm fine." I forced a smile. "I'm okay, really. Tired, though. That's really neat about the poem, Mom, thanks."

"He was very popular when I was younger," my mom said almost dreamily. "I wonder whatever happened to him? You could probably look him up on the internet. I wonder if he had any other books published?"

Only after he was dead. He'd been dead, in fact, when this book was published, if I remembered correctly. I didn't tell her that, or about the fugues, or the "coincidence" that Johnny had been one of Ed D'Onofrio's best friends way back when.

"Your dad never liked the other poems," she confided suddenly. "Just that one. It was his idea to name you Emmaline, actually. We couldn't agree on a name, and, oh, we argued and argued. He wanted something trendy and different, and I thought a more old-fashioned name would work better. We compromised. You were always the only Emmaline in your class."

"I'm the only one I know," I told her.

"You're the only you," my mom said, and hugged me again.

Later, after we'd said our goodbyes and she made me promise to call her soon, my mom left and Johnny arrived. He brought Thai food, fragrant and still steaming, and he set it out on my kitchen island while I grabbed plates and chopsticks. I poured us both hot tea and warmed my hands on it while I watched him open the cartons of food.

He caught me staring. "What's up?"

"Just looking."

He smiled and came around the island to kiss me. "Like what you see?"

"Oh, very much." I squeezed his butt. "Feel, too."

He looked over his shoulder at the food, then at me. "How hungry are you?"

"Depends on what you're planning on feeding me."

Johnny took my hand and moved it around to the front to cup his crotch. "How about some of this?"

"I'm so glad to know," I said, "that even after several months of fucking me, you still can be so romantic."

He rubbed my hand around in a little circle while we both laughed and kissed and parted with shining eyes and wet mouths. I hugged him then, tight against me. The day had been strange. Being with Johnny made it somehow better.

"What's going on?" he said into my hair.

I squeezed him harder, then pushed him back so I could look at his face. "Am I too young?"

His brows went up, the corners of his mouth went down. "Kimmy been after you again?"

"No. It's not her. I want to know what you think."

Johnny let out a breath and let go of me to lean against the island directly across from me. "You're young. Yeah. Or maybe I'm just old."

"But does it still bother you?"

He looked at me very seriously. "Why? Is it bothering you?"

"No." I wasn't really sure what was bothering me. I wanted to kiss him, maybe unzip his jeans right then and there, take him in my mouth and make us both forget I'd ever started this conversation.

"Emm. Talk to me, please."

I loved that he'd insist on talking about this, whatever it was. That it was important to him not to just shove awkward silences under a rug woven of mutual pretense. I loved him for so many reasons, but they were tangled and wouldn't lay smooth.

"Does it bother you that I knew so much about you before we met?"

He laughed. "You mean does it bother me that you saw me naked before you ever saw me naked?"

"That, yes. But everything else." He knew I'd seen his movies, looked him up on the Net, but we'd never talked about it. "Do you ever worry that I just weaseled my way into your life because of who you are?"

Johnny laughed again and moved forward to kiss me. "Emm, I *want* you to want to be with me because of who I am."

"But not who you were," I murmured.

"Same person," Johnny said against my mouth, then stroked a hand over my hair and looked into my eyes. "Do you want to know how many lovesick girls…and boys, have tried getting in my pants because of something I did thirty years ago?"

I frowned, hard. "Not really."

"A lot," Johnny said, anyway. "Are you like them?"

"No!"

He shrugged and traced my lower lip with his thumb before kissing me again. He tasted good. Felt good against me. I closed my eyes and let him try to distract me, but it wasn't working.

"I love you," I said to him. "But…honestly, all that other stuff—the movies, the pictures, the interviews…"

He nodded. "Yeah."

"That's not why I love you now," I said.

"It wasn't why you loved me then, either," Johnny said.

I froze. I stared at him, searching his expression for any sign he was teasing. Anything. "What do you mean?"

"When you saw me in the coffee shop that first time," he said, "you didn't know all the rest of that shit, did you? So let's face it. It was my ass, wasn't it?"

It wasn't the answer I expected, not that I knew what I expected, but I burst into laughter. "Yeah. That was definitely it. Your epic fucking ass."

This time, his kiss really did distract me. It wasn't until later that I thought about what he'd said. He hadn't hesitated in his answer, hadn't looked like he was trying to hide something.

So why, then, did I feel like he was?

"C'mon, you know I don't know anything about art." I ducked away from Johnny's reaching hand and stepped back, almost knocking over a statue displayed on a pedestal. I caught it before it could fall. "See? I'm a menace."

"You have a good eye, and I want your opinion," he said seriously. "And this is your friend's work, so maybe you could just give me a hand here, huh?"

"I think it looks great!" I pointed at the plain white wall where he'd already hung three of Jen's pieces. "There's plenty of room there for at least four more."

"Yeah, but which ones?" Johnny sounded annoyed.

"How am I supposed to know? You pick." I looked over the framed photos laid out on the gallery floor. I didn't even want to come any closer, in case I accidentally stepped on one.

Johnny pointed at one of Jared taken in soft light. "That one?"

"It's nice. It's good, I mean."

He pointed at another. "This one?"

"That one's good, too! They're all good!"

He started laughing, shaking his head. "Jesus, babe, you really don't know art, huh?"

I feigned insult. "I told you."

"You just think you don't," Johnny said. "If you let yourself go, you'd have great instincts. See a lot. But hey, it's okay, I can do this myself. Don't worry your pretty little head about it."

I stuck my tongue out at him. "Now you're being a turd."

Johnny scoffed and put up his hands. "Ooh, wow, that hurts."

He bent back to arranging the frames. I watched him. A few days had passed since our conversation in the kitchen, and something was still niggling at my brain.

"Johnny."

He didn't look up. "Yeah, babe."

"What made you decide to become an artist?"

His hands, moving over the prints, slowed. He sat back on his heels. He didn't look up at me for a few seconds, but then did, expression guarded.

"What do you mean?"

"Well…you started off in the movies and stuff, and I know you took a break before you started doing art—"

"I was always doing art," he said quietly. "I just didn't show it. I didn't try to make anyone else think I was an artist. There's a difference between deciding to be an artist and just accepting who you are."

"I know." I chewed my lower lip briefly. "So…when did you?"

Johnny got to his feet, dusting off his hands. "I need a drink. You want one?"

Without waiting for me, he headed for his office. It didn't have the best memories for me, that office. I couldn't step inside it without remembering my embarrassment about the time I'd kissed him and he'd pushed me away.

Johnny opened a drawer in his desk and pulled out a bottle of Glenlivet. He poured out two glasses and gave me one. I sipped, grimacing, and coughed.

"God," I said.

"Nope," Johnny said. "Just whiskey."

He drank his back and sucked at his teeth for a second before setting down the glass. He looked at the bottle like he might pour another, but didn't. He looked at me.

"What is it you really want to ask me?"

"I want to know what happened to you. What made you accept who you are, if you want to put it that way. Why you decided to start showing your art and keep doing it instead of just putting it away in a notebook."

His head tilted. "You know about the notebook."

His reply meant I hadn't invented it, so at least I didn't look too crazy. "Sure, doesn't everyone?"

Johnny poured another drink.

"I want to hear it from you, that's all. I don't want secrets between us. I don't want to know details about your life that you didn't tell me, like I know all your secrets and you don't realize I know them. I don't want you to not tell me stories because you think we already know them, even if I do. I need to hear them from you. That's what I want."

My long speech had left me a little breathless, so I finished the whiskey to keep myself from babbling more.

"What do you want to know? About the parties? About the drugs, the sex, the movies?" Johnny swirled the amber liquid around in his glass. "It was all a long time ago, Emm. You'd get a better story from one of those books or the documentaries."

"Not just that stuff." I ran a finger down the buttons of his shirt, but didn't linger. "Can you tell me about what happened to you after 1978?"

"What happened after '78, huh? I'm told it was 1979."

I rolled my eyes and poked him. "Smart-ass."

"Epic smart-ass, right?"

I didn't really like my own words thrown back at me, even

if he was just teasing. "After Ed D'Onofrio committed suicide at your house."

Johnny let out a long, slow breath that sounded a little shivery. "You really wanna hear about that? Really, Emm?"

"I guess…not if you don't want to tell me. But I know about it. At least what the fan blogs say, what the documentaries say. But that's really all just speculation, isn't it?" I put my glass down and put my hands on his hips. Looked up into his face, so familiar, so handsome, so beloved. "They say you went crazy."

Johnny snorted a low, harsh laugh. "Yeah. You could say so."

"Did you?" I put my finger on his lips before he could reply. "Before you answer, I want you to know that I don't care if you did."

He kissed my finger, then bit it gently before taking my wrist and moving my hand from his mouth. He tucked it up against his chest instead. "You don't care if I went nuts and had to be locked up, huh?"

I shook my head. "No."

Johnny sighed. "Fuck, Emm. It was a long fucking time ago, you know? Can't you just ask me about the women I fucked? Hell, ask me if it's true I once let Elton John blow me backstage at one of his concerts. Those are the kinds of stories you're supposed to speculate about."

"Did you?"

He kissed my mouth. I tasted whiskey. His breath, hot, caressed me when he spoke.

"Maybe."

I sighed. "Johnny."

His laughter didn't last long and faded into weighted silence. "If I say yes, will you still want to know about the rest?"

I nodded. Then I shook my head. "If you don't want to tell

me, I guess I understand. It's not really any of my business. I mean, you had this whole life before you met me—"

"So did you," he pointed out. "A whole life. We both did. Mine was just longer."

"But everything you know about me is something I told you!" The words came out louder and more vehement than I'd anticipated. We both flinched. I rubbed my palm over his heart, feeling the thump. "I'm sorry."

"Don't be. I'm sorry this is bothering you so much. Whatever you want to know, just ask. I'll tell you, okay? If you really need to know."

I hesitated. Did I really want that? There was so much floating around in my head, rumors and bits and pieces of history, all mingled with whatever it was my imagination had created when I went dark.

"I just want to know you," I whispered. "Really know you. That's all."

"Oh, Emm. Do you think you don't?" His hand slid to the back of my neck, cupping it. His fingers massaged the base of my skull, beneath my hair. He looked down at me, face grave.

"I don't know." I sighed unhappily. "It feels uneven."

"We feel uneven?"

"Yeah. We do."

He pulled me close to him. I pressed my cheek against his chest. The steady thump of his heart was soothing. So was his smell and the weight of his hands on my back.

"I love you," he said quietly.

I put my arms around him, held him tight. "I love you, too."

"I'll tell you anything you want to know. Just ask. Okay?"

"What happened in 1978?"

He sighed. The steady thump under my cheek skipped a beat,

or maybe it was just my own heart I felt. He kissed the top of my hair.

"Things were nuts. We were all living in that house. My house, but they all stayed there. Candy, Bellina, Ed. Paul was coming by every coupla weeks to make those damn movies of his, you know?"

"I know that."

"He was gonna be the next Warhol or some shit. Something big. And the pictures, they were art, you know? They were art," Johnny said. "They still are. I'm not ashamed of what we did back then, Emm."

"You shouldn't be."

"Me and Sandy had broke up. She was getting crazier into the drugs and shit, and she was bringing Kimmy around all this stuff. I finally told her she needed to either let me take the kid or give her to her mother."

I pushed away to look at him. "You did? But I thought you said you weren't there for Kimmy the way you wanted to be."

"Yeah, well, I wasn't. I told Sandy I wanted her, but I didn't, you know? I was a kid. A stupid, fuckdrunk kid high on the attention. Life was spinning around and all these people were telling me how fucking gorgeous I was. Offering to blow me at rock concerts. Jesus Christ, what was I gonna do with a kid there?"

I couldn't begin to imagine that life. I'd seen it when I was dark, and it hadn't seemed real. But it had been, for him.

"So, what did she do?"

"She gave Kimmy to her mom, thank God. And she went off and spent a year in India following some maharajah or some shit, some guru. Came back all scrawny and full of parasites. But that was later. And maybe… Shit." He sighed. "Maybe she went a little crazy herself. I think we all did. Ed was just the first one."

Ice punched my guts at the mention of his name. "The writer."

"Yeah. Fucking brilliant guy. Just…so fucking above the rest of us. We were all making our little shit movies, drawing shitty little life studies—"

"They weren't shitty," I broke in.

Johnny looked at me for a long few seconds. "You don't know anything about art, babe."

Technically, I also hadn't seen his life studies or anything else; I was just extrapolating from the early pieces I'd seen on the internet and what I knew of his work now. "Nothing you do could've been shitty, that's what I know."

He smiled faintly. "If I didn't get better, I wouldn't be much of an artist, would I?"

"I guess not." I didn't want to keep pushing him; I wanted Johnny to tell me on his own terms, in his own time. Even if it wasn't all at once, right now. I just wanted to start the conversation. I'd already learned some things I didn't know. I was feeling better, overall.

"It was a fucking hot summer," Johnny continued. "We were all full of this…I dunno what to call it. There was this pulsing, growing…just…this creation. We were all full of it. Knocked up. Pregnant with making art. Candy with his cooking, Bellina with her plays, Paul with the movies."

"And Ed with his poems."

"Yeah. He wrote books, too, did you know that?"

I nodded. "Yeah. I haven't read any."

"Well, he wasn't no J. D. Salinger or anything, but his books were good. I mean, they were weird, but good. But his poems… they were art. Really art, Emm."

"Yeah, which I can't appreciate," I murmured.

I thought of Ed's face across the kitchen. The stink of him. The sound of him reading that poem aloud. It would've been so much prettier in my mom's voice, why couldn't I remember that instead of the fugue?

"Pffft," Johnny said. "You keep talking like that."

"My mother named me after one of his poems."

Johnny went still. "Did she?"

I studied him. "Yeah. 'In Night She Walks.'"

Johnny drank his second glass of whiskey.

"She brought me the book," I said. "Told me she used to read me that poem over and over when she was pregnant with me. And after the accident. She said she named me after that poem, but I don't remember her reading it to me, ever."

"I love your name," Johnny said.

"It's not a nice poem," I told him, frowning.

"It could've been worse. She could've been a big e. e. cummings fan, and then who knows what she'd have called you."

"Were you close with him?" I asked.

"Ed? Nobody was close with him. He lived in his own head a lot," Johnny said. "He hung out with us. But were any of us close to him? I don't think so."

"But when he died, that messed all of you up. Didn't it?"

Johnny looked like he was thinking that over. Whiskey on his breath wafted over my face. "It was a big mess, yeah. Is that what you want to know?"

"What happened?"

"He was…Ed. I mean, he did his thing, you know? We all were doing our own thing. But he got into the drugs. Hard stuff. Shooting up. Not sleeping, drinking too much. Crazy shit, Emm. And he just lost it, I guess. He couldn't deal with it. Life. Whatever." Johnny rubbed at his eyes, then pinched the bridge of his nose. "He drank too much, shot himself up too much, then slit his wrists and jumped in the deep end of the pool after everyone was out of it. Hell, maybe he thought someone would find him. Any other night, someone would've been there. But not that night."

"And…he died."

"Yeah, he fucking died." Johnny pushed away from me to go around his desk. Pacing. He ran both hands through his hair and linked them behind his head. "Made a fucking mess of my swimming pool, too."

I waited quietly, my glass in my hands but not drinking from it.

"Do you really still want to know what happened?" Johnny asked quietly, facing away from me.

"Only if you want to tell me."

He turned. "Ed went crazy. We all fell apart. I guess I went a little crazy, too. I let what other people said about me, what they wanted, get in the way of what I knew I should be doing. So I went away for a while to get my head on straight."

I thought of the Johnny-then I'd made in my own head. Could he have lost it all? Become overwhelmed, lost his shit, gone away? Maybe.

"To rehab?"

He shook his head. "No. Loony bin. Straight-up state hospital, no private fruit-loop facility for me. They took me away on a stretcher. I couldn't have paid for something fancy even if I had the sense to put myself away. By that time, the money had disappeared up my nose, down my gut, whatever. My mother was the one who did it, finally, God bless her. I'd probably have died myself, otherwise."

It hurt to hear this, though he said it in a matter-of-fact voice without shame, the way he'd said everything else. I wanted to hug him tight. Kiss him all over. But I wasn't sorry I'd asked. I needed to get these things straight in my head. The real from unreal.

"How long were you there?" I asked.

"A year. Got out in '79. Cleaned up, sobered up. Maybe still a little crazy." He smiled.

"You weren't crazy to begin with."

His smile became a little sad. "No. I know that. But being in that place was good for me. Yeah, it was hard. 'Love the sinner, not the sin' sort of place, not that it was religious. I had a great doc, really got my head on straight. Made me think about a lot of things that had happened that summer. Made me see a lot of truths."

"About Ed?"

"No, babe," Johnny said. "About—"

The door to his office opened and his assistant, Glynnis, stuck her head in. "Johnny, that guy from—oh, sorry. Didn't know you had company in here."

She looked back and forth between us with a curious stare, but since we weren't touching, weren't even on the same side of the desk, at least she couldn't have thought she'd interrupted anything embarrassing.

"It's okay," Johnny said. "What guy?"

"From that website. The blogger guy?"

"Oh, that guy," Johnny said with a facepalm. "Yeah, I told him I'd do an interview with him about the new show. Glynnis, can you just…fuck, I dunno, entertain him or something for a few minutes? Show him around the gallery?"

"Sure, Johnny." She gave me a timid smile and ducked out.

"Sorry," Johnny said. "I need to get back to this stuff."

"It's okay. I'm glad we talked. I'm glad…well, just that we got some things out between us."

He gave me a curious look. "Was it that bad, Emm? Were you really that upset about it? I'd have told you anytime. I just didn't think you'd want to really get into it. It's all old history."

"I just wanted to hear it from you, that's all."

From outside the office we heard voices. Johnny came around the desk and kissed me thoroughly. "You okay?"

I nodded. "Fine."

"Good." He kissed me again, longer this time.

I forgot where we were. Not a fugue, just lust. I laughed when he pushed his erection against me.

"You'd better tame that thing before you go out there, or Bloggy McBloggerstein will have a lot more to say about you than he expected."

"Wouldn't be the first time my cock was all someone could talk about," Johnny said as he walked backward toward the door, my hands still held in his.

Our fingers touched until the last possible second, and then he let go.

Chapter 27

It was different looking at pictures of Johnny with him instead of giggling over them with Jen or even sighing over them by myself on the internet. He had a thick album full of prints, some kept neatly in place by sticky corners, others falling off their pages. Some were signed, not just by him but by others in the photos. Some had names and dates scribbled on the back. Some were formal, some were snapshots, some eight-by-ten and others in smaller sizes.

"I haven't looked at it in a long time," Johnny said when a fistful of photos slipped from between the bulging pages and fell onto his thick carpet.

I picked them up, sorting carefully. The paper was thick, the colors a little faded, but compared to shots I'd flipped through in my parents' albums over the years, they were really well-preserved. "Why not?"

"Do you look at old pictures of yourself naked?"

"My mother has some hanging up on the wall," I answered drily. "Bathtub shots. Totally embarrassing, yet there they are, for everyone to see."

"I'm going to have to take a good look when I go over there."

I rolled my eyes. "Yeah, not really the same thing, is it?"

Johnny looked at the pictures in my hand, then took one. I recognized it as one of the famous Roman statue photo shoot. I'd seen them on the internet and, of course, in my own convoluted fantasies. They looked different in his hand. He shook it a little.

"No. It isn't." He leaned closer to look at the others I had in my hand. "What do you see when you look at those?"

"I see a beautiful man," I told him quietly.

Johnny snorted. "Yeah."

"I mean it, Johnny."

He looked at me. "And what do you see when you look at me?"

I kissed him. "Same thing. Just better seasoned."

The kiss deepened. He pulled me closer. His hands moved down my back to cup my ass, and he pulled me up tight against the front of him.

"What do *you* see?" I asked.

His gaze cut to the album, then to me. "I see a kid. A young kid with his head up his ass, didn't have a clue about life, what to do. I see a fuckup ready to show off his cock for a coupla bucks."

"Was that what you were?" I pushed onto my tiptoes to find his mouth with mine, then to hold his face and look into his eyes. I thought of Johnny-then, who'd been young, brash, a bit arrogant, but not a fuckup.

Johnny's gaze got harder for a second before he smiled. "Sure."

"I don't think so."

He studied me, something moving deep in those hazy green-brown eyes I thought I should be able to figure out but couldn't quite. "You...didn't know me."

I lowered onto my heels and took his hand, pulled him toward the couch so we could sit and snuggle. "You know what

I think? It's not really what someone says about themselves that matters, it's what other people say about you. And what people say about you, Johnny, is not that you were a fuckup. Not that you had your head up your ass, without a clue."

"People," Johnny said, slightly derisive, "don't always have a fucking clue."

I dug into the box of memorabilia he'd brought and pulled out a folded movie poster. I'd seen ones just like it selling on eBay for hundreds of dollars, and this one was signed by the entire cast. "'To Johnny, with love, Marguerite. To Johnny, always ready with a joke, Bud. Johnny, thanks for all of it, you know what I mean, Dee.'"

I looked at him. "People liked you. They gravitated toward you. And you were a generous friend."

"Too generous, maybe," he said after a second, looking over the poster.

I wondered if he was thinking about Ed but didn't ask. "You keep in touch with them, don't you?"

"Some of them, yeah. Off and on."

"You all went off and did your own thing, you all became successful at it."

"Some of us more than others," Johnny said.

Again, I wondered if he were thinking about Ed or Bellina, or about Candy, with his own megamillion-dollar television show and cookbook empire. Or about himself.

"I'm going to own up to my internet stalking. I read a lot about you." I laughed when he rolled his eyes, but put a finger to his lips to keep him from answering. "A lot. From famous interviews to lowly blog discussions, and the consensus is the same, sweetheart. You're not only gorgeous, but smart and talented, too."

"You obviously missed all the bad reviews," Johnny said. "And anyone who praises some of that shit I did back then is just blowing sunshine."

I laughed again. "Yeah, well, it's true that you weren't always at your best. But that doesn't matter. Who is? Where it counts, your talent shows. Your art."

Again, his gaze flickered and I wanted to know what that meant. "It saved me."

This wasn't the answer I was expecting. "Did it?"

In answer, he kissed me again. Long, slow, sweet. The pressure of his mouth urged mine to open, the sweep of his tongue encouraged mine. I loved kissing Johnny. All mouth and breath. Teeth and tongues. I found myself on his lap, straddling him, my knees pressing deep into the couch cushions and my crotch pushed against his.

His hands cupped my ass, moving me in slow circles against him. His kiss deepened. His cock got hard between us, and I shivered, thinking of how it would feel in my mouth. Between my legs. Inside me, deep.

I unbuttoned my blouse and my flesh humped into goose pimples at the touch of chilly air—Johnny kept his thermostat lower than mine. It felt good, though. Like phantom fingers, urging my nipples into tight, hard peaks. I shrugged out of my shirt, unhooked my bra and let it slide along my shoulders, though not off. I cupped my breasts with the satin still covering most of them, pushing them together to create cleavage.

He took my offering, moving his mouth from mine and down my throat, over my collarbone. His tongue traced the swell of my breasts. I let the satin fall away, and Johnny closed his mouth around one tight nipple, sucking gently until I moaned. Every gentle suck echoed in my clit. I'd always loved having my nipples played with, but my few other lovers had never spent much time there, preferring to dive straight between my thighs.

Johnny took his time.

I let my head fall back, my hair tickling my skin as I rocked against his crotch with the barrier of layers of denim, cotton and silk buffering the sensation. He sucked slowly, gently, on my nipples, one and then the other. When he bit down on the flesh around them, denting it, I bucked against him and cried out.

He laughed against my skin, and I laughed, too, though mine was breathless, panting, sodden with lust. Johnny nuzzled against me, lightly, smoothing over the small marks his teeth had left with his tongue.

I arched my back, giving him my body, and he took it. He put his hand flat on my back, between my shoulder blades, the other one under my ass. Before I knew what he was doing, he stood. My legs went automatically around his waist, my arms clinging as he gripped me.

I gasped. "Johnny—"

"Shhh," he said. "Bed's only a couple steps away."

I clung to him as he walked us over. We half fell onto the bed together, rolling until I was beneath him. His shirt scratched my bare skin. We kissed. We rubbed. We got his shirt off, mouths fused as we fumbled with buttons. Then his jeans, half-undone, pushed just over his hips while I slid out of mine and lay before him on the bed wearing only my silk panties.

His eyes gleamed. He got on his knees, looking down at me, my legs spread wantonly, my chest already flushed with arousal I could feel as heat spreading upward. I could see the jut of his hips, the dark gold fluff of his pubic hair, the delicious spot on his lower belly I wanted to kiss.

I drew in a deep breath suddenly, almost a gasp, certain this wasn't real.

"Emm?"

I ran my hands over my body, cataloging the feeling of my fingers moving along my flesh. I was real. I was here. The bed moved as Johnny did. That was real, too.

"Touch me," I whispered.

My eyes wanted to go half-lidded and heavy, but I forced

myself to look at him full-on. Keeping him in front of me. All of this, centered. Anchored.

Johnny licked his lips and ran a hand back over his hair to push it off his face. He nodded. "Yeah. I'm going to touch you."

Nerves tingled at that, the accent I adored. The sentiment. Mostly the masculine, slightly arrogant tone that should've made me roll my eyes.

I spread my legs wider, lifting my hips. My panties were damp, my cunt already slick. My clit rubbed at the silk when I moved.

Johnny drew a fingertip down my belly, over the lacy hem of my panties, and across my clit. He circled there for a second, pressing just hard enough to make me bite my lip on a moan. The material between his finger and my flesh didn't deaden the sensation, but heightened it.

"How you want me to touch you, huh, Emm? Like this?" I had no trouble reading his expression now. Nothing in his gaze was hidden from me.

"Yes, Johnny."

He rubbed a little faster. "I can feel how hot you are. You're wet, too."

"Yes," I breathed.

"You're wet for me."

I grinned. "Yes, Johnny. For you."

He slid a finger under the leg band of my panties and pushed it inside me. Then another. Before I could thoroughly revel in this, he drew them out and over my panties again, working the wetness into the silk.

"Take these off," he said.

I eased them over my hips and down my thighs, and he moved aside to let me push them down the rest of my legs. When I lay back again, every inch of me exposed, I had a moment's hesitation.

Johnny saw it. "What?"

"Nothing." I didn't want to think about or dwell on how many beautiful, gorgeous, tight-bellied women with tiny asses and huge tits Johnny'd fucked. I especially didn't want to tell him I was thinking about it.

His hands paused in pushing his jeans over his hips. "Emm. Talk to me."

I ran my hands over my body again. "Nothing, really. Get to touching."

He took his jeans off and instead of moving over my body to enter me, the way I'd hoped, or even sliding down between my legs to use his mouth the way I'd have also enjoyed, Johnny stretched out beside me and propped himself on one arm. His cock pushed my hip. He looked down into my face while his other hand rested flat on my belly, too far from my clit for my taste.

"You know you're beautiful, right?" he said, quietly.

I wanted to point out to him that this wasn't the question of a man with a head up his ass, one who didn't have a clue. Maybe it was the years that had changed him, made him grow up. It happened to everyone. I thought it would probably happen to me, too.

"I'm glad you think so." I turned a little onto my side to look at him. "You are, too."

Johnny's hand slid a little lower, tracing the edge of my trimmed pubic hair but again not moving against the spot I really wanted him to touch. "I mean it, Emm. Not just your face or body. I don't want you to think it's just that."

"Hmm," I said, pulling a frown. "Are you going to tell me it's my inner beauty? Because that sounds kinda like saying I have a great personality."

He chuckled and kissed me, rubbing my lower belly in smooth, slow circles, inching closer and teasing me. "It means

I'm not just fucking you because you have great tits or a fine ass."

I laughed, I couldn't help it. I should've been annoyed, maybe even angry. I knew other women who certainly would've been with a statement like that, said in a moment like this. "So, what is it, then?"

Johnny didn't laugh, though he did smile. His hand, at last, slid lower, stroking through my curls and finding the sweet spot so desperate for his touch. "You want a list?"

"Yeah," I breathed. "I kinda sorta do."

His fingers moved at just the right pace, just the right rhythm. We hadn't been together for very long, but he knew my body so well. Just how to touch, and when to pause. Where to press. How to stroke.

I closed my eyes and drifted on his voice and under the sweet pressure of his fingertips on my skin.

"You don't take shit," Johnny said. "Not from anyone, but especially not from me."

Slowly, slowly, his moving hand was bringing me close to the edge. But it was his voice that pushed me faster. I listened. I gave myself up.

He kept his voice low, not distracting, just loud enough for me to ride the way I was starting to ride his hand. "You don't let anything keep you from doing what you want. You're stubborn that way, Emm, and I admire that. You're good to your friends. Good to your family. I like that you still like your parents."

I laughed, breathless. "Let's not talk about my parents…right…now."

Johnny chuckled, low, fingers slowing, then moving faster. Making me crazy. "I like the way you wear your hair."

"Better."

"I like the way you do that thing with your mouth when you're thinking hard about something and you're not sure what to say."

I sighed, arching.

"I like the way you cried when you came into my office that day, because you were embarrassed something bad had happened."

I cracked open an eye, hovering too close to orgasm to pull back, but still not quite there. "Dude. Sexy things! Talk about… sexy…"

He could've talked about the price of tea in China just then, and I'd still have tipped toward coming, but Johnny bent to kiss my mouth. He sucked my tongue in time to the stroking of his fingers, which had gone maddeningly slow. I wanted to push my hips upward to force my clit against his hand, but I steadied myself.

"I like the way your nipples get hard when you pull your shirt off over your head on the way to the shower. How's that?"

"Much better…"

"I like the way you taste when you're coming on my tongue. I think about the way you taste and I get so fucking hard I think I'm going to break."

I murmured his name. I couldn't move, couldn't speak. Could only listen. And feel.

"The first time I saw you in that coffee shop," Johnny whispered into my ear as his hand drew me ever closer into ecstasy, "I knew you, Emmaline. I had to keep walking past you because I didn't have words to say what I already knew, that we'd end up like this. Together. I didn't have a choice, and it pissed me off."

My eyes flew open, my body tense and hovering, ready to burst into pleasure. "It…did?"

Johnny moved his hand low to push his fingers into me, fucking just as slowly as he'd stroked. A different kind of pleasure, easing off and pushing me forward at the same time. "Yeah. It did. Why do you think I was such a raging prick to you?"

More breathless, panting laughter trickled out of me, and I

thought I was finally going to tip over the edge. But I didn't. "Oh, baby, you have such a fucking strange way of being sexy...."

I loved it, though. Just like I loved him. Everything about him, including the fact I'd pissed him off the first time we met without ever having said a word.

"You're so hot, and wet. I can feel how close you are. You're gonna come for me, Emm."

"Yes."

He nuzzled into my ear, tongue flicking the skin of my neck and sending sharp, bright sparkles of pleasure coursing through me. There could be no more talking, not on my end. Voiceless, I moved with his touch. Closer and closer. Nothing would stop me, nothing could.

"Seeing you was like being hit by a truck going ninety," Johnny whispered. "I walked past you like you weren't there, but I thought I was going to trip on my own fucking feet. That's what you did to me that day, when I saw you there. And you looked at me."

Somehow, I found words and the breath to speak them. Somehow, I found my voice. "I saw you. Didn't know you, but I felt...I felt like... Oh, God, Johnny, just like that. Just a little more."

It would only take a bit more. Just a bit. I was surging, cresting. Falling. Flying.

"You hit me, too," I managed to say, not sure what words were coming out or what sense they'd make. Speaking from my heart, not my mind. "We crashed, didn't we? Right then. You and me, moving toward each other...at the right time...."

"Finally, the right time," Johnny murmured into my hair, and I felt his cock throb against my hip, though I wasn't touching him at all.

I came. Hard. I heard his moan in my ear and felt him pulse and throb against me. I felt his heat, the wetness. I smelled him, and aftershocks rippled through me hard enough to make me gasp.

I drifted again after that, dozing and quiet with Johnny's hand still on me. It was sticky between us; I idly thought I should get up, maybe take a shower. I didn't, though. I wanted to lie here forever with him, not moving.

"We didn't crash," he said after a few minutes, in a sleepy voice.

"No?" I turned to cuddle against him, tangled up in arms and legs.

"No, what's it called when two objects in motion…fuck," he murmured. "You gotta get special insurance for your car."

I loved that I could follow this, even though he was obviously fuckdrunk and on his way to sleep. I laughed softly, nudging my face into the sweetness of his neck. I thought back to high school physics. "Two objects in motion collide, Johnny."

"That's what we did," he whispered. "Collide."

Chapter 28

Things were good.

Not just with Johnny and me—I wasn't so swept up in love that I believed our relationship should matter more than anything else. I loved him, but that didn't mean that's all there was to me, or to him. I understood that.

No, *everything* was good. I wasn't going dark. I was firmly entrenched in the now, and even though I couldn't pretend I didn't sometimes miss the excitement—the sheer freedom of those imaginary days with Johnny-then—I was much more appreciative of what we had for real.

I thought often of what he'd said, though. Of what had happened to us both that first day in the coffee shop, when he'd walked past me and pretended I didn't exist. I thought of what he'd said we'd done.

Collide.

I thought, too, of what he'd said just toward the end, when orgasm was making us both mindless. The right time, he'd said. Finally.

I couldn't stop thinking about it.

"Who knows what he meant," I told Jen over tall coffee drinks and plates of pastry in our old hangout.

The Mocha was crowded as usual, but it had changed for me. I still loved it, but I didn't look up hopefully every time the bell jangled. Carlos had finished his book and stopped coming every day—taking a break, he said, before starting in on the next novel. I saw some new faces, missed some old. I understood, too, that the Mocha hadn't changed; I had.

"I don't know. Maybe it was just fucktalk, you know. People say some crazy shit when they're coming." Jen sipped her drink, then leaned forward. "I mean, once, Jared yelled out, 'Saint Peter on a pogo stick!' when I was giving him a blow job and I rang the back doorbell, if you know what I mean."

I burst into laughter. "What the hell?"

Jen laughed, too. "You know what I'm talking about. Don't act like you don't."

I raised a brow, feigning innocence. "Not a clue."

She gave a quick glance around and then demonstrated, miming sucking a cock while she used one finger to…well, ring the back doorbell. "Girl, I thought he was going to take the top of my head off, he came so hard."

I laughed harder, covering my face for a second, trying not to picture it and unable to stop myself. "Wow."

"He loved it," she said with a satisfied nod. "Don't get me wrong, I'm not really a fan of that sort of action, you know what I mean."

"I know what you mean."

She shrugged, looking happy. "But when you love someone…and you want them to be happy…not that I'm saying Jared needs that to be happy."

"Of course not."

She grinned. "But he fucking loved it."

We laughed together. "I'll take your word for it. I'm not sure Johnny would love it."

She scoffed, waving a hand. "You never know."

I shook my head and sipped coffee. "That is some kinky shit, girl."

"I know it." Jen waggled her eyebrows. "Who knew, right?"

A matronly woman passed us, her hair in tight gray curls and her sweater set perfect. She gave us a stern look. Jen waited until she'd gone by us before rolling her eyes.

"Different sort of crowd in here today," she said. "Old people, geez. No offense to your main squeeze."

"None taken. He doesn't count."

"Nope." She licked icing from a fingertip. "Johnny fucking Dellasandro doesn't get old. So, when you two get married, are you going to change your name?"

I laughed. "I don't know that we will get married—God, you and my mom. Let us just…you know…hang out for a while."

"You're not just hanging out. Girl, you are full-on in love," Jen said. "Fuhrealz."

"Fuhrealz," I echoed. "But I don't know about that marriage business. He's been married, what, three, four times? Maybe he doesn't want to go through that again. And since we can't have kids, does it really matter? We don't even live together."

"C'mon, you think just because he went through it before he's burned? Let me tell you something, a dude doesn't get married four times without being the sort to get married."

"Very deep," I teased. "Wow, that was philosophical."

She tossed a napkin at me. "Shaddup. It's true. I bet you're married before I am."

"You planning on getting married?" This was news, and good news. I leaned forward. I'd been a little worried that things with Jared were rocky.

She shrugged. "Maybe. He says it's a shit life, being the wife of a funeral director. I said how is it any worse than being the girlfriend of one, except for the part where I have to live with a basement full of dead bodies instead of just visiting them?"

I made a face. "You don't have to live there, do you?"

"No, but it makes his life easier." She shrugged again, toying with her brownie, breaking off a piece and nibbling it. "I don't know if he's trying to convince me, or just hold me off. Then other times, he's all over me about it. Talking about how we could elope to Vegas."

"Do you want to marry him?"

Jen looked thoughtful. "I don't know. But I don't know if I'm not sure because I really don't know, or because I don't want to be sure in case it doesn't work out."

"Complicated," I said sympathetically.

"Yeah," she said cheerfully. "But back to you. So, change your name or not?"

"Why does that matter if I'm not even sure I'm getting married?"

"Because just think," Jen said as the gray-haired woman started weaving her way back down through the tables, "if you did, you'd be Mrs. Emm fucking Dellasandro!"

I burst into laughter again as the woman gave us a snooty glare. "Oh, yeah. Think of how I'd answer the phone at work. 'Hi, this is Emm fucking Dellasandro, how can I help you?'"

Jen giggled. "You have to admit, it's catchy. Maybe I should stop calling him that, now that you're all smoochy with him and shit."

"No," I said. "Don't stop. He's still Johnny fucking Dellasandro to me even now."

She looked a little more serious. "Really?"

"Yep."

"That's cool. He's cool," she added. "Even if I can't watch his movies anymore since all I can think about is the fact he's banging my best friend."

"Oh, like I'll be able to look Jared in the face after hearing about you ringing his back doorbell?"

We laughed, loud and hard, turning heads and not caring.

That's what friends are for—raucous, slightly rude laughter in coffee shops. Jen ate more brownie, and I finished my apple dumpling.

"I'm so freaking nervous about the gallery show, though," she confided. "I mean, joking aside, he is Johnny effing Dee, you know what I mean?"

"You shouldn't be nervous. Johnny loves your stuff. He told me, and he's not just saying it because you're my friend. I might be fucking him, but he's serious about art. He wouldn't mess with you, Jen. It's going to be great."

"My first show." She pointed at the blank spots along the wall where her pieces had hung. "Not like this, that doesn't count. This is real. It's important. I don't want to screw up, you know?"

I nodded. "I know."

"Not that I think I'm going to have some great, famous career or anything," she said hastily. "I don't expect to quit my day job. I just want people to see my stuff and like it. It's not about the money."

"I envy you. And Johnny. I don't have a creative bone in my body..." I paused, thinking of the complicated stories my brain wove. "Not anything I can do anything with, at least."

"Yeah, well, I can't add or subtract without a calculator. The world wouldn't spin without people who can do math."

"The world wouldn't spin without people who can create beauty, either," I told her. "Your show is going to kick ass. I can't wait."

She made a face, but the grimace became a smile. "I guess I can't, either."

We chatted and drank coffee. We judged the outfits of everyone who came through. I looked at my watch after a while and sighed.

"I should get going. I promised Johnny I'd make dinner tonight, and I thought I'd actually make something. Stupid."

"So. Fucking. Whipped," Jen said.

"Not," I protested, without much heat.

"You're totally gonna marry that guy," she teased. "Next thing I know, you'll be answering the door in high heels and pearls, a little apron on. Cooking him a heart-shaped meat loaf."

It wasn't such a bad idea. Not the heels and pearls, not even the meat loaf, though I thought it sounded cute. Just the idea of being domestic like that.

"I never thought..." I began, and stopped myself, dismayed to discover I was suddenly close to tears.

Jen, like the good friend she was, didn't tease. "Didn't think what?"

"That I'd ever have it. Any of it. I thought I would have to live at home forever." I drew in a shaky breath, fighting tears. "Sorry."

"Hell, no, girl, don't you dare apologize. How's it been lately, anyway?" She made a whirling gesture by her temple.

"The insanity?" I asked, just to give her a hard time because I knew she didn't meant it that way. "I haven't had a fugue since the day we tried it. I keep waiting, though. I'm always waiting."

"Probably always will, don't you think?"

She'd hit that right. "Yeah. I guess so. Though when I was clear for that couple of years before I moved here, I was hoping... Well, I guess I was always waiting then, too. Just more hopefully."

Jen nodded. "I bet. But maybe they're gone for a while now."

"Yeah. I think so, maybe." There was no way for me to tell, of course.

"Do me a favor, though."

"What's that?"

She laughed a little, looking sheepish. "Don't try to make yourself, okay? I thought Johnny was going to slaughter me."

"He was just worried. He's not mad at you."

Jen shook her head. "Girl, you should've seen him. He was scared out of his fucking mind. Not like the night of the dinner party. I mean, then he was anxious, I could tell. It was very sweet, very cute. But that day when you put yourself under, I really thought he was going to bust something. Probably my face."

I laughed uncomfortably. "It was a pretty stupid thing to do."

"Was it?" She eyed me curiously. "I don't know. If you could make yourself go into one, don't you think you could learn to bring yourself out? Forget it. Johnny was right—it was dangerous, and I'm a shitty friend for even suggesting it."

"No, you're not. I think you have a point. It's just that I promised him I wouldn't try to do it on purpose again, and..." The truth was, I was afraid to.

"I get it. I do. And I'm not a doctor or anything. Jesus, girl, I don't even watch any of those doctor shows on TV. I shouldn't be suggesting you mess around inside your head. Johnny's right."

"The thing is, most seizure disorders can't be mind-controlled. If they could, people wouldn't need meds, you know? But I've always had success with the meditation, with acupuncture, alternative medicine and stuff. More than the traditional drugs. And it's not a seizure disorder anyone has ever been able to really diagnose, so I've had different doctors saying different things all along. There's a shadow on the CAT scan but it doesn't get bigger, and it doesn't go away." I sighed. "Lame."

"Totally," Jen agreed. "The fuck were you thinking, breaking your brain like that?"

I was glad to laugh with her about something that anyone

else would've made utterly humorless. "I don't know. Stupid little kid, I guess."

"Well, hell, weren't we all? I once jumped off a two-story landing with a Superman sheet tied around my neck. Thought I could fly."

"When did you figure out you couldn't?"

She snorted. "As soon as I jumped."

We laughed again at that, shaking our heads at our stupid, youthful selves. I looked again at my watch. "Okay, I really have to run. I think I might need to get some ground beef for that meat loaf."

"Don't forget the apron and the pearls," Jen advised as we both got up. "And the heels."

I thought of what we'd talked about while I went to the grocery store, pushing my cart up and down aisles and buying food not just for myself but for Johnny, too. Making sure to get the kind of olive oil he preferred. Toilet paper in the brand he liked better, though it was more expensive. His favorite salt-and-vinegar potato chips.

It didn't feel wrong, making these choices that were different than if I'd made them for myself. I didn't feel compromised, or pushed aside. It was a bigger part of something, this simple trip to the store. It wasn't about which brand of butter or how many boxes of rice I bought. This wasn't about a single dinner, or even a month of dinners.

This was about making a life with him.

This stopped me cold in the middle of the candy aisle, my fingers tight on the handle of the shopping cart. The floor slipped under me in a familiar way. I thought I detected the faint, drifting scent of oranges. I waited for the fugue to come and take me away, make me dark, before I realized it wasn't that. I wasn't slipping and sliding at my broken brain's whim, but from emotion.

I couldn't be sure I'd fended off a fugue or if I'd simply

assumed this topsy-turvy sensation was the precursor of one, since I'd never had such an uprush of emotion that knocked me so unsteady without also going dark. At any rate, the world didn't fade out in front of me. I didn't end up in a field of flowers, or riding a canoe over Niagara Falls.

"Excuse me," said a young mother with a cart full of groceries and a happy-faced baby in the seat.

I stepped aside to give her access to the candy bars, and I pushed my cart off down the aisle. I felt it again at the checkout counter as the cashier weighed my organic tomatoes and chatted over her shoulder with the bag boy. As I paid and slipped the backpack containing my purchase over my shoulder so I could walk home. The world, slip-sliding and swirling. It was like the twitch of a curtain on a stage. Like a hand knocking on a door.

The question was, would I answer?

Chapter 29

My mind made up itself. I spent my days with Johnny without going dark. When it came time for bed, tucked up close beside him in the dark, beneath the weight of blankets we usually kicked off as the nights got warmer, I slept. And dreamed.

Of Johnny.

It wasn't like those times I stumbled into a lust-wrought fantasy of slick, hot flesh, long hair, summer heat. It was still Johnny-then in my dreams, still that house. Still that summer. But there was something else there, too.

It seemed useless in a dream to pay attention to a clock or a calendar, but I tried, when I remembered, to look. It was a couple weeks before that fateful party that tore them all apart, and I was glad my unconscious mind had sent me here. They were all happy. Getting high, having sex, arguing over politics and art. Eating, always eating the delicious food Candy provided.

And there was Johnny in the middle of it, holding my hand. Kissing me casually. Capturing my hair at the base of my neck and lifting it off my skin to give the air a chance to reach it. Letting me drink from his bottle of beer, eat from his fork, taking my head into his lap and tracing every line of my face as we lay in the grass of the backyard and looked up at the blue summer sky.

"Wish you'd stay over," Johnny said to me as he drew deep on a joint and passed it to me.

I declined; he shook his head and tucked it back in his mouth. "Can't. You know that."

"I know you say it," Johnny said.

I was content, just now, the dream sugar-sweet. I laughed, just because it felt good to laugh. I shifted in the green grass, looked at blue sky. Looked at the face of the man I loved.

"What's funny?" he asked.

"Nothing. I'm just...happy."

He leaned to kiss me, breath fragrant with pot but not gross. "I'm glad you're happy, Emm."

"Aren't you?"

He put on an exaggerated frown. "Sometimes."

I sat up, playing along. "Awww. Poor Johnny. What's wrong?"

He shrugged. "Like I said, wish you'd stay."

"Oh...you wouldn't like it half as much if I did," I told him, giddy with my own sense of joy and with the freedom of dreams.

"Yeah, I would."

"No. You'd get tired of me like you get tired of all your women."

Johnny laughed. "I never get tired of women, baby. I love them all too much. That's my problem."

"See? I don't want to be just another woman!"

He shook his head slowly, looking into my eyes. "You're not, Emm. Not even close."

I settled back onto his lap, feeling his bare flesh against my cheek. He wore truly horrible red short shorts lined with white piping, further proof this was a dream. My Johnny would never be caught dead in something so yuck—well, not now. Back in 1978 they were probably superhot.

"Trust me, you should be glad I don't hang around all the time," I said.

"Well, I ain't." He put the joint away and rested his hands behind him in the grass to look up at the sky.

I sobered a little. "We'd have a fight."

"About what?" he asked, like he didn't at all care.

"Something. I don't know. People always have fights eventually. I mean…I'm a raging bitch sometimes."

He laughed at that. "You think I can't handle that?"

"Well, you shouldn't have to, that's all." Not here. Not in a dream.

"Maybe I want to," Johnny said in the same nonchalant tone I didn't believe for a second. "Didja ever think of that?"

Everything was topsy-turvy, all switched up. I could remember the fugues, our conversations, the lovemaking, but where they fit into this time, this dream, I couldn't quite figure out. Everything had gotten chopped up into pieces.

I sat up and looked at him. "I love you, you know."

He looked pleased. "Yeah?"

I poked his bare chest—short shorts aside, he was naked. "You're supposed to say it back, you ass."

Johnny leaned in to kiss me. "I love you, Emm."

From the pool in front of us came a giant splash, and Ed surfaced, blowing out a spray of water. The others weren't around. We'd been alone until now. I wished we still were.

"Even if I am a bitch," I said, "it doesn't last long."

"No?" He kissed me again, and his hand found the spot on the back of my neck he liked so well to cradle.

"No," I said against his mouth.

"Good to know," Johnny said.

Someone called his name. He looked toward the house with

a frown. Bellina stood at the back door, holding the phone stretched tight on its long, curly cord. She said a name.

"My agent," Johnny explained, and looked apologetic. "Gotta take that, babe."

"You go." I stretched in the sun, lazy and sated.

He got up, looking down at me, silhouetted by the sun. "Will you be here when you get back?"

"I hope so."

But I wasn't.

Another night I was back again. Same place. Slightly different time. Johnny walked out of the kitchen and found me standing in the front hallway. He looked me up and down.

"Hey. That was Freddy. Says he got a gig for me set up in Italy. Horror flick." He took me in his arms. "Wanna go to Italy with me?"

Why not? "Sure."

He grinned. Kissed me. Then a little harder. "Wanna go upstairs with me?"

"Sure to that, too," I said with both my hands on his ass and squeezed.

A clatter of something in the hall made us both turn. It was Ed. Annoyed, I frowned. Was he following us, or what?

"Sorry," Ed muttered, weaving a little. "I thought...you'd gone, Emm. You were there and then I thought you... Never mind."

"I'm right here," I said, annoyed.

Johnny laughed. "Go sleep it off, man. That guy," he said when Ed stumbled into the living room and collapsed on the couch, "should cut back on the booze."

Upstairs in Johnny's bedroom, he stripped out of those god-awful shorts and stood naked, his erection already thick and gorgeous, begging for me to get down in front of it and take it in my mouth. Which I did, gladly, the hem of my lightweight nightgown crushing under my knees. His fingers ran along the spaghetti straps, pushing them off my shoulders so my breasts pushed up and out of the material.

I stroked my hand down his cock and took the head in my mouth. I sucked. He moaned. He thrust. I licked and nibbled gently, and Johnny tugged on my hair until I looked up.

"Stand up," he said. "Turn around."

I did. I put my hands on his dresser, my fingers flat on the polished wood. Behind me, he slipped up my gown, found me bare beneath. His fingers toyed with the crack of my ass, then slid between my legs to stroke my clit. I shivered, head bent, legs spread. I was already wet.

"You always go without panties?" he murmured, not like he expected an answer. Appreciative.

I slept in this gown without panties, yes, and would never have gone out in public this way if it hadn't been a dream. But that was too long an explanation. "Just for you."

He grunted. His fingers slid into me, then out. He used his thumb and forefinger to tug gently at my clit, and a low noise eased from my throat.

"You want me to fuck you, Emm?"

"Yes."

"Just like this?"

"Definitely," I answered.

Above Johnny's dresser was a mirror. When he pushed inside me, he also gathered my hair at the back of my neck and pulled until I looked up. I gazed at both of us, captured there in glass, a frame around us like a painting. Making us art.

His face looked grim as he moved inside me. Concentrating. His brow furrowed, mouth thinned. My gaze blurred as pleasure built, but his hand in my hair kept me from looking away. Our eyes met in the mirror.

His other hand moved against my clit, stroking in time to every thrust. My fingers curled and bent on top of the dresser, sliding and unable to grip. We moved together. The dresser shifted, squeaking on the floor, nudging the wall. The mirror shook, and we shook inside it.

Everything shook.

I was coming, fast and hard. Johnny closed his eyes, head back, his hand still gripped so tight in my hair I couldn't move without pulling. I watched ecstasy wash over his face and wanted to look away from my own twisted features. Then, over Johnny's shoulder, in the doorway, I saw him.

Ed. Watching us. This was worse, somehow, than having Sandy walk in on us, because it could be said that even in a dream I wanted to prove to her she'd lost Johnny and I had him. But this voyeurism didn't feel sexy to me.

I gasped, orgasm ripping through me. Johnny let out a low cry. I said his name, urgently, and he opened his eyes. He blinked, gaze hazy, thrusts slowing.

Then he blinked, half turning, letting go of my hair but still inside me. "What the hell?"

Ed shook his head, hands up, muttering apologies. He ducked out of the room. Johnny pulled out from me and wet heat slid down my thighs. I gasped at the sudden withdrawal and turned as he stalked to the doorway.

"Ed! Hey!"

"Johnny, don't." The hem of my dress fell around my thighs, covering me. I pulled up the straps. "It's not worth it. I don't think he meant anything."

"The hell," Johnny said, sounding confused. "Drunk son of a bitch."

I didn't think Ed was so drunk, so high, that he hadn't known what he was doing. I don't know why I lied to save him, either, other than just as I knew this was a dream, I knew what happened to him, eventually. "Don't worry about it. He got an eyeful of your ass, that's all. And who hasn't."

Johnny didn't laugh. Still naked, he slammed the door and

turned to face me, his cock still half-hard and glistening. He put his hands on his hips. "He's been acting like a freak for weeks."

I wasn't sure how he could tell Ed had been acting like more of a freak than normal, but what did I know? "Don't worry about it."

"I ain't worried, just pissed off." Johnny jerked a thumb over his shoulder. "Give the guy a place to crash, he does that sort of shit?"

"Maybe…maybe you should stop giving everyone a place to crash." I didn't know where that came from, either. I knew they all broke apart after Ed killed himself, but technically that hadn't happened yet.

Well, it had. Just not here. Not in this now. In this time.

My head whirled.

I looked down at my dress. My hands, which had left no marks on the dresser, though I could still feel the tingling from the pressure I'd used. Johnny was talking, but I couldn't make out the words.

I was dreaming. Or had I gone dark? Was this a fugue? I couldn't tell. I looked at him, his face, his body, his mouth, moving. I could still feel him inside me. Still feel the aftershock rumbles of my orgasm.

He was at my side in a second when I crumpled. "Emm, you okay?"

"Fine," I managed to say. "Just a little light-headed. That's all. It's hot in here."

"Let me get you a drink."

I let him lead me to the bed. I put my head between my legs, smelling our sex. Johnny brought back a cool cloth for the back of my neck and a cup of water from which I could only manage a few sips before my stomach turned. I pushed it away with a shake of my head. I took deep, slow breaths, learned from my meditations. I pressed my two fingers to a spot on the inside of my wrist, a trick I'd learned about acupressure.

"You sick?" Johnny rubbed my back. "Or upset?"

"Just a little woozy, that's all." I breathed in through my nose, out through my mouth. The nausea was fading too slowly for my comfort. The piece of the floor I could see between my feet wasn't staying still.

Johnny rubbed my back in slow circles and kept the cool cloth on my neck. I breathed. I breathed.

I breathed.

"I'm going to go," I told him.

"You shouldn't go anywhere, you should stay here," Johnny said.

"No. I have to go." I stood. My feet planted, anchoring me. I didn't fall.

Johnny sighed. "Fine. Go ahead. Leave."

I didn't want him to be angry, but did it matter? Really? My head whirled again, all of this confusing and too much to take. To understand.

"Where do I go?" I took the cloth from my neck to press to my face, hiding it.

"Hell if I know. You won't tell me." He sounded sullen but resigned. "No phone number. No address. You show up, you leave."

"But I always come back, right?"

"So far," Johnny said, as though he didn't believe it would always be the truth.

I took the cloth from my face. "But you never see me go or come?"

"I've seen you come plenty," he said with a grin I'd have returned if my stomach weren't still doing the Hustle.

This was a puzzle with a few pieces missing. I could see the picture. I could even see what parts yet needed placing. I simply couldn't find them. Or maybe I didn't want to—I was suddenly very tired.

If this was a dream, I could leave it now. Same with a fugue. Just…go. Without leaving the room, or Johnny in it. I could vanish like a genie. I should.

Yet I backed up toward the door, never looking away from him. Not willing to vanish. Not willing to be made a ghost, an unreal thing. Not in front of him.

"I'll be back, Johnny. I promise."

He bent to grab up his shorts and put them on. He turned without looking at me, his shoulders slumped. He didn't answer.

"I will," I said.

He nodded.

I left.

Chapter 30

I woke with a start, my stomach still twisting and turning. I was in my bed but so disoriented I couldn't figure that out for a good thirty seconds. Johnny snored lightly beside me, one arm flung over his head.

My guts forced their way into my throat. I tossed off the covers and stumbled to the bathroom, where I fell to my knees in front of the toilet and tossed up everything I'd eaten for the past year and a half—or so it felt. Heaving, sweating, the tile cool under my knees, I closed my eyes.

I already knew.

I hadn't been thinking about it. The slight bit of extra tightness in the waist of my jeans was easily explained by too many brownies in the Mocha. The tenderness in my breasts was PMS. My late period and the spotting in between was from nerves.

That wasn't it. I wiped my mouth with a handful of tissues, then bent over the sink to splash my face and rinse my mouth. I spit, then spit again. I closed my eyes as my fingers gripped cold porcelain almost the way they'd gripped the dresser the night before, in my dream that wasn't a dream.

"Emm? You okay?"

It was so much like what he'd said to me last night I was

afraid to look, afraid to see Johnny-then somehow in my *now,* like those old commercials for Reese's peanut butter cups. Chocolate in my peanut butter. I rinsed and spat. I splashed my face. I heard his feet on the bathroom floor.

"Can I get you something?"

"No." I cleared my throat. "I'm okay."

I did feel better. Hungry, in fact, despite my still-tumbling stomach. I looked at my reflection. Pale face, circles under my eyes. I'd looked better.

I smoothed my hair from my forehead. "Must've been something I ate."

"Huh," Johnny said. "You going in to work?"

I nodded. "Yeah, I feel okay. Just need to eat some crackers or something. Settle my stomach."

"You sure?" He looked doubtful. Also, beautiful, even with sleepy eyes and messy hair, his pajama bottoms riding low.

"Yep." I pulled my toothbrush from the holder and spread a thick layer of paste on it. Brushed. Spat. Again, until the taste was driven from my tongue.

Johnny watched me, and I felt him looking but neither of us spoke as I turned on the water in the shower and shrugged out of my nightdress. He stooped to pick it up off the floor, which was nice, as I thought if I bent I might end up back in front of the toilet. Johnny fingered the cloth as he hung it on the hook.

"I like this gown," he said. "I always did."

I shuddered, one hand under the still-cold water. It could take forever to heat up. My nipples peaked from chill, not arousal, and I put a hand across my chest. I cupped a breast, then laid my palm flat. Feeling my heart.

"You bought it for me," I reminded him.

He'd brought it home and presented it with a flourish normally reserved for something like the crown jewels. I liked the nightgown, too, with its funky retro vibe and soft fabric. It was what I'd worn to bed and worn in my…dreams, too.

"What made you pick it?" I asked.

Johnny looked at me. "It looked like something you'd wear, that's all. It looked like you."

I sipped some breaths, willing my stomach to stay in its place. The world, too. I got in the shower with a hiss at the water, now too hot. I fiddled with the faucets. I pressed my face into the stream of water and hoped I wasn't crying.

"You sure I can't get you anything?" Johnny pulled aside the curtain and looked in, his face concerned.

"Some toast," I said. "Dry toast would be great. Peppermint tea? That would be great, baby. Thanks."

"Sure, okay." He sounded doubtful, but closed the curtain.

I waited until I heard the bathroom door close before I sank onto my hands and knees. I didn't feel like I had to puke again. Didn't feel faint. But I was trembling and sought the comfort of being low to the ground. I put my face in my hands, pressed them to the tub's slick surface. Water hit my back.

I'd seen the movie *The Time Traveler's Wife.* The heroine, desperate for a child, and angry at her time-traveling husband, meets up with his prevasectomy self and urges him to make love to her so she can get pregnant, though her present-time husband doesn't want her to. In other words, she fucks her husband-then in order to have a child with her husband-now.

Never once in any of the fugues or the dreams had I made Johnny wear a rubber. Hell, they had them in 1978, didn't they? Even if hardly anyone in that pre-AIDS era used them? And I was, albeit haphazardly, on birth control. We'd been careful, but even if we weren't, Johnny-now couldn't knock me up.

"Oh, fuck," I said miserably into my palms. "Oh, shit. Oh, fuck."

A baby. I was going to have a baby with Johnny. I slid my wet hands over my belly.

But how could I tell him?

I felt sicker to my stomach about facing him and telling him that by some miracle, some unbelievable, fantastic, impossible occurrence, we were going to be parents. He was going to be a dad again when he was already a grandfather. I could only imagine what Kimmy was going to say.

In the kitchen, I found him with tea brewed, toast browned, waiting for me. He was looking over a folder of invoices or something from the gallery, but he took his glasses off and stood when I came into the kitchen. He looked me over.

"You feeling better? Sure you don't want to stay home?"

"No." I shook my head and took my seat at the table. The toast smelled good, and suddenly I was ravenous. "I'm okay. Really."

I forced a bright smile for him as I shoved toast in my mouth and washed it down with tea. The crumbs scattered on the table. I wiped them with my fingertips.

Johnny leaned across the table, surprising me with a kiss. "Love you."

"I love you, too."

I managed to keep up a conversation with him as he drove me to work, and if he noticed I was quieter than normal, he didn't remark on it. At work I sat at my desk, a zombie, filling in forms and answering the phone without really paying much attention.

The worst part of all this was not actually that I thought I might be insane. That part seemed almost…expected, giving my history of brain damage. The worst part wasn't trying to get my brain to wrap around the concept I hadn't just dreamed about 1978. I'd gone there. This time I wasn't Alice, slipping through the looking glass. I was the White Queen, believing impossible things.

The worst part was the fact that after spending a lifetime guarding against unwanted pregnancy, about being careful, making sure I was responsible for my body, after all that, I'd still ended up pregnant by accident.

I buried my face in my hands at my desk and let out a low, almost-silent moan. Pregnant. A baby. How could I have a baby?

I'd long ago given up the idea of having children. After all, how could I expect to make it through nine months with another life growing inside me when I couldn't always be counted on to know where I was or what I was doing? How could I be a mother, be responsible for another life, when at any moment I could slip sideways into darkness?

Or backward, I thought. I had a sour taste on my tongue. Rotten orange. But I didn't smell it. Just taste it.

When I opened my eyes, I expected to find summer heat, a swimming pool. A young Johnny looking at me with that gleam in his eyes. Instead, I saw my computer, my face reflected in it like a ghost.

I put my hands on my belly, rounder always than I'd like. What small life swam inside me? Daughter? Son? Would he have his father's eyes, would she have my smile?

I clicked on my web browser and looked up time travel. I didn't learn a lot. I found a lot of sites with a lot of fancy words and descriptions of tachyons and particles and physics, which I'd never understood. I found many book and movie reviews, some even from books or movies I'd read. I read a lot and learned very little beyond what I already knew.

Time travel didn't happen.

It most certainly didn't happen from falling off a jungle gym. It didn't make sense, and yet it was the only answer I had. I went dark; I went back. I'd been having fugues for years, but none had been like the ones that started after seeing Johnny that first time in the Mocha.

Again, I rested my head in my hands. None of this made

sense, yet it made perfect sense. All I had to do was suspend my disbelief.

At lunch I went out to the pharmacy and bought a quadruple pack of pregnancy tests. I didn't wait until the morning, the way the instructions advised. I went into the bathroom at work and peed on the stick and waited for the lines to show up. One, or two.

Two.

I did it again.

Two.

I went back to my desk and drank a bottle of water even though I really wanted a Diet Dr Pepper. I forced myself to eat a salad instead of the bacon double cheeseburger I was suddenly craving, though I allowed myself the cookie for dessert. I might be eating for two now, and I wanted to make healthy choices.

I broke into tears at three o'clock, sitting at my desk with my face muffled in most of a box of tissues. The tears became laughter, semihysterical, but genuine. I laughed. Cried. I went to the bathroom, certain I was going to barf up my lunch, but I didn't.

At three forty-five, Johnny pulled into the parking lot. I could see him from my window. I was leaving early today so I could go to the gallery show tonight. I pressed my face against the cool glass and for the first time in a very, very long while I prayed.

It seemed about as useless as wishing on a star, but if I could believe I'd somehow managed to travel back and forth in time I could also believe some higher consciousness was listening and might be moved to help me.

I had never wanted a child. I'd never thought I'd be a mother. I'd never held a friend's baby and yearned for my own. I wasn't cut out for it. Liked kids from a distance, enough to coo at a baby in a stroller but always happy to give them back to their beaming parents. Babies smelled, they cried, they were tiny, expensive, consistent pains in the ass.

Looking down at Johnny's car idling in the lot, I slipped my hands once more over my belly. It was too soon to feel a difference, but I imagined how it would be in just a few months from now, my belly out in front of me like a basketball, if I were lucky. A watermelon, if I weren't.

It would grow inside me like a parasite, sucking out every nutrient I consumed and making me crave stuff like paste or pasta or Jolly Ranchers candy. My feet would swell. I'd get stretch marks. I'd puke for months, then gain so much weight my body would never be the same, and at the end of it I'd spend hours in agony pushing a human being the size of a bowling ball out an orifice much smaller. I'd bleed. I'd be unable to have sex for weeks. And then I'd have milk squirting out of my nipples at inopportune times.

After that would come the diapers, the screaming, the childproofing. Car seats, cribs, bibs, spit-up. I couldn't have a pet because I couldn't deal with poop, how was I going to deal with a baby?

This was pregnancy, childbirth, motherhood. This was what I had to look forward to, the rest of my life spent putting someone else first, making sure this life I had been so foolish as to create was safe and happy and loved.

"Please," I murmured, my forehead still pressed to the glass. I watched Johnny get out of the car and pace a little. I knew he craved a cigarette, though he'd given them up. I knew he was wondering why I was late.

"Please," I said again.

Please. Please. Whoever is listening, whatever can hear me, please, oh, please, oh, please.

My hands pressed lightly on my belly, and my fingers linked.

"Please," I said. "Please let this be real."

Chapter 31

The gallery had been transformed. It was always beautiful, of course, no matter what was hanging on the walls, but Johnny's staff had hung even more strands of fairy lights from the roof's old beams and soft mosquito netting from the pillars with lights nestled inside. The uneven wood floors were waxed and polished, and I clung to Johnny's arm, certain that in my high heels I'd slip and fall. Make a fool of myself.

Or worse, hurt myself.

I'd taken the other two pregnancy tests an hour or so apart, at home, hiding them carefully under a wad of paper towels in my bathroom garbage can even though I had no reason to suspect Johnny had or ever would bother to dig through it. Both had come up without a doubt, two blue lines that said I was pregnant. While a false negative could be likely, there wasn't much of a chance for a false positive.

I kept my secret drawn close to me like a cloak. A shield. I couldn't stop thinking about it. It made me distracted and clumsier than I could blame on the slick, polished floor. Johnny caught me before I could wipe out the refreshment table.

"Careful, Emm."

"Sorry."

He shook his head, his arm around my waist, fingers resting lightly on my hip. "Nah. Don't worry about it. You want a drink?"

"Just water, thanks."

He looked at me carefully. "You don't want a glass of wine? A beer? I made sure we got that dark stuff you like."

"Maybe later. Oh, cheese!" I was starving, my intermittent nausea in hiding for the moment.

"I gotta go check on some things. You go getcha cheese, I'll be back." Johnny's accent was a little deeper tonight, and I snagged his hand before he could walk away.

"Hey."

He didn't try to pull away. He let me pull him closer. There in front of everyone, he smoothed a curl of my hair behind my ear, and he kissed me.

"Hey," Johnny said softly. "What."

"I love you," I whispered. "Don't forget it."

"Never have." Johnny brushed his lips over mine, then kissed my forehead. He looked into my eyes. "You need something, Emm?"

I shook my head. "You go. I'm going to get something to eat. See if I can find Jen. She's probably nervous."

"She'll be great. She's showing her best work. People will like it."

"Doesn't mean she won't be nervous," I told him.

"I know that." Johnny kissed me again, patted my ass and headed off to do whatever it was he needed to do.

I met up with Kimmy at the buffet table. She looked nice, dressed in a sleek black dress, her hair piled on top of her head. I could see a lot of her mother in her, but I could see her dad, too. She nodded at me with a glass of wine held in her hand.

"Hi, Kimberly," I said sweet enough to rot her teeth. "I'm so glad to see you here."

"My dad invited me," she said. "He serves good wine."

"He does." I piled my plate high with cheese and crackers and a dollop of some kind of mustard dip.

"You're not drinking any, I notice."

She caught me with my mouth full, so I just shrugged. Kimmy looked me over. She sipped her wine.

"I like your shoes," she said at last, which was as close to being friendly as I ever expected her to be, especially when she found out I was going to be giving her another brother or sister.

I spotted Jen from across the room, Jared at her side. He had one hand on the small of her back, steadying her. She was grinning, but it looked a little strained.

"Hey, girl, hey!" I said. "Hi, Jared."

He nodded. "Hey, Emm."

"Girl," Jen breathed. "Would you look at this? All these people? Omigod, I think I might barf."

"Please don't," I said automatically. "If you do, I will, too."

Jared laughed and pulled her close to kiss her mouth. "You're fine. How many times do I have to tell you?"

Jen didn't look mollified, though she did allow herself to relax into his embrace. "Easy for you to say."

"Well, yeah, but that doesn't make it any less true."

We talked about the show. Jen's pieces were in the back room, which was why she was out here. She didn't want to watch anyone studying them.

"You want me to go look in?" I asked.

"No!" she cried. "Okay, yes!"

"I told her I'd go," Jared said, "but she wouldn't let me."

"You stay with me," Jen told him. "Emm, would you just check it out? I don't want to know if anyone's saying mean stuff."

"I would never tell if anyone was," I promised.

I looked for Johnny as I wove through the crowd toward the

back room, but didn't see him. I tossed my trash and grabbed a bottle of ginger ale from the bar, not because I was feeling sick but just in case. I sipped it as I went through the doorway into the back room.

I saw Jen's artwork at once, displayed on the white walls and lit by tiny spotlights. She'd picked her favorite pieces after agonizing for weeks, and I agreed with her choices—even though I knew my opinion meant very little beyond that of a friend. I studied them, admiring the way she'd taken photographs of local landmarks and used photo editing and hand-painting to enhance or even change them. To my surprise, I saw myself in one of her pieces.

She must've kept it a secret from me, as a surprise, because though I remembered her taking the picture—with her cell phone, no less—I'd had no idea she'd used it. It was of my face, eyes to the side, mouth pursed. I'd been trying to catch a surreptitious glance of Johnny. She'd trimmed out the background and placed my face in the window of a tall brownstone, one of the unrenovated ones from my block. Next to it she'd added a shot of my house with me and Johnny standing on the front step.

"Nice piece," said a husky feminine voice from beside me. "Shocked Johnny let it in the show, though. That is him, isn't it? Jesus, you'd think I'd be able to tell."

I turned to face the woman who'd come up beside me. She wore a black dress, too tight, and red shoes that would've been nicer without the scuff marks on the toes. Her bleached blond hair was pulled into a high ponytail, stretching her skin back from her face—either that, or she'd had some very bad work done. She turned to me at the same time.

"Oh, shit," she said.

I blinked rapidly and took a step back. It was Sandy. Older, of course. Worn, definitely. But I knew her right away, and she seemed to know me, too.

"Oh, shit," she said again, almost conversationally, and faced the framed pictures. She had a cigarette in one hand and she put it to her mouth like she was smoking, though it was unlit.

"You must be Kim's mom." My voice shook, so I cleared my throat. "Sandy, right?"

"And you're Johnny's teenage girlfriend."

"I'm way out of my teens," I said, hoping this wasn't going to turn into a fight…but on the other hand, part of me was ready to tear it up with her.

"Not by much," Sandy said derisively, and waved the cigarette at me.

"Why does it matter to you? You haven't been together for years."

Her smile was hard, but not without humor. "True. But that doesn't mean…"

She stopped, eyes narrowing. She looked me up and down, focusing on my face. She moved toward me.

"Have we met?" Sandy asked.

"No." It tasted like a lie, but all I had was a crazy through-the-looking-glass theory, nothing real.

Sandy studied me again. "You sure?"

"I'm sure."

"You look familiar."

I forced a laugh, thinking of blurry-eyed Sandy in Johnny-then's upstairs hallway. Of her walking in on us fucking. Of her demands for money, her lack of consideration for privacy. That had been a long, long time ago for her.

"So do you," I said.

This seemed to satisfy her. She smoothed her hair, then her dress. She held the cigarette between two fingers while cradling her elbow with the other hand.

"Just one of those faces, I guess," she said. "You, I mean. Obviously, you've seen me in photos. Johnny's pictures."

She didn't say *pitchahs* the way she had in the fugues. Sandy had either made a conscious effort to change her manner of speaking or I was just crazy and never really had met her. She looked a little smug now, and that wasn't different.

"Oh, you were in pictures with him?" I asked with an innocent blink.

Of course I knew she was. There were several famous ones of the two of them frolicking naked in a field of flowers, both with long flowing hair and holding daisies. I was just being a bitch.

Sandy's smile told me she knew it, too. Maybe even respected it. "But that was a long, long time ago."

"Yes," I said. "It was."

Without another word, she turned on her heel and left me there. I didn't mind. The less I ever had to see of Sandy, the better.

I looked at the rest of Jen's pieces, then the others. I didn't have to appreciate art to prefer hers. The others were good, but Jen's had something special about them that stood out. I admired them all while trying to be subtle in my eavesdropping about what people were saying. It was all good, and I knew she'd be glad.

I was just about to head back into the main room to tell her when something caught the corner of my eye. Along the back wall, set apart from the rest of the art, was a display I'd never seen yet I instantly knew. The crowd parted, moving away, and I moved forward.

Blank Spaces.

The work that had first given Johnny recognition, real respect as an artist. Not a single piece but a series of sketches and paintings, all with the same subject in slightly different poses. The most famous of them, the biggest, the one in the center of the display, I'd seen dozens of times in .jpgs of varying quality on the internet.

A woman, head turned so her hair fell over her face and

shoulders, in a yellow sundress. She stood in green, green grass. One hand outstretched. There was a hint of water in the background I'd always thought was a river or a lake, maybe an ocean, but in this version, at least eighteen by twenty inches, I could see it was a swimming pool.

The other pieces were smaller, some of them no more than pencil sketches, though the frames made them more impressive. I could see the progression of some of them from first pencil strokes to the final piece. Fascinated, I studied them all, for the first time able to have a glimmer of understanding about what made the difference between a picture and a piece of art.

The woman wasn't the same in every pose. In some she was facing away altogether. In others, her hands were at her side. Sometimes it was as though a wind had tossed her hair and hem of her dress.

I didn't smell oranges. The world didn't waver. I didn't even blink. One minute I was standing in front of Johnny's most famous painting and in the next I was in a dark kitchen smelling booze and pot, staring at an empty chair and an ashtray full of crushed cigarettes.

"No," I whispered.

The calendar said August 1978. I could still smell sweat and booze. Ed's notebook was still on the table, but he was gone. From outside, the sounds of the party got a little louder, more frantic.

I left the kitchen, went into the backyard. People spoke to me, and I ignored them. I knew the date on the calendar. I knew this place, and what was going to happen.

I found him on the far side of the swimming pool, on the grass, in a pocket of shadow.

"There you are," Johnny said. "Been lookin' for you."

"Johnny."

"Yeah?" He pulled me closer, and I let him kiss me.

So much to say, no words to say it. I knew so much, but

nothing. I took his hand and put it on my belly. I kissed his mouth. I looked into his eyes.

"I have something to tell you."

Something shifted in his gaze as his palm moved in a slow circle over my stomach. I didn't say anything. He smiled.

"Yeah?"

"Yes," I said.

"Really?" Johnny looked at my belly, his hand still rubbing. He looked back at my face. "Emm, really?"

"Yes," I said.

He kissed me, taking me by surprise. His lips bruised mine. He laughed into my open mouth and pulled away to put both hands on my stomach.

"I'm gonna take care of you, Emm," Johnny said. "I want you to know that, okay?"

I knew he meant it. I could see it in his eyes. Hear it in his voice. And my heart broke, knowing I was breaking his.

From somewhere, a breeze rose up. It blew my hem. It blew my hair. I stepped away from him.

"I have to tell you something, Johnny."

In a few hours, Ed would take his own life, slitting his wrists and bleeding to death in the swimming pool. His death would break up the Enclave and push Johnny into a spiral of drugs, booze, sex and excess, then into the mental hospital, taking away the opportunities that had been laid out for him on a golden platter. It would change his life forever.

I couldn't let that happen. I could stop this. I could warn Johnny what Ed meant to do. They could keep him alive, at least for tonight. And that would, could, might change everything.

I had a butterfly beneath my foot, ready to step and crush it into the mud.

I looked at his lovely, perfect, beautiful face. His young face, young body. I looked at Johnny-then and felt like I held his future in my hands. I could do this for him. Give him the life he'd surely have had if not for this night.

A life without me in it.

I knew that as certainly as I knew everything else. If Johnny went on to trade his face and that body for fame and fortune, he would never become an artist. He'd told me so himself, several times. If I changed this for him, it would change everything else, and some thirty or so years in the future, I would walk into a coffee shop and never find him.

I couldn't do it.

"Emm?" Johnny reached for my hand.

Another breeze came up. My hair blew over my eyes and I pushed it away, desperate to keep anything from blocking him from my view. I loved him—both the young man he'd been and, more importantly, the man he was now. I wanted him, and I wanted this child of impossibility.

"I'm crazy," I said aloud.

"I told you, I don't care." Johnny reached for my hand. "I'm gonna take care of you, Emm. I told you that, too. It don't matter about anything else. Okay?"

"I love you," I told him. "No matter what else happens, promise me you won't forget that. And…forgive me?"

"For what?" Johnny said.

The smell of oranges swept over me, overpowering, and I fought against it. I turned. I had never gone in front of him. I didn't want him to see it. But I was going, I couldn't stop it, and somehow this time felt different.

This time felt like the very last time.

"There's more to you than a pretty face and an epic ass," I told him. "And I love you. Remember that. I'll see you again. Just hold on to that, okay?"

Chapter 32

"You're back," Johnny said.

I blinked and sat up. A wet cloth fell from my forehead into my lap, making it damp. I was on the couch in his office.

"Oh, no."

"Shh. Don't worry. Nobody saw."

I shook my head. "Johnny—"

"Shh, I said. Emm, it's okay." Johnny took my hand, stroking each finger. Soothing. "I'm taking care of you."

I squeezed his hand. "I have something to tell you."

He smiled. "Yeah. I know."

I waited for my mind or the world to whirl, but it all stayed steady and still. "How?"

"You told me."

"When I was dark? Just now?"

"Not now." Johnny shook his head. "Then."

I gave a small groan and rubbed at my forehead. "I don't believe this. This can't be happening. Can it?"

"I don't know, babe, but it did." He kissed my hand and then handed me a glass of water with ice in it.

I sipped gratefully, then swung my legs over the couch to face him. "How?"

He shrugged. “Don’t know that, either.”

My laugh surprised me. “Am I crazy?”

“Nope. I’m not, either, though I thought I was for a long time.”

“I tried to tell you. About Ed. I wanted to warn you,” I said, guilt filling me with heat. “So you could stop him, or at least not let it get to you….”

“Emm, Emm, shhhh. Listen. That bullshit with Ed, that wasn’t what… It’s not what made me lose my shit.”

“No? But you said—”

“I said what you thought you knew,” Johnny told me. “The truth is, I lost it all when I lost you, back then. I was so fucking crazy in love with you, and you kept leaving me. Then you left for good, right in front of me, and I knew you weren’t ever coming back. Shit, I figured you were dead or something. A ghost. Whatever it was, I knew I’d lost you for good. That’s what made me nuts, baby. Not Ed, that prick, God rest his soul.”

“I don’t understand any of this. I don’t know.” I shook my head. “All these years, all those times I went dark. And only when I met you did it change. It’s like…”

“Fate,” Johnny said. “Karma. Kismet. Whatever the fuck you wanna call it. That’s it.”

I thought of what he’d said before. Two objects meeting at a great force. “Collide. That’s what we did, we collided.”

“We sure as hell did.”

“Tell me what really happened,” I asked him. Ready to believe the impossible.

“I told you most of it. You disappeared right in front of me. I went a little nuts. Best thing for me, in the end. I kept thinking about what you said. What you told me I could be. I believed you, Emm. Nobody’d told me anything like that before. Sure, I had people crawling so far up my ass they ate my breakfast for me before I could, yeah, but it wasn’t the same. Nobody really believed in me. But I kept thinking about what you'd said, and the doctors said it would be good for me to draw. So I started. Shit at first, real shit. Talent but no skill, you know?"

"I don't believe it," I said.

"I could show you, but you wouldn't be able to appreciate it."

We laughed together, a strange feeling in the midst of all this chaos.

"And then, I got my life straightened out. Got out of the hospital, got sober, got my head on straight. I tried some acting work, that shit, because, hey, someone was willing to pay me for it. But I knew it wasn't going anywhere, not after all that time. They'd moved on to the next big thing. But it paid the bills, and gave me time to work on the drawing."

"And then you did *Blank Spaces*."

Johnny nodded. "Yeah. Big break. From then on it wasn't wine and roses, but it sure as hell beat panhandling. I was doing something I was proud of, you know? Something I was good at."

I squeezed his hand again, looking at it. His age showed here the way it did in the corners of his eyes, but I put the back of his hand to my mouth and kissed it, because it belonged to him. I cupped my cheek with his hand.

"It was you," Johnny said. "Without you, I'd never have done it."

I didn't want to take credit for it, the blame of sending him into crazy easier to bear somehow. "That's not true."

Johnny laughed. "Emm. It is fucking true. Don't you get it? You don't, do you. How could you?"

He got up and went to the armoire in the corner, unlocked the door, pulled out a thick sketch pad bound with rubber bands that looked worn and cracked, ready to give at the slightest tug. One broke when he pulled it, and Johnny tossed it to the side.

He opened the book. Showed me some sketches. Turned the page. "See?"

Harsh, bold lines, the strokes of pencil cut through the paper in some places, and yet created a delicate and intricate pattern of graphite on paper. The same woman from *Blank Spaces*. Similar pose. Only in this one, she wasn't turned away, and her hair wasn't obscuring her face. I could see her every feature.

It was me.

I gasped, and yet...wasn't surprised. Hadn't I somehow known all along? Had some part of me not guessed this, from the first time I'd stumbled on the ice into his arms and into his past?

There are some things that make no sense. Love is one of them. Falling in love is jumping face-first into a vast abyss, hoping the person you love will be there to catch you. Love is a connection.

Something had brought us together, Johnny and me. We didn't have to understand it. We just had to accept it.

I looked at the bottom of the picture. Johnny'd scrawled his name and the date. I traced the lines of it with my finger, and even now, years later, the pencil smudged my fingertip.

"This was the first one I did," Johnny said. "I just sat down one day and started drawing. I couldn't stop."

"You started on that day?"

"Yeah."

I traced the date again and looked at him. "I know why."

He looked back at me. "Do you?"

"It's the day I fell. The first day I went dark."

We both looked at the picture he'd drawn so long ago. The lines and swirls he'd created that made my face. Everything had started and ended on that day, and we'd never know why. Was it important? I didn't think so.

Johnny closed the sketch pad and set it aside. He kissed me. He put his hand on my belly, over the place where we'd made a miracle. I kissed him, too, no longer afraid the world would spin out from underneath me. Knowing that no matter what had brought us to this place, or what might happen in the future, this was exactly how everything had been meant to happen all along.

I knew all of him in that moment. I no longer feared this was a dream. I knew it was all real.

★★★★★

Author's Note

I could write without listening to music, but I'm so glad I don't have to. Here's a partial playlist of some of the music I listened to while writing *Collide.* Please support the artist through legal sources!

"Breathe Me"—Sia
"Bulletproof Weeks"—Matt Nathanson
"City Lights"—Mirror
"Closer"—Kings of Leon
"Collide"—Howie Day
"Damn I Wish I Was Your Lover"—Sophie B. Hawkins
"Don't Pull Your Love"—Hamilton, Joe Frank and Reynolds
"Dream a Little Dream of Me"—The Mamas and the Papas
"Ghosts"—Christopher Dallman
"Goodbye Horses"—Psyche
"I Think She Knows"—Kaki King
"I'm Burning for You"—Blue Öysters Cult
"If"—Bread
"If You Want to Sing Out, Sing Out"—Cat Stevens
"Incense and Peppermints"—Strawberry Alarm Clock
"Je t'aime moi non plus"—Serge Gainsbourg and Jane Birkin
"Joy to the World"—Three Dog Night
"Kiss You All Over"—Dr. Hook
"Labor of Love"—Michael Giacchini's *Star Trek*
(Music from the Motion Picture)

"Lascia ch'io pianga Prologue"—Antichrist Soundtrack
"Life on Mars"—David Bowie
"Purple Haze"—The Cure
"Shambala"—Three Dog Night